Kid Stuff

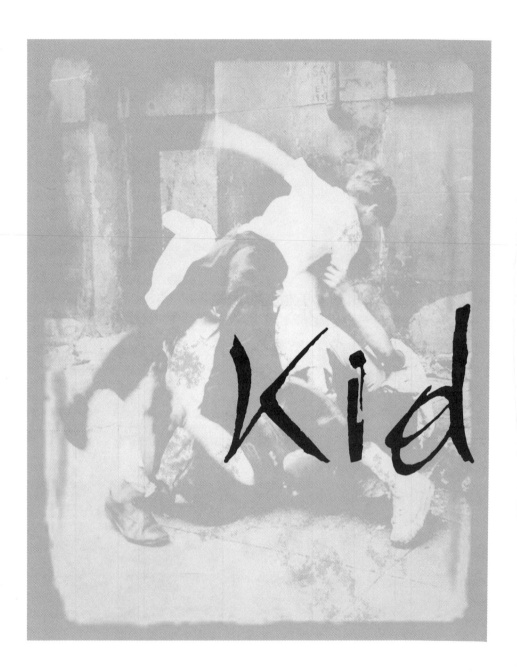

Kid

Tom Walmsley

Stuff

ARSENAL
PULP PRESS
Vancouver

ARSENAL PULP PRESS
103 - 1014 Homer Street
Vancouver, B.C.
Canada v6b 2w9
arsenalpulp.com

The publisher gratefully acknowledges the support of the Canada Council for the Arts and the British Columbia Arts Council for its publishing program, and the Government of Canada through the Book Publishing Industry Development Program for its publishing activities.

Design by Solo
Cover photography by FPG/Getty Images

Printed and bound in Canada

This is a work of fiction. Any resemblance of characters to persons either living or deceased is purely coincidental.

National Library of Canada
Cataloguing in Publication Data

Walmsley, Tom, 1948-
  Kid stuff : a novel / Tom Walmsley.

ISBN 1-55152-153-9

  I. Title.

PS8595.A583K52 2003   C813'.54   C2003-911201-2

For Pam, who has
given me everything

Summer

CHAPTER ONE

i

Moth was lost. He recognized nothing and no one. The overhead lights were scorching and making him squint. He knew the time and place but the scene was alien, with no rounded corners of familiarity. Everything looked scratchy and sharp-edged, like his bedroom when he ran a temperature. It would all dissolve any moment from the heat of the lights. Was somebody filming this? He felt cold and exposed under his robe but his face was sticky and fevered and covered in vaseline. Sounds and faces suddenly bloomed, then shrunk, like a drug scene in a B movie.

The Godin brothers, Roy and Henry, crowded him along. A large guy in a white shirt who looked like a bouncer stood directly under the lights a few feet away. Moth tried to squint past the strangers in the far corner surrounding a man in a terrycloth robe. He needed to see the man's face.

There were people out there in the dark, on every side. Moth focused beyond the lights for a moment and could see them in smoky attendance, more men than women. He looked down and saw a pock-marked man with a greasy ducktail smirking at him. The woman leaning against the man had no eyebrows and looked worried and disapproving. She shook her head at Moth.

Roy and Henry moved him away from the ropes and pushed him into a corner. He looked for the man in the terrycloth robe and saw him raise both hands in the air. The large guy, the bouncer, shouted, the White Trapper! Moth just then understood that the guy had been speaking since the woman shook her head. There was applause from the darkness and somebody yelled, Mike!

The White Trapper. It was insane, a name in a dream. Roy pulled off Moth's robe and Henry tapped him on the arm. He didn't know what he was supposed to do. The guy in the white shirt wasn't shouting, he was speaking into a microphone. Timothy Watson! he said.

What name? Moth asked Henry.

We told him Moth, Henry said.

His name, I mean his name.

Travis, said Henry, Mike Travis.

They moved him under the lights while he was still getting used to the name. He looked away from Henry and saw Travis right in front of him, two feet away. Moth was a couple of inches shorter and at least five years younger, even seven or eight. Travis had a leaner body and less hair on his head. He had a man's face. The referee stood beside them and told them things they already knew, then rapped their protective cups with his knuckles, checking. He looked enough like the announcer that they might have been brothers. Travis was calm and dismissive and Moth beheld him wide-eyed. They touched gloves.

Good luck, Timothy, Travis said.

Moth was back in his corner before he could think to reply.

Good luck, he said to Roy.

Roy and Henry looked at each other, but neither of them asked what the hell he was talking about. Moth opened his mouth to say something and Henry stuck in the mouthguard. The bell rang.

Travis took a couple of steps out of his corner, then held his hands in front of his face and glided the rest of the way to the centre, where the lights were brightest. Moth trotted toward him, the way he'd heard Marciano used to cross the ring.

Roy and Henry watched Moth jog up to Travis with his gloves in front of his chest. They saw him take two jabs in the face, not stiff enough to make his head jerk. Travis came down off his toes, his right held back like he was miming an archer, and Moth threw his first punch. It was the kind of right hand a guy might throw in a bar fight, wild and looping and easy to avoid, but it caught Mike Travis on the side of the jaw and knocked him across the ring. Roy, Henry, and everyone in the club shouted at once.

Moth ran after him and roundhoused another right. It landed high on the head and Travis threw a very straight, hard right hand back at him. Moth took it on the mouth, heard a strange grunt from himself, and had the lights full in his eyes as his head snapped back. He stopped moving. Travis pawed out with his left and Moth swung the right, then ran into him. They clinched.

He's hitting with an open glove, Henry told Roy.

Two fingers of Moth's right hand were taped together. A stranger had wrapped his hands, an ex-fighter who had travelled in the car with them from Bresby. They had turned chairs around and straddled them in the dressing room and Moth had watched his hands thicken and mummify under a roll of gauze. Something felt strange about his right, but he hoped it wouldn't make any difference once the gloves were on. He told the man doing the taping that there was something wrong.

You'd be surprised how many fellows come back to me after I've taped them the first time, the ex-fighter said. He was drinking rye from a paper cup. He had asked the woman driving them if she'd mind if he drank in the car and she'd said she would mind. The car radio had played "Little GTO" and "House of the Rising Sun" on the way there, two of Moth's favourite songs. Now he had two fingers taped together and couldn't close his hand.

The referee pulled them apart and Travis stepped in and hammered a mighty right hand to the jaw. They were both fighting as though their left hands were broken. Moth lowered his head, grabbed Travis and held on, breathing in the smell of his sweat and deodorant. Travis needed a shave. His stubble burned along Moth's shoulder and the side of his face. Moth only shaved a couple of times a month. He'd never been hit like this before, not in the gym or his imagination.

An older, heavier kid from school had knocked him down the year before. They were sparring in the basement without mouthguards and the understanding was they'd restrict themselves to body punches. Moth had turned his head and the kid had hit him on the jaw and the next moment he was lying on the gritty concrete floor with broken teeth and he couldn't open his mouth. A half hour later, hiding in the bathroom, Moth cried into a towel from the pain. He couldn't eat dinner. The doctor told him his jaw was badly bruised, not broken, and asked him twice if his father had done it. That punch had hurt. It hurt when it landed and it hurt for a long time after.

The right hands from Travis weren't like that. Moth knew he'd never been hit harder, but he wasn't being damaged in any way he recognized. He was being moved to places far off the main road, spots he'd never read or heard about. He was frightened and eager. He wanted it to stop, but he wanted to reach the destination in whatever wilderness the punches delivered him.

Travis stuck out his left twice, then threw a right. It bounced off Moth's forehead without serious effect. Henry Armstrong had never taken a backward step in a fight. Neither had Lew Jenkins, Jack Dempsey, or anyone named Rocky. They wrote that about every slugger. Moth had been summarizing and examining his own projected career for the last couple of years and he knew the reputation he wanted to establish and how he wished to be remembered. This was his first fight in the ring. He took no backward steps.

He missed with a right, got clipped on the shoulder, and they clinched. They breathed heavily in each other's ears. The referee pulled them apart and they went toe to toe for two or three punches each and found themselves too close to do anything but hug. In the gym, Moth could hit with short, hard punches on the inside and favoured a body attack. He threw combinations and had worked relentlessly on his left hook. Roy often told him he had a great jab. Travis might have been a dazzling example of artistic brutality in his own gym. On this night of formal combat, they fought like drunk hockey fans.

Moth pushed over a left and threw his right. It hit Travis in the middle of his face a blink before a solid shot pounded Moth's left eye. They stuck out their left gloves at the same time; they both landed right hands. Moth threw another one. Travis backed up, tried to circle and got knocked into the ropes. He stepped into Moth and landed a perfect right hand to the jaw. Moth grabbed him in desperate embrace. The crowd hadn't stopped shouting since the first solid punch of the fight.

There it was. It only happened when Travis caught him on the magic spot near the point of his jaw. Everything else was just a punch.

They were falling through time together. Moth was being clubbed by Travis in perpetual night, in foreign landscapes. It was Day One. The sky was blue and Moth was dead. He fought Travis in the ring, in a palace, on a barge. He could see every fight imposed on the fight before, the past getting smaller the closer it got to the bottom of the tunnel. This fight was miles and centuries away from the first. They fought in a dream. Travis had a moustache and Moth was a boy. His hair hung down like Stanley Ketchel's. He killed Travis with one thunderous blow to the temple. Hundreds of men surrounded them in a clearing in the woods without a woman in evidence. He had always known Travis.

The referee separated them and Moth swung a right and missed. He was here, now, in Toronto, in 1965. This was this. The bell rang.

They grabbed him and pulled him into his corner and sat him on a stool. He was exhausted. Roy pulled the waistband of his trunks away from his body, like on TV.

I thought his name was White Trapper, Moth said. He opened his mouth for the water bottle, took a slug and gargled for a second, then spit into the bucket beside him. The bottle was wound in black electrician's tape and Moth wondered what it had held originally.

Where's your left hand? Jesus Christ. Use your left.

Set him up with your left, said Roy. He smeared two fingers of vaseline over Moth's nose and under his eyes.

The referee shoved his red, sweating face over Roy's shoulder.

Close your fucking hand, he said. You're hitting with an open glove.

Close your hand, Roy said.

He can knock me out, Moth said.

You can knock *him* out.

Roy gave him another mouthful of water. It could have been one of those big Coke bottles they left for you when you were babysitting. The mouth was maybe a little too big.

Listen to me, said Henry. Keep your hands up. Hit him in the body. Use your fucking left.

It sounded rehearsed and corny, the two of them acting out a tired old boxing scene and talking the way you're supposed to talk. They had seen it on TV. Moth wanted to tell them that, but decided it could wait. He wanted to laugh.

Henry was the president of a bike gang. That was a little corny, too.

Moth spit water into the bucket. Everything was coming to him as a jigsaw of random scraps that would never lock into each other.

Understand?

He nodded and one of them pushed in his mouthguard. It was cold and wet. Henry pulled him up by the waist and Roy took the stool out from under him. He wanted to sit there and think a while longer. He wanted to talk. The bell rang.

Travis glided out the same way as before. Moth walked across the ring and into a right hand on the jaw. He almost vomited. Travis was never going to understand him. Maybe this whole fight was a misunderstanding over something neither of them could remember.

Moth used to spar with Ricky Charles and afterward they'd pull down their shorts in a corner of the basement. Ricky was nearly two years younger and they did this every time they boxed. Moth's legs once turned blue from the dye in a wet towel and he didn't notice until he went to bed that night. He thought the colour was a consequence of what he did with Ricky. Once people saw his legs, they'd know.

The dye washed off in the shower and Moth and Ricky kept hiding in the corner. They stopped boxing altogether. Travis could not possibly know any of this. Moth hit him.

He knew how to duck, slip and counter, but he did none of these things. The rules seemed to be that he would hit Travis and then Travis would hit him. They would stand upright and do almost nothing to avoid a punch. It was an unbreakable pattern, preordained. Moth felt his nose fill and his mouth wash in a foul taste that did not resemble copper pennies. Like jumping into the deep end and getting a noseful of chlorine that made you cough and spit when you surfaced. This was jumping into a pool of blood.

Henry Armstrong lost his first three fights but later achieved spectacular success. He knocked out twenty-eight men in a row, held three titles simultaneously, and never took a backward step. Moth could lose, but not by a knockout. No one started his career like that. He was dimly afraid of it happening, but he needed to be hit to get anywhere. Moth gaped at this insane conviction while it formed. He had no time to ponder. His punch hit nothing but air.

Travis could smash him in the face and leave him suddenly alone, surrounded in the woods by a surly audience and no opponent. There was no journey without Travis. Or he could knock Travis cold and figure it out later.

The referee pulled them apart and said something about the open glove, his words no louder than the crowd. A looping right hit Moth on the ear, knocked him off balance, and he grabbed the top rope. A very pretty woman looked up at him, horrified, her hands framing her face. Moth winked at her. Travis hit him again and made everything immediately clear. They weren't in the past, but the future. Moth recognized every blow and movement, but only the second it happened. He had seen all this before, this future that was now the present.

This is now, Moth said. Water ran out of his mouth and down his chin when he spoke.

Spit it in the bucket, Roy said.

He was sitting on the stool in his corner. Henry and Roy leaned over him, as clear as in a dream.

Did he knock me out?

It's the last round, Henry said. You okay?

Moth knew the secret to this fight and all fights. If he could remember what Travis did before it happened rather than at the same time, he could beat him. He could kill him.

I'm really tired, Moth said.

He *did* know what Travis was going to do: paw with two lefts, then throw a straight right hand. Travis carried his left too low and tried to back away when Moth threw the right, rather than blocking it, ducking it, or countering. He backed right into the curve of Moth's crazy, open-gloved punches. That was the past and it would be the future. Destiny had overridden their tactics and training and Moth's gift of foreknowledge was irrelevant.

You want to throw the right, then throw it all the time, Henry said. Keep throwing it until the bell. You can knock him out.

No one gets knocked out in their first fight, said Moth.

This isn't his first fight.

Roy poured in another mouthful of water. Moth rinsed his mouth and spit. If this was the future and he'd already seen it, then why the barges and palaces and woods? Had he seen it all from the beginning of time? He breathed deeply. It was night, about nine o'clock, and he was in the ring fighting an amateur fight in a small club in Toronto. Travis was not Cain and Moth wasn't Abel. This was this.

Henry Armstrong lost his first fight, he said.

By a knockout, said Roy.

Henry cuffed Roy on the shoulder and lifted Moth off the stool. The bell rang. The crowd began to clap as he walked across to meet Travis. The referee stood at centre ring and made them reach out and touch gloves. Then he stepped back quickly. Moth and Travis started throwing punches.

The young guy with the greasy ducktail kept his eyes on the ring and one arm around his girlfriend. His name was Todd and chicken pox had given him a face tougher than his capabilities. He'd been in high school with Mike Travis and they had once almost fought over an empty chair in the cafeteria. They'd argued over who deserved the chair and Travis asked Todd if he wanted to step outside. Travis didn't look tough, but the challenge had made Todd weak and shaky, a reaction he couldn't control. He was ashamed and he walked away. He was still ashamed.

He hoped the kid from Bresby would kill Travis.

He's just a boy, his girlfriend said. She had been saying this ever since Moth stepped into the ring.

He's kicking the shit out of Mike, said Todd.

That's not true. I think Mike is winning and he should be ashamed of himself.

Her name was Carol and she'd plucked out her eyebrows and drawn new ones. She had been dating Todd for six weeks and he was okay, but Mike had been more fun. Mike didn't look like he was having much fun tonight fighting this kid. Carol had a very trim figure and either of these guys should have been grateful she even knew them. They both liked talking dirty and she wondered why they thought that any girl would enjoy that. It was stupid and they sounded like little kids.

She hoped this boy would kill Mike.

Moth held onto Travis while the referee tried to pull them apart. This was more like fighting. He was too tired to sustain an attack and the punches felt just like punches. They landed with a meaty thud on the side of his face and turned his head, like an adult version of a punch in the gym. Travis had lost his accuracy and taken the cosmic significance out of their encounter.

I'd call it a draw, said Roy. They both look like shit.

They'll give it to Travis, Henry said.

Sure they will, Roy said. He's from here.

No. He's not fighting so fucking crazy.

Travis hit Moth and they clinched. They were strong-armed apart and Moth hit Travis. He looked around while he held on and saw a large clock on the wall with no second hand and a white face. It looked like two or three minutes before nine, which told him nothing. He'd seen tired fighters on TV look up at the clock in the last round and Moth had added it to his carefully compiled list of things he had decided against ever doing. It showed the judges you were tired. He had also decided never to clinch or lead with his right hand.

He's looking for the fucking clock, Henry said.

Probably seen it on TV.

Henry was a middleweight who could do everything and Roy was a welterweight who couldn't punch. Henry had seriously considered turning pro, but became the president of a bike gang instead. He had never regret-

16

ted his decision. Roy worked in a liquor store and lived with their mother. Neither of them would be fighting that night and both of them wanted to get drunk.

That fucking Jack, Henry said. I should never have let him tape the kid's hands.

In the ring, Moth and Travis swung wildly, fell into each other's arms, and staggered into the ropes. The referee was pulling them loose when the bell rang. They fell back against each other and hugged.

Do you think I'm pretty good? Moth asked him.

Travis looked at him and snorted a fine bloody mist. He turned away and walked to his corner. Henry pulled Moth across the ring and Roy hung the robe around his shoulders. The house lights came on, sucking the drama out of the night. Maybe they'd come on after every round, Moth couldn't remember. He looked over the top rope at Todd and Carol and waved. With the lights on he could see that she had eyebrows, but they looked like a doll's.

You know him? Todd asked her.

No. Do you?

Why is he waving if you don't know him? Todd said.

It isn't my fault he's waving, said Carol. He was looking at us before it started.

The kid wasn't waving at them for no reason at all. Todd could give her a smack outside and tell her never to talk to him that way again, but he wasn't about to do that in here.

Maybe I'll have to teach that kid some manners, he said.

Carol looked away from him so she wouldn't laugh in his face. If Mike couldn't teach the kid manners then Todd wasn't about to either. Timothy. He probably had a crush on her. It was sweet, but he was probably the same age as her brother. Any other guy would have laughed and got a kick out of it when he waved. She felt suddenly embarrassed and sorry for Todd. It was the closest she'd felt to being in love with him since they'd started dating. Carol leaned over and kissed him lightly near the corner of his mouth. Todd didn't look at her, but he took her hand and squeezed.

Look at this guy, Henry said, pointing at Todd.

Moth and Roy looked at him and Todd stopped glowering immediately. He turned toward Carol and gave her three short kisses on the lips.

What was he doing?

He's not doing it now, Henry said. That's for fucking sure.

17

The bell rang four times, quickly, and the announcer spoke into the microphone. Moth watched Todd and Carol kissing. He heard the announcer's breath and loud, slurred words: split decision, Mike Travis. There was applause and booing. Carol looked up at him and shook her head, the same as before. Moth shook his head back at her. Todd didn't look at him.

Roy raised Moth's right hand and most of the crowd applauded. Travis had started across the ring, but stopped when he saw this. His seconds were two friends with violently scarred and misaligned faces, the result of a drunken road accident. They sneered at Moth's corner, but no one except Travis saw them do it. They stepped on the bottom rope and lifted the middle strand and Travis ducked through and took the three steps down to the floor.

Moth gave Carol and Todd a final look, but they were staring at each other. Henry and Roy led him across the ring and opened the ropes for him. Roy carried the water bucket with the taped bottle inside it and Henry stood on the ring apron, pinning down the bottom rope with his boot. Moth hunched over and Henry guided him through and preceded him down the steps. A fighter about Moth's age stood politely to one side, waiting to enter the ring. He wore a red satin robe and his father and brother held the water bottle and bucket. Moth nodded, but none of the three returned it.

The fight was over.

ii

Beryl climbed down the TV antenna without making it creak or shake. She'd practised during the day when her mother was home and she knew how to step gently onto each rung before letting it take her weight. It was more difficult in the dark, when even her fingers touching the metal made a soft ringing noise. The night was empty of sound. Beryl knew why drunks howled on street corners after midnight.

She ran across the grass in her bare feet and then took five long steps from the swings into the field. Her running shoes were within six inches of her left foot when she stopped and looked for them. She laced them, then stood up and began looking for the path.

Terry parked his car on a dead end street, ran across the road and through the school parking lot and then down the hill behind the school. He stopped at the oak, the boundary between field and school, the one she'd shown him last time. The night was so silent he felt deaf, nothing as loud to his ears as the sound of his own breathing. He had planned to walk casually along the street and then saunter inconspicuously behind the school instead of racing like a man pursued by a wolf. A dozen people were probably writing down his licence number, calling the police, slashing his tires so he couldn't drive away. He was nervous and he hated this. He had to get home before his father finished his shift. In ten minutes he would leave. In five minutes. If she wasn't here in half an hour, he was gone.

The field was lost in the dark, the foliage an unbroken black surface. The homes on the other side were backlit by streetlights and looked like they awaited the invasion of Earth from another universe. Terry watched the pebbled bathroom windows glowing in every house. Any minute something was going to happen. He almost screamed when Beryl stepped out from behind the tree.

I scared you, she said. She rubbed her bare arms and he shrugged off his jacket and handed it to her.

The suede jacket overwhelmed her from shoulders to thighs. Terry took a step closer and she stood on her toes, reaching for him and lost in the sleeves. They kissed a hard, wet kiss. He opened the jacket and stuck in his hands. Beryl kissed him on the neck. They were behind the tree, they were tripping over branches, the long grass of the field was bending under their feet. Terry didn't know if he was pushing her or she was pulling him. She began a slow fall to the ground and he followed her down. He could smell the earth and her hair and she could smell him. They unbuttoned and unzipped each other without a pause or fumble, their fingers settling lightly and exposing flesh to the night and then moving on. They breathed into each other's mouths.

Terry had touched her there before she'd even had hair. Before she'd had hair. There. She raised her hips and when she lowered them she could feel the rough edge of his jacket against her bare skin and the tough yellow shoots of the field sticking into the backs of her legs. His hands were hard, hot and gentle. She took his wrist and pushed his hand against her and herself against his hand. Terry's teeth scraped over hers. He was beside her, then above her, and then on top of her and Beryl yanked down his pants, one side and then the other. She let go of his wrist and circled his waist with her arms, moved her hands down onto the smooth hill below his spine, dug in her fingers and licked his face. Terry lifted his hips against her grip and guided himself into her with his right hand. Beryl gasped and Terry groaned.

She could see nothing, her face against his chest and shrouded by his open shirt. They could have been lying in her room with the covers over their heads. The smell of him was everywhere. She needed a sheet from his bed, she would ask him to bring one. A sheet of his she could cover herself with at night and hide beneath. Beryl pushed her hand between them and felt Terry where he entered. She touched herself. He started moving with a familiar violence that made her feel like she'd been grabbed and was being shaken. Wear a skirt next time. Or take the pants right off. She whispered words neither of them could hear, her voice bumpy and broken like the efforts of a bouncing baby. The muscles in her thighs tightened and jumped. She wanted to wrap her legs around him but the pants held her like leg irons. Beryl touched Terry and herself and her lower body twitched and jerked and couldn't be controlled. She bit him on the chest in the middle of a word.

Terry's face was a couple of inches above the dirt, his eyes covered by the leaves of some tiny plant and his elbows and knees balanced on small, sharp stones. He was in love with her. She would have his child. She is here because this is what she likes. She likes this. She wants him to do this to her. This idea arrived, took his imagination hostage, and finished him off with a loud, heaving sob. He fell onto Beryl and she kept moving her hips until he rolled off. They both stared at the sky.

No moon, Terry said.

Hush, said Beryl.

She put her head on his shoulder and both of them suddenly felt the cool air of the night. They had been lying down together in fields for more than two years, in every season. When Beryl lived in the old neighbourhood, Terry's house had been a block away and he'd had a bicycle. He would coast past her front window and then circle back, riding over the front lawn and along the side of her house. Beryl's window was the only one on that side of the bungalow. She kissed Terry as she knelt on her bed, leaning out the window while he sat on his bike. He reached down the neck of her flannel nightgown and lightly pinched her. He wanted to lift her out of the window and sit her on the crossbar and pedal away with her arms around his neck. Beryl wanted him to pull her outside and lift the nightgown over her head. All last summer they'd spent the evenings hiding in bushes, touching each other under their clothes and then kissing at her window until Terry's neck was stiff.

He was getting cold. There was a song by the Supremes loud in his mind, but he couldn't remember what it was called. Beryl would know, but it was the wrong time to ask. It was the right moment to say I love you, but he didn't feel like it. If he pulled up his pants it would be a mistake. It was irritating, knowing everything you felt like doing was the wrong thing. Maybe she didn't feel the cold and it was just him. What time was it? He could take his father in a fist fight, he was sure of it.

Beryl started singing in a whisper. It was the song by the Supremes. Terry tilted up her chin and kissed her on the mouth, their first soft kiss of the night.

That's our song, he said. Let's make that our song.

There were many songs that made Beryl think of Terry. Every song she liked, really. But they had never had a song that was their song and it was shockingly romantic for him to suggest it. It wasn't her favourite group and it wasn't her favourite song, but there were worse choices. He could have picked one about cars or surfing. Her favourite song, and the best Terry song, was "Needles and Pins." It began playing for her that instant. She couldn't even remember the tune to their song when she thought of "Needles and Pins." She pushed Terry onto his back and leaned over him and touched his lips with her own. The soft ones worked better than grinding your mouths together. Beryl rolled on top of him awkwardly, keeping her mouth on his. Next time she would pull the pants right off.

The night air became colder on her body. Terry put his hands on her hips and then moved them lower. She wanted him to stay until sunrise. She wanted them to do it again. She tried to think of things they had never done before that they could do now, alone in the field. They could take off all their clothes and he could kiss her everywhere. They kissed. She could feel his muscles caught between having to leave and wanting to stay. He was small and sticky and then large and sticky. Beryl pulled one foot free of her pants. Needles and pins.

She got into bed without taking off her clothes because she didn't want her mother coming in after ten minutes with a bamboo stick and whipping her. That had happened once, a little more than two years ago, and she had been asleep until the covers were pulled off and the beating began. It was for stealing change from her father's coat, not for being out at night. Beryl was still ashamed for screaming.

She had a pink record player that looked like a makeup case. It separated into two parts, turntable and speaker. At the time of the beating, she had owned only one 45, "Big John" by Jimmy Dean. All her other records were LPS that had come with the record player and they were soundtracks from Broadway musicals. After her mother had used the stick, Beryl couldn't listen to the records without reliving the night. "Gary, Indiana" and "The Night They Invented Champagne" were the worst. They made her feel like killing her mother, setting the house on fire, blowing up the car. Wearing her clothes to bed brought it back as strongly as the songs. She could get Terry to break into the house and pour honey over the rugs and rip apart the couch.

Her mother would cry over that god damned couch. Beryl didn't want her mother to cry; she wanted her to scream.

She opened a couple of buttons and pushed her fingers under her clothes. It made her feel weak and unprotected, the skin too soft to be hit with a length of bamboo. She wanted to fall into a dream of her body and the night and instead she was rigid in a landscape of injury and revenge. The Supremes had vanished and couldn't be found.

Terry used to chase her in the field behind her school, throw her into a snowbank and stick his cold hands up her sweater. After a while, he started sticking them down her pants. His hands would be warm by then. They didn't kiss for weeks. Or maybe it was only a week. It seemed like forever, anyway. His face would be so close to hers and their mouths would be open and his hand rubbed her where she had only rubbed herself and she still hadn't been kissed. Her brother Moth was sometimes right beside them, lying on top of that Catholic girl from Wayne Street.

She wanted Terry's bedsheet and pillowcase. It was hard to concentrate on him and her mother at the same time. In the early days of summer vacation she'd fallen out of a tree and her mother had yelled at her that she had no right to climb trees and wouldn't take her to a doctor. After a few days the swelling around her elbow went down. She didn't stop climbing trees or stealing change from her father.

Someone walked down the hall toward her room. The floors didn't creak like the ones in the old house and it was harder to tell who was out there. Most of the time it was just a visit to the bathroom. Beryl started breathing between her teeth. She had no plan, but she wasn't going to lie there if she was attacked with a stick. The bathroom door closed quietly and there was the small click of the lock. It could be her mother, playing with her. If she could hear them, it was one of her brothers. Almost every night Beryl thought about jamming her dresser against the bedroom door and she could hear her mother saying that she had no right to block the door. Screaming at her from the other side with her fucking stick. No. She wouldn't try anything with the stick until Beryl's father was working nights.

She heard Moth splashing in the bathroom and tried to let herself go limp so the knot in her shoulders would disappear. Her father was home this week. He wouldn't protect her, but her mother was more violent when he was away. Like she didn't want him to think ill of her.

Beryl saw herself underwater. Her room was filled to the ceiling and she floated out of bed and swam to the window. The world was submerged, the surface of the water reaching the clouds. She could slide open the window and glide above the ground all the way to the field, just like she was flying. Cheryl was a lovely name and Beryl was an ugly and stupid thing to be called. Cheryl flew in slow motion through water as clear as light and Beryl lay in bed wearing all her clothes.

One beating with the stick, for stealing. Slapped across the face when she was washing the dishes and it had made her gasp. She was smacked on the head for bedwetting, hit for making mistakes. Pretty average. Her friend Susan had to take off her clothes for a beating, which was a thousand times worse and something Beryl would never stand for. Terry's father hit him with his fists and she had never even thought about it. It was just because they'd moved that it seemed weird, now. Maybe that's why she hated her mother. Because they lived here.

In the old house she wasn't afraid of taking off her clothes for bed, except for the first few days after she'd been whipped. Now they were in a neighbourhood where parents told their kids that they were very disappointed and made them stay home and babysit or mow the lawn or something that wouldn't scare anyone. They should have never moved.

Or maybe she hated her mother because she knew that having sex with Terry was worse than stealing change. She was afraid of getting caught, afraid of the punishment, and it made her mad. And that's all she could think about when she thought about her mother, now. Every stupid, mean thing she'd ever done. Just because it made her mad thinking about what her mother might do if she found out about Terry. It had nothing to do with Mom. Maybe she felt guilty, maybe she knew she shouldn't be doing what she was doing.

She thought about getting up and writing it all down. There were reasons behind reasons. Her insight staggered her. If she lay there long enough, it was conceivable that she'd figure out *everything*. Writing it down would be a mistake because her mother would find it and read it and Beryl wasn't making that up. She had written a love letter to herself and signed it Richard Chamberlain just to see what it looked like and her mother had showed it to Moth and her father and they had laughed at her and had never forgotten it. This would be different. Nobody would laugh if they knew what she did with Terry. She was getting angry again and she couldn't remember her breathtaking insights.

She swam. Not like a fish in water, but like a bird in the sky. She flew through the ocean like a gull on a breeze and never had to take a breath. There wasn't another living creature anywhere to be found and it didn't bother her a bit. She remembered a fat girl named Cheryl she used to see on her brother's paper route and realized it wasn't such a great name. Girls with braces or dark hair on their arms could just as easily be Cheryls. No one was called Beryl. She took off her clothes under the covers and kicked them onto the floor. It was the greatest way to swim. Naked, underwater, and never having to surface.

She hated public pools and she didn't like the beach. The lake was good, if you could find a place nobody liked. But even swimming holes were better than a pool. She missed the creek. Another thing she'd lost when they moved. It wasn't quite a mile from the old house and there was only one really populated stretch where boys smoked and fought each other. South of that, a couple of orchards separated the creek from the road and there were more woods and fewer people.

Melody Creek had deep pools where kids swam, usually naked boys who liked to stand up and show themselves if a girl walked past. If you followed the path for about an hour the trees thinned out and the creek ran through fields that had no end until they climbed into hills far away. There were no houses and the only people you saw were tough teenage boys with their hard-looking girlfriends. They stood still and stared at you until you went away. Farther along, the creek became suddenly deeper and wider and curved under a railway bridge made of huge, dark stones. This bridge was Blue Arch.

The Arch was reached more easily from the highway a mile below it. An exit ramp for westbound drivers turned onto a dirt road running almost all the way to the creek. At that point the water was sluggish and changing into a swamp. Bugs were fierce and the creek road was the last refuge of desperate teens and crazy anglers. Few of them were motivated to venture as far north as Blue Arch, where the water was deeper and wider than at any other spot. The bridge was as high as a two-storey house and looked dramatic and medieval, even on an afternoon in August. Knights on armoured steeds could have trotted across the Arch after midnight. A rectangular dab of white paint covered one block of curved stone at the apex. The single word *Blue* had been painted on the stone beside it.

iii

Beryl had arrived at the Arch one Saturday in late summer, sweating and thirsty and with no intention of swimming. Her ambition had been to undress and roam the fields. She had climbed up the hill beside the Arch until she found a section of wire fence that was trampled flat. Honeybees flew into her face from the clover that covered both sides of the tracks and she lowered her head and crossed the rails and slid down the hill on the other side. On the south side of the Arch, weeping willows leaned over the water and tall grass began a few feet from the banks. It was Beryl's favourite place on the creek. There were frogs no bigger than dimes and water beetles that looked as big as her foot. The water hardly moved.

She saw a small pile of clothes beside the first willow tree, rubber boots standing next to a shirt, pants, and socks. A white beach towel rolled like a newspaper lay between the boots. Beryl was close enough to see ants crawling over the towel and she stayed at the edge of the tall grass, looking around. They were men's clothes.

A grey Volkswagen was parked far ahead on the creek road and there were no lovers or fishermen anywhere in sight. She walked along the smooth clay of the banks and looked left and right. It was quiet enough to hear the hum of dragonflies and theirs was the only sound she heard. A bead of sweat ran from Beryl's armpit down her ribs like an insect under her shirt. Darning needles. That's what her parents called dragonflies. In England they were called that because people used to think they could sew your eyes shut.

She heard a rhythmic thunder, faint and far away. She knew a train was coming, just around the bend from the bridge, sounding as distant as a truck on the highway because of an acoustical trick of the Arch. The noise got louder every moment until the engine was in sight and then there was nothing but the sound itself, covering everything beneath it. A huge belch of air broke the surface of the water in front of her as the train crossed the bridge and a long, black shadow ascended from the bed of the creek. She tried to watch the train and the engineer waving and the shadow emerging a short distance from her feet at the same time. She waved at the engineer. A tall man rose up in the middle of the creek and looked at her. The noise of the train filled every corner.

The man wore a diving mask that caught the sun and shone as though the light came from his eyes. He pulled it off as he waded toward her, his hair straight and wet and its colour a mystery. Light radiated from him. Beryl knew it was the time of day and the position of the sun in the sky that made it look that way. She knew that later, remembering him. While he came through the water to her, she knew nothing.

He lifted the scuba tank from his back and she saw its harness was homemade, covered in foam rubber and electrician's tape. The dull metal cylinder was twice the size of the air tanks she'd seen on TV. She watched different parts of his body grow firm and distinct with muscle while he hoisted the equipment and put it down at her feet. The regulator was double-hosed and looked official, like the mask in his hand.

Hold this, he said. That's what his mouth looked like it was saying and it made better sense than cold tits, which she also considered.

Beryl steadied the tank, a hand on each side. The man lifted one foot out of the water and removed a monster-sized black rubber flipper. He took the other one off the same way and then stepped onto the bank and put one large hand on the scuba cylinder.

Thanks, he said. The caboose had just crossed the bridge and the word was clear and deep.

Beryl squinted up at him and wished the sun wasn't in her eyes. It made her feel like the fat, evil women in her brother's war comics. Her face became too round when her eyes were scrunched and gave her cheeks like a chipmunk. The man smiled, looking over her head, and Beryl wondered if he smiled because she looked like Petunia Pig. He was about the same age as a substitute teacher and he smelled of the creek, just like any of the boys.

26

They were that close, she could smell him, and he was wearing almost nothing. He stood in front of her at the greatest place in Bresby and they were all alone. Beryl stepped into a dream.

He lay the tank down on the grass, he washed out his mask, he told her his name. Gordon. She said her name was Beryl and when he said Cheryl? she said yes. She said things so stupid that she would remember them for years. How much she liked *Sea Hunt* and Volkswagens. How fat her father looked in a bathing suit. She told him the worst places for swallows, where they almost flew right into your face, and he looked like he was watching TV while she talked. It made her panic. She asked him where he worked, where he lived, and how long had he been diving, in a single sentence.

Gordon said, Would you like to try it? If you don't have a bathing suit, keep your underwear on.

Beryl floated to a bush a few feet behind the willows and began removing her clothes, gracefully and without hurry. She watched him through the leaves while he loosened or tightened something on the air cylinder. The hair on the back of his head reached just below his ears and was plastered flat against his neck. She wanted to put her face against that spot. Her undershirt had a permanent stain from chocolate ice cream and her panties flapped on her thighs, the elastic stretched and broken. There was one large hole and a line of smaller ones just below the waistband and the colour was so faded there was really no colour at all. Her fingers vibrated as she slipped off the undershirt and dropped it on top of her clothes. She hesitated mindlessly for a long moment and then quickly yanked down her panties and shoved them inside a shoe. She stood up and peeked through the bush, a breeze touching her body and verifying her nakedness. Gordon hadn't turned around.

Beryl had already halved the distance between them before he looked over his shoulder. She didn't cover herself with her hands or hunch forward. She wanted to look bored, as though she was so accustomed to nudity it didn't rate mention. A Wild Child. Gordon looked surprised, but not shocked. She wondered if he'd take off his bathing suit.

I don't wear underwear, Beryl said.

He picked up the tank and mask and walked into the creek, saying nothing. Beryl stepped carefully along the slick mud and saw that her legs were covered in bumps larger than a chicken's. She looked at the hair stuck to the back of Gordon's neck and felt the cool water close over one foot and then the other, the stones in the creek bed smooth and flat beneath her soles. Water spiders skated away from her shins, then her knees. Gordon turned around just as the water reached the top of Beryl's thighs and she hurried toward him to cover herself. He was waist deep and she was up to her breastbone. He handed her the mask and had her spit on the inside of the glass and rub it around with her fingertips. She hated spitting in front of him.

He told her the tank was an old air force bottle and she nodded as though she knew what he meant. He said it would be very heavy, and it was. Too heavy to need a weight belt. Gordon took the canvas straps that hung from the harness and snapped them together around her waist. His knuckles rubbed across her stomach and she had a sudden urge to pee, but was afraid he'd know. He told her what to do in a low, calm voice. Beryl put the rubber mouthpiece against her teeth and bit on the nipples on either end of it. He turned a valve behind her head and she blew through the mouthpiece, then breathed. Gordon took a deep breath and put his right hand between her back and the tank of air, taking some of the weight. They slid under the water together.

She wanted to surface immediately. It was unbelievable, as clear as a scene on that TV show. She had no idea it would really look like this. Not in real life and not in Melody Creek. It frightened her to see every rock and weed exposed and sharply visible. Light slanted through the water the same way it came through clouds in religious paintings and her hands gave a pale glow, like the hands of a movie ghost. Maybe she had drowned and was in heaven. Gordon was an angel.

He wasn't right beside her, but a bit higher. She saw his white, shining arm, but she was afraid to look at his face. He was lifting the tank slightly and she thought his hand was hovering directly over her ass. Beryl hoped it didn't look fat, then remembered Gordon wore no mask. She was nothing but a soft blur, probably. It was a real world down here, with too many things going on and too much to think about.

The tank on her back was so heavy she had to push herself off the floor of the creek and swim with all her strength just to keep from getting pinned. After two or three strokes, she sank and started again. She began walking along the bottom of the creek on her hands, her legs stretched straight out, the way a child pretends to swim. She could breathe. Beryl Watson was naked with a grown man and she was breathing underwater.

She tucked her knees up against her chest and leaned back, her feet touching down. Gordon's hand fell away and she saw him stretched above her, as white as the belly of a fish. She pushed herself toward the surface with all the strength in her legs, her arms spreading wide, then dropped her head and flattened herself out. It was a long, diagonal drift to the bottom and she fought to make it last. Gordon was nowhere in sight and she didn't need him. The creek was too narrow. Beryl wanted to be in the middle of the lake.

Gordon kicked his way in front of her and touched his mouth, then her own. She had the wild thought he wanted a kiss. He was fighting to stay down at her depth and he gripped her by the shoulder, but Beryl had no idea she was his anchor. His hand held her in a hard, unfriendly way. Gordon's face looked intense and peculiar and it was an odd place to see anyone's face, you didn't see faces underwater even in a dream. Maybe in a picture of a dream. That's what made her feel strange. That and his hand. He didn't want to kiss her. She wasn't scared, it was just very strange. All of this washed through her mind while she looked at the stranger who held her arm. Beyond him, darkness began at the edge of something that looked like vast, open jaws.

Beryl was suddenly so scared she wanted to scream. They were invisible, on another planet with no one around for miles and anything could happen, all the things she'd heard about. Gordon touched her mouth, then his own. He was telling her not to scream. He was warning her not to tell anybody. She shook her head and his eyes widened, confused. He wasn't warning her. Beryl nodded. Gordon nodded back and reached for her mouth.

She realized he wanted air. He had told her about this while she'd spit on the mask. She took a deep breath and pulled out the mouthpiece, a stream of bubbles gushing free as it floated above her head. Gordon pulled it down and bit on it, his face very close to Beryl's. He exhaled and took a couple of breaths, then handed it back. He smiled. She wished they could talk.

Beryl pushed the rubber bit into her mouth and remembered to blow through it. She took a breath and water trickled coldly over her tongue. Gordon swam over her back, holding the tank, then turned around so his head was just above hers. His hands touched her ribs then circled her waist, pulling her against him in a hug, the air cylinder between them like a steel chaperone.

Beryl stayed perfectly still. She wanted to know what he was doing, but had no way of asking. She wished he'd let go of her so she could repeat her trick and she wished he had the tank and could hold all of her close to him. She saw them weightlessly holding hands, side by side. There was too much to think about. Water was coming in both sides of the mouthpiece and she couldn't make it stop. She felt Gordon lift her and begin propelling them toward the dark.

They flew. A crayfish, larger and darker than the ones she always saw in the shallows, crawled up ahead. It backed away very quickly as they approached and they shot by at the same time it disappeared under a rock. They were moving fast, like outlandish fish mating on the run. A black hole was ahead, sucking them toward it. Gordon's hands were strong against her stomach and when she moved her feet they touched his legs. Water started to pour into her mouth. It was the Arch they were approaching, its mammoth stones rooted in the mud like prehistoric molars, its ceiling keeping light from ever reaching the water. Beryl couldn't face a mystery anchored within another mystery. She grabbed Gordon's hands and tried to pull them away and he released her immediately.

She kicked herself to the surface and spit out the mouthpiece as Gordon bobbed up beside her. The Blue Arch stood right over them and it made her dizzy and anxious. She tried to stand and she disappeared underwater, her feet finding nothing solid. She came up coughing. Gordon hooked an arm around her and pulled her to the shallows in a smooth glide. Their feet touched the bottom.

Water was getting into my mouth, Beryl said.

My fault, he said. We should have practised. Let's try it here, where it isn't deep.

She realized that his eyes were bright green and it made her aware of how seldom he looked at her. It was as though he was afraid of being recognized. Or he was very shy.

I don't want to try it right now, Beryl said.

She didn't know why she said it. Everything had turned creepy all of a sudden. Maybe it was just the Arch.

Gordon touched her stomach and made her jump. He unhooked the belt and lifted off the tank as though it was as light as a pillow, then turned his back and waded to shore. The banks were steeper this close to the bridge and vegetation grew along the very edge. He pushed the air bottle into the grass and left the creek with one long step, without looking back. Beryl moved downstream, watching him.

It isn't my fault I'm not an expert.

No, he said. It isn't.

She reached the willow tree and walked out of the water and onto the mud. Gordon was doing something to the regulator again, or maybe he was just staring at it. He hadn't moved and wouldn't hear her unless she shouted. The sun was hot and Beryl rubbed her wet body with her palms. There was nothing scary about Gordon.

Hey! she yelled.

He said something she couldn't hear, but he didn't raise his head.

Look!

He looked. He knelt beside the tank and pulled it in front of him.

You're a little girl! Gordon shouted, like he was calling her names. Go put your clothes on!

He was lying. She knew it and it made her angry and at the same time she felt like she was five years old standing up in the bathtub. If she shouted back something stupid would come out of her mouth. Beryl ran to the bush and found her clothes. It seemed like yesterday she'd taken them off here. She pulled the panties from her shoe and dropped them, then started getting dressed. He was a fish. That's what she wanted to scream at him. You're a fish.

Gordon had almost reached the creek road by the time she came out. He carried his clothes and diving equipment and he gained on the Volkswagen with long, rapid strides. Beryl had no idea how he'd managed to get so far away without actually running. She hated him, but she felt even worse watching him disappear.

iv

Beryl's mother was standing over the bed and Beryl sat up and grabbed her by the hands without thinking. There was no stick in her mother's hand.

Don't, her mother said. Don't do that. You're having a bad dream.

What's the matter? What is it?

You were crying, her mother said. It woke me up.

She sat on the edge of the bed and Beryl lay down and took a deep breath. It rattled in her nose like she had a cold and she knew she must have been crying. Maybe she'd fallen asleep thinking about Terry. That day with Gordon never made her cry.

Are you all right?

Yes, Beryl said. It was just a nightmare.

Her mother looked a hundred years old, even in the dark. Her face was too thin and there were always pouches under her eyes. Beryl wanted to know how her eyes got that way so she could take any steps necessary to avoid getting them herself. When her mother was a young girl she'd looked almost the very same, but without the deep lines by her mouth. Beryl had seen the photographs. She didn't like her sitting on the bed like this.

Are you all right now?

Yes, Beryl said. It was just a bad dream about that time I fell out of the tree. Sometimes I have nightmares about it and it makes me cry.

Her mother nodded in the dark, silently, then moved closer to speak. She said nothing, leaning over her daughter and moving her head in a tiny affirmative motion. Beryl tried to keep her eyes and face neutral. Her mother sat up, then stood and slowly walked out of the room. She closed the door gently behind her.

Beryl reached over and dragged her clothes into bed. She slid into her pants and pulled on her shirt, her ears straining for footsteps. Then she tugged the covers up just beneath her chin.

She tried to remember a song by the Supremes.

Chapter Two

Beryl was eating breakfast when her mother told her they were going to move to Quebec. Her mother spoke from the other end of the kitchen, where she was pouring boiling water into the teapot, and she didn't look up. It made so little sense that Beryl didn't know what to say. She looked at the spoonful of milk in the bottom of her bowl and the four surviving Rice Krispies. She hated cereal that floated.

Did you hear me? her mother said. Then answer.

Why are we moving to Quebec?

We're moving. I don't have to explain it to you.

She covered the teapot with a thin, stained cozy and put it on the table. A crime magazine, a new one, lay face up beside her cup.

When are we moving?

Her mother put two pieces of bread into the toaster, then put the rest of the loaf back into the breadbox and took out a butter dish and a small knife. She watched the bread turn to toast and didn't answer Beryl.

It wasn't the new neighbourhood, Beryl knew. She'd been wrong about that. It was her mother. Maybe they weren't even moving. Or maybe they were.

When are we moving to Quebec?

Her mother gave her a warning look, bright-eyed annoyance at being harassed.

We can't move while you're in school, can we? After that.

Moth came downstairs, his hair still wet from the shower. He poured a bowl of cornflakes for himself, just like his father, and said nothing to either of them. The toast jumped up in the toaster and their mother took it out and began buttering.

Where's Trevor? she asked Moth.

33

Colouring, Moth said. He sat next to Beryl and began eating his cereal at a measured pace.

Tell him to come down and eat before school.

I'm eating.

Beryl, her mother said. Tell Trevor.

We're moving to Quebec, Beryl told Moth.

What did I just tell you to do?

Beryl left the table and walked out of the kitchen. She shouted her little brother's name from the bottom of the stairs.

What's this about moving to Quebec?

If she didn't have that to sulk about, she'd find something else, his mother said. Don't you start.

Start what? We're moving? Since when?

Your father got a promotion.

So what? Moth stopped eating and pushed away his bowl. So what?

Try that tone with your father.

I will when he tells me. If it's even true.

I'll tell him you said that, his mother said.

Beryl came back and stood in the kitchen doorway, saying nothing.

I'll tell him myself, Moth said. He was standing and his voice got louder with every thought he spoke. Moving? What do you think we are, boxes of clothes?

So brave, his mother said. So brave when he talks to his mother.

Trevor walked around his sister and came into the kitchen with a piece of paper and two crayons, blue and red. He put the paper and crayons on the table, then went to the Rice Krispies box. Beryl followed him and took a bowl down from the cupboard, which Trevor refused. She took down an identical bowl and this one passed muster. She fetched him milk and a spoon while he poured cereal over the counter, on the floor and into the bowl.

Look at that damned mess, their mother said.

Trevor carried his bowl to the table and sat down. Beryl poured milk over the cereal until he shook his head.

When are we supposed to be moving? Or is it a surprise?

Talk to your father, she said. She opened the magazine in front of her and turned to the middle, where there was a black-and-white photograph of a nearly naked woman, bound and bleeding. It looked real.

We have to leave soon, Trevor, said Beryl.

34

Trevor ate slowly with one hand and drew on his piece of paper with the other. He made a broken circle, a v, and a number of unconnected lines that looked random. It was probably a monster, Beryl thought. The v could be a tooth.

I'm making a picture, Trevor said.

Eat, said Moth. I'm taking that picture away if you don't hurry up.

His mother read her magazine and didn't look up. Trevor carefully folded the paper and pushed it into the middle of the table, laying the crayons on top. He knelt on the chair and leaned over his bowl and ate noisily with extraordinary speed.

Moth knew his mother would be cold, quiet and calm. The more he shouted, the quieter she'd become and finally she would start smiling. If he could find the words that immediately drew blood, she would start shouting back and make herself cry. But he was too enraged to have any accuracy and he knew it. He looked at Beryl and she stared back, morose and confused, a comrade in rage. Trevor picked up his bowl and poured the milk into his mouth and down the front of his shirt. He picked up his paper and crayons and got down off the chair.

Put your shoes on, Moth said.

Trevor got his shoes from the hall. He talked to himself as he sat on the bottom stair and put them on. Beryl waited for Moth to speak to their mother, but he said nothing. He sat at the table and looked at his hands, which Beryl could see were shaking.

We're moving when school's over, Beryl said.

It nearly made her mother speak, but she took another bite of toast instead. Beryl went into the hall and a minute later Trevor shouted goodbye.

Bye, Trevor, said their mother. Be a good boy. She didn't look up from her magazine.

Moth looked at his hands and thought about wiping the irritated look off his father's face with one good left hook. A left and a right, no more than that. His mother would scream her head off when he did it. He could feel her across the table, aware of him but not looking up. Quebec. It was nuts.

He wanted to know if they'd move at the beginning of the summer or at the end and he knew he wasn't going to find out from her. She had always managed to make any bad situation worse. Now she'd be able to make his father mad, too, telling him what he'd said. If Moth hit his father he'd have to leave home and they'd call the cops. He wasn't sure he was ready for that.

He thought about beating them both to death and burning down the house. Maybe everyone would think he was dead, too.

Why are you so mean? Moth asked his mother. As soon as it was out of his mouth he wondered why it had taken him so long to ask. It was the only question he had for her and the only one he'd ever had.

She blinked rapidly at her magazine. The question had never been put to her and it had never occurred to her to ask herself.

Who the hell do you think you are? she said, looking up. You have no right to talk to me that way.

You beat my sister, Moth said, his voice low. She was just a little girl and you beat her with a stick.

She knew better than to steal again, after that.

No she didn't. You think I stopped because you hit me with your stupid shoe? You beat her because you like beating little kids.

Wait, she said.

Yeah, I know, said Moth. You'll tell Dad. You can tell him that I'd better never see you do anything like that to Trevor.

He could see she was ready to jump out of her chair and attack him. Moth would sometimes lower his head so she could hurt her hands on it. Other times he would block her with his forearms, which would make her so angry her face would swell. He liked to smile at her when she was like that. All she could do was tell his father. His father was full of tired threats, but he wasn't going to swing on Moth, ever.

You didn't have to tell us about Quebec right now, he said. You just like being mean.

Where do you get your bloody nerve? she said. I speak any way I want to in my own house. You are never going to talk that way again. Never.

He knew he'd be late for school if he didn't leave. Late, serve a detention, get home after she'd told her side of the story. He smiled at her and she smiled back, her face mottled with patches of red. She was breathing quickly and sitting up very straight in her chair. Moth kept his eyes on her when he walked by and she grabbed him by the wrist with both hands. Her voice sounded strange to him, soft and excited.

Don't be bad, his mother said. I might have to come to your room with the stick. Beryl wasn't wearing anything at all. It must have hurt like hell. What do you wear to bed, Moth?

She let go of his wrist and saw his eyes turn damp. She listened to him

36

walk into the hallway, then down the steps to the side door. It opened and then closed without being slammed.

She turned the page of her magazine.

ii

Beryl was made to stand in the hall for passing a note in her history class. The teacher was a young man who was as round and white as a peeled potato. He had tried to embarrass Beryl by having her read the note to the class and she read it in a loud, clear voice.

We are moving to Quebec. I wish Terry would kill my parents.

It wasn't what the teacher had expected. He sent her out to the hall and her brother walked by not two minutes later. They ignored each other at school, but now she waved him over.

Where you going?

Cafeteria. I'm on a spare.

I'm not going to Quebec, Beryl said. It even looks ugly on a map.

They'll make you go. Terry can't look after you.

What are you going to do about it?

Fuck it, Moth said. I want to finish high school.

It isn't fair, Moth.

No, he said. It isn't.

He walked away, rubber soles hardly audible in the hall. Her brother was the only boy she knew who didn't make noise when he walked. Most guys had half moons on their shoes, suicide in a fight on this type of floor. No way of keeping your balance. She'd heard this from Moth and Terry both, but at least Terry didn't wear rubber soles. Moth had bad shoes, dumb clothes, a stupid haircut. Terry didn't dress like every other tough guy, but he dressed. Moth would even wear old shirts of their father's.

Beryl had hemmed her skirt to mid-thigh with safety pins in the washroom before her first class. She had applied a tiny amount of bright red lipstick and some mascara, but not eyeliner. Too hard to remove and it made her eyes red when she did.

She would stay awake tonight, all night. When her mother made her move, Beryl would be ready. She wasn't a little girl now and she wasn't going to get beaten *and* sent to Quebec. Get the stick out of her hand and whip

37

her across the face. Nothing would matter after that. Reform school would be worth it. If Terry was her brother instead of Moth, none of this would be happening.

Moth walked into the cafeteria without looking around. He sat where he could see the teacher and piled his books on the table in front of him. He opened a button on his shirt, slipped out a copy of *Ring* and flipped to the middle, where the top ten contenders were named in every division. *Ring* had the only reliable ratings system. Moth had looked through the flyweight and bantamweight divisions before he realized he was paying no attention to the names.

Mom with a stick. He wished she'd try it. He'd pull the god damned thing right out of her hand. Moth imagined himself jumping out of bed naked and disarming his mother. He rubbed his feet on the cafeteria floor. Kitten Hayward. Curtis Cokes. Luis Rodriguez. He would take the stick from his mother's hand. Hold her down on the bed and beat her like she beat Beryl. Joey Archer. If Archer could punch, he'd be the champ for twenty years. His mother is wearing her robe and he pulls it off. They would call the cops. They would. They can beat you but you can't beat them. His mother pulls the covers off him while he's still sleeping and he wakes up to being whipped. He rolls over on his stomach. Harold Johnson. Willie Pastrano. I can't let her do it. Pastrano doesn't have a real punch, either. Johnson looks like the perfect fighter.

He thought about waking up when she was whipping Trevor. Moth would pull on his pants and not bother trying to grab the stick. Smack her face hard enough to knock her down. Show his father Trevor's welts. Yes. She beats Trevor and Moth knocks her down.

Zora Folley knocked Doug Jones flat on his back in one of the earliest fights Moth had seen on TV. It was the first round and Jones got up. He managed to survive and close ground over the next few rounds and then he knocked Folley out. It must have been in the seventh. The picture of Zora Folley heading for the canvas was on the cover of every boxing magazine the following month. Jones gave an interview and said, Take away his punching room and he's nothing.

Body punching was the best attack. Body punching and fighting inside. They were forgotten arts. There was Emile Griffith, Wayne Thornton, and Jones. Everyone else was a head hunter. No more Bobo Olsons. He could have broken Travis in two if he'd fought like Olson.

Moth was breathing normally and his heart didn't pound. He calmly turned to the last section of the magazine and looked for the fight results from Montreal. It might be a nice place. Maybe it wouldn't be as pinched and crabby as Toronto, which looked like six Bresbys stuck together. He might like it. He might have sex. Maybe he'd turn pro.

His mother with a stick, standing in the dark. Moth looked at the pictures: Eddie Machen, Liston, Cleveland Williams. Where did she get the stick?

Moth wished he'd seen Cleveland Williams fight Sonny Liston. Years ago before he'd ever thought about boxing, they'd fought. Maybe twice. He wished he'd seen it on TV when Trevor was asleep, his parents were out, Beryl was with Terry. It must have been a hell of a fight.

Cleveland. It was a better name than Moth. Sonny was better, as well.

Did she keep the god damned stick in her closet, just in case she needed it?

Moth thought Doug Jones had a good name, too.

iii

Terry found Jimmy O'Hara pissing against the wall behind Buster's and told him he wanted whiskey. It was a warm, clear night and it made Terry nostalgic and miserable. The other guys were already down at the lake waiting for Henry Godin to fight Richie Bender at eleven o'clock in the park.

Get a case of beer, Jimmy said. We'll take it with us.

I don't want to go anyplace, Terry said. I just want to get drunk.

They walked into Buster's through the back door. There were six pool tables in the back of the store and cigars and magazines out front. Buster himself served the customers. He was an old man of forty-three, small and tough and unpleasant. All the regulars liked Buster because he acted like an unpleasant thug, not an unpleasant proprietor. He watched Terry and Jimmy walk in, then went back to looking out the front window.

Lights shone above two tables, the only two in use, and left the rest of the room dim and muddy. A couple of Buster's quiet, fat pals sat reading newspapers on benches against the wall, but otherwise the backroom had no business. No one knew how the fat men managed to read their newspapers every night of the week in the dark or why they were the only customers allowed to use the washroom. No one asked.

Randy Zed was the only guy Terry recognized. He was as wide as a door across the shoulders and trim around the waist, like a cartoon of a tough guy. He was shooting and missing. His opponent was a large, soft kid who watched without speaking.

We want to get a case of beer, Jimmy said to him.

Whiskey, said Terry. I don't want beer.

Yeah, Randy said. So?

I'll give you a couple of bucks if you get it for me.

I'm playing.

I meant, Terry explained, when you're finished.

I need a ride to the lake, Randy said.

Okay.

Godin has no chance, Jimmy said. Richie's twice his fucking size.

You're twice my size, Jimmy, said Randy. Doesn't mean much, does it?

Jimmy's face went blank. Randy looked at him, calm and patient, like a good teacher waiting for an answer. Terry stepped away from the table as though to read a sign on the wall, getting out from between them. No, the sign read. The bottom half was covered in a large scab of dried paint or blood or tar. He heard the two guys at the other table talking about a girl in their social studies class.

I don't know, Randy, said Jimmy. It might.

Randy Zed almost took a step backward in surprise. He carefully put his pool cue on the table without looking away from Jimmy, who watched him with a dull, sullen stare. Terry tried to think of where he could find someone to buy him his bottle if they fought. Jimmy O'Hara licked his lips.

I'm just saying it might, said Jimmy. With Bender and Godin.

It won't, Randy said, and smiled.

They walked to the liquor store and Randy went in alone. Jimmy stared at him through the store window whenever he could get away with it, watching Randy produce the bogus birth certificate and make a joke with the guy at the counter. Terry knew Jimmy wasn't going to try it; he just wasn't. It was more likely he'd start picking on Terry and if he did that, he was going to lose. Terry saw it clearly. He was going to close ground to nullify Jimmy's boots and then keep hitting him until someone pulled him away. He'd had no idea until now that he could take him. Now he knew.

The notion of fighting Jimmy or anyone else tonight made him hollow in the stomach. He felt like everything inside had been scooped out of him like cat food from a can.

They walked back to Buster's and passed the bottle around, one drink each. Terry capped the whiskey and the three of them climbed in the car, Randy riding up front. They drove to the lake without speaking and none of them noticed the silence. Terry wondered where he was going to get drunk. Maybe in the field behind her house? It would make him feel too much like a girl doing something like that. Go to their spot, drink, start crying. He could park somewhere and drink in the car. Don't play the radio. Or he could drink right now and hit Jimmy O'Hara in the mouth.

There were no bikes near the park, but Randy wasn't surprised.

He's not coming here with his gang, he said. He's just going to show up and act like Henry Godin, which is fucking plenty.

A rusted Ford stopped next to them and six guys from school piled out. Their hair shone stiff and wet under the lights spaced around the edge of the park and they had turned up the collars of their shirts. They looked like TV actors playing delinquents. Randy got out of the car and gave the Ford a hard kick, big flakes of coppery metal rattling off its body and heaping on the asphalt.

Move your fucking car, Randy said.

It took them a second to see who it was. The hard looks turned polite, then apologetic, then sheepish, in the time it took for a moth to circle the streetlight. They looked anywhere but at Randy and all of them quietly got into the car. The Ford backed up and drove away.

They think they'll come down here and look tough, Randy said. Just because they're around tough guys.

Terry locked the bottle in the car and followed Randy and Jimmy into the park. He could drink on the beach later. The thought lasted a second. The cops stopped a lot of cars coming from there and they'd be stopping plenty tonight. He'd be too drunk to be ignored. He didn't want to see Godin fight Bender. He didn't know what he wanted.

About thirty guys were standing around the baseball diamond, near home plate. Not many girls that Terry could see. He knew about half the crowd, from school and dances, and the other half probably worked at The Plant with Henry. A space as wide as Randy's shoulders separated the two groups. The workers were stocky men who made Randy Zed look like a kid. They stared right at you and drank from bottles of rye or helped themselves to beer from an open case on the ground. Terry scanned their faces, looking for his father, but all these guys were in their twenties.

Four girls leaned against the chain-link backstop, smoking and staring. A loose hierarchy had formed in front of them, starting with some lacrosse and football players nobody knew and followed by eight or nine guys who were fixtures at every dance in the South End. In the front row were the tough guys from both tech schools, different from the others in everything but their haircuts. Randy Zed joined them and left Terry and Jimmy on their own. Everyone was too tough to talk.

The Righteous Brothers sang on a car radio off in the distance, then suddenly boomed from the other end of the park. The treble hummed and the bass buzzed and the song was almost too loud to hear. No one could make out the car that had crept into the lot and run over the silence. The headlights were on, too far away to cover the crowd, but the music eliminated the distance. Either the driver was ignorant of the battle, or he was an imbecile. The headlights shone and the radio rattled until the song ended. Terry had just decided it must be a couple of girls when the car shut down, the door fell open, and Richie Bender got out and stood under the streetlight.

He started walking across the grass toward them, flanked by no one. His stride was long and easy and he covered ground quickly without seeming to hurry. Just about six feet tall, maybe one-eighty, heavy in the shoulders. His face seemed made of nothing but bone. As quiet as they'd been, the crowd now held its breath. Terry shifted his weight and set his feet as though expecting an attack.

Shadows entered the park behind Bender from both sides and fell into a ragged v, like a convoy of malevolent birds. It was an action silently appreciated and envied by every spectator as a great movie tactic, but none of them knew what movie had inspired it. The shadows numbered ten or twelve and strode behind their man, expressionless and ready, their allegiance clear and beyond question. Terry heard the hollow clink of beer empties being lifted from the case nearby and he scanned the ground quickly for a weapon. It would be a brawl between the guys from The Plant and Bender's tribe, and he didn't want to get caught in it. He found no stick or branch or even a large rock. When he looked up, they had arrived.

Where is he? Richie Bender said.

No one spoke. Bender was only about three giant steps away, almost exactly midway between the two groups. His supporters stopped in an uneven line behind him and stared blankly at the crowd around home plate. It was a placid, insane gaze that chilled even the hard guys.

Henry Godin, Bender said. Where is he?

Terry recognized one member of the backup line, a burly lunatic named Soldier. He had seen Soldier beat up two guys at the same time outside the Settlement House, two guys who'd been looking for a fight all night. Soldier had giggled from first boot to final punch and his head seemed as invulnerable as a basement floor. Terry wondered if Soldier was the toughest they had, then realized it couldn't be true. They had Richie Bender.

I'm not asking you again, Bender said.

Somebody laughed. It came from the other side of Terry's group and his mouth went dry at the sound. This was not going to be thirty tough guys on one side fighting half their number. Randy Zed's row had the only real fighters and there was no unanimity among them. Maybe three of them would do battle and how many of the workers? And how many of those could fight?

He turned his head and faced a sea of ducktails, every man present trying to find the source of the laugh. It came again, a loud, jeering hee-haw that mocked their dramatic pretensions. The working guys broke up their tight knot, making room for the hidden comedian pushing his way to the front and Bender took a half-step forward, squinting for a better look. Henry Godin stopped laughing, but kept a grin on his face as he stepped out of the crowd and onto centre stage. A moment later Henry and Richie were surrounded by a wide circle of friends, foes, and witnesses.

Terry stood between Jimmy and a guy he didn't know who was shrouded in a choking aura of aftershave. The four girls drifted out of the shadows and toward the action, but didn't join the circle. It was a quiet group for a fight crowd. There were no shouts of encouragement or advice and, above all, no jokes. Henry was still grinning, dwarfed by Richie. Terry looked around on an impulse and saw Soldier grinning as well. Most of the time guys grinned because they were terrified, but not here. Terry knew two things immediately: Soldier wanted to fight Henry Godin and Henry was going to beat Richie Bender.

Richie stood with his back straight and his right leg stretched behind him, the toe dug into the earth. His left leg was bent at the knee and it brought him down closer to Henry's height. Henry's legs were spread, but at no great distance, and most of his body was turned toward Bender. He leaned forward suddenly, without moving his feet, then pulled his upper body back. Richie's right leg moved an inch and he stiffened. Now everyone knew what Henry Godin knew: Richie was going to start with a boot. They even knew which boot.

Henry made the same move and took a half-step forward. Richie's boot came as fast as a punch and missed Henry's face by the width of a thumb. Henry hit Richie once to the body and six times in the face. The body punch dissolved Richie's stance and the first two heavy shots to that bony face snapped it back and forth as quickly as a speed bag. His knees dipped and he might have been trying to retreat when the next four punches hit him. His nose spurted blood, he stared up at the sky, his head turned all the way to his left and then all the way to his right. Richie's arms and legs went limp and he deflated like a beach ball, losing his shape as he folded. Henry kicked him hard in the stomach and the terrible sound of Richie trying to scream gave everyone goosebumps. He pitched forward in the dirt and he bled and gagged, trying to push himself up. Henry stamped on his right hand and Richie's face met the ground. He held his broken hand beneath him and began to cry.

Terry wanted to vomit at the sound. He wanted to put his hands over his ears and close his eyes and erase the whole event from his memory. Henry Godin walked away from Richie and picked a beer out of the case. His friends from The Plant watched him as he did, but no one went to him or made a sound. He opened the beer on his belt buckle, took a long swallow from the bottle, and walked out of the park. Richie Bender cried like an infant and the circle around him remained unbroken. Terry looked at Jimmy and saw that he was pale, the skin stretched tight on his face and his pupils so large they blocked the colour from his eyes. The school jocks were the first to begin drifting away, trying to make an unobtrusive exit. Terry looked over and saw that Soldier was still grinning.

Terry.

One of the girls from the fence was standing right behind him, young and lost, looking like a kid experimenting with makeup. Terry didn't realize he was afraid until he saw how afraid she was. Darlene. She'd been in his English class last year and now he recognized her and remembered.

Can you take me home? she asked him.

Okay.

He backed out of the circle, took her by the arm and began hurrying her out of the park. She tugged on him hard enough to make him stop, then kicked off her shoes and picked them up. They hurried on. No full-scale rumble was going to break out, Terry knew. The sound of Bender crying seemed louder the farther they left him behind and it was the only thing they were trying to escape. Terry wondered whether Randy was going to follow him and demand a ride and he risked a quick look over his shoulder. Bender's troops stood like the same supernatural shadows, gathered around their man but doing nothing. The tips of cigarettes glowed like red punctuation all over the baseball diamond. Terry pulled Darlene along until they reached the lot, then let go of her arm. She followed him to the car.

Why was he crying like that?

Jesus, Terry said. Why do you think?

I thought only little kids cried when they were fighting.

Terry wanted her to shut up, but he wanted her to be right. He'd seen guys crying in frustration and rage, swinging at the air while bad nosebleeds soaked their school sweaters, but those guys weren't Richie Bender. Little kids cried and guys who weren't expecting a fight. Maybe Richie had made his reputation on guys like that. Maybe he really had no guts at all, like one of the bullies they tell you so much shit about in school. But guys with no guts didn't fight Henry Godin. Richie wasn't a little kid, even in his heart. Maybe Henry could make tough guys cry.

He drove out of the lot and started north. Two police cruisers went by, heading toward the lake.

Terry imagined crying. He had been kicked, but no one had stomped on his hand. No one had hit him so many times in the face and *then* stomped on his hand. Maybe it was everything happening at once that did it to Richie. It was all too much of a surprise.

Do you know where I live?

Where?

Well, Darlene said. You're driving and you're not even asking me where we're going.

Okay, where are we going?

I don't know. Where do you *want* to go?

He gave her a sideways look. She still looked younger than she was and more afraid than she sounded. Maybe she looked like this all the time. He tried to remember Darlene's face from the classroom, but he couldn't attach anything to it.

45

What are you talking about, Darlene?

I don't know, she said. I don't have to be home. I'm supposed to be sleeping over at Diane's.

I'll take you to Diane's.

You don't like me, do you, Terry? she asked him without a change in her tone.

Terry could see her thighs every time they drove past a streetlight and he imagined what the rest of her looked like under her clothes. She had a nice mouth except that it made her look like she was always on the verge of complaining. The whole school would know, but it was nearly summer. It would be ancient history by September and who could prove it was even true?

Beryl would be gone long before anyone knew anything. She was leaving without making any effort to stay.

I like you okay, he said. But I have a girlfriend.

We could park. You don't have to do anything.

He had heard about this but never really believed it. The girl doesn't know you, you're not on a date, she wants to park. It sounded too much like a dream come true. He started remembering things he'd heard about Darlene and who she liked. She went with the worst of the South End guys, the ones hanging around the dances who beat up on any guy with a nice-looking date. They never fought alone and couldn't punch and their boots were the only weapon they had. Randy Zed didn't even slug guys like that; he backhanded them. Terry didn't want to have anything in common with them.

Darlene had a full lower lip and she pouted naturally. All he had to do was stop the car somewhere they couldn't be seen. Being with her wasn't going to turn him into one of the cowards from the South End. He had to do *something* and this would be better than getting drunk. But there was no reason he couldn't get drunk, too.

You want to park, she said. I can tell by the way you're breathing.

Darlene, said Terry, Do you like me? You don't even know me.

I don't know.

She turned on the radio, usually the first thing Terry did when he got into the car. He wondered if everything he did was different and weird tonight. The deejay was saying something about the Righteous Brothers and Darlene turned it off. For a couple of seconds they could both feel the silence.

Did you ever go with Richie? Terry asked.

46

Darlene said nothing. She reached for the radio again and withdrew her hand without touching it. Terry leaned down at a stop sign and pulled out the paper bag holding the bottle. He passed it over to Darlene, who put it in her lap.

Let's wait till we park, she said.

Terry drove. She'd been with Richie Bender. She wasn't his girlfriend or she'd be famous. Maybe they had just parked and he'd done nothing except sit behind the wheel looking scary while she did the rest. It didn't matter. Darlene had been with him, close with him, they had done something together. And now she had seen him bleeding and crying in the dirt like a little boy. Terry felt like they weren't driving toward anything. All they were doing was driving away from Richie.

He drove past his old junior high, Melody Creek to his right. There were the ugly beginnings of a subdivision he hadn't seen before and he could smell the clay and stacks of lumber on the site. He drove by an abnormally flat piece of land two minutes later and couldn't remember what had been there before. Sewer pipes were heaped on top of each other in neat rows. He wished it was daylight. There was a road that ran all the way to the dump, but it was hard to find without landmarks. Only the garbage trucks used it.

Terry turned east on the first road he reached and found himself driving through a corridor of fir trees without a single streetlight. He reached a dead end at an unpainted construction shack that sat on concrete blocks in the middle of the road. A semicircle had been cleared beside it for trucks to turn around. This wasn't the way to the dump. He pulled around the shack and onto the rutted curve of road and stopped the car. When he turned off the headlights, the world disappeared.

Darlene took the whiskey out of the bag and unscrewed the cap. He heard her gulp from the bottle and catch her breath. She started to take on a shape for him in the dark. It wasn't pitch black, just dark enough. Darker than the field behind Beryl's.

I like this place, she said. Why don't we get in the back seat?

The bottle bumped against his chest as she passed it to him. Terry didn't touch it. A wash of heat rolled through him from his hips to his throat, choking off his breath. The way whiskey was supposed to make you feel, but didn't. He found the bottle and took it from her, but didn't drink. Darlene began climbing over the seat and he reached out with his free hand and touched the top of her thigh. Her skirt had climbed high and his fingers felt the plump flesh at the rear, just before it stopped being a thigh altogether. Darlene slid back to where she'd started and Terry's hand stayed where it was. She was on her knees, almost leaning against him, and he sneaked two fingers into her underwear.

What are you doing?

I'm touching you.

Terry. Get in the back seat. Don't do anything. You'll like it.

I have a girlfriend, he said.

I know. You said. Have a drink.

They're moving to Quebec, Terry said. Which is, like, I don't have a girlfriend.

He felt Darlene's fingers on his wrist, carefully guiding his hand off her leg. Making sure it didn't feel like she was forcing him to move it.

Terry, Darlene said, I'm not going to be your girlfriend. You're giving me a fucking ride and now we're parking. That's all it is.

All the heat moved to his face. She had become older and wiser and he was an eighth-grader getting reprimanded on his paper route. She was like Beryl. He didn't like it, but it made him excited. She didn't think he was cool, he didn't make her feel lucky, she didn't even like him. She'd been with Richie Bender.

Terry unbuckled his belt and unsnapped his jeans. He unzipped and raised his hips, then slid his jeans and underwear down with his free hand. The seat felt like a damp blackboard eraser against his bare skin. Darlene sat quietly beside him, then leaned over. Her hair covered his lap and she pouted her mouth around him. Terry thought of nothing except that she was doing this because she wanted to do it. It was the thought that always worked. He brought his knees together and held Darlene by the back of her neck and she gave a little hum as she swallowed. She sat up and took the bottle from him and sucked down a drink, coughed, and took another. Then she took a deep breath.

Diane lives near the Settlement House, Darlene said. I'll show you the way.

Terry wanted to laugh. He wanted to lean out the window and howl, but he'd never tried it before and didn't think he could hit the high note. He leaned the heel of his hand on the horn and it sounded as loud as a church organ. Two short and one long. It was Morse for what?

You guys and your fucking horn, Darlene said. That's why I like the back seat.

48

Terry pulled up his pants and started the car.

iv

The next time Moth fought Travis, the referee stopped the fight in the third round. Moth was bleeding heavily from the nose and leaning on the ropes with his hands down, incapable of self-defence. When he realized the fight had been stopped, he lunged at Travis and threw a left hook that missed by three feet. Then he started crying.

Ali fought Liston in their rematch the same night and it was shown on a screen in the stadium. The ring was dismantled and the screen assembled while Moth developed raccoon eyes and the upper half of his nose turned a deep purple. He wanted Liston to lose again, to be disgraced, to know humiliation. He wanted Liston to feel the way he felt and he knew it wasn't likely. Sonny Liston had fought cops on the street, run with gangsters, learned to read and write in the penitentiary. He was the last bad man.

The fight was broadcast from a hockey arena in Maine and shown in black and white. Liston went down in the first round from a punch invisible to Moth, got up and resumed fighting, and the referee jumped in and stopped it. The referee was Jersey Joe, who had fought one incredible battle with Marciano and then was belted out in a single round in the rematch. He said that Liston had been down for ten seconds, knocked out.

Henry said, This is the first time I've been ashamed of being a fighter.

The crowd around them shouted and swore. Moth didn't feel any better. Travis had landed a right at the end of the second round that had disengaged him from the proceedings. There had been no epiphanies or journeys through time. Liston changed none of it a jot.

Henry drove them back to Bresby. Roy sat up front with his brother and Moth rode in the back seat with a bantamweight named Callahan and his girlfriend Nancy, who was twice his size. Everyone was drunk except Moth, and he snapped the caps off bottles of beer as they were needed. He had never been in a car travelling this fast.

What if it gets scratched up? Roy shouted. What if you're in an accident?

I *had* a fucking accident, Henry said. My legs were on fire.

Your legs? Nancy said, leaning forward.

49

My pants. They were on fire from the knees down.

Two thousand dollars on a god damned motorcycle, said Roy.

It was noisy inside the car. The front windows were rolled down and Henry and Roy threw their empties into the night. Moth and Callahan had so much vaseline in their hair from fighting that the breeze didn't even ruffle them. Nancy's hair blew around her face and made her look wild and unpredictable.

Your poor legs, said Nancy.

Would you put two thousand into a bike? Roy asked anyone.

I don't know, Moth said. What's normal?

Good question, Henry said. What's normal?

He's a kid, said Roy. Callahan?

What?

Two thousand bucks, Callahan. Would you spend it on a bike?

Why not? Callahan said, rubbing the back of Nancy's neck. One thing's as good as another.

Moth made them drop him off at the top of his street. He didn't want them throwing bottles onto the road and arguing right in front of the house. Nancy looked out the back window as the car pulled away. She reminded Moth of the woman with no eyebrows who had given him the same look at the first fight. He hoped that woman hadn't been there tonight.

Every house he walked past had its bathroom light burning, but was otherwise dark. There were no sidewalks, as though the street was part of a scheme to turn the neighbourhood into a suburb. Not a dog barked. His running shoes squeaked from streetlight to streetlight and he touched his face, exploring a wider, flatter nose tingling under his fingertips. Before the fight a doctor had listened to his heartbeat in the dressing room and squeezed his hands, searching for broken bones. He had given Moth a bored, vice-principal stare and asked him if he played the piano. Soft hands, long fingers. The very opposite of his father's.

When Moth reached home, the living room curtains were pale with light. He cut across the driveway next door and onto the lawn, then went around to the backyard. The lights were never left on at night. There was a rusted swing set at the end of the yard and he sat carefully on the metal seat of the sturdiest. He stared at the kitchen window, wondering who was waiting.

Beyond the swings was an open field that ran all the way to the high school. He didn't know that his sister had sex in that field with Terry. Sometimes when he walked across it in the morning, a grouse would explode from underfoot in a furious racket of ascent, stopping Moth cold and making his heart pound. Some kind of large bird dragging a broken wing had hopped into his path one day and jumped away from him. He had approached cautiously and the bird continued to hop just enough to keep the same distance between them. Moth didn't know what he'd do when he reached it, but he moved slowly so it wouldn't panic. When the bird became more agitated in its retreat, Moth started taking long, quick strides and finally ran after it. The bird flew away, both wings in perfect working order. Moth knew he'd been lured away from a nest and he was angry enough at being tricked that he wanted to find and destroy it. The nest proved impossible to find. He had no idea where he'd first seen the bird and he wandered back and forth across the field, feeling stupid and betrayed.

A shadow moved across the kitchen window. If he stayed out much longer they were going to grill him about it. Tomorrow was a school day. His face wouldn't heal before morning and the fight wasn't going to end any differently no matter how long he waited. The swing gave a low, horror-film groan when he rocked back and forth, louder than a shout to Moth's ears. He kept still.

The bungalow next door had an absence of light that gave it the atmosphere of a house under construction. Moth looked at its back windows and the windows stared back with dead, vacant eyes. The house belonged to a couple in their twenties who had a nine-year-old daughter. After the first Travis fight they'd asked Moth to babysit, which they had never done before. The woman was dark and pretty and Moth had often watched her through his kitchen window when she lay in the sun. No other married women in the neighbourhood had interested him.

The little girl had been asleep when he arrived and made no sound all evening. Moth and the couple had made the bright, empty talk of babysitters and parents, as though they were old friends and he was doing them a favour. They had shown him the daughter's room, the bathroom, the selection of chips and soft drinks he knew he would never touch. He had always been wary of the father, a man of his own height who was muscular and quick-tempered. The father had shaken his hand as they were leaving and Moth had felt the same hard palm and thick fingers as his own father's.

He had brought a recent *Ring* with him and began reading as soon as he was alone. He sat in a high-backed easy chair with the room behind him and after a few minutes he became aware of the magazine, of his hands holding it, of himself sitting in the chair with the magazine. Moth realized he was watching himself as though he was someone else, standing behind the chair. He jumped up and turned, facing the room. Hot and cold waves ran up his arms to the back of his neck and his face itched terribly, like it was thawing out. His heart thumped, loud and hollow, and his limbs twitched with every pulse. The room was empty.

Moth could see down the hallway from where he stood and it was dim and unoccupied. The parents' bedroom was at the very end, the door shut tight. The girl's room was a few paces closer, directly across from the bathroom. Between the bathroom and living room was the archway to the kitchen. He would have to cross the kitchen to reach the back door or he could step around the corner and into the hall to gain the front entrance. Anyone could be hiding anywhere.

Moth saw the room, the unlighted hallway, and himself. No doorknobs turned or floorboards creaked. His mind filled, flooded, and drowned.

The child needed his protection and he was a coward and he hadn't known this a second earlier. Everything about himself suddenly scared him. He knew the little girl he was babysitting. He had found her behind a bush in the field a month ago, squatting to pee, her red shorts covering her knees. She smiled, confusing and exciting him. He hadn't touched her, but he walked her home and he was scared the whole time. Now he wanted to run but was afraid of turning his back on the hall. He imagined that Satan was in the house and would appear at any moment, robbing him of all the faith and courage he possessed. Everything was possible and made sense.

There was nothing between Moth and the night. All ancient and evil things were nocturnal and roamed abroad and he was without weapons or will. He saw what he was: a sixteen-year-old high school kid lacking the essential hostility of the Godin brothers, of Stanley Ketchel, any of his heroes. No one feared him. He was a dreamer, a liar, a child afraid of the dark. Without looking away, Moth scooped a handful of chips from the bowl and crushed them into his mouth. It was his first TV food in months. He felt bottomless and empty.

Something was hiding, waiting in the darkness. He ate the entire bowl of chips while he stood scrutinizing every shadow. There was a chair to his right that would have given him the same view of the hall, but Moth knew that relaxing was a mistake. That's when they came, when you were no longer alert. He waited another five minutes, then sat down, feeling bloated and pathetic. His lips and tongue were stinging, but any drink was to be found in the kitchen and Moth would never be thirsty enough to leave this room.

He hated boxing. He marvelled at the thought, but he was relieved to acknowledge his secret. He wanted a gun. There was another bag of potato chips, but it was in the fucking kitchen and he needed it. He wanted to cry. He wanted a girlfriend so he could pick up the phone and call her right now. If he had a girlfriend, she would already be here. Moth wondered if he would run outside and leave her behind as well. If he stayed where he was and didn't move, nothing would happen. You couldn't act brave when you were this scared. Maybe he wasn't even brave enough to use a gun.

He had pulled down his pants with Ricky Charles all summer. The little girl down the hall had made him hot and nervous, standing up with her shorts down. He had had dreams of being punished by his French teacher, a stern woman with pale skin. He was too ashamed to fight anyone over anything. The night was too big and he was too small in it. There was no defence and no way to beat it, any more than he could beat the rain or the morning or his dreams. He could neither defeat nor defend himself against the girls at school who wore tight jeans and high heels and pretended they didn't understand dirty jokes, which they would repeat with wide eyes, asking Do you know what this means? Moth wanted to kill them. They were animated proof that emptiness was in control and even sought after. He wanted them and he wanted them to want him.

The couple had come home just after midnight and the woman had looked in on her daughter while her husband paid Moth. They had both been drinking and they looked relaxed and attractive. Moth was stiff and exhausted from vigilance. He had gone home and broken his New Year's resolution to read a verse of the Bible every night before going to bed. He hadn't done fifty push-ups or said his prayers. He had lain beside his younger brother in the bed they shared and wondered if Satan had followed him home.

Now Moth stood up carefully. The swing made scarcely a sound. His face felt bigger than it had an hour ago. He was suddenly so tired that he could have stretched out on the lawn and slept until sunrise. It had given him hope, or something like it, remembering the babysitting episode. Fear had ruled that night and followed him for days after.

He had felt nothing tonight, not even the faint tingle of apprehension he had before a race on Field Day. He had panicked when the fight was stopped, but he had never been afraid. Calm and empty in the dressing room before, beaten and hollow afterward. He had never been afraid.

Moth walked across the lawn to the side door of the house and went inside.

v

Terry was waiting by the front door of the school when Moth came out after his last class, trying to catch up with a lean, dark-haired girl who was ignoring him. Moth reached for her books and she held them closer to her chest and kept walking. She stopped when she saw Terry and he recognized her when she looked at him. Francine. Terry knew her brothers.

Moth turned toward him and Terry saw what a beating he had taken. His eyes were still underlined by dark blue pouches and most of his face had turned crayola yellow. His nose had moved slightly to his right.

Jesus, Terry said.

Lucky punch.

Francine walked past Terry and Moth hesitated, wondering how it would look if he ran after her.

She's mad at me, Moth said.

Terry wasn't interested. He was impressed by the amount of damage a boxing glove had produced. It looked like Moth had taken a boot or two to the face.

You didn't look this bad the first time, he said.

I was too close the first time, Moth said. This time I was standing back, right at the end of his arm. Take away his punching room and he's nothing.

You want to take a ride?

Moth followed him across the school parking lot to the car. He wondered what Terry would be like in the ring and how he would have fought Travis. Too heavy. Terry looked more like a light-heavyweight now.

They climbed into the front seat and Terry started the car.

You heard about Richie Bender and Godin, I guess.

54

Yeah, Moth said. I wish I'd seen it.

It takes all my time, seeing your sister, Terry said. I've got no time for anything. So what is this shit?

He drove slowly through the lot, waiting for knots of students who refused to move or hurry past. Once he reached the sidewalk, Terry muscled his way onto Myrtle Road.

So? he said.

What shit? Quebec? My old man got transferred. Beryl must have told you.

She says she can't see me, Terry said.

It's my mother, said Moth.

So that's true? It's your mother?

Yeah, said Moth. Of course it's true.

Terry drove down Myrtle toward the shopping centre. He took a left just before the main intersection and Moth realized he was heading toward the old neighbourhood.

I can't stay out too long, Terry.

I'll take you back, Terry said. I want to show you something.

They drove past The Plant, where the day shift had just ended and the night shift was arriving. In ten minutes the road would be dense with new cars.

The hourly-rate guys always have the best cars, Terry said. You notice that?

Moth hadn't, but he'd heard his father say it. The Plant had always scared him. It covered twice as much ground as the shopping centre and stretched out behind a high chain-link fence. It looked like an orphanage in a silent movie, or a reform school.

Would you want to work the same shift as your father? Terry asked him. Just my luck, I'll get on the line right across from my old man.

I'm not working at The Plant, Moth said. Never.

Half a dozen warehouses stood at odd intervals along the road beyond The Plant. Fields of broken asphalt surrounded them. After that the road narrowed and small bungalows with tiny lawns appeared. Hedges. Moth had a theory that no one except office workers had hedges.

How long is this going to take? Let me call home about dinner.

Terry pulled into a Sunoco station and stopped at the air compressor and Moth got out of the car. He recognized the gas station and remembered

55

the phone booth on the corner, but something had disappeared and something else had taken its place. He couldn't tell what was gone or what had
been added. Moth shut himself in the phone booth and watched Terry check
the pressure in his tires. A light-heavy for sure. Beryl answered and asked
Moth where he was and then the connection was broken. Moth didn't have
another dime.

What happened?

Moth got into the car and slammed the door and Terry hung up the
hose. He slid into the front seat.

My mother is a cunt, Moth said.

She's your mother, Moth.

Listen, Moth said. Beryl answers the phone and when she hears me she
wants to know where I am. My fucking mother grabs the phone and hangs
up. Because she thinks Beryl is talking to you.

How do you know? Maybe Trevor was playing with it.

I just know. I know her.

Don't call your mother a cunt.

Terry drove out of the station and a block later turned right on Winslow.
Moth prickled when he realized where they'd turned. He couldn't make
sense out of it. There was an apartment building on the corner and a play-
ground beside it and neither of them had existed when he was here last.
He knew the Sunoco station and a block away knew nothing. Trees. That's
what had been erased. The trees were gone and nothing had a background
any more.

This is crazy, Moth said. We didn't move that long ago.

Tell your father you don't want to go, Terry said.

They passed the school, which was in its rightful place. He could see
the woods behind it.

I mean, move from here, said Moth. They're changing everything.

Wait, Terry said.

Winslow looked much as it always had until they passed a flat plot of
land. Something had once been there but Moth couldn't remember it. He
looked at the ordered rows of sewer pipes and saw those flat, pointed sticks
poking out of the ground. They were tied with red or blue ribbons and divided the plot. You always got a handful of slivers from them and the ribbons
were some kind of stretchy plastic. After that came the muddy clutter of the
new subdivision. There were no workers, only the indestructible yellow ma-

chinery of construction sites. Moth didn't know why it upset him.

When they reached their old junior high on the corner of Winslow and Melody, Terry pulled over and stopped the car. He slid out and crossed the road and started climbing the most familiar hill in town. Moth couldn't think of what to do except follow him. He got out and looked around. The orchard was there, farther up the road, across from the raspberry field. Behind him, the school looked as dark and old as The Plant and the same bungalows with their wrought-iron porch rails ran along Melody.

Terry was already close to the top of the hill, treading the path they'd used most of their lives. It ran from the road all the way up and was as deep as a ditch. Moth jogged over and started up the long, shallow slope. Some of the bloodiest fights he'd seen had taken place beside Melody Creek and Terry had established his legend there. Moth wondered if Terry wanted to fight him. He stopped hurrying and caught his breath and climbed the rest of the way with measured strides. Terry stared down at him as he came, his expression inscrutable.

Moth stepped off the path as he reached the top, keeping more than an arm's length between them. Terry wasn't looking at him.

Don't you want to kill somebody? asked Terry.

Moth looked down the other side of the hill and felt swallowed up by a dream. He had a sickening instinct that he was still in the ring with Travis, transported to another strange land. It would never end until one of them was dead. He looked over at Terry, then looked back at what had been Melody Creek.

He didn't know what they'd done or how they'd done it. From the base of the hill a grey infinity of pale clay extended in every direction and covered everything that had come before. It reached as far as he could see to his left and right and only paused at another hill directly ahead, a mile away. The creek was just a crack in the clay, a trickle running down its leg. There were no boulders, weeping willows, long grass, pathways, or brush. Not an insect, butterfly, or swallow. No kids, tough or otherwise. It looked like it had all been removed with a giant eraser, leaving no trace.

It's like this all the way to the bridge, Terry said. They've just started behind the orchard.

Moth said nothing. He couldn't remember the last time he'd been here and he didn't know why it made any difference to him. Beryl should see this, he thought. She'd feel better about Quebec.

This place was practically the whole story of my relationship with Beryl, Terry said.

It dumbfounded Moth to hear it. He had no idea that there was either a story or a relationship. It was just something they did.

This is crazy, Moth said.

Somebody told me it's going to be a golf course.

I can't see where anything was, Moth said. Shit. Gordie Bly. Where did you fight him?

Fuck Gordie Bly, Terry said. I used to come here with Beryl. I had to carry my bike down this hill and you couldn't see anything at the bottom. You couldn't see anything and no one could see you.

Terry almost whispered the last word and Moth didn't look at him. He stared at the empty landscape and waited. The creek held no memories of love or victory for him, but he felt angry and empty and his feelings embarrassed him. In a war, they bombed the town you lived in and destroyed everything. Your friends died or had their legs blown off or your parents were killed. People lost it all. This had been nothing but a patch of trees and a little creek he played in when he was a kid. Only a baby would cry about it.

Do you know Darlene Bain? Terry asked.

No, Moth said.

This moving thing has fucked me up, Moth. I came down here because – I don't know why. I just came here. And now it's gone, too. Do you think it means something?

Moth didn't speak. Terry made it sound like God was sending signs. Beryl leaves town so Melody Creek is flattened like Sodom. Terry was a god damned fool.

I'm fucked up, Terry said.

It's going to be a golf course. That's all it means, man.

Look, Terry said. Darlene Bain. Beryl's leaving and I'll probably never see her again.

We'll never see Melody Creek again, that's for sure.

Are you listening to me, Moth?

Terry, Moth said. She's my sister. What can I say about it?

They both looked at the clay below and the silence lasted long enough for Moth to adjust his balance. Tough guys always liked to slug someone when they were upset and Terry was just like the rest of them. Moth felt calm at the prospect. It was Melody Creek that scared him.

Terry leaned over and picked up a stone, then stepped back and pitched it far to his right. Moth watched its long arc to the ground, where it surprised him by bouncing. The clay looked like quicksand.

No, Terry said.

He found a larger rock and threw it harder. It rolled more than bounced when it landed, about twenty feet to the right of the first stone.

Shit, said Terry. See where the second one landed? Go a little ways in front of it, then maybe ten yards to the right.

Yeah, okay.

That spot? I figured it out. That's about where I beat Gordie.

They looked at the spot, which was as featureless as everywhere else.

That was a hell of a fight, Moth said.

Yeah, Terry said. Come on. I'll drive you home.

He led the way. Terry knew that if they stayed any longer he was going to start talking about his mother.

CHAPTER THREE

i

It took Beryl and Moth almost an hour to walk to the arena, twice as long as it would have taken him on his own. She hated side streets and liked going into stores along the way to steal candy, which was beneath Moth ever since he'd been arrested for break and enter. He wouldn't stop walking or even slow down for her. They had argued about it and then stopped talking altogether. Five minutes later, Beryl was bored by the silence.

Terry can beat you up, she said.

So what?

So be nice to me.

Shut up, Moth said.

Terry says he'll kick your head in if you get me in trouble. He says he can beat you with one hand. You're nothing to Terry.

He didn't say that and you know it.

Ask him, said Beryl.

I will, Moth said.

They entered the park at the north end and crossed it in silence. Beryl stepped over the broken slats of a fence two paces ahead of her brother. She half slid down a short hill and Moth followed, running to keep his balance. They took a path that was as hard and flat as pavement all the way to the creek.

Do you come home this way, too?

Yeah, Moth said, although he didn't.

Aren't you scared?

Scared of what?

A tree trunk stretched from bank to bank and they trod slowly along its length to the other side of the creek. Beryl hoped he was lying about coming home this way in the dark. She couldn't stand the idea of her brother being so brave. He was no braver than she was. Terry wouldn't walk through here, but he had a car. Terry thought that hanging around the creek and walking across logs was for kids. He was right. You never saw an adult down here and if you did, he would be a maniac.

They followed the path up a steep hill that had wooden steps running pointlessly down half its length. At the top of the steps there was an unpaved road that took you all the way to the arena.

Wait for me when this is over, she said. I'm not kidding.

You say anything else and I'm going home. *I'm* not kidding. Fuck you, Beryl.

They reached the top of the hill and stepped out into the road. Beryl could tell he was becoming enraged and in a moment he'd be capable of anything. So would she. Her back teeth ground together and made a brief, high squeal. She had to see Terry. She had to shut up. She wanted to kill her brother.

They both started running without a word or a glance between them. Moth had a long stride that made it look effortless, but he strained to put distance between them and strained more to look like he was barely trying. Beryl pumped her legs in a pneumatic fury. They kept their positions all the way to the arena, separated by no more than the length of a bicycle. If they had reached out, they could have held hands while they ran. Moth slowed and stopped in front of the concrete stairs and Beryl took an extra step and jumped onto his back. She covered his eyes so he'd know she was playing and Moth grabbed her legs, holding her in a piggyback position. They sucked in air and didn't try to speak.

Three men in their thirties got out of a pickup in front of the building and walked past Beryl and Moth without saying a word. A young guy with a little boy about eight years old walked around the corner and the boy yelled Piggyback! before they went inside. Beryl straightened her legs and Moth slumped, letting her slide down. They were still breathless.

I'll go get him, Moth said.

He paid for his ticket just inside the door and then went to the snack bar to find Terry. There was a lineup, but Terry wasn't in it. Every guy in line was about Moth's age and they were all buying giant cups of Coke. Moth wanted one. What he really wanted was any kind of orange drink, which was the only thing that worked when you were really thirsty. Terry wasn't in the line, he wasn't looking at the candy bars, he wasn't in the washroom. Moth hurried around the corner to the open space of the arena.

The stands were about three-quarters full. Every seat on the floor near the ring was taken and he didn't check any other seats. There was no chance that Terry would be sitting down, but now Moth could say he had looked. He gave the bleachers a quick once-over from where he stood. Faces stared back, but they had none of the hostility of a boxing crowd. In a few minutes the first match would begin and he had no seat and no drink and all because his stupid parents wouldn't let his stupid sister see Terry. He trotted back to the window and told the ticket taker he was going outside.

Beryl was sitting on the steps and she didn't even look up when he told her.

Yeah, she said. His car isn't here.

You want to come in? Moth asked her. She looked too sad to leave alone.

Beryl shook her head.

I'll wait for him here. His father is probably trying to kill him. Terry's going to show up.

Moth walked away slowly enough to indicate that he shared her misery, then ran back to the bleachers. The spot he'd seen earlier was still open and he sat down just as Gentleman Jim Hady walked out. He looked no taller than Moth but was about a hundred pounds heavier. The crowd knew him and cheered his approach. Both of Gentleman Jim's ears were terribly cauliflowered, like a popular idea of a punchy fighter. Moth had seen plenty of cauliflowered ears on wrestlers, but none on boxers except in old photographs. Maybe in the future wrestlers wouldn't have them either. It was a stage in their evolution.

Gentleman Jim walked with his back very straight and his arms held away from his body, like one of Henry's friends. It had taken Moth a long time to accept him. His nickname belonged to the conqueror of John L. Sullivan and it was the title of one of the very few good boxing movies. But now Moth liked Jim Hady. There wasn't a hint of the exotic about him. If he was a gentleman it was a case of blue collar good manners, not the refinements of a man on a fox hunt. He looked like a guy you might know.

Hady had just stepped between the ropes when Sweet Daddy Siki strutted onto the concrete. He was as dark-skinned as Gentleman Jim was dough-coloured and he grinned as though he was about to laugh. Jim exuded a grim sense of duty. There were friendly catcalls as Sweet Daddy stalked the ring in his high-topped white tasselled boots. It was hard disliking either one of the men.

The bell sounded three times to get their attention, the same as it did at a boxing card. The referee looked like the ref from the first Travis fight. Referees looked like the bartenders in movies. Moth wished he was a professional wrestler, giving and taking fake punches and everyone having a good time. The only time a boxing crowd acted like a wrestling crowd was when someone was being beaten unconscious. Or you were going toe to toe and hammering the shit out of each other. Neither Gentleman Jim nor Sweet Daddy looked tight and nervous. No one was going to get hurt.

Jesus, how many times are we going to see these guys? said the man next to Moth. He wore an open-necked shirt and a sports jacket, like a tough guy at church.

I've seen you here before, the man said. We've seen these guys, right?

Yeah, said Moth. He didn't remember the man.

Yeah, the man said. He smiled and winked at Moth, as though they had just shared a secret.

The crowd cheered Jim and shouted at Sweet Daddy. Neither of them had rabid fans or enemies. Moth tried to watch the ring and the man next to him at the same time. If he changed seats it was like saying he was scared. The guy was in his twenties, a grown man. He looked trim and hard, even in those clothes. It made Moth nervous and it made him angry. The man moved closer, his shoulder touching Moth's, just as Sweet Daddy and Jim Hady went head to head.

The bleachers were crowded. It might have been an innocent move, an accident. Moth's breathing turned ragged and he knew his voice would tremble if he spoke. He hated this part. If they could just start throwing punches he'd be fine, but the buildup wore on his nerves. Shoulders touching, then thighs, then more and more friendly pats on the back. At what point did you threaten the guy or start punching?

Sweet Daddy got Gentleman Jim in a headlock and started walking him across the ring. Moth couldn't concentrate on what he was seeing and he wanted to scream at the injustice being inflicted on him in the bleachers. What if he turned and faced the guy and screamed at the top of his lungs? No one likes sitting next to a lunatic. Sonny Liston got spooked at the weigh-in the night he lost the title and it was all because he suddenly believed he was going to fight a man who was insane. All Moth wanted to do was watch a wrestling card. It wasn't fair, going out for a good time and having to smash a stranger in the face.

Their thighs touched, then the man moved away. Jim Hady body-slammed Sweet Daddy.

Crowded, the man said to Moth.

Yeah, Moth said. I'm going out to the parking lot.

The man's eyes opened wider, as though encouraging Moth to repeat what he'd said. Moth stood up from the bench and moved past a couple of pairs of knees, then climbed down from the bleachers. Young guys were shouting threats at the ring and tight-lipped older men shook their heads at Sweet Daddy's tactics. Moth's legs were unsteady and he felt two punches away from stability. You have to give one and take one and then everything was okay.

He walked through the deserted space in front of the snack bar and a kid about his own age watched him with suspicion from behind the counter. Moth had a yearning to attack him. They were about the same weight and he had just cause, being stared at like that. He kept walking, past the ticket booth and outside the arena. It would be dark in another fifteen minutes. He wished he was fighting the kid instead of the man in the bleachers.

Beryl wasn't on the steps and Moth couldn't see her in the parking lot. Maybe Terry had shown up. He breathed deeply and watched the door. It must be like this for a girl every time she goes out. The man he waited for was probably in good shape, good with his boots, hard to beat. Moth tried to stop thinking beyond the moment. Don't argue with him. Once you let them talk, you're lost.

He had heard it all before. It was an accident that his dirty mind blew out of proportion. It was something he secretly wanted, like it was all his own fault. They looked at you like they didn't know what you were talking about and sometimes they smiled or laughed. Hit them and they stop smiling. What happened with the last guy who did this? It was a bus ride, thigh to thigh. Moth got off the bus at a stop blocks from his destination and thought the guy was right behind him, but the doors closed and the bus drove away. The guy was sitting next to the window but didn't look at Moth as he went by. Not that guy. Who was the last one who followed through? That kid in the shower at school, a sprinter from the track team. Once they got out of the shower the kid quickly dried off and left. Moth hurried to catch up, but there was no one outside the school. Didn't count. Who was the last guy?

All the guys who looked at him that way were well built. Their muscles seemed to grow while Moth watched. They became more formidable the longer he thought about them and maybe that was happening right now. Maybe this guy tonight was soft all the way from his neck down and one good shot would break him in two.

The door to the arena stayed shut. He might be getting a weapon. Or washing himself, hoping for the best. The top half of a broken bottle lay near Moth's feet. It had one long, lethal tongue of glass extending about four inches. He left it where it was, only a step away if the man had a knife. No one had pulled a knife on him so far. Had they? The image was familiar, but Moth couldn't remember the details. He stared at the broken bottle, trying to bring a memory into focus and wondering how the hell they made bottles, anyway. Some kind of mould they'd cover in hot liquid glass. You'd think they would have poured it over enemies back in the early days and there would be a museum of naked glass people frozen in their agonies. Maybe there was. Somewhere a sultan had a palace full of them. .

The last guy. Someone had touched him, mocked him, fought him. No. It was after the last one that Moth had become convinced that fighting was the only way. They didn't listen when you spoke. He didn't invent their actions and it wasn't his fault. The guy had said, You really like doing this, don't you? Moth could see him, excited and looking like he was in love. Ricky Charles.

Moth looked up and in that very second he knew he was waiting for nothing. No one had ever followed him anywhere. He'd heard every argument, but no man had spoken the words. Every voice was his own and there had never been an opponent or a punch thrown. Moth knew this for only a moment and then lost it forever. He stuck the words into the mouth of a faceless, mocking enemy whose name was a mystery. Some overweight teacher smiling fatly at him and telling him it was all in his mind. He tried to pick the perfect speaker. Terry. Too stupid to understand anything but absolutely convinced it was Moth who was too thick. Terry was saying, A guy bumps into you in the bleachers and you make up the rest.

Terry would have said to the guy, What are you – queer? Then there would have been a fight or the guy would have vanished. But it would never have happened to Terry. He looked too violent to rub.

Moth picked up the half-bottle and thought about shoving it right into the centre of Terry's face. Right through the eye of the guy in the bleachers.

He thought about the football coach who taught health and he saw the bottle bury itself into his sagging gut.

Don't sweat it, Moth would say to them. It's all in your mind.

He dropped the bottle and it cracked on the gravel, losing all use as a weapon. He couldn't go back inside and it was going to take a long time for Beryl to get back.

It was turning to night very quickly.

ii

It was already dark when Beryl left the road. She knew as soon as she was on the hill that she'd have to hurry if she wanted to find the log where they'd crossed. She almost sat while she crawled down the slope, digging in her heels with every step and holding herself off the ground with stiff, unbending arms. She felt like a crab, or as though she was doing a push-up upside down. Something about it felt like sex, but maybe it was because she'd been expecting Terry. She stopped near the bottom to make her arms stop shaking and held tightly onto the long grass. Imagine if she'd had to crawl down the bank of the creek like that when she used the scuba tank. Gordon trying not to stare and pretending it happened to him every day. Could Terry beat up Gordon?

He shouldn't have gone home. He knew he was meeting her and he should have known he'd have a fight with his father. Not even a fight – his father would hit him and Terry would take it. Moth would knock their father flat if he ever tried something like that. But their father wasn't Terry's. Beryl slid the rest of the way down the hill, leaving the path altogether. The ground was barely visible. Her brother thought he was so brave, but there was really nothing to it.

She got up and looked toward the creek, trying to find the log that spanned it. It was getting too dark, too fast. She scraped her shoes through the weeds and dirt, feeling for the path. All at once her feet stopped moving and Beryl felt like she was looking through one end of a roll of wrapping paper, or a telescope that made nothing larger.

The dark shape of a man stood tall on the log, looking at her. She could see him because he was so devoid of light that everything else almost shone. Beryl looked to one side to focus on him and she realized he was moving.

66

He was on the log, then at the end of the log, then he was gone. He was coming for her.

She crouched low and didn't scream. He already knew where she was and kneeling on the ground wouldn't make her invisible. She wanted Terry and her brother to come down the hill. Beryl wanted her father. Closer than she would have thought possible, a boot made a dull thud against a rock. He was almost there. She was just a little girl. He wouldn't do anything to a girl.

Beryl started running.

She ran at the hill and fought her way up, digging in with her feet and tearing out clumps of grass. The steep hump near the bottom was the hardest and slowest part to climb and she had to put it between herself and the stranger as fast as she could. She climbed and clawed, wetting her pants just a little but too scared to cry. As soon as she began leaning over to grab at the grass, she knew she could almost run to the top. Beryl gave a quick look over her shoulder and there he was, as close behind as a rabid shadow.

It was nightmarishly unexpected. Monsters had hidden in closets and basements and under beds all her life, but now they had entered the world. Beryl stopped climbing and sat down, trying to think of the magic words that would stop this. All power had left her legs and her skin was electrically charged. He stopped when she did, only a lunge away. She could hear his breathing and smell his body. This was their appointment. He was here and it was now, all of it impossible and unjust. He smelled like a dead animal, like the ones you find under wet leaves in a ditch.

The hill was too high and too steep and there was nothing she could do about it. The stranger moved up closer, on his knees. He was saying a single word she couldn't understand, repeating it with every breath. He had no face but wore no mask. Her bladder emptied. Beryl screamed. She felt his fingers on her leg and screamed again. It gave her back her legs. She rolled away from his hands and started to stand up and he knocked her feet out from under her. She landed heavily on her hip, felt herself start to roll and went with it.

She bounced into space when the hill fell away. He was reaching for her when she started to fall and she would have screamed again if she'd had the time. Beryl braced herself and hit the hard, flattened path on her right side. She saw how unbelievably tall the stranger was as he hopped down in front of her. He came no closer, sounding like a man trying to catch his breath after being hit in the stomach. It destroyed his supernatural aura. He coughed out his secret word and took two long steps toward her and Beryl got to her feet and fell into the bushes to her right. She got up just as he reached her and at that moment somebody called down from up the hill.

What the hell are you doing?

It was a man's voice. She looked up quickly and then back at the monster in front of her. There was no monster. No stranger, no man, no pursuer. Nothing but the blank, black stretch of field.

What's going on?

She could see the new man now. He stood on the last step of the abbreviated stairway, looking down on her.

Help me, Beryl said.

The man stepped onto the hill and slid down without losing his balance. He jumped the last few feet and landed right on the path. It must be easier for adults. Beryl wondered how he could see in the dark.

What's the problem?

Someone is chasing me, Beryl said. A man. Please.

Where is he?

He had a grown-up voice, low and sure of itself. You had to answer when he asked a question.

He chased me up the hill. He was right here when you yelled.

She looked around and saw nothing, which didn't mean there was nothing to see. She could smell beer on the man in front of her, beer and cigarettes. He wasn't as big as the stranger, but those things worked differently when you were older. Being big wasn't everything. She wanted him to put his arm around her shoulders or even pick her up and carry her. He was looking out at the dark.

I saw you fall down the hill, he said. Then you fell into the god damned bushes. I thought you were drunk.

It was the man, Beryl said. He was chasing me.

She had moved toward him and now he started walking. She had to hurry to keep up. He had no trouble staying on the path.

I didn't see anybody, he said.

He stepped onto the log and she grabbed him by the back of his belt. She couldn't get left behind. He said nothing about it while they crossed, but he stopped and faced her when they reached the far bank.

You're going too fast, she said. I'm scared.

He looked her over and she could hear the change in his breathing. She wondered if he'd kiss her. She wanted to be pulled against him so she couldn't see anything else. Terry had it coming, leaving her alone in the dark.

How old are you?

Sixteen.

Bullshit, he said. What's your name?

Beryl Watson, she said without thinking.

Your old man at The Plant?

Yes, Beryl said. Tim Watson.

He started walking, but more slowly. Beryl thought about taking hold of his belt again, but she wouldn't be able to explain it. She could smell the oil in his hair now, some brand she didn't know. He smelled tough and capable.

Your dad's a general foreman, he said. He's a good guy.

We're going to Quebec, Beryl said. I don't want to go.

That's right, that's right. Quebec. Are you going to tell your father somebody was chasing you?

I don't even speak French and we're moving to Quebec.

Somebody was chasing you, he said. I scared him away.

You didn't even see anybody, Beryl said.

I saw the guy, he said. I saw him. I just didn't want you to be scared. My name is Peck. Can you remember that? Herbie Peck.

Are you going to Quebec too?

No, Herbie said. It's guys like your father. He'll get a promotion. But I wouldn't mind going. They made me a foreman, I'd go.

They reached the short hill that ran down from the park and Herbie Peck covered half of its length in two strides. He stopped and waited for Beryl as soon as he remembered he was her saviour. She took a run at the hill and grabbed his jacket. Her hand found the back of his belt again. He squirmed.

Let go the belt, he said.

He took her hand away and led her back down the hill, then leaned down and grabbed her around the legs. For a wild second, Beryl thought it was some secret grown-up way of having sex. Herbie straightened up and she fell over his shoulder and he strode up the hill as though she didn't weigh a thing. He put her back on her feet in front of the broken fence. Beryl was thrilled and breathless.

Where do you live?

Just off Myrtle. Near the school.

Jesus, he said. Look, it isn't late. The guy's gone. You can get home all right, can't you?

Beryl didn't know what to say. Maybe he didn't like her. She wanted to sit under a tree with him, but she could tell he was in a hurry. The scary man, the monster man, wouldn't leave the creek to follow her, she just knew it. He lived by the creek, like a troll under a bridge. All you had to do was stay away.

I can get home, she said.

Peck. Herbie Peck. Tell your father.

Beryl followed Herbie Peck out of the park and onto the street. Under the streetlight she saw he had a chin like Jiminy Cricket. She wanted to go home.

iii

Terry was hiding under his bed while his father moved around the house. He had crawled under when he had heard the front door open and now he wished he'd gone out the bedroom window. Beryl was waiting for him and he was hiding like a kid. She would think there'd been a fight. She would think the old man had punched him in the ribs and knocked him down and that Terry couldn't bring himself to fight back. Beryl would think this because that's what Terry would tell her.

He saw his father's feet enter the bedroom and heard his noisy, open-mouthed breathing. Already drunk. The closet door creaked open and shut and the dresser drawers scraped on their runners and were slammed closed. It wasn't the first time this had happened. Terry wondered what he was looking for or if he ever found it. The closet and the drawers were searched, but his father never looked under the bed. Next he would go into the living room and turn on the TV. If he didn't move for ten minutes, it meant he had passed out and it was safe to leave the bedroom.

The mattress bulged above his chest and Terry watched his father's feet rise and disappear, one at a time. A moment later, the whole mattress sagged above him. Father and son lay parallel, separated only by a few inches of cheap stuffing. Close enough to smell. Terry breathed softly and tried to keep his mind neutral, afraid that violent thoughts would sound a telepathic alarm. He hated having his father in his bed. Maybe it would put him to sleep faster than the television.

Above him, he heard what sounded like a sob. A pause, then a noisy clearing of the throat. Terry felt his whole body clench as he listened. He had never seen the man cry. The same low, moaning catch in the throat sounded and Terry's own throat tightened when he heard it. His mother was dead and they had never discussed it. Or she had left not long after he was born. His mother's fate depended on the amount of beer consumed and Terry hadn't heard about her for a long time. He believed she had died. No matter. His father had lived with a broken heart ever since; you could see it when he drank. Anyone who drank as much as he did had a broken heart.

His father began singing "Sixteen Tons." There wasn't a hint of melancholy in his voice and he was as far from tears as he was from China. He sang it from beginning to end and then breathed deeply and evenly for about a minute. Terry could feel his voice through the floor. He sang it again. He sang "John Henry," "Ghost Riders in the Sky," and "Jezebel" before he passed out. He rolled onto his side and his arm dangled over the edge of the bed, his hand nearly touching the floor. It was a thick hand with short fingers and the skin of his palm felt more like a fingernail. It was only eighteen inches away from Terry's face, but he didn't see it. He'd been asleep since "Ghost Riders."

His father snored as loudly as a go-kart engine and Terry woke throughout the night, usually from the middle of a dream. None of his dreams were familiar that night. Twice he woke up thinking he was in a coffin with a lion on his chest.

It was still dark outside when the lump in the mattress changed shape and feet were planted on the floor. Terry watched them walk out of the room, heard water run and the toilet flush. The refrigerator opened and closed. There was the gravelly noise of vomiting in the kitchen sink. A return to the bathroom, then the front door opened, closed, and was locked. Terry waited until he heard the car start up and drive away.

He crawled out from under the bed feeling like he had the flu. He pulled the covers off the mattress and took the case off the pillow, then turned out the light. There was no trace of a lion in waiting. Terry lay down with all his clothes on and fell asleep.

Moth hated the night. He hated cars pulling into his driveway and the phone ringing downstairs while he was lying in bed. The street was a dead end and his family's house was the last chance to turn around. He would hear wheels crunching over the gravel and a moment later headlights made half his bedroom radiant and the other half shadowed and sinister. Moth crept to the window, expecting to see a police cruiser behind his father's car. He never saw one and he never stopped getting out of bed to check.

His father had entire telephone conversations without giving any hint of who was on the line or what they wanted. His tone was always weary and guarded. The suspense was crushing, worse than the cars. Moth would sit on the edge of the bed until he heard his mother ask who had called and if their voices weren't raised he would lie down again.

He lay on the very edge of the mattress to minimize squeaking, his right elbow jutting over the side. His brother never woke or moved. Moth thought about his French teacher, the Inquisition, swimming naked with Henry's girlfriend. A car pulled in and he hurried to the window, then went back to bed and started again. Directly beneath him, his parents watched television. Moth imagined being arrested by women cops and strip-searched. He imagined Beryl.

The police had phoned one night when he still lived at the old house. He had heard his mother's voice, high and breathless, asking questions. Moth had pretended to wake up when his father came into the bedroom, as though sleeping through the phone call was proof of his innocence. He slept in an upper bunk then, and his window faced away from the driveway. He got up, got dressed, denied everything, and left the house with his father. On their way downtown he admitted breaking into his school and stealing an acetylene torch with Roger Gondek. He'd been expecting the call for a week, ever since Mr Gondek had beaten a confession out of Roger.

The cop at the station had asked Moth why he'd done it and Moth had said he didn't know, and when they asked whose idea it was, he said he didn't remember. He answered these questions the same way a dozen times and then they typed out his statement.

Roger and Moth had spent most of the school year stealing typewriters, bicycles, whiskey, Christmas presents, and anything else they fancied from homes, cars, and businesses. They had broken into a factory near the lake one night but had gotten spooked before they could take anything. The factory had a vault and they had decided to return and cut the door open once they had the acetylene torch from the school. Roger's father beat him up before they could visit the factory again.

The cop who took his statement had told Moth that he might as well come clean because they were going to find out about everything anyway. Moth thought if they were going to find out anyway, there was no point in hastening disaster. He said they'd stolen the torch because it was neat, a motivation he'd heard used by kids on TV. His father had driven him home and made much of his being a liar and his mother had attacked him with a shoe when he walked into the house. Moth had gone to bed.

His French teacher makes him stay after class because of his wretched marks. She tells him that in Europe he would be caned for being such a terrible student. She locks the classroom door and fetches the yardstick. Makes him fetch it. He bends over a desk and she tells him he has to pull down his pants. Holy shit.

His mother would do it. She wanted to do it. Maybe she'd do it tonight.

There was always this moment when his rage at the very idea of being caned or whipped had to be weighed against the high, flushed thrill of his imagined submission. Moth paused in the dark between cars and phone calls and let his body make the decision. Saw a blonde woman wearing a man's white shirt, bunched and knotted beneath her breasts. The blonde licked Henry on the neck. Moth had been there and seen it happen. Henry had been showing him the hole a shotgun had blown through a kitchen drawer and the shoe brush that had had half its bristles neatly removed by the blast. Someone had tried to kill him. The woman licked his neck. Connie? Carol?

Moth imagined two women cops making him undress in an interrogation room. Cops watched too much television. Juvenile delinquency was a frequent theme on TV, mostly involving bored, unloved teenagers and the rich parents who ignored them. Kids got drunk, went joyriding, ran over a hard-working immigrant at a crosswalk. Later they said they had taken the car for kicks. They broke into homes, stole money they didn't need, stabbed people to death for kicks. The first time the cops had come for Moth, they'd asked him why he'd been smashing the windows of empty homes. He told them he had done it for kicks.

Someday worms would crawl into his dead brain and eat the memory of his thoughts. Moth stared at the ceiling and imagined his brain jumping with slimy life, like a rabbit's body heaving with maggots.

Beryl had found him sitting behind the house on the swing. He had expected her to arrive later, after she'd gone back to the arena and seen he wasn't there. He thought there would be a fight when he saw her coming across the lawn and he stood up, whispering at her to keep quiet. Even in the dark he could see she was covered in dirt and grass stains, like a little kid. Beryl ran the last few feet and grabbed him around the waist and he put his arms around her. It felt like they were living in the old neighbourhood and she was going to tell him what kid had hurt her. Moth hoped it wasn't Terry. She had raised her head and just as he was about to speak, she had kissed him. The tip of her tongue had rubbed the end of his own. Moth's head had jerked back like he'd been probed by a clumsy dentist.

Fifty push-ups at bedtime, fifty first thing in the morning. Ten seconds to get to his feet after he opened his eyes. He wanted to get into the habit of standing upright before the count of ten. There was a man in the land of Uz whose name was Job. If he read a chapter a night, then how long to read the whole Bible? He had no idea. He wanted to read about Emile Griffith, Rip Randall, Hurricane Carter before turning out the light. He wanted to think about Francine. She let him walk her home from school, but wouldn't allow him to carry her books.

And that man was perfect and upright, and one that feared God, and eschewed evil.

Moth thought about Ricky Charles and his hairless skin. He imagined girls at night and then pulled down Ricky's shorts the next afternoon. It sneaked up on him every day as a fresh idea.

Beryl was his sister and his mother was his mother. Ricky was a boy.

Job was a short book and he'd heard of it before. It was a better place to start than the Garden of Eden. He didn't think he was Job and didn't see his life reflected in the story. Christ was too much a fantasy figure and the big stories were cartoons. None of it made any sense and the only things Moth knew were that God existed and He wanted the Bible read. Moth was uncircumcised and had found a verse that said he'd never go to heaven. He had friends who had never read the Bible but were also uncircumcised and they all knew this verse. It didn't motivate Moth to commit crimes, nor did it make him repent. It was no more confusing than what God had done to Job, which was insane.

And not God, or the police, or Henry, or his parents would find Ricky Charles acceptable. You had to stop doing that when you were twelve. Up until then you were okay.

His mother and the stick didn't count as sex. What about the kids they knew who took off their pants for punishment? It wasn't sex.

Beryl had given him one kiss and then they'd gone into the house and told their parents she'd fallen down the hill on the way to the arena. You were only okay with your sister until you stopped taking baths together.

Moth ran three miles every night after dinner. He watched about an hour of television and then went upstairs, did his push-ups, read the Bible, lay down for a restless hour and fell asleep. He thought his anxiety probably sprang from a heightened sense of self-importance, from thinking he was too special. It made you the centre of everyone's attention. The police were after him, classmates didn't like him, his every move was scrutinized. He hated the night.

He lay on the bed, watching the darkness and not thinking about Beryl or his mother or Ricky Charles.

Fall

Chapter Four

i

Kate Watson waited in the bedroom and took her husband as soon as he came home. Trevor was at the community centre and Moth and Beryl always came home on the late bus, after wrestling. The house would be empty for another hour, but her madness was over in less than fifteen minutes. Every feral thought she'd ever had jumped into her skull and seized focus for a rabid moment or two. That's how it felt. She imagined being watched, thought of her husband sharing her with a friend, saw Beryl get her beating. Saw Moth, bursting with muscle.

She said, Tim.

Her husband said, Kate.

He rolled off and they breathed deeply, side by side. Fury overtook her, doubling with every breath. They had no business living in her imagination. It wasn't fair.

What are you going to do about Moth? she said.

Why? What's he done? Tim sounded exhausted, tired from the bottom of his soul.

Look at him. He sits there like he's going to burn the house down. I can't sleep when I think about it.

Well what the hell can I do about that? he asked her.

My father would say, I'll wipe that look off your face.

Her husband sat up on the bed, picked his pants off the floor and stood up. He was thick around the middle, getting thicker. His arms as big as his son's, but with none of the contours. She hadn't seen Moth without his pants in years.

Jesus, Kate, he said. Tell him to stop looking like he's going to burn down the house?

You're afraid of him.

One of us is, Tim said.

79

She was looking at his back, thinking about clawing him until she drew blood. He'd turn around and she'd bite him hard, just above the nipple. Pull him back down and do it again, do it again and then again. Do it until she couldn't think.

He was putting on his shirt. She was naked and he was nearly dressed and he would lean down and hold her by the hair, hold her head against the pillow so she couldn't move, give her breasts a half-slap when he felt them. She tried to will it telepathically.

Tim left the bedroom without looking at her. Kate touched herself and felt him leaking thickly past her fingers and onto the sheet. She rolled onto her side and tried to make herself cry. All she found were a couple of dry sobs. She didn't know what to think about any more.

The Watsons had visited the country club twice since they'd arrived in Valentine. Neither of them golfed, but Tim was considering it. He got almost no exercise these days and he knew men from The New Plant who played on weekends. Kate was never going to become a golfer, but she liked the class of people who belonged to the country club.

They went to a club dance with a couple her husband knew from work. They were a tense pair who tried to impose humour on every observation and Kate tired of them quickly. Tim laughed so fraudulently at their un-funny talk that Kate was afraid they'd take it as mockery. She recognized five other couples at the club who were former residents of Bresby and who had also been transferred to The New Plant, and she saw Judy Arnold from the community centre. She found these people more bearable.

They took over the corner farthest from the band and divided them-selves amongst three different tables. Almost none of them danced, but everyone drank. Kate had downed a calming tumbler of wine before leaving the house and her first drink at the club made her drunk immediately.

They promoted Tony because they couldn't fire him, Judy told her, nod-ding toward a pear-shaped man a table away. He was sleeping with the plant manager's wife. See that little mouse? His wife. Doesn't know a thing.

Tim never mentioned it, Kate said.

Oh, he knew. Everybody knew. Phil and Doris? Just the opposite. The woman's a god damned mink. Everyone says Bill Webb is queer, do you know him? Check the wife.

Well, Kate said, faking a laugh, Why do you think they gave Tim his promotion?

Oh, don't get me wrong, said Judy. It isn't the Foreign Legion out here. I'm sure your Tim got the job for the same reason as Frank. At least I *hope* they gave it to Frank because he's good at his job.

Kate looked across the room at Judy's husband. He looked intensely average.

The club was full, the tables forming a ragged perimeter around the dance floor. Most of the younger couples danced. Cigarette smoke lay like fog and the band was only slightly louder than the crowd. Kate couldn't remember going anywhere like this, ever, in Bresby.

Bill Webb sat down across from her and Kate asked him to dance. Judy stared with exaggerated disbelief and Kate winked. She walked across the floor with Bill a step behind and wondered what the wink was about and what the hell she thought she was doing. The band was playing Sinatra.

I winked at Judy, she told Bill. I don't know why.

You've been drinking.

I hate it when people say that, she said. It's true, but so what? I can wink if I want.

Her breasts were pushed against his chest and she wondered how it looked to Tim. Bill Webb moved her more deeply into the group of dancers. He was taller and slimmer than Tim and not bad looking at all.

You're smart, aren't you?

Yes, he said. And I'm not queer. Judy Arnold is the worst gossip you'll ever meet.

She didn't say anything, Kate said.

Oh yes, she did, said Bill. Judy can't have a coffee without pouring a shot in it. It doesn't help her.

Are you holding me close to prove you're not queer?

I thought you were holding *me* close. You and Tim are from England.

You *are* smart, Kate said.

And you're a little brat, aren't you?

The song ended and they separated and added their polite applause. Kate squinted through the smoke and saw Bill's wife looking at them. It was an appraising stare of curiosity without a hint of hostile emotion or insecurity. Kate smiled and waved at her.

Your wife, she said.

Joanna. Let's get a drink.

He led her through drunk and sloppy dancers to the bar. A good-looking man in his late forties smiled absently at them as they passed.

Marc Cloutier, Bill told her. He owns this place. You'll hear that he's a gangster. A town this size, they have one club, so everyone decides the Mob has to be involved. It's like Chinese restaurants in small towns – you always hear about the dead cats in the kitchen. In Valentine they have one bar owned by the Mafia and one restaurant serving fried cat. What are you drinking?

White wine, Kate said. She had never imagined that the dead cat story could be untrue.

Bill fought his way past the herd in front of the bar and Kate looked back at Joanna. Her eyes were on Kate, but she looked as unoffended as if she was watching a sunset. Kate didn't know what to do; she could hardly wave again. She looked away.

Your wife is staring at us, she told Bill when he handed her the drink.

She's staring at you. Is your background Irish or is that an insult?

My father was Irish, said Kate. I'm a brat. A British brat.

It's your skin, Bill said. Damn. *I* must be drunk. I mean your complexion. It caught Joanna's attention. She believes it's an Irish trait.

Joanna Webb was a tall, athletic-looking woman with the posture of a ballet dancer. Kate watched her walk across the room toward them. Her stomach developed a cold knot and she needed to pee. She looked at Bill, but he was smiling at his wife.

Joanna, you've met Kate, haven't you? Kate Watson.

Oh, Kate met everyone all at once, didn't you? Joanna asked her. Too confusing.

Kate's father is Irish.

Bill, go tell Kate's husband she's in good hands. He's looking for her.

Bill Webb gave his wife a look that was darker and deeper than he seemed capable of, then he found his smile. He walked back to the tables.

Bill wants you all to himself, Joanna said.

Maybe I'm drunk.

I'm sorry. Are we making you feel intimidated?

I don't know, Kate said.

You do have a fabulous complexion. Please don't feel strange. Did Bill mention that I paint?

No.

You'd make a wonderful model, Joanna said. I've never said that to anyone else here, you can be sure.

82

I don't look like a model, Kate said. Her face burned. Any second now this woman was going to laugh at her and then tell every table about her cruel joke. A model. If you can imagine.

You mustn't say that. You're a lovely woman.

My God, said Kate. I'll really have to come here more often. People say the nicest things.

You're not afraid of me, are you?

I'd better sit down before I fall down, Kate said.

Oh, hell, Joanna said. You're offended.

She took Kate lightly by the upper arm and walked her past the dancing couples. Kate had the urge to ask her to dance and laughed out loud at the thought. That would give Judy Arnold something to talk about. Joanna gave her arm a sudden squeeze.

You're enjoying yourself, aren't you?

Sure, Kate said. It's about time.

They sat down beside each other at the same table as Tim. He was smiling at a woman who appeared to be relating the story of her life. Tim laughed and shook his head. The woman looked across the table at Kate and tried to pout.

Tell your husband to dance with me.

If he doesn't dance with me, he doesn't dance with anyone, Kate said.

Hey, said Tim. You were dancing.

Because you won't dance.

A challenge, Tim said. Let's dance.

He stood up and held out his hand and, for reasons she didn't understand, Kate leaned over and licked his palm. Tim sat down and looked at her like they were both twenty years younger.

Bravo, said Joanna.

It's okay, Kate said. We're married.

Judy Arnold already had her mouth an inch from Tony Babcock's ear. They were both looking at Kate, a table away. Tim smiled at his wife and it was the first time she'd thought of him as handsome for many months. Maybe years. The tables were full of smiles. Joanna had a fresh, excited feeling about her and Kate liked that. She could see that Joanna had beautiful skin, too. Bill was standing behind his wife and Kate liked him as well. She liked him, and them, and everyone at their tables and in the club. She loved Valentine.

83

Tim took her by the hand and they went out on the dance floor. The band played "The Shadow of Your Smile." Kate licked her husband on the neck and he let his hands rest on either side of the small of her back. He danced her past the bar and to the side door and they went out into the warm night air and the darkness of the golf course, which was somehow darker than the night itself. They knelt on the grass and kissed and Tim turned her around and slid the tight skirt above her hips and Kate wondered how lovely her skin must look and whether he could see it. He dragged her panties down to her thighs and she felt an excitement and shock she hadn't known since the first time he'd seen her this way. Maybe she could be painted like this. See who gets scared then.

Tim pushed his way inside her and Kate held the short grass in her fists. She was young and he was young. They would never die.

ii

Moth arrived in Valentine to a brand-new game. No one gave him a copy of the rules, nor did he want them. Valentine enraged him. It was a large patch of new homes jammed between two small towns, thirty miles from Montreal. A thousand families lived there. That's what the real estate agent had said: a thousand families. There were woods that circled the town, ending at the main road to the south. The country club and golf course had flattened an enormous area to the north. A weak trickle of creek ran through the golf course and all the way south past the road, emptying into a grimy river with gravel banks.

The high school was in St Lucy, right next door. Four miles beyond the school was the shopping plaza, a row of a dozen stores. There were larger groups of stores in bigger towns the closer you got to the city, but downtown was in Montreal. Moth imagined living back in Bresby and having to travel to Toronto to get downtown. It would turn anyone into a madman.

We've got two championship teams, the principal at St Lucy's told him. Football and wrestling. You look like an athletic fellow.

I'm a boxer, said Moth.

I don't consider boxing a sport, said the principal.

Moth had hitchhiked into Montreal every day the summer they moved. It was the only summer he would spend in Valentine. He had joined a boxing club and put on the gloves with tough French fighters who made no distinction between gym work and fighting a main event. The heat in the club had been suffocating and Moth was thirsty all the way home. Three times he had been picked up by men who gave him five dollars to lower his pants while they put their faces in his lap.

He met Jake when school began and two weeks later they were sparring partners. Jake was on the football team and he gave Moth decent opposition. Moth joined the track team for roadwork and the wrestling team because he was weak as an infighter. The toughest guys in school were the jocks. They looked just like Moth.

He had always imagined that if he travelled, he would confront the same cast of characters he already knew. The same guys, but speaking French or Italian or German. Everyone liked to say that people were people and then add a few tidbits about human nature. Teachers liked to say it; teachers and parents.

Now he knew it wasn't true. There were guys with greaser haircuts who fought in the halls and were known to the cops by name, and then there were guys who pulled pranks at Halloween and sneaked liquor from their parents' cabinet. The cops knew the pranksters as troublemakers and the trouble was never a felony. There were guys who went to dances to fight and guys who went to dance. Guys who skied and guys who didn't.

The guys in Valentine weren't like the guys in Bresby. They acted like the school teachers of tomorrow.

He wrote it all down, every night, in a large notebook he kept between the box spring and the mattress.

His mother read it over breakfast.

Reading through the summer was a waste of time, Kate Watson thought. July and August could have been reshuffled and dealt again with no one being the wiser.

Over an hour getting to the club. Jumped rope, speed bag, heavy bag. A guy named Simard did three rounds and I never landed a solid punch. I should have made him come to me instead of chasing him. I am WAY too slow.

Moth hated school and she wasn't surprised. He had to repeat grade nine in Bresby and now he has to repeat grade ten. Completed it last year, but has to take it again because they think they are a year ahead here. He'll be old enough to get married before he gets out of high school.

Moth might never finish high school. He might spend the next two years or five or ten in the penitentiary, no matter what the lawyer predicted.

He must have thought about the robbery, planned it, set a date. Not a word of this could she find.

School pages. All kids hated school; she wasn't interested. Moth doesn't think teachers should be addressed as "sir," doesn't like the Lord's Prayer, hates discussions about future salary based on education. Moth hates money.

His mother turned the pages.

Moth wants to beat the captain of the football team bloody because the kid threw snow in Moth's face. Realizes he'll look like an out-of-control freak if he hits him. Kate could see, as her son could not, that the football player wouldn't go any further than throwing snow, even though Moth had cursed him as probably nobody had before. They are afraid of one another. Boy stuff.

Moth meets Donna Mesrine.

Suddenly, Valentine re-establishes its dominion in the narrative. There was a short description of Donna's eyes (brown), her overbite and the smell of her hair, and then she disappeared altogether. Valentine is a swamp of banality, a compound for the brain-dead, a training ground for the conformist of tomorrow. His mother was reduced to scanning the page, looking for Donna or any reference to female anatomy. Math teacher is a cunt. Not the right context.

She wished Beryl kept a diary. It was something girls were supposed to do, not boys who boxed. Girls wrote about the good stuff, the things that mattered. They didn't make lists of all the horrible shortcomings of everyone else. They wrote about love and sex and jealousy and they knew what jealousy was and admitted it when they had it. Boys acted like they'd just been arrested. They thought they had a right to remain silent and they knew that anything they said could and would be used against them.

They thought they ruled the world and they didn't. No. They did not rule the world.

Lifting weights isn't taking the snap out of my punches. Maybe if you didn't hit the bag or spar it would make you too big and stiff. I am better on the inside.

Ran three miles after school. Donna stayed late. There is nowhere to go in the school. I think the bench press is best for a fighter. I don't have any money to take her out.

Jake has his grandfather's trunk in the basement. The old guy is dead.
The trunk is full of guns.

That was how it started, she thought. Boys and guns. She wished she'd read it before the police came to the house, wished she'd talked to them instead of leaving it to Tim.

Look, she would have said. He found some guns. That's why they did it. Boys aren't girls. You have to keep things out of their hands.

The diary didn't explain that welding torch or whatever the hell it was he had stolen before. Maybe Moth was nothing more than a bad seed. It didn't matter what he had or didn't have in his hands. When his hands were empty, he made fists.

iii

Two detectives had come out from Montreal about two weeks after the robbery. They had sat on either side of Moth at the kitchen table and put the single-action Colt on the table top in front of them. The gun had been close enough for him to breathe its scent of Three-in-One oil. He'd never before been in the company of such big men outside of a gym and it made him feel young and innocent.

Where did you get the gun? asked the one on his right.

It was in a trunk in Jake's basement, Moth said. It belonged to his grandfather.

Quite a gun.

The detective hefted the .45 and smiled at Moth's father, who stood by the front window and didn't look their way. The cop looked back at Moth.

Whose idea was the gun?

I don't know, Moth said. He showed it to me and then we ended up taking it with us.

Planning to shoot somebody?

I thought it would scare them.

Moth didn't want to sound too remorseful, because he believed it was cowardly to suffer regret once you were caught. He didn't want to sound like a smartass, either. He kept his voice as toneless as possible and there was no defiance in the way he looked at the police. There was also no pleading. Moth monitored every breath he drew and he hoped his father was learning a lesson about him.

You took a loaded gun to scare someone? the cop on his left said. Come on.

87

I thought I might have to fire a warning shot or something to show them it was real, Moth said. It looks like a cowboy gun.

A real six-shooter, the other cop said.

Shotgun shells. Whose idea?

Mine, said Moth.

You've done this before, haven't you?

Johnny Ringo. It was a western on TV. He kept a .410 shotgun shell in one chamber of his gun. I tried it and it worked. They wouldn't sell us the real bullets.

Television, said the one on the left to the other one.

Television didn't make him rob the place, the other cop said. You can learn about dum-dums on TV too.

I had to cut the ends off the shells to make them fit, Moth said.

You ruined a beautiful gun.

They wouldn't sell us the bullets.

The cop on his left leaned over toward him. He smelled like Travis; maybe it was his after-shave.

You were the one with the gun. You pointed it at Gilles Cloutier and told him you'd shoot him. What happened to that warning shot?

He was too close, Moth said. I made a threat, but I wasn't thinking. I knew he was close enough to recognize us, so there wasn't any point trying to get away.

You were going to shoot him.

No. If I wanted to shoot him, I could have shot him. He was right there.

So you lost your nerve, the other cop said. Moth was surprised. He thought that one of them was supposed to act like his friend while the other one accused him.

I never intended to shoot him, Moth said.

The two detectives stared at him. He looked from one to the other and then settled on a spot in the middle distance between them and let his eyes unfocus. The three of them sat silently for a long minute. Moth's father was watching the neighbour across the street wash his car.

There's no point you taking this attitude, one of the detectives said. They were becoming one cop to Moth.

I'm trying to answer your questions.

We don't want answers. We want an explanation.

I don't have one, said Moth.

One cop exhaled and the other clicked his tongue. Silence took them again. Moth realized that they wanted to make him so uncomfortable he'd be forced to talk and he decided that in itself was a good reason to shut up. Both of the cops had huge hands and he watched them while he stared at the top of the table beyond the gun. He wanted to be careful they weren't aware it was a contest. They were cops; they knew. This is what they did.

Look, Moth said wearily, I don't know what you want me to say.

You don't have to say anything. We can sit here as long as you like.

Moth almost gasped. He nearly began shouting, then pressed his palms against the table and took a breath. He looked from one pair of hard eyes to another.

Okay, he said. Fine.

They were here, in his kitchen, because he'd robbed the country club. Tried to rob the country club. Broke in and been surprised by the owner's son, who then called the police. The gun made it armed robbery. Now these two shitheads were treating him like he'd cut classes or stolen a volleyball. Maybe it was always like this, no matter how old you were. Maybe when you were forty cops still said, You should have thought of that before you did it. They would always act like vice-principals and you were always the bad kid. He had tried to rob the country club in the middle of the night while armed with a .45 loaded with shotgun shells. Moth wanted to be treated like a bandit.

We broke into the place, he said. I was carrying the gun. We tried to open the cash register and we couldn't, so we took a bunch of other stuff.

Chocolate bars, said the detective on his left. Pop. Like a couple of kids.

I guess we woke the guy up when we were trying to open the register. I looked up and he was right there. I pointed the gun at him and he turned on the lights. That was that.

Tim, said the same cop. Do your friends call you Tim or Timothy?

Tim, said Moth. He knew they'd make much of his name if he told them.

Tim, we know what happened. What were you doing there in the first place?

You've done this before, said his partner.

Yes.

The cops relaxed.

Tell us, one of them said. You don't have to be afraid of us, Tim.

I broke into a school in Bresby about three years ago and stole an acetylene torch.

One of the cops took out a notebook and started writing in it.

I got caught, Moth said. I got a year's probation.

The cop stopped writing and frowned.

Tell us what we don't know, he said.

There's nothing else to tell you, said Moth.

It was almost true. He could have talked for ten minutes without pausing for breath if the subject had been his criminal hijinks in Bresby, but in Valentine he was nearly a virgin. They had decided to break into the snack bar at the community centre the week before and found the lock smashed and the hut ransacked by the time they arrived. Moth had shot out a window, but it was hardly worth mentioning.

The country club is really the only place in town you can rob, said Moth.

What?

There's the community centre. Other than that, there's only the club. Even the variety store is over in St Lucy.

You robbed it, said his left-hand cop, you robbed it because it was there?

Yes, Moth said. Because it was there.

The cop on his right opened his mouth, paused, and looked across the table at his partner. Moth's father had turned around and stared at his son, blinking quickly as though to clear his vision. Both cops started laughing at the same moment. The one on the left was actually not bad looking when he laughed.

Well, Tim, the good-looking cop had said, That's about it, I guess.

They had stood up.

My friends call me Moth.

You have friends? Guys you like? Or just because they're there?

Moth had looked up into their eyes, and had seen that no answer was expected. One of them scooped up the gun.

Let me tell you something, the cop had said. They'll be calling you Butterfly in prison.

Moth's father had followed the detectives into the hall, closing the kitchen door behind him.

Butterfly, Moth thought. There were worse names than that.

CHAPTER FIVE

i

Beryl came home drunk and went straight upstairs to the bathroom. She stood under the shower for five minutes and then gargled with mouthwash while she got dressed. It didn't sober her up, but it made her alert and explained away her bloodshot eyes. She always showered as soon as she came home from school and always with the same motives. All she had to do now was stay awake for an hour and not talk much.

She got drunk almost every afternoon. Usually she made it back to school in time for the late bus and she'd ride home with Moth. If she missed the bus there was no point in hurrying. She'd missed it tonight. Her father was on nights and with any luck her mother had been out since dinner. Moth always got stuck with Trevor because Moth never went anywhere.

There was a song she was trying to learn, a French song about a doll. She played it many times a day on the jukebox and it was the most beautiful song she'd ever heard. Marcel was trying to teach her the words, but she felt ridiculous singing in French. She needed the record. What she wanted to do more than anything right now was to lie down in her room in the dark and listen to that song.

Marcel bought her drinks at the tavern near the shopping plaza and kept her hidden in the back, close to the exit. Beryl handed in notes at school that excused her absence due to afternoon sessions of physiotherapy. Marcel had missed most of grade ten because of physio and he was invaluable in supplying details. A driving instructor who hung around the tavern wrote the notes. Beryl could forge her mother's signature but she couldn't spell.

She opened the bathroom door while she towelled her hair and listened to the house. When her father worked nights, her mother usually went out. Beryl had no curiosity about where her mother went.

Her parents watched TV from dinner until bedtime on the nights they stayed home and they only spoke to her or each other during commercials. Most of the time Beryl sat alone in the kitchen and played the radio while she pretended to do homework. Moth jumped rope in the basement or stayed in his room reading boxing magazines while Trevor slept in the next bed. Beryl was glad her brothers didn't share a bed any more; it was too creepy.

Her father still worked three rotating shifts, each of them two weeks long. On the two weeks of days, he liked to watch television and go to bed early. He was only home without fail on the evenings he worked graveyard. He napped after dinner until ten, watched an hour of TV and left. On the night shift, he went to work right after eating. Most of those nights her mother went to that weird woman's place for a glass of wine. Mrs Webb. She would even go over after eleven.

Twice Marcel had met Beryl on the golf course at night. It was exciting and sad and no song played for her. Beryl felt she had taken a jump from one end of the alphabet to the other without learning a single letter in between. All she knew was A and Z, Terry at the beginning and Marcel at the end. She hadn't jumped – she'd been dragged by her parents from a place and a boy she knew to a place and boy she didn't. She had done everything with Terry that her friends had done with their boyfriends and all of them had the same feelings she had and thought no one else could know the way they felt. Beryl had learned this and she could face it. You arrived at the same place as everyone else and after that there were places that would only belong to you. You and your guy, your boyfriend. She and Terry had just reached their beginning and now they couldn't go anywhere else.

Bill Webb worked the same shifts as Beryl's father and he was a handsome man. He was the only married man in Valentine she could imagine kissing. Sometimes she thought about lying on the golf course with him and getting caught. Beryl would say she had never felt like this until they moved away from Bresby. See how her mother liked that. One true thing was that she had never wanted to get drunk so much before they moved here.

She had met Bill Webb at the community centre just after her fifteenth birthday when she was trying to sober up by swimming. He told her that exercise only made you more drunk and recommended a shower instead. The kind of man who asked you to call him by his first name and spoke to you like you were the same age. His wife sat there smiling, like she knew something nobody knew and she looked at you like she was seeing someone else. Maybe she was crazy.

Three letters to Terry and nothing back. There was no reason she couldn't fall in love with Marcel, but she couldn't. And even if she did, they wouldn't get any further. They'd do it over and over again until they were tired of doing it and then they'd find someone else to do it with. Movie stars lived their whole lives that way. You couldn't keep getting married like that unless you were a movie star.

In Valentine, a girl met a guy in grade eight and they went together until they graduated. Or one of them met somebody else in their final year and had a horrible breakup. You went out with two people all the way through school, maybe three. More than three and it might as well be thirty. That's what Marcel told her. The guys didn't even fight over a girl. They didn't have cars and they didn't go to jail and if they fought, it wasn't over girls. Everybody went together for years and broke up just at the end or stayed together and probably got married. Or you had to move to a town where they didn't know your reputation.

Beryl was never going to fall in love with Marcel or Bill Webb or anybody else.

She wrapped the towel around her head and went to Moth's room at the end of the hall. She rapped lightly on the door and heard the creak of the bed and the thump of her brother's feet on the floor. Moth opened his door a couple of inches and panted in her face. He was red and sweating and Beryl looked away in embarrassment. She wished he'd said he was getting changed and given himself a minute. Even better, why didn't he use the bathroom?

God, Moth, she said.

What do you want?

Where is she? Mom? Beryl asked him.

She won't be back until after the news, Moth said. She's over at Joanna's and that's when she comes home.

Who's Joanna?

Joanna Webb. I can't talk to you right now.

That's disgusting, said Beryl, stepping back. Don't tell me that.

Moth looked at her, red and gasping and licking his lips. She wondered if he was going to get violent. He didn't look or sound the way her brother usually looked and sounded. Beryl heard a solid thump against the wall behind him.

Is Trevor awake? she said. What's going on?

Moth whispered so quietly she couldn't hear, but she stepped no closer. He opened the door enough to stick his head out and mouthed a word like he was speaking to the deaf. A dozen variations of what he was trying to say filled her head. Moth said it again, this time in a low voice instead of a whisper.

Donna.

Donna? said Beryl, as though it was a code.

She's here, Moth said. Don't tell Mom.

Beryl stared at her brother until he closed the door. She wanted to hammer at it in outrage, shouting at them to stop. Donna. Beryl could think of three girls with that name. She was furious and didn't look for reasons. Poor little Trevor. Yes. You never did those things around a little kid. Bringing her here, using the bed, not losing your underwear on the golf course. It wasn't right. Moth got to use the bed, just like he was married. Even if their parents found out, nothing would happen. It made her breathless with rage. Donna wasn't a French name. She must go to their school.

Her brother knew everything. Knew about the tavern, about Marcel, the physiotherapy notes, all of it. He had too much power for her to throw a fit. She ran downstairs and remembered she was drunk when she missed a step and bounced down the last two, sitting up. Like riding a toboggan. It was such a bright, white scene that she could smell the cold. And then it dissolved and she felt stupid.

She caught her breath and leaned back on the stairs, looking up at the closed door of Moth's room. It didn't open, even though he must have heard her fall. She wanted to scream. Poor Trevor was in the same room, this girl was no older than Beryl, Moth didn't have a broken heart. He had a stupid crush on Francine, but he had never had a girlfriend. Moth had robbed the fucking country club. Probably he was in love with Donna and they didn't have to lie down in a field.

She got to her feet and walked carefully into the kitchen. No tailbone damage. The wall phone was ringing and she took a glass from the cupboard, ran the tap until the water was cold, filled the glass and drank it empty. The phone stopped ringing while she drank. You drink, then you stop and then a miracle happens. The water turns to wine. She felt back where she'd started, before the shower. She put the glass in the sink and went outside through the back door.

Fireflies had dotted the lawn during the summer, glowing and fading like malfunctioning neon, and Beryl missed them. They were the only thing Valentine had that Bresby didn't. With the fireflies gone, there was no point.

It was cold, colder than it had been when she came home. Or maybe it was because she had taken a shower. She tried to think whether a hot shower would make her feel hotter or colder if it was cold outside, but she had to give up. There was an empty lot behind the yard, uglier under the streetlight than it was in daylight. June bugs would bounce off the light and make a buzz like mechanical insects and she didn't miss them. Beryl looked up at the stars, ten thousand more than she'd ever seen in Bresby, and almost fell on her back. She couldn't understand why she would be this drunk. When had she eaten?

She crossed the lawn to the lot and her balance was fine. You'd never know she'd been drinking from the way she walked. Or was she was being too careful or moving too slowly? She wished Moth would come downstairs and watch her. She held her wet hair away from her face with one hand and squatted at the edge of the lawn. Look at that. As solid as a statue. She picked up a rock that was half the size of a brick and stood up.

The towel was lying near the back door, nearly gleaming on the dark grass. Beryl walked over to it, bent down with no trouble at all, straightened up and took a deep breath of the night air. She put one foot behind her and leaned back, then threw the rock through Moth's window.

The glass exploded with a hair-raising racket, louder than Beryl had ever heard a window break. She heard a girl's scream and nearly screamed herself. Trevor. Beryl ran into the house and was at the bottom of the stairs when Moth came out of the bedroom, shirtless and running. He materialized in front of her before she could take another step.

Somebody's throwing rocks at the house, she said.

He smacked her across the face as the last word left her lips and he grabbed a handful of her hair, jerked her off her feet and onto the floor. Beryl was on her back before she had even registered the slap. Moth held her around the throat and squeezed so quickly and with such strength, the edges of her vision whirlpooled. Her brother looked terrifyingly calm and grim. A girl stood beside him, leaning over and shouting, but Beryl could hardly hear her.

Moth took his hands off her throat and stood up and Beryl rolled over and vomited. It burned and jumped out of her like the first few splashes from a water pump. She curled up, then stretched, with every heave. Moth and Donna stood over her and watched and she wanted to beg them to go away. Having them gape was worse than the way it felt puking out this mess and she thought the pain in her throat might kill her. She wanted to cry and she couldn't as long as there was anything to bring up and even when there wasn't, her body continued to flex and stretch.

Moth ran back up the stairs when he heard Trevor fumbling with the doorknob. He reached the bedroom just as the door opened and scooped his brother up in his arms. Took him back inside and kicked the door shut behind him.

War, Trevor said.

Moth turned on the overhead light. One end of the curtain rod was still in place, the rest of it twisted and hanging straight down, the curtains a lump of fabric on the end. The glass hadn't gone beyond the cloth and splinters large and small were scattered beside Moth's bed. The rock had made a dark scratch on the wall above his pillow and now lay on the throw rug only a couple of feet from where Trevor slept.

Somebody threw a rock at our house, said Moth.

Who?

It was an accident. They were trying to scare away a skunk.

Moth sat Trevor down on his bed.

Stay right here, he said. I need my shoes.

He ran back down the stairs and saw Donna helping Beryl stand up. His sister's face was swollen and dark and her eyes looked tiny. The downstairs smelled like the alley behind the Pinklon Hotel. Moth stopped next to the front door and pulled on his running shoes.

You'd better clean this up before Mom gets home, he said.

Moth, said Donna.

He went into the kitchen and looked quickly through cupboards and drawers and found nothing he needed. He yelled for Donna and she came to him immediately.

Don't shout at me, she said. This is bad enough.

Would you go and keep an eye on Trevor? Moth asked her. I'm afraid he'll cut himself.

You could have killed her, Moth.

She could have killed Trevor with that rock, Moth said.

He opened the basement door and went down the stairs. Donna used the wall phone to call her parents and she told them that Debbie was nearly finished copying her school notes and she'd be leaving in about ten minutes. Then she called Debbie.

If my parents call, tell them I just left, she said.

I won't answer the phone, Debbie said. My mom and dad are still out. Did you do it?

I'll tell you tomorrow.

You're still there. You did it, didn't you?

Almost, Donna said. You won't believe what happened.

She hung up just as Moth came up from the basement. He was carrying newspapers and a roll of masking tape.

Where's Trevor?

I had to call my parents, Donna said.

Moth left the room without another word. Donna fetched the sponge mop that stood in a corner near the back door. She stuck it under the kitchen tap and soaked it, then squeezed it out.

Beryl was sitting on top of the shoes next to the front door. Donna went to her and leaned the mop against the wall.

I'm sorry, she said, but I have to leave. I'm not even supposed to be here. Can you hear me?

You get to use the bed and everything, Beryl said.

Nothing happened. We were just talking.

Don't be so fucking stupid, Beryl said.

You're sitting on my shoes.

Beryl moved as slowly as her math teacher. Donna picked up the shoes and sat on the stairs while she put them on. She tried not to look at the lumpy pool on the floor.

You're lucky it's tile, she said. It's pretty easy to clean.

Go home, Beryl said.

Donna got to her feet and went back into the kitchen. She opened the cereal cupboard and took out her school binder. Now she couldn't remember why she had hidden it. The phone began ringing. Donna stood still, as though the caller would be able to tell she was there if she moved a muscle. The ringing stopped.

That was enough. Donna went out the back door and closed it quietly behind her. She looked up at Moth's broken window and thought about calling his name. At least tell him she was leaving.

97

She crossed the backyard and went through the lot behind it. There wasn't a real path, but if you stayed to your right you wouldn't get muddy or cut yourself on the trash that had been dumped there.

You just had to know where to step.

ii

The suburbs are a mask for trash, Joanna Webb said. At least real trash is honest. They live in horrible bungalows and swear at their kids and everyone can see that they're trash. But out here you look and think, How nice. How nice.

Bresby is an awful damned place, though, said Kate Watson.

Yes. And they don't like Bill there, either. Think he's queer because he's read a book. He shouldn't be an engineer. That was a bad choice and it's a weird thing between Bill and his father. I hate that father-son thing that they take their whole lives to sort out. Bill, an engineer. You should meet his father, Joanna said. One of those men who is very proud of being stupid.

Kate loved listening to her talk. It wasn't gossip and it was full of opinions and ideas. The suburbs were a favourite topic of Joanna's. It was so difficult being an artist in a sterile environment. Kate wished she had some artistic pursuit of her own.

They'll ostracize you, too, Joanna said. Now that you know me. The women hate me here. They want me to have thick, terrible thighs as white as the belly of a fish. Broken veins. Their skin looks like curdled milk. Think about those people making love. Their husbands have enormous stomachs and no ass. Why do their asses get so flat?

Tim doesn't look like that, Kate said.

No, my dear, said Joanna. And you don't look like curdled milk, either.

She leaned forward and gave Kate a small kiss on the lips. What she would call a sisterly kiss. Kate held tightly on to her glass of wine, wanting to giggle. Talking like this always made her want to giggle, especially when she was given a kiss. She wished she had more to contribute to their conversation. Joanna could talk all night about movies Kate had never heard of, books she was reading, an idea she had for a painting. She had been to Italy. Kate had never wanted to go there until she heard Joanna describe it. No wonder she hated Valentine. It must be hard liking any place after Italy.

Sometimes they hardly talked at all. Near the end of the summer, they had sat in the backyard drunk and covered in insect repellent, watching what remained of the fireflies. A hedge over six feet tall ran around the entire yard and the neighbours were invisible. It was easy for Kate to imagine they were somewhere in a forest. She wondered if Joanna sunbathed out here and what she wore.

Kate had only been to the country club once since Moth had robbed it and she had wanted to apologize to Marc Cloutier. He wasn't on the premises and she felt as though every pair of eyes in the place was fixed on her. Joanna walked her back outside before their drinks had even arrived.

You see? she said. It's because you're with me. They hate me.

They had never spoken about the robbery.

Some nights Kate posed. Not every night and especially not during day shift. Tim had no idea she was being painted and she wondered what Bill thought. He must see his wife's painting and know it was Kate. Bill must imagine her naked every time they met. Kate certainly thought about it whenever she saw him.

They drank wine and some nights Kate took off her clothes and stood in the living room having odd feelings while Joanna worked on the painting. Other nights they just drank wine and talked, and in summer they had sat outside and looked at the stars and tasted bug spray in their drinks. School had begun and the bug spray ceased. They drank wine.

She hated the pose. Joanna had her standing with her back to the room and leaning forward, hands against the wall, like a thug being frisked. Kate couldn't remember ever being naked in a living room and she thought that probably had a lot to do with the way she felt. She might feel more at ease if she were standing in the bathtub or sitting on a bed.

Do you know what Bill would say if he were here? Joanna asked her. He'd say 'I'd like to bite your bum.'

Kate almost rubbed her legs together, thinking of it. The way she leaned forward, she was in the right position for Bill to do that. Or Joanna. Anyone at all. She thought of herself standing like this while various people gave her a nip on her bottom. Kate fought to keep the image quietly to herself. She didn't feel merely unclothed, but the same as when the very first boy had taken off her dress. Stark naked, very naughty and heated with erotic shame. It was a lovely feeling.

She wasn't drunk but she knew she shouldn't have any more wine.

99

Why don't we take a break and have a glass of wine? asked Joanna.

I'd like that, Kate said.

There was a man's terrycloth robe on a stool beside her. When they took breaks, Kate would cover herself with it before turning around. Tonight she turned and crossed the room and left the robe where it lay.

My goodness, Joanna said. That isn't all Bill would say.

I don't need the bathrobe, said Kate. We're both girls.

Joanna took the bottle from the top of the desk and refilled their glasses. She handed one to Kate, then fetched her the robe.

We can't start running around the house naked, Joanna said. That isn't the way I work.

Kate put her glass on the coffee table and pulled the robe over her shoulders. She felt foolish, but covering herself up completely would be humiliating. She'd feel like a chastened schoolgirl.

Joanna was wearing white shorts that were tight enough to show the action of her muscles when she walked. Kate sat down in the easy chair and watched her move back to the desk with the wine. You could have a body like that or you could have kids, but you couldn't have both.

Would you let Bill bite my bum?

Joanna turned and looked at her carefully, over the top of her glass.

Well, she said, would you let Tim bite mine?

Kate felt confused, as though the conversation had suddenly shifted to lacrosse.

Tim? I don't understand.

What don't you understand? asked Joanna. I'm saying how would you feel if the shoe was on the other foot?

You don't want Tim to do that.

No, said Joanna. And I don't want Bill doing it to you, either. I was paying you a compliment, that's all.

Kate felt like screaming in her face or bursting into tears. She had had whole weeks of wanting to scream or cry, but hadn't felt that way in this house until now. The second she felt wonderful, someone had to start acting like a family doctor. Playing at maturity and adulthood because they suddenly notice they've gone too far. She had never imagined that Joanna would do this, too. It was betrayal. Maybe a trap. Joanna had started it. Now whatever Kate said would be a mistake. Too much wine. If she said nothing, then it would be awkward and awful and their voices would sound strange for the rest of the night. She wanted to go back to the very beginning or open her eyes and find out it was tomorrow.

Kate?

She opened her eyes. Joanna was standing in front of the chair with a hand on her shoulder.

You poor thing, Joanna said. You're passing out right in front of me.

I'm sorry.

Did I sound cross? said Joanna. I should have kept my eye on the wine.

She helped Kate to her feet and tried to keep her covered at the same time. The robe slid to the floor and Kate hugged her.

You could bite me there, she said.

You're drunk, dear, said Joanna.

Kate rested her head against the strong and solid shoulder. Such a nice, clean girl's smell. She told herself to keep her mouth shut. Don't say another word. Just keep quiet and let things happen. Let anything happen that wanted to happen.

She opened her eyes and then sat up quickly, lost and afraid. The room was dark and a streetlight outside the curtains gave the furniture a ghostly hostility. Kate was naked, but partly covered with the robe, which had bunched midway between her breasts and hips. She was dying of thirst and her mouth tasted foul and foreign. All of her needs were pressing and immediate and, more than anything, she had to know the time.

She put her feet on the floor and stood up, pulling on the robe. Pain covered the front of her face and made her head feel like her brain was being pushed into the back of her eyes. This was Joanna's house, Joanna and Bill's. She was in the living room, and the bathroom was just down the hall. Kate whispered this information to herself, then sneaked past the closed bedroom door to the bathroom.

The light had been left on and as soon as she closed the door, Kate vomited into the toilet. She turned on the taps in the sink to cover the noise, then vomited again. It was the god damned light making her throw up, but she needed to see. She flushed the toilet and found mouthwash in the medicine cabinet. Kate tried gargling while she peed, but it made her gag and she had to wait for her endless stream to finish before she spit the mouthwash in after it. She heaved twice, but nothing came up.

This was the first time that drinking had made her sick, so the sickness likely had nothing to do with the drinking. The logic seemed unassailable. Something she ate had poisoned her. She squeezed a line of toothpaste onto her finger and rubbed it over her teeth, then rinsed out her mouth. Very carefully she scooped up small handfuls of water and drank. Too much would make her sick again, or maybe drinking it too quickly. She thought it out very clearly as she filled her cupped hands and drank and drank and drank. There was no aspirin in the cabinet and she wondered about the possibility of a brain tumour. She didn't look at herself in the mirror.

Her clothes were folded and piled on the same stool she used for the robe. Kate realized it wasn't only the streetlight that made the room milky. The sky was getting lighter. She found her watch tucked in the pocket of her shorts and turned on the coffee table lamp once she was dressed. It was just after six. Her mind was beginning to find itself. She had been posing for Joanna and she must have lain down. Tim would have come home just before one. Bill must be here now, in bed with his wife. She felt like she'd been on public display and everyone knew her business.

She left by the front door and started home. Thank God it was half an hour too early for the day shift to be pulling out of their driveways, staring at her and knowing Tim Watson's wife had been out all night. The streets were empty and she tried to hurry. She thought she could hear the water sloshing around in her stomach and she slowed and took deep breaths. If she vomited on the street she might as well go home and hang herself. Someone, somewhere would see her. That was the way it worked.

She eased open the front door and closed it almost noiselessly. Slipped off her shoes. The soles of her feet felt sticky on the tiles, as though someone had spilled a pop and wiped it up without washing the floor. Every step she took made a small noise, like tape being peeled off a roll. She walked into the kitchen and her stomach and heart jumped away from each other in dizzy fright at the sight of Moth sitting at the table, staring straight at her.

Where have you been? he said.

I drank too much wine at Joanna's and I fell asleep, Kate said.

Moth stood up and Kate backed away without thinking. Maybe he'd slap her and make her stay in her room all day. It was a mad thought, but the only thought available. Moth had seen her naked at the Webbs', had seen her hug Joanna, knew she'd been a bad girl. He knew she'd thrown up. Her legs trembled but she couldn't think of anything to say. She had been bad.

The soft, early light made Moth glow, just slightly. Or maybe she was seeing him through tears. Kate wiped her eyes and Moth crossed the floor quickly and they put their arms around each other in a long, tight hug. He felt as hard and solid as a wall under her hands. He let go and stepped back as though the ref had just told him to break. Kate let her arms fall to her sides.

Dad didn't tell me anything, Moth said. He went to bed and I thought you'd be home any second and then I started worrying. I couldn't sleep.

Could you get me a glass of water? Cold.

Kate pulled out one of the chairs and sat down while Moth ran the tap at the other end of the kitchen. He brought her water in one of the big glasses and she drank it straight down and then handed him the glass while she caught her breath. Moth poured her another glass and put it in her hand, then sat down at the table. She took a gulp and set the glass in front of her.

What were you worried about? she asked him.

I don't know, Moth said. Some kids hit a baseball through my window. They broke it.

Moth, I can't think very well.

Kids, he said. They were playing out on the road and they broke my window. They ran away before I came outside.

Your window is broken, Kate said.

Yes. I covered up the hole. Trevor thought there was a war.

Trevor, she said.

Nothing happened to Trevor, said Moth. I thought you and Dad were maybe breaking up. I don't know why.

His face was becoming more distinct. Kate leaned over the corner of the table and gave her son the kind of kiss Joanna had given her. It felt as odd and completely unfamiliar as their hug and conversation.

Why the hell would you think such a thing?

I don't know, Moth said. You've never been out all night before.

Your father is probably angry.

Who knows? Moth said. How could I tell?

Kate pushed back her chair and stood up. Moth did the same.

I'm going to have to go to bed, she said. You'd better, too.

It's Saturday, Moth said.

They stood facing one another, unsure whether to try another hug. Kate smiled at him, but didn't know if he could see it. She took one final drink of water and turned away, taking the glass with her.

What the hell had they spilled on this floor?

Moth fought his last fight in the basement of a church forty miles from Valentine. The crowd was polite and applauded after every round, but made hardly a sound while the punches were being thrown. None of the overhead lights were extinguished and there was a constant buzz of fluorescence. He lost a decision to a good-looking guy his own age from the YMHA, and punch for punch it was his most painful fight.

Everybody says you don't feel the punches, but you do, he told Jake. They don't hurt as much, but it isn't like a fly lands on your face. You look at a picture of guys boxing – does it look like they're not feeling the punches?

They sat across from one another at an empty table in the school cafeteria. These tables, near the windows, were always vacant because of the noonday sun and Moth and Jake squinted at each other. They were hot and Moth's shirt had begun to stick to his chest.

I know what a punch feels like, Jake said.

But this was different, said Moth. It was like getting punched by surprise. Every fucking punch. I know this guy couldn't hit like Travis, but it felt harder.

Why?

I don't know why, said Moth. But I know that he wasn't feeling my punches the way I was feeling his. That's a nightmare, a fight like that.

Maybe you should quit the wrestling team, said Jake.

I fought this guy wrong, that's all, Moth said.

They hadn't spoken much since the robbery, but Jake was no longer terrified. He'd been given a suspended sentence and now he didn't care who saw them talking. Moth was waiting for a pre-sentence report before trial. He had become a strong but very limited wrestler and he won more matches than he lost. He thought it had made him a better infighter.

What the hell does it have to do with wrestling? Moth asked.

I don't know, Jake said.

Montreal was too far away and during school he could only go to the boxing club on weekends. Soon there would be mountains of snow and he had no idea what he'd do then. He might be boxing in prison.

Moth had fought in the ring for the last time, but he wouldn't know it for another year or two. He would believe that Valentine had killed boxing for him and he would hold his father's transfer responsible, as he would the distance, the weather, and the impossibility of training regularly and improving. He would believe these things had been his undoing. He would never accept that he'd quit boxing, left school, and returned to Bresby because of Donna Mesrine.

She wasn't in the cafeteria and Moth had a queasy vertigo, wondering where she was. What she had brought for lunch. She had probably made it herself and put things in it that Moth would never think of eating. Maybe she knew how to use wax paper. Knew what kind of bag to use for lunches and even where to get the bags and how much they cost.

I hate it when seven and eights are in the same school as everybody else, Moth said. My old school wasn't like this. Most schools in Bresby start high school with grade nine. Seven and eight is junior high.

Jake said, If you don't feel the punches, then why do guys wrestle, but they won't box? Guys don't box because they get punched.

I felt every punch, said Moth. And he kept hitting me. After the fight he said I shouldn't crouch.

You're harder to hit when you crouch, said Jake.

Not for this guy.

The day of the fight he'd felt as sick and awful as he felt on every other day. It made no difference knowing he would be in the ring with a stranger that evening. Maybe this is what they meant by falling in love, but he doubted it. No one ever talked about this feeling and they would have if they'd felt this way. It was like going back through time in the Travis fight. Someone else would have talked about it if they knew what it was like.

He had taken the bus downtown to the club, where cars were waiting for the fighters. He had always travelled blind. Donna would know every landmark, but she had been on this road how many times? It didn't matter. Moth would be no wiser or more observant if he made the trip every day for a decade. He had looked out the window trying to commit each building to memory and wanted to sob when he gave up. He knew he could never catch up with her.

She took this bus downtown and she went shopping. She knew the stores, large and small, and Moth had never bought himself a pair of socks. Donna knew east from west and north from south while he could only distinguish left from right. He was stupid. She was smart. All of her school notes were organized and divided neatly in a binder and she did homework every night while Moth read about fights that had been won and lost before he was born. She skied, she read, she knew the names of flowers and trees. She could tread water for twenty minutes. Moth could identify the Big Dipper and Donna could point out constellations in every corner of the sky. Everything about her diminished him.

Each morning Moth woke up and felt like he was starving to death. His stomach had been scooped out and someone was standing on his chest. It was worse than any feeling he could imagine because he had no idea what he felt or why. It had no name. Everything about it was embarrassing. Donna did things right and he did things wrong. She had never said this to him even by insinuation.

Details ruled his mind and crushed him. He saw her pick up a paper clip with her left hand even though she wasn't left-handed and he found it perplexing. He tried to visualize himself picking up the same paper clip. Left hand or right hand? She knew Casablanca was in Africa. She could skate.

He saw her standing at the cafeteria doors, looking for him. He raised his hand and she waved at him to come over. With her left hand she made a motion as though she were splashing water on her face. Moth tried to imagine how he'd do it. He wouldn't wave; he would walk over to the table. She was too smart to sit in the sunlight.

She wants you to go over, said Jake.

I'm thinking, Moth said.

He had no idea how you waved someone over. Maybe he had never done it. If he ever had to do it, if there was no choice, he wasn't sure what he would do. She figured out things like that with no trouble at all. He couldn't stand it.

Donna came over to their table but didn't sit down.

Couldn't you see me waving? she asked.

It was a weird wave, Moth said. I didn't know what you were doing.

You want to go outside?

Jake raised his eyebrows and smirked at Moth, unseen by Donna.

There's less than half an hour, Moth said.

Up to you, said Donna.

Moth stood up without another word to Jake. Donna grabbed his hand and they almost ran downstairs and outside into the cool light of noon. The halls were empty except for the monitors who watched with frowns or tight-lipped stares, rehearsing for their future as obedient citizens. They were the irksome informants of tomorrow and Moth had decided to flatten at least one of them if he didn't get jail time.

The school was only five years old and it rose from a clearing a quarter mile off the main road, with overgrown acreage on every side. The football field looked like a landing strip carved in the middle of the badlands. Moth and Donna ran down the hill toward the bridge where other students smoked out of sight of the teachers. As soon as the school disappeared and before they could be seen from the bridge, they ducked into the tall grass and ran to a thick grove of trees.

Donna looked at her watch. We have to be really quick, she said.

Moth pulled her close and kissed her. She dug her fingers into his biceps then ran her hands down the sides of his body. It made him feel strong and fit. He lifted her skirt and felt for the waistband of her underwear. A sudden breeze turned her flesh to goosebumps under his hands and Moth felt his own skin prickle. They kissed perfectly. He took his hands out from beneath her skirt and held her face. Donna pulled down the zipper on his pants.

Let's lie down, she said.

They had never come here when it was this cold. On their first time they had taken off all their clothes and run away to another tree, unsure exactly where they had stripped. Donna had led the way and the effect of surrendering control made Moth crazed and insatiable. That same week they had returned to the wrong spot and found no trace of their shirts and shoes and for three endless minutes thought someone had sneaked in and stolen it all. They fell onto the grass and bit one another's mouths, delirious. They would have to walk back to school naked, Donna whispered, and Moth had moaned and bucked on the ground like a landed fish.

On other days they had crept through the long grass until they could see the kids smoking. Their nakedness was defined and electrified by the school sweaters and white blouses on the bridge. Donna's hand held Moth and he touched her, their fingers moving on one another while they watched the boys and girls they knew. The world opened up and Moth fell into it.

They brought their lunches with them and bolted sandwiches while they raced back to school. Donna sliced bread diagonally, like they did in restaurants, and Moth cut his straight across, like a kid. He noticed it one noon hour and his throat went dry. It was the very first thing to take hold of him.

The first of that kind, but not the very first thing. She'd had a boyfriend the year before who had moved to Texas with his family. They had written to each other until he met another girl and that was the end of it. That much Moth knew.

He was okay, Jake told Moth. Nothing special.

Big, small, good-looking, what? asked Moth.

Taller than you. He played football.

Did you like him? Moth asked.

He was funny. A nice guy.

You liked him.

He's in Texas, Moth, said Jake.

You think they did it? He ever say?

He wasn't the kind of guy who'd tell you, said Jake.

Beryl had thrown a rock through his window while Moth and Donna lay side by side on his bed, their pants to their knees and shirts unbuttoned. Their teeth scraped when they kissed and Moth knew the time was upon him, and it all dissolved in a burst of glass.

He spent the rest of the night in a fever dream, neither sleeping nor awake. It was all kid stuff. His mouth had covered most of her body and she had journeyed from his lips to his thighs, but he had never entered her. They ran naked in a field and had muffled orgasms while they watched the group on the bridge and it was kid stuff. Moth had pushed his face between her thighs, which seemed very adult and advanced, but it came to nothing. No guy talked about doing that to his girlfriend. The guys carried condoms in their wallets and had secret stashes at home, liberated from their father's sock drawer. They said they got laid, got fucked, that she was tight as a bug's ear. They nailed girls, put the blocks to them, threw one into them. Meanwhile, Moth played with Donna.

He didn't want to play. He wanted to be inside her, like every other guy had been inside girls. Like they were married. Moth would think about marrying her, being in love, having a baby. Not caring that she could figure out when the next leap year would fall. A minute later he would be sitting up, wondering why his mother hadn't come home and where the hell she'd gone.

Now they were in the field kissing and had only twenty minutes at most. Soon it would be too cold to come here. Moth kissed Donna and held her face. She had managed to dig him out of his underwear and she gently moved her hand, but he wouldn't let her kneel down.

Tell me you love me, he said.

She said it. He said it back to her. He kept her face on his and their lips together. He wanted to tell her the whole thing, from the very beginning to her waving in the cafeteria. Confess every humiliating moment of it. That was the only way his mind would feel empty of its madness. If he could tell her now, he would be cleansed, reborn, ready to start again. He could stop asking questions she couldn't answer. Donna was smart. Maybe she would tell him what was wrong with him.

Don't you want to do anything?

Moth kissed her and didn't answer. He wanted to do everything. He wanted to be normal. It would mean returning to the starting line and he didn't have the energy. Maybe he was as normal as hell and didn't know it. He had a weird quirk about – what? What was it? Moth wanted a name for the way he felt and he wanted reasons. It could be a small corner of his brain acting up, like people who couldn't stop shoplifting. Or it could be his very essence. He kissed her miserably.

I guess I just don't feel like it today, he said.

He felt himself slip out of her hand and her arms went limp. He had never said this before and she looked carefully into his face.

What's wrong? Did I do something?

Let's get back, Moth said.

They pushed their way through the grass and onto the road, then trudged up the small hill without holding hands.

It's because I was late, Donna said. Is that why?

I don't know, Moth said.

I had to help her find her stupid watch, she said. She was really upset.

Do you know where Mount Everest is?

Of course I do, Donna said. Why?

Forget it.

She was mystified and hurried to keep up with him. Often he asked her questions that were dumbfounding, as though he was giving her a secret test.

You know what I think? said Moth. You keep trying to prove how smart you are. I don't think you're so smart.

It came as unexpectedly as the sky raining turtles. She thought she knew his sensitive points by now and didn't number intelligence amongst them. Her last boyfriend had been more her academic match and they had struggled mightily to defeat one another in final exams. Moth was a different proposition. He seemed oblivious in the classroom and never carried home a book. His binder was a prop, a couple of pages covered in his own rating system for the greatest middleweights of all time. He told her the story of Stanley Ketchel being gunned down by Walter Dipley and he talked about Dempsey riding the rails. It wasn't very interesting, but it wasn't as dull as football. None of it had to do with being smart.

You can't walk past a fucking weed without telling me all about it, Moth said.

Why didn't you just say it bothered you?

I'm saying it now, aren't I?

You ask me a lot of questions, Moth, she said.

Don't worry, I'll stop, he said. Why do you swing your arms when you walk, anyway? I don't.

She looked at her feet and watched them hurry. If she started to cry she wouldn't be able to stop. The thought of crying made her want to wail. She knew this tone of his and she felt old and tired every time she heard it. He would attack from every side and no resolution was possible because she had no idea what he was talking about. It would be unpredictable and relentless and it made her head ache. Swinging her arms.

Stupid, said Moth.

Her feet slowed and halted. They were in front of the school and Moth went a few more feet before he stopped and turned around.

We can't stop, he said. We're going to be late.

She wondered why he buttoned his shirt right up to his throat. His face was hard and angry and his neck looked swollen. Two more words and the top button would pop. One night when her father had stood in the living room and yelled at her, she had seen a small spot of ink over his heart. He had told her she would be grounded for the rest of her life if she ever saw Moth again and all she could think about was the leaky pen in his breast pocket. She had wanted to tell him about the pen and she wanted to ask Moth about his buttons.

Why do you button your shirt right to the top? she asked.

Moth stared at her, as stunned as if she'd hit him in the face. Donna heard her own question and closed her eyes while her shoulders trembled. Moth stepped toward her and laughter burst from her like a shout. She had no control over it. It shook her body and made her bend over, holding her stomach. Tears wet her face. She straightened up and it started again, right from the beginning. Moth looked scared and that was funny, too. But not as funny – nothing was as funny – as asking him about his stupid buttons.

You see? she said, trying to catch her breath. It's funny. You're funny.

Moth frowned at her in warning and it enraged her.

You know why I swing my arms, Moth? she asked him. Because I'm so smart. That's right. I shave my legs and I don't cut myself because I'm a genius. I'm sorry it makes you feel so bad.

She closed her eyes and covered her face with her hand. Her body still shuddered in waves, and her eyes were hot and wet. Maybe she'd cry, she wasn't sure.

When she wiped away the tears with her sleeve, she saw that Moth was gone.

She started laughing again.

CHAPTER SIX

Okay Terry fuck you.

Stupid. This is letter number 3. I learned to write in about grade 2 how about you? I was really really upset becuse I was so much in love with you and you had a hold on my heart. Chek mail every day but no Terry. I even think it was my mother but I give you my freinds adress and nothing. So it is you Terry. I loved you and you are an asshole.

Needels and pins is for somebody else now.

I cant even return a ring becuse you didnt give me one in fact nothing. Never one thing.

My heart broke now I dont care. You make me puke. I hate you now and for good.

Jerry Delaney read Beryl's letter and decided it was about time his son read one of them. He'd never even known about this kid until the first one arrived. On TV they always steam letters open but in life you burn your fingers and it must take forever. It even took the kettle too long to boil. He'd say he opened it by mistake.

The first letter had been so good, so funny and so pornographic, that he'd taken it to work and read it in the cafeteria. His whole table broke up. How old were you before some babe did this kind of shit? She was sucking Terry off all over the place. He has a big one, just like his old man. And he's fucking her while the old man's on the night shift.

Her heart cries tears. Terry's eyes take her far away to another land. Jesus Christ. The price a guy pays.

The second letter had been a disappointment. Almost no sex, but lots of stuff about her poor, suffering heart. It was amazing. The kid was maybe fourteen or fifteen and she acted the way they all act no matter how old they get. He didn't read that one in the cafeteria. It was too depressing. This letter,

Terry could read. Let him bite the bullet.

He told himself it would give the kid some character, but even Jerry Delaney knew he shouldn't be so overjoyed. He nearly giggled. The letter was printed in blue ink on notebook paper, with three holes punched along one side. He folded it carefully and stuffed it back into its tiny envelope, then hunted down a pencil in Terry's room. Above their address he wrote Open by Mistake, then left it on the pillow in the middle of the bed.

Jerry got himself a beer from the fridge and sank into the couch. He wondered if he should keep the letter until he was working days, then he'd be here when Terry read it. Day shift was too far away. Maybe he could rap on Terry's door when he came home, ask if he was okay. No secret that he'd read the letter. Or he could call from The Plant. Don't push it.

Shit. He hated working second shift. You missed everything.

Terry shot pool with Randy Zed all afternoon and they only spoke to each other in reference to a shot. Buster's friends watched them quietly, drank from coffee mugs, and read their papers. No one played at the other tables. Terry wasn't a good player and he and Randy weren't friends; he was there from the weight of the day. Buster sat and looked out the front window, slapping his thigh with a rolled-up magazine.

At four o'clock Soldier walked in through the back door, alone. He came straight to their table and picked up the cue ball just as Randy Zed was about to shoot. Terry looked at Randy and Randy kept his eyes on Soldier. Buster left his post at the window and moved behind the counter.

What's the problem? Randy Zed asked.

I'll talk and you listen, Soldier said, starting to grin. Okay?

Randy shrugged, his face frozen in sleepy unconcern.

I'm looking for a big Wop named Angelo who shoots pool here. Where is he?

One of the men on the bench laughed and Soldier turned around, looking like he was about to laugh himself.

Buster, the guy yelled. This kid wants to find Angelo.

Why? Buster asked, staying behind the counter. Both of his hands were hidden beneath it.

He doesn't play with us, Jerry said. We don't even know the guy.

These guys do, said Soldier, looking from Buster to the man who'd yelled.

Why do you want to find Angelo? Buster asked again.

Just tell me where he is, Soldier said, and maybe I won't hurt anybody.

The two large, older men slowly put down their newspapers and mugs and stood up. Neither one of them looked nervous. Randy picked up the eight ball from the table and held it by his side. Buster stepped briskly from behind the counter, wrapping one end of a bicycle chain around his knuckles.

South End scum, Buster said.

Soldier laughed. He ran at Buster, leaving the two men in front of him standing foolishly, trying to change gears. Buster leaned forward and swung the chain low, slapping the floor at Soldier's feet, making them suddenly kick in mid-air. Soldier hit the floor on his back and the first old guy got there and knelt on him. His friend jogged over and sat on the thick, struggling legs. Buster walked around them and looked down into Soldier's face. Soldier grinned back.

You're not going to smile again for a long time, sonny, Buster said. You two go home.

Randy and Terry put their pool cues down on the table and walked out the back door without looking behind them. They were halfway across the parking lot when they heard the lock snap into place.

Jesus Christ, Terry said.

He has it coming. If anyone has it coming, it's Soldier.

Maybe they'll kill him.

If they do, Randy said, I wasn't here and I didn't see anything. I was someplace else. With you, at the lake.

Terry got into his car. The key was wet and it shook between his fingers. Randy walked away from him, through the alley and onto the street. Terry was afraid he'd hear Soldier screaming if he didn't get out of there. It was too much like Richie. He flooded the engine, jumped out of the car and ran.

The Plant was changing shifts and the street was getting crowded and he couldn't see Randy. He ran half a block to his left, past the front of Buster's. The green blinds had been pulled down and the front door had the Closed sign hanging from it. Maybe they had taken Soldier down to the basement. He started running back to his car, then stopped in the alley and caught his breath. He was making everyone stare at him, running around like a week-old kitten. They'd remember he was here and then Buster would kill him too. It was a long way from a fight at a dance. These guys were grown-ups.

He left the alley and walked two blocks to the first movie theatre on his side of the street. The day was bright, but it felt cold. There was a poster of Julie Andrews with her mouth open and arms spread, looking at him from a wall on the other side of the road. Bresby had four theatres, all within a quarter-mile of each other, and two of them showed double features. Terry's theatre had the James Bond guy and he bought his ticket and went inside.

The movie had already started. Only half a dozen guys were there and the god damned movie was black and white. Not James Bond, just the same guy. He was in prison, a prisoner of war. No. He was in a military prison for doing something wrong in the army. Terry didn't like the look of it. Four other guys were locked up with him and it looked like a cave, not a cell. It didn't have the order of an American prison, the ones where breakouts were planned by guys who were working with lathes in the shop. They didn't even know the other prisoners in the movie and there wasn't a cafeteria. They were treated like shit, always running, doing pointless things outside in the heat.

Maybe prison was really like this. Any asshole who doesn't like you can make you run up and down a hill all day in the sun. Not feed you. Tell you you're queer and push his face right up to you when he does it, like some shrimpy teacher. Prison movies made him angry; this one made him scared.

Maybe he'd tell the cops the truth. He didn't start it and it had nothing to do with him. Buster wasn't supposed to be protected by him. Buster was a man.

The smallest guy in the cell dropped dead from running all day in the sun. James Bond was obviously the toughest and smartest guy in the movie. He was going to start trouble over the guy dying. Terry knew how it would end.

He'd have to leave town after he talked to the cops. There was Buster's friends and there was Randy Zed. He wouldn't be able to walk down the street. All he had to say was that Soldier had started trouble and he didn't know what happened after that. Or he had to come up with a better story with Randy. We were at the lake. Jesus. Doing what? What time did we go and what time did we come back?

The guys in the prison acted a lot like the guys at school. Terry had never seen that in a movie before and he knew immediately it must be true. The head guy comes out, the guy who runs the place, and he bullshits them and calms them down when they're going to riot. They all lose their nerve. Everybody except James Bond.

He couldn't talk to the cops. He was thinking like a kid.

The guard who hates him asks for a fight and they go into an empty cell. Two other guards go in with him, three against one.

Terry felt cold. He wished that Soldier hadn't been laughing. Three old, hard men who wouldn't feel sorry for him at all. Buster would whip him with that bicycle chain or maybe they'd cut off his fingers. No one would see him being brave, and all we'll ever see is what they did to him. If they don't kill him. Terry knew then that they wouldn't. They'd let him walk around with his chain-scarred face and deformed hands and Soldier would stop laughing for all time.

James Bond – his name was what? He was back in his cell with the other guys. He looked beat up, but Terry had seen worse. Three guys against one and he just had some bruises and a broken foot. He was in pain, but it was movie pain; his mind was still the same.

Terry left the theatre.

ii

Darlene's mother was baking a thousand muffins. At least a thousand. She hummed loudly while she greased the pans and poured out the thick, sweet mix. The kitchen was small and wallpapered and the corners of the paper were peeling, showing the ugly brown underside. A red-and-white coffee pot was repeated endlessly as a pattern. The light switch guard was a plastic coffee pot that matched the ones on the paper and Darlene's mother was still delighted to have found it.

The heat had turned her face shiny with sweat, but she kept humming. Harry Belafonte played on the stereo and cued her. It was a live recording and she laughed every time Harry made a joke, even though she had heard the record as often as she'd made muffins. She knew the words to every song, she was familiar with every pause, and she had made many muffins. Darlene never helped. She hated baking and she hated Harry Belafonte. It took the fun out of the whole experience for her mother.

Darlene lay on her bed, talking on the phone. Her father was working nights and her mother was playing that fucking record and turning the house into an oven. Terry listened to her describe it to him.

We don't even eat the muffins, Darlene said. They're for her church group and they're always doing something where they need to eat. They have meetings and sales and all kinds of shit and they always want muffins. Probably they think it's all she knows how to make. My mother can bake anything. My dad has a huge gut, like a bag of groceries under his shirt. He takes off his shirt in the summer and I can't even look at him. It isn't beer, it's my Mom's cooking. If I ate half of what she cooks I'd look like Mary Ferrini.

Why don't you meet me? Terry asked her. I can pick you up on the corner.

It was just getting dark. Terry was standing in a phone booth ten blocks away from Buster's, on the main drag. He had parked his car in the lot behind the Pinklon, where he could keep an eye on it. The Pinklon would serve you as long as you had ID.

You're not even listening to me, said Darlene.

Yeah, I am. Your mom is a good cook and your dad is fat. I need to see you.

It's late, Terry, Darlene said. I can't just say I'm going out.

You've come out before.

Terry didn't see any women enter the Pinklon under the Ladies and Escorts sign. There always seemed to be women there, but you never saw them come in. Maybe they lived in the hotel. They were always old, at least thirty, and they looked like they worked in a cafeteria. Terry liked the way they looked and he liked their confidence.

You always want something else, said Darlene. You're never happy. I hate that.

I promise I won't ask you for anything else.

Yes you will. You always promise. You're the first guy who's ever complained.

Listen, Terry said. Do you have to keep on talking about other guys? I don't want to know.

He saw Randy Zed go into the hotel.

You're not my boyfriend.

Maybe I'd like to change that.

It was out of his mouth before Terry knew what he was saying. His eyes were on Randy and his mouth worked on its own.

117

Darlene didn't answer. She listened to him breathe in her ear. Looked at the hairless Teddy bear as old as she was, sitting on a tiny chair in the corner. *Little Women* and half a shelf of Nancy Drew books. *Fanny Hill* wrapped in the broken cover of a geography school text. She listened to Terry breathe.

I'm not sure exactly what you mean, she said.

Maybe I'd like to be your boyfriend. I mean, I'd like you to be my girl-friend. What do you think?

Terry's heart raced. It was crazy. He wasn't sure he meant a word of what he said, but it might be true. He felt like he was listening to himself, not knowing what he'd hear next.

All I think is that you're sure saying maybe a lot.

Okay, Terry said. Do you want to be my girlfriend?

I don't know, Darlene said, trying to keep her voice steady. I think you could still be in love with Beryl.

There was a long pause. Darlene looked nowhere. She waited for him to say it.

Terry wondered if Soldier was dead.

Well, Terry said, I'm not. I'm not in love with Beryl.

Darlene kept quiet.

He could be dead or in the hospital. Maybe he had no face any more.

What do you want me to say? Terry asked her.

Nothing. I don't want you to say anything you don't want to say.

Come and meet me.

It's late, Darlene said, letting all her breath out at once. I have to go.

The night looked longer than the highway. It started at the phone booth and ran all the way to his room, where it would end with the rising sun. The sun had barely gone down. It had to give a whole day to everywhere else in the world before it returned.

I love you, he said.

You just want me to meet you tonight.

Christ, Darlene, Terry said, I'm in love with you.

He sounded like he might start to cry. Darlene felt like everything had gathered in her chest, like when you shake a bottle of pop. She felt too rest-less to keep still.

I'll meet you in half an hour, she said, and put the receiver down before he could say anything else.

Terry hung up and left the booth. He wanted to go into the Pinklon and talk to Randy. He wanted to get drunk. He couldn't understand why he'd said what he had just said. He shouldn't have called her.

Darlene was already on the phone to Diane.

iii

Shirley was waiting in the parking lot when Jerry Delaney's shift finished. He was sweaty and tired and he wanted to go home and drink. She looked heavier in that skirt, especially where her blouse tucked in behind the wide belt. It divided her into two parts. Her hair looked almost green under the big lights that circled the fence.

Shirley, he said.

You think I'm being pushy, don't you? she asked.

I kind of wanted to get home.

No time for a drink?

Sure, Jerry said. Where the hell are we going to get one?

I've got it in my purse. Let's take a ride.

Jerry opened the passenger door and she slid inside while he hurried around the car. He tried to scrutinize the lot, but it was as confounding and noisy as a wartime evacuation with one shift leaving and the graveyard starting. Headlights randomly combed the dark, cutting through the spooky dimness of the company lights. He wondered how many guys had seen her besides the ones at the gate.

Isn't Walter on graveyard? he asked her as he pushed himself behind the wheel.

That's why this is the perfect time.

Yeah, perfect if you want all his god damned friends to see you here.

I'll tell him I tried to catch him before he went in, she said. I just missed him.

What are you going to say you wanted?

Oh, Christ, I don't know, she said. I've got all night to think of that.

Jerry realized she was drunk. He started the car and backed out of his spot and eased into line. They'd drive right past the guards at the gate and those guys knew everyone. She must have taken a cab here and she could say she ran into him and he gave her a ride home. Or maybe she'd tell Walter that she had been sleeping with Jerry for the past three months.

Shirley pulled a mickey out of her purse and took a shot right from the bottle. Rye, the colour of light maple syrup. Her mouth was red and wet. She drank anything, but Jerry liked rye. He pulled it out of her hand and stuck it between his legs as they drove past the guard.

They won't arrest me, Shirley said.

I'm taking you home. You're drunk.

You're taking me to the lake, she told him. I've got another one in here.

She pulled the stubby head of a mickey out of her purse. Her hand flashed white and black from the shadows and lights. Long fingers and sensible nails. Jerry took the opened bottle from between his thighs and swallowed two mighty gulps. He could taste her lipstick on it, nearly as good as a kiss. It cut his fear in half. He took another one.

Don't take it *all*.

You're already drunk, he said. Give me a kiss.

He wedged the bottle snugly between his thighs and against his crotch. Shirley moved closer and pushed her tongue into the corner of his mouth while he watched the road. She dropped her hand on him, just above the open mouth of the mickey.

Take it out, she said. I'll do it while you drive.

Wait, he said.

He heard the croak in his voice. Shirley's face was almost against his and her breath was warm and tickled him. The kind of tickle you get between your legs when you know you've slept in and there's going to be trouble. She'd do it; she'd do anything. As long as that was true he was going to see her no matter how stupid it got. This he knew. He also knew that he was going to start carrying a wrench or the head of a ball-peen hammer in his pocket. Walter was strong and bad-tempered. That was one side to consider. The other side was that Jerry could unzip and she'd do it while he was driving. You can't turn down a girl like that. She must do it to Walter all the time. It was a dirty thing to do, it was great, but sometimes you need more than dirty sex. Shirley didn't understand that. She had the same kind of mind as that kid who had sent Terry the letters. Too hard to turn down. You can dress it up all you want but it was still dirty sex.

The one thing about Shirley, she had that face. Such a pretty face and she was such a dirty girl. It would drive anyone crazy. That was one reason why putting it in her mouth was so irresistible. It makes a big difference, a hell of a difference, when the girl has a pretty face. Ugly girls think they have to do it so you'll like them, but it doesn't work. A pretty face is everything.

Shirley's head was in his lap, but his pants were still closed. Like she was hoping to change his mind by rubbing against him. Tonight he was going to take her out of the car and walk her up the hill to the bushes. Make her take off all her clothes. It was cold this time of night and she'd be shivering just a little bit, like a virgin. She'd wrap those shaking white legs around him and kiss him with her pretty mouth. If he was going to hit Walter in the face with a wrench, he wanted a good reason.

They were halfway to the lake before he knew she was sleeping. He was the only driver on that stretch of road and he had begun feeling as light and dangerous as a new razor. The dark horizon of the lake would be discernible, even in the dark, after he crossed the tracks. That close. Shirley's deep, noisy breathing changed his vision. He became an unhappy man bound for a dying lake with a woman, drunk and married, in his horrible automobile.

He thought about turning around and taking her home, but it was just another big pain in the ass to add to the others. She shows up drunk right at the god damned Plant and now she was out cold. He knew if he woke her up at the lake she'd be chilly and complaining and there wasn't enough booze for either of them to get back their mood. He decided to go home. It wasn't any crazier than anything else.

Jerry slowed and signalled a right turn. He drove down a residential street at the posted speed, a polite and intelligent driver.

He owed a lot to The Plant. It had made it possible for him to buy a house and raise a kid. It paid for everything he ate, the clothes on his back, the car he was driving. Shirley worked in the office, so you could say The Plant had supplied her, too. Pretty much everything you could want or need. There were no jobs a guy without a trade could get that paid so well and the union was strong enough that you'd have to intentionally crush someone with a forklift to get fired. They'd had women working on the floor until just after the war, then they all got sent back home. Betty had worked on the same line he was working now. You could say The Plant had given him Betty, as well.

By the time he pulled into the driveway he knew that coming home was madness. The lights were on, but Terry's car wasn't out front. He couldn't have Shirley walking into the place even if it was empty. Everything could be explained and lied about except that.

Shit. Terry's letter. He had forgotten about it once he'd left The Plant, but he'd looked forward to Terry's reaction all day.

Jerry stopped the car and he waited a full minute while he heard the thought reverberate. Even Shirley wasn't as important as that god damned letter. There was something awful about that. The main thing was – well, the main thing was where the hell was Terry? It was late and he wasn't home and there was no way Jerry would stand for it. Maybe that was one reason he was glad that girl had shafted him. Terry never did what he was told and his attitude was something the cops would have fun changing. That's really what he needed, the cops. That girl was probably underage, too.

His hands began to hurt and grow numb on the wheel. Shirley snored, very softly. The girl didn't shaft him. Right at the beginning she'd said it was the third letter. He'd been so pleased about what she'd written that he'd forgotten that. Third letter. Terry would know he'd kept the other two.

He lifted Shirley's head and slid out from under it, gently opening the car door and holding the mickey at the same time. She didn't move when he lowered her face onto the car seat, nor when he pushed the door closed with a single click. Terry might not have even come home and seen the letter. Grab it and tear off the beginning. Maybe spill ink on it.

The lights were on. He'd seen it.

The front door wasn't locked. Jerry carefully pushed it open without stepping inside the house and he could see the TV set on its face, the centrepoint of dark shards of thick glass. He stepped inside, soaking his shoes on the beer-sodden carpet. The living room smelled like the Pinklon on Saturday night. He walked over the torn cushions of the couch and broken empties to Terry's room. It looked about the same. He had smashed the place up and left.

Jerry was mustering his fury when fear shot through him like the jolt from a bad tooth. The kid wasn't scared of him. Terry had gone this far and he obviously wasn't afraid. He might not even be finished. He could come back at any second and then all the threats in the world weren't going to mean a thing. A wrench. A wrench or a hammer head he could close his hand around before he started swinging. There was an old pair of vise-grips under the sink that would work if he came home now.

Jerry was navigating his way to the kitchen when he looked into his bedroom and changed his mind. The dresser lay on its side, blocking the door. He could see the splintered drawers beyond and a scattering of beer-soaked clothes when he approached it. His bed looked intact. He saw the open box lying on a pillow and he booted the dresser away from the door.

The box had been hidden underneath the dresser for maybe fifteen years, ever since he'd bought it. It had originally contained cutlery and been lined with a gold-coloured fabric that felt like the top of a pool table. Later the fabric had been torn out and three spoons in the back of a kitchen drawer were all that remained of the cutlery. Jerry walked over his shirts and socks to the box, seeing the neat pile of papers beside it and a corner of a photograph poking out below the lid. He sat down as though any sudden move would trigger a bomb.

Terry had seen the letters, the marriage licence, the photographs. It wasn't right. These things were his personal property and were none of Terry's business. You get rights over a wife that you don't get over your mother. You don't choose your mother and she doesn't choose you. Terry had always made a big deal about it and it wasn't fair. He had a father who fed him and protected him and all he would say was that he didn't have a mother. Well, *he* didn't have a wife. Think about that sometime.

The letters from the box weren't written by her. Jerry had composed a letter every night when she had first left and never sent them. There was no good reason to keep them, but he had. He wanted to kill Terry.

She left him and later, only a little bit later, something awful happened. Maybe.

They'd had three beautiful years together before Terry was born and one smack across the face had ended the whole thing. He was pretty sure that's what happened. What woman leaves you over one clout across the mouth? That part didn't make any sense to him, even now. He had never done anything like that for the first three years, but none of that counted all of a sudden. One smack.

He thumbed through the photographs and then stood up holding them in his hand. This time he looked at each one carefully and put it on the bottom of the pile. The two of them standing in front of their first car. On the beach, facing the camera like mannequins. Sitting on a couch beside a Christmas tree. There were over a dozen snapshots of the two of them holding their spines straight and grinning strangely. The photographs of her alone were gone.

Jerry let the pictures fall on the bed and took a giant step toward the wall, throwing a punch straight from his shoulder. He smashed a hole between the studs and heard the pieces rattle as they fell between the walls. God, let him come home. Please let him come home so I can give him just one shot like this.

He kicked drawers and clothes out of his way and left the bedroom. Held his breath when he opened the door to the fridge, but the little bastard had smashed the whole case. He nearly ran from there to Terry's room. The letter was still on the bed, but when he snatched it up he saw it wasn't the letter, but just the envelope. Terry had written SLEEP WITH YOUR EYES OPEN.

Jerry crushed it in his fist and began yanking open drawers. He had opened three before anything penetrated his brain. Terry had taken everything. He was gone. Not like he didn't expect it. Jerry had been searching through the closet and drawers a long time, waiting to find them empty.

The mickey was sitting on the window ledge where he'd left it when he entered the house. He'd forgotten having it and forgotten putting it down. But he had never needed a drink more. There were three good swallows left in the bottle and he took a small pause after the first and second.

The only three pictures of Betty by herself and he would never see them again. In one of them she had been sitting on a swing in the park. Looking like she was surprised that he was taking her picture. He remembered everything about that day and he'd taken the last three shots on the roll during it. Betty sitting in the car, putting on lipstick and trying to turn her head away. Betty asleep on the couch, looking ten years younger. Terry had stolen the only pictures he had of his wife. The only ones of her without him.

Not quite a year after she left she had been killed in a car accident in Boston. Her mother had sent him a letter about it. They'd buried her somewhere down there because they couldn't find out who she was or where she was from. That's what her mother wrote. Her mother had always hated him. She'd found out about the accident because she was trying to find Betty. Jerry didn't know why the hell she'd go to Boston or who she knew there.

When it first occurred to him that it was all lies, it was too late. By that time, her mother was dead. Not in Boston and not from an accident. She had probably lied to him because he was trying to get Betty to come home and the old bitch knew that she would. Other times he was sure it was the truth because of the hex you'd put on your own child by making that up.

There were even times when he remembered Betty leaving for Boston. They were in love, they had plans, and she was just going away for the weekend. And Terry was where?

124

If she wasn't dead, she'd have come back for Terry. It was hard enough keeping her from taking him when she left. Jerry knew that if he let her take the kid she'd never come back. That's how he remembered it. Other times he thought he'd tried to force her to take Terry and she wouldn't. Every time he thought about her it started as a straight road and then branched off into a hundred dead ends. The only thing he knew for sure was that Betty wasn't here and Terry was.

And now he wasn't there, either.

Shirley woke up when he tried to pull the other mickey out of her purse. She sat up quickly once her eyes were open and looked around.

Give me that, she said, grabbing at the bottle.

She took a long drink and stopped to cough. Her eyes watered. She took another.

I feel awful, she said.

Jerry started the car. He'd take her home and he wasn't sure what to do after that. He didn't want to come here. He wanted Terry to come back and clean up all the mess and give him back his pictures. He needed them. They were the only pictures where she didn't look like she was having her picture taken. She didn't stare and she didn't grin and she looked like herself, just the way he remembered her.

She had that face.

iv

Terry was drinking a beer in the Pinklon, trying to stretch Darlene's babysitting money to closing time. He sat at a table with his back to the wall and read initials on the tabletop. In his section were half a dozen other guys who sat by themselves and there was no correlation between their ages and their solitude. A man entering the room alone would proceed to that area as though by decree.

Terry had slept poorly the Night of the Letter and last night he had nodded out for ten minutes at a time, awoken, then drifted under again. He'd parked in the brush downstream from the Blue Arch both nights and woke up in the back seat freezing and blinded by the sun. He hated being dirty and not brushing his teeth and he hated needing money and somewhere to stay. There were so many things to figure out that he was exhausted before he began.

He could drink until closing time, if he nursed every glass. It was a terrible way to drink and the only cumulative effect was on his bladder, but he had no choice. He'd be back in his car in an hour otherwise. He could try phoning Beryl again, but money was scarce and if anyone answered it would wipe him out. She didn't even have to be home and it would still leave him broke. He had no idea how he could convince her that his father had stolen two pieces of mail but delivered the third. Terry didn't know why his father had done it. He didn't know why his father kept pictures of his mother hidden. Or why he wrote letters he never sent.

He didn't know why he had told Darlene that he loved her. Maybe he loved her.

He took out his wallet and pulled out a picture of his mother, the one of her on the swing. Even young people looked old back then because they dressed in old people's clothes. You couldn't tell if she was thin or chunky. Her face was an average size, but that didn't mean anything. He wanted to know everything about her: height and weight and the sound of her voice. And many other things he didn't want to think about tonight.

He replaced the picture and put his wallet back in his pocket.

Everyone drank at the Pinklon except the nights he was there. If he left, he was sure the room would fill up with guys he knew. He had friends. Moth. Randy Zed wasn't a friend, but he knew him. A bunch of guys from the South End, but they didn't count. Jimmy O'Hara. Was he really going to count Jimmy as a friend? The point was, he knew a lot of guys. A lot. He didn't need some guy to hang around with like he did with Moth when they were young. Girls had friends.

That was it, right there. He was with Beryl and now he was with Darlene. That's why he didn't make friends with a lot of guys. It made sense.

It might still be too early. There were faces he recognized, but none well enough to join their table. He wanted someone to buy a lot of beer and he wanted them to talk about anything except mothers, fathers, and girlfriends.

He looked up and there was Soldier, right in front of him. He wasn't grinning, but looked like he was waiting for Terry to laugh at a private joke. His face was unmarked.

I know you, Soldier said.

He pulled out the chair opposite and sat down like a man who had spent too much time on his feet that day. The solitary drinkers nearby looked at

126

him and then back at their glasses. His presence was noted, but he wasn't recognized.

I'm looking for a guy named Angelo, Soldier said. Big guy.

I don't know him, Terry said.

Soldier picked up Terry's glass of beer and drained it, then put the glass back where he'd found it.

Okay, Soldier said. Then I'm looking for Henry Godin.

Terry gave the tables a sweep with his eyes. He didn't think anyone had seen what had happened to his beer. Maybe he was the only one there who could see Soldier, like when someone meets a ghost in a movie. The guys near them had seen a chair move by itself and wondered if they should quit drinking. Soldier should be anywhere but here. He should be dead or in the hospital or hiding somewhere crying over his wounds.

Henry Godin, Soldier said.

I know who he is, Terry said, but I don't know him.

Me neither, said Soldier and he laughed the moment he said it. Isn't that something? I don't know this fucking Angelo, either.

Yeah, Terry said.

But I know you. And I need a ride, said Soldier.

Terry would think about this day for the rest of his life. The dialogue with Soldier would change many times in recollection and in his memory the fabric of the hours would strain with approaching violence. He would remember looking at the picture of his mother and wanting to beat his father to death. He would recall struggling with revenge scenarios, barely able to maintain his balance, although there was not a jot of truth to this. In his history, it would be written that at any moment in that day he might have descended into the valley to smite at random.

Soldier appeared, having been humiliated at the hands of three old men, and tried to reclaim the ground he'd lost.

Soldier appeared and Terry won his respect.

Soldier appeared.

They crossed the street and Terry told him he needed gas and had no money. Soldier went back into the Pinklon without a word. The night was fresh and quiet after the airless din of the beer parlour and Terry wished they'd sell to him at the liquor store. At least he'd be able to drink somewhere that had windows. He tried to imagine where that place might be, but arrived at the swamp by the Arch. Somewhere.

He sat in the car and thought about driving away, but so fleetingly he couldn't remember the impulse even later that very night. It did not become a piece of the lore of that terrible twenty-four hours. Soldier got into the front seat and placed a five-dollar bill on the dashboard and Terry filled his tank a block away.

Richie joined the navy, Soldier said.

It was the first time he'd spoken since leaving the bar and he said nothing else until they drove across the tracks.

He was a heavy hitter and he was hard to tag, said Soldier. That doesn't mean tough. You saw him with Godin. You dig around in Richie like a box of crackerjack and there's no prize.

Terry drove. He felt like he'd had just enough to drink. He wasn't drunk or light-headed or slow to respond, but his sense of fear had been dulled and his imagination lumbered. Fear and fantasy were of no use in this situation. He didn't think he could beat Soldier in a fight, but he wasn't afraid of him either. Just enough to drink. He felt calm and alert and unbelievably hungry. Never had he been more ravenous. Without preamble, his stomach moaned loud and long, like it was haunting a house.

That happen when you're scared? Soldier asked.

When I'm hungry.

Stop at the A & W.

It's closed, Terry said.

Soldier contemplated the news in silence. He weighed the issue and his options according to his own esoteric code while Terry marvelled. Everything with Soldier would turn on the hazard of the moment and nothing would be known until the moment arrived. Being prepared wasn't possible. Terry's stomach made a deep, noisy plea.

I think you swallowed a fucking owl, said Soldier. Here. Right here.

Terry turned into the parking lot of the Mohawk. No one he knew or had ever met went to the Mohawk to drink and its reputation didn't exist. Too far from downtown. The customers were tool and dye workers and men from the bottling plant. South End men. There were rusted pick-ups and cars no better than his own in the lot.

I'll get us something, Soldier said.

Terry watched him walk from the car to the hotel. They were about the same height, but Soldier was wider. He didn't strut or swagger, but he didn't sneak quietly along, either. He walked like everywhere he trod belonged to him, like a conqueror in a movie. He wore a loose black shirt, open at the neck, and his jeans were rolled in a single turn at the bottom of each leg, the same as Terry's. Motorcycle boots, although he owned no bike. Soldier dressed like a guy who fought, not like a guy who wanted to look like a guy who fought. They had that much in common.

Henry Godin belonged to a different division. He dispatched enemies with brutal economy and no one had seen him fight the same way twice. He appeared endlessly adaptable and inventive. Randy Zed once claimed to know whether Henry Godin was fighting just by listening. His punches didn't connect with the full, meaty whack of a roundhouse; they sounded like he was hitting clay with a stick. Henry could throw a punch in a phone booth.

Henry was above the ordinary theatre of dance club violence since the founding of his gang. They fought other bikers north of the city in towns smaller than Bresby and they were the envy of every South Ender. Terry didn't understand bikers or why they fought. It was easier understanding Soldier.

He had no idea why Richie Bender had challenged Henry. No one had done it in years and it didn't seem likely anyone would again. Until tonight. This utter lack of ceremony was exactly Soldier's style. There would be no announcement, no gathering of spectators, no appointed time and place. He would appear and violence would ensue. And Terry had no more sense of his motive than he'd had of Richie's. He was guessing that Henry Godin was the one obstacle between Soldier and immortality.

No one was coming out of the Mohawk. It was taking Soldier a long time to get potato chips. Terry hoped he wouldn't come back with pickled eggs.

Soldier's legend was written in the shadow of Richie and, before that, John Tate. He was seen as the mad dog at his owner's right hand, but he was always seen as having an owner. Tate had been tougher than Richie and as crazy as Soldier. He was the original unifying leader for the bad guys of the South End and he killed almost a third of his own gang when he drove into the side of a tractor. He died with the rest, drunk and unconscious and burning up on a dirt road with no streetlights, his mission that night a mystery for all time.

Richie was smarter than Tate and probably smarter than Soldier. Smart enough to join the navy when his time was up. Now it looked like Soldier was going to establish independence in ways indisputable. Terry wondered if he would make himself the leader of the South End boys, but he didn't believe it. Soldier didn't want to be president, he wanted to be king. He didn't need a master and he needed no gang. What he needed was to leave Henry Godin bleeding in the dust. It would add a dimension to his celebrity that would relegate John Tate to a mere footnote. You needed more than strength and skill to beat Henry Godin. You needed character.

Maybe none of it was true. Terry sat behind the wheel of his car and recognized that he couldn't understand his own father or himself and it was therefore pointless trying to decipher Soldier.

He was probably drinking, Terry thought. He would return drunk and empty-handed, accountable to no one. Soldier appeared in the instant of the thought and walked to the car twice as fast as he'd left it. He had bags of chips and peanuts and all his teeth showed in his grin. He jammed the bags under one arm and opened the car door.

Get going, he said.

He slid in and slammed the door, his eyes on the entrance to the Mohawk. The snack food fell onto his lap and the floor. Terry could smell Soldier's sweat and see blood on his hands. The shoulder of his shirt was torn. He started the car.

No one came bursting through the doors in outraged pursuit. Terry backed up and got on the road as quickly as he could without appearing to be rushed. He forgot all about being hungry.

We're having quite a night, said Soldier.

What happened?

That fucking Angelo was in the hotel, Soldier said. Right there. That's what you call luck.

Not if you're Angelo, I guess, said Terry.

Soldier's eyes were bright when he looked at Terry and he smiled. It wasn't like his mad grin at all, but a wide, happy smile of delight.

That's good, he said. I like that.

Terry kept his eyes on the road. He affected a neutral expression as a police cruiser drove by and a few minutes later he saw the club off to his right. It looked and sounded like a place of good cheer, like a hangout in a beach movie, with no hint of its sullen realities. They were playing Jan and Dean. He could see the parking lot by the lights surrounding it and there were probably as many guys standing outside as there were inside.

He drove past the park where he had seen Richie beaten and crying.

Where he had met Darlene. Small groups were gathered in circles and drinking. Car radios were tuned to the same station listening to a boisterous idiot playing requests. This was such a bad night to go looking for serious trouble and he wished it could have happened during the week. Aimlessness spread itself more widely around town than it did on weekends. For the very first time he wondered why the hell anyone would come here to stand around with the same guys every week and drink beer. He wondered what everyone was waiting for.

Soldier had him pull over another mile down the road. He could hear the lake once he opened his door and its smell was strong and carried him back through his life. A few yards ahead, the grass gave way to sand. Somewhere along this beach his mother and father had sat together, having a picture taken. His father had no friends, but someone must have been with them that day. He wondered if the same person had taken every snapshot.

He followed Soldier up the incline and saw the lake, not nearly as close as it sounded. A bonfire was burning farther down the beach, much closer to the water. A handful of shadows stood nearby in the same postures that everyone had that night. They were immobile, but restless. Terry had the absurd conviction that everyone was following orders. They had been told to wait and they waited.

There were three motorcycles on the grass, a long way from the fire. One of them gleamed and shone, catching every piece of reflected light. It was the most famous bike in Bresby.

Soldier stayed close to the crest of the hill and began moving along toward the bikes. Terry followed him without any good reason. Maybe he was following orders. He could see that the shadows were three men and three women. One of the men pushed a long piece of driftwood into the flames and dark smoke spread from it. The others stepped back and cursed him. Terry and Soldier were closer now, and they recognized Henry Godin. A blonde woman with wide hips stood beside him, holding his upper arm with both hands.

Soldier stopped walking when they were opposite the fire, the bikes very close. He watched the couples for a minute while he took deep breaths, then stepped back and grunted to himself, like he was preparing to take a running jump. Terry said nothing and they didn't look at each other. He wondered how old Soldier was, where he lived, whether he had brothers and sisters. He knew nothing about him.

He looked up as a cloud covered the moon and at once the moment contained everything. He saw himself staring at the sky and he saw a fire and people on a beach. Nothing was connected or had meaning or was anything other than it appeared. He saw a fire and people near a lake and that was all. It looked desperate and unreal and nothing any of them did was going to make any difference to the moon or the world or even to Bresby, Ontario. He had no thoughts at all. It was just a matter of seeing. What he saw was a small fire and tiny people on a fragment of sand. He could see. It lasted only until the cloud moved on, but for that duration he could see.

By the time the moon shone again, the world was a different place.

v

The police came to Jerry Delaney's door as he was about to leave for work. They were detectives and they wore baggy suits, like Sunday school teachers. One of them was younger than Jerry and the other was about his age.

Nothing had changed in the house since the night Terry had laid waste, except that the smell had become excruciating. The broken TV still lay face down and the rug had taken a new identity. Any piece of exposed floor was sticky with dried beer. The cops looked at the ripped cushions of the couch and the field of broken glass crunching under their shoes and then looked at one another.

Somebody broke in, Jerry said. They didn't take anything and I didn't report it.

How long ago was this?

A while, said Jerry. I don't know.

We're looking for Terry.

He's in there, Jerry said, pointing. He's hiding under the bed.

The cops went into Terry's room, which was unscathed, and called his name. He crawled out from under the bed.

He's always done that, his father said. He thinks nobody knows.

What the hell is going on here? one of them asked Terry.

I don't know, he said. Nothing.

You know Clarence Barnes?

No, Terry said.

No? You were sitting with him in the Pinklon. You left together. Satur-day night.

132

Clarence? Terry asked. Is that Soldier's name?

Mr Delaney, the same detective said, we're taking Terry down to the station.

What'd he do?

Nothing. But he might be a witness to something.

Jerry smiled at his son and Terry didn't bother looking innocent. He knew how much he was going to tell the cops. He'd tell it a little at a time, so they'd think they'd forced it out of him and when he stopped they'd be sure it was all he knew. He didn't look honest, but he didn't look tough. He looked like a guy who knew just a little bit.

Beryl heard a slightly different version of the story. The cops showed up just after Terry and his father had wrecked the house in a fist fight. They dragged Terry off his old man before he killed him and then they took him downtown. This is what he told Beryl and she believed every word.

Terry had never been questioned at the station before. The thought only occurred to him when he was talking to Beryl that Moth had had more experience with this than he had. Moth also knew Henry Godin. Terry started feeling like her brother had the edge and he didn't like it.

The detectives confused him. They didn't get right to the point and they didn't push him or call him names. They had no warmth or mirth, but they weren't stupid. One of them kept going backward while the other one asked harsh questions about the night at the lake. They wanted to know about Soldier coming into the pool hall and they wouldn't tell him what had happened to Buster and his friends. Who was Angelo?

They asked him about his father and his mother and why he hid under the bed. Why he had given Soldier a ride and whether he knew a hotel called the Mohawk. Why he had smashed up his own home. Where he'd taken Soldier. Clarence. What time, what happened, what had he done next?

The room where he was questioned didn't look like the ones in the movies. It was just an office, with no wall-length mirror or stark tableau of metal furniture. There were four desks, all heaped with paper that was spread around prehistoric Underwoods. Reports and handwritten notes were pinned to cork boards on the walls. Both of the cops smoked and dropped the butts into coffee mugs. There was only one ashtray and it was as big as a candy dish and almost invisible under a pyramid of filters and ash.

The story came out of Terry's mouth in pieces, with no chronology. He

133

couldn't keep track of what he was saying or where it was leading. He told them about Beryl's letter, his mother's pictures, sleeping at Blue Arch. He didn't know why Clarence was called Soldier. He didn't know if his mother was alive or if Beryl was his girlfriend or what Soldier had done at the lake. He did not know Angelo.

They read their notes to him and Terry had to correct numerous mistakes. He couldn't believe they had paid so little attention to what he'd said. He was not waiting for Soldier at the Pinklon, he had not gone into the Mohawk, he wasn't hiding under the bed from the police. One of the cops started typing and the other one left the room. When he came back, he handed Terry a Coke and put two dirty white mugs of coffee on the desk. He looked relaxed and pleased.

You know what happened? he asked Terry. You drove him to the lake and then you saw Henry Godin kill him. You're afraid of Godin, aren't you?

I dropped Soldier off at the park.

No sand at the park, the cop said. I'll bet your car has little tiny bits of it all over the wheels. We have equipment that will find it. Or on your shoes or in your socks or between your toes. We know you were right there and you saw everything. We can prove it.

Terry didn't look at his feet. The car tires were bald and he was sure they'd picked up nothing. He held the cop's stare while he made up his mind, then he looked away.

I don't know anything about sand, he said. Soldier wanted to get out at the park and I let him out.

You're in big trouble, Terry.

All I did was give him a ride, he said.

Accessory to murder.

Terry counted to twenty before he spoke.

Okay, he said. Look. I knew he was looking for Angelo. When he came out of the Mohawk he had blood on his hands and his shirt was ripped. I knew he'd found him. He wanted to go to the park and I took him down there, but I was supposed to wait for him. I went home instead. I thought maybe he'd killed Angelo and I didn't want to hang around with him any more.

The cop's eyes were hard and steady.

I thought maybe he'd killed Buster, too, Terry said.

You were supposed to wait while he did what? the detective asked.

He didn't tell me, Terry said. He said he was going in the Mohawk just to get some chips and he came back with blood everywhere. I didn't know what he'd do at the lake.

He looked at the floor and peeked at his shoes as he did. He couldn't see any sand.

Look at me.

When Terry raised his head, he tried to look confused and remorseful and a little bit afraid. The other detective had stopped typing and they both stared at him. They saw a kid who looked shell-shocked.

Soldier was a bad guy, Terry said. I thought maybe he'd burn our house down because I didn't wait for him.

Is that why you don't want to tell us about Godin? said the cop. Because you thought Soldier had it coming?

Was this Angelo a friend of Godin's? asked the cop at the typewriter.

Terry slumped in his chair without faking it.

I went home, he said. I don't know what happened after that.

Beryl heard how they had kept Terry awake all night, asking the same questions over and over again. How he had refused to answer.

He was at the police station for three hours and he told them everything except the truth. He didn't tell Beryl, either. He didn't say he knew Soldier had been beaten to death with a rock or that he'd seen him fall like a bird with a broken neck. No one except the cops knew about the rock.

They let him go home because they were convinced he would have fled at the sight of Henry Godin. They already had a terrified, underage girl who had been at the fire and was ready to tell them whatever they needed to hear. Terry was just another dumb kid who fought at dances and thought he was a gunfighter in Tombstone. His father was drunk and stupid and probably violent. Both cops had lived Terry's life before he had and saw no reason to give him misery.

Terry told Beryl he loved her and she said it back to him and then he hung up and wondered how he'd pay the phone bill. He called Darlene and arranged to meet her in half an hour.

The police had never heard of Soldier and it astonished him. There was no legend more fortified except for Henry Godin's. At least they knew Godin. He was sure they'd heard of Randy Zed, if only he could give them a last name instead of a first letter. A minute after he'd mentioned Randy they were asking about Richie and then he knew they knew nobody. They wrote down Richie's name and put *navy* beside it. The entire pantheon was obscure to them and it was unlikely they'd be impressed even if all the tales were told. It was stunning. There was an alternative universe like in a Superman comic. Two histories were being read and written concurrently and they only intersected at the point of the dead Soldier.

There weren't only two, he realized. There was the endless biography of The Plant, which would endure, as immortal as the police department. It employed the fathers of all the major players in his life and it had employed Henry Godin. There was the short and violent life of Henry's gang. Darlene and Richie, Moth and Henry, Soldier in the ground. Too many connections to make every narrative separate and too many divisions to form a single world. There was Terry, his father, his mother, and Beryl. It was the story he lived and the only one he knew and he barely knew it at all.

That night Darlene lay down on the back seat and lifted up her skirt and Terry lay on top of her for the first time. He didn't blast the horn afterwards. They moved to the front seat and Terry walked around to the back of the car in darkness that was nearly total. He emptied his bladder and looked up at the sky and thought he was being scrutinized by the stars. Maybe he was surrounded by police with cameras that took pictures in the night. He was being followed everywhere and his phone could be tapped. They knew about Beryl, about Darlene, about hiding under his bed. They knew the truth.

It was a thought, not a feeling. He didn't have to act on a thought and he didn't let it scare him. Thoughts came and went, but two girls kept making his stomach turn over and it didn't matter what he thought about it. He felt like Luke from the South End, who had set a garage on fire and then been trapped inside. You didn't escape just because you started it. He knew that thinking was a waste of time and didn't have anything to do with the way you lived. Fear wasn't a thought. Neither was love or fighting or your parents or getting drunk. Richie Bender thought too much and Soldier hadn't thought at all. Henry Godin was a mystery.

He felt his way around to the driver's seat and opened the door. The car light made Darlene squint. She gave him a morose look as he climbed inside and then the light went out. Terry started the car and turned up the radio. He didn't want her to speak and he didn't want to answer any questions.

The Supremes were halfway through the greatest song they would ever perform.

It was the soundtrack to the movie Beryl was living. She felt like an actress watching herself from the front row of a packed house. Her boyfriend was involved in a murder. Bikers, detectives, and interrogations populated the story and all of it was real. It was a drama beyond the appreciation of Valentine and her school, where the football team was the designated supplier of extracurricular excitement. Valentine was a TV show.

Moth and Jake robbing the club and Marcel at the bar weren't much like television and neither was her mother in any circumstance. Neither was drunk Judy Arnold, for that matter, or the very weird Mrs Webb. Whatever her brother was doing with Donna Mesrine probably wasn't something that Ward and June talked about with Wally and the Beaver, either. Valentine looked like a TV show and tried to act like one, Beryl decided, but it was losing the fight. There was always trouble between kids and their parents because the kids wanted TV parents and the parents wanted TV kids.

She understood immediately that the same thing had happened in their last neighbourhood in Bresby. She had meant to write it all down when they lived there and now she wished she had. TV parents didn't hit their kids and their kids didn't kick other kids in the head. That only happened on serious crime shows where the people were too rich or too poor. Her mind was flooding with ideas, but she was lying underneath Marcel behind the country club and there was no way to record them. There was definitely no point in trying to talk with Marcel, then or later.

Murder. Even on TV they took it seriously. It was the last word someone said before the commercial. The bad guys were mouthy and asked what the charge was, then they were stricken with fear at the sound of the word. Now she could say it. She knew what it meant and it belonged to her.

Someone had been killed while Terry was there. Maybe the last person to see the guy alive, besides the biker. Her boyfriend knew the victim and her brother knew the murderer. No other girl in Valentine would be able to say that, ever. They would have skating and skiing and the keys to the car, but they would never have what she had.

Terry dropped Darlene off at the bottom of her street after a wordless ride and Beryl kissed Marcel goodbye under the streetlight near the empty lot behind her house. Everyone went home.

Winter

Chapter Seven

i

Tim Watson went straight to the bar. The club was empty, except for a few golfers and the evening staff setting up. It looked smaller in the daylight. Marc Cloutier watched him approach and nodded assent, as though seeing a prophecy fulfilled. He wore a wine-coloured jacket with the club's crest on the breast pocket and he held an unlit cigar.

Tim extended his hand and Cloutier squeezed it like he was trying to crack a walnut. They had seen each other on the night of the robbery and hadn't met since.

Mr Watson, Cloutier said.

Mr Cloutier, said Tim. I know I'm late in saying this, but I apologize for the actions of my son. I wish I could make it up to you.

This is exactly the right time, said Cloutier. If you were any earlier, I might have been suspicious of your motives.

Tim blinked at him.

I mean, Cloutier said, you may have wanted me to drop the charges. Which would have been impossible, in any case.

Oh, no, Tim said. No. He made his bed.

Yes, he did.

This isn't the first time, either.

Mr Watson, I don't hold parents responsible for the criminal behaviour of their children. There would be no end to it.

My wife and I like this place, Tim said. She looked for you here one night, to talk to you herself.

My number is in the book, Cloutier said, pleasantly.

Tim looked at him, unsure what was being said. He tried to keep his face blank, but friendly.

If you knew me, said Marc Cloutier, you would realize how generous

I've been. A few years ago, some snowmobiles were stolen from behind the club. The young men who did that weren't as lucky as your son. I had their arms and legs broken.

Tim tried to look properly respectful, but he was disappointed. A man named Tremblay worked as an inspector at The Plant and his kid had stolen the snowmobiles. They had transported them to Ontario and sold them. It was common knowledge and Tremblay was happy to relate the story. All of his limbs and those of his son were intact.

Marc Cloutier liked being thought of as a man connected to the Mob and now Tim knew he was just another make-believe tough guy. He'd known them in the war.

Your son held a gun on my son, Cloutier said. I thought about meeting him on the street and beating him within an inch of his life. But I didn't. Do you know why?

Yes, I do, Tim thought. Because Moth would have absolutely pulverized you. He'd beat you into a coma.

He fought against smiling. He felt proud of Moth, which was rare enough.

I did nothing because I am a good judge of character, Cloutier said. I know people of real class when I meet them. You and your wife have nothing to do with the actions of your son. Why should you suffer? Let me buy you a drink.

It was the accent, Tim knew. When you first got off the boat you were there to steal their god damned jobs and once you advanced beyond coveralls you were a man with real class. Cloutier was a peasant. Kate would laugh when he told her.

Marc Cloutier poured the drinks and they toasted one another silently. Joanna Webb appeared at Tim's elbow and leaned against the bar.

Curiouser and curiouser, she said.

I didn't see you, Tim said.

I was in the Ladies. I had no idea deals were being made and plots hatched.

Mrs Webb is our early bird today, said Cloutier.

You're keeping your wife from me, she said to Tim.

Marc Cloutier moved away from them with a neutral smile. Tim didn't look at Joanna. He hated people who demanded a confrontation when they knew damned well what had happened and why. It was as though they thought a fear of arguing about it would make him drop the issue altogether.

Kate has a home, he said. We have children.

Your son didn't break in here because Kate was at my place.

I don't want to be rude, Tim said, but it's really none of your damned business.

Joanna laughed in delight.

My God, she said. There's a real tiger under there, isn't there?

I have nothing against you, he said. Or Bill. I don't blame others for leading my kids astray and I don't blame you for Kate's drinking.

She poses for me, Joanna said. I think she needs a drink because she's naked.

Tim took a large swallow of his brandy.

You didn't know about that, did you? she asked. Bill isn't there when she does it.

You paint her, he said. And she doesn't wear any clothes.

Correct.

Bill has seen the picture.

Oh, Christ, Joanna said. Yes. Big deal. Would you feel better if you could see a picture of me naked? Or I could let you have a look at the real thing.

Bill Webb came into the club and beamed at them from the door, like a salesman. He glided across the floor in the way that so many men at The Plant found suspect.

Are you recruiting Tim to come with us? he asked. You're certainly welcome.

I'm just having a drink, said Tim.

I was asking him if he'd like to see me naked, said Joanna.

Who wouldn't? Bill said. You're beautiful.

What did you do about the paint shop? Tim asked.

They're going to have to come in, Bill said. There's no other solution.

To hell with the paint shop, said Joanna. I want to pose for Tim.

He downed the rest of his drink and stepped away from the bar. He looked for Marc Cloutier, who had disappeared.

Why are men afraid of me? asked Joanna.

Listen, Bill said. Did you know Henry Godin? In Bresby. He was in maintenance.

I know who he is, said Tim.

He was arrested for murder. I only just heard.

Henry Godin, Joanna said. He was the biker? That's a man I would have painted.

Did he kill somebody at The Plant?

I have no idea, Bill said. I just got the news.

Tim looked for words. He wasn't going to tell them that Henry Godin ran the boxing club and had trained Moth. Trained him. He knew what Kate meant, finally, and why she was afraid. If Godin had murdered someone, then Moth could do it too. There was no logical bridge there, but he knew it was true. Moth had pointed a loaded gun at a boy right here, in front of the bar. Murder had hung in the air between heartbeats.

You're thinking about it, aren't you? Joanna said. Me without my clothes.

Bill smiled at them both.

Tim gave them a meaningless nod, then turned and walked out of the club. He saw that Bill Webb had parked beside him and he fought the urge to drag the paint off their car as he backed up. He was sure the man was a homosexual. You would never let your wife talk that way to anyone else. Maybe he liked to watch.

He went cold at the thought of Kate lying down with Joanna and Bill leering politely from one end of the bed.

He changed his mind about going home once he'd turned onto his street. The blind inequity of his life made him want to drive with his eyes shut and the pedal to the floor. Kate posing naked closed the distance between them and their neighbours. It was as good as saying there was no difference between the Watsons and anyone else in Valentine. It was worse than that; she had chosen the couple who were the strangest and most disliked. Rumours and gossip would cover the family like moss. As though Moth hadn't done enough to promote that on his own.

Tim didn't want to know about Beryl. Kate and Moth were enough. The news at home was never good and he had no heart for any more of it. He turned into the first driveway, backed up, and almost drove right into his children as they walked home. He saw the late bus behind them, heading for the main road.

Moth stepped over to the window as Tim rolled it down. Beryl didn't move toward him.

You're going to work?

I just came from work, Tim said. I went up to the club and talked to Mr Cloutier.

Moth nodded impassively. Father and son looked at one another without a thing to say.

Tell your mother I had to go back to The Plant, he said.

Moth stepped back from the car. Tim started rolling up his window, then stopped and leaned forward.

You know what Cloutier said? he asked. He said he was going to beat you up, but he changed his mind.

I'm shaking, said Moth.

Tim smiled at his son and drove away. Moth watched him leave, wondering what the hell that was all about. Beryl resumed her slow, steady walk toward the house.

The car stopped with a jerk and backed up ten yards until it was beside them again. Beryl felt like running, for unaccountable reasons. Moth wondered if his father was going to fight him.

You might want to know this, Tim said. Henry Godin was arrested for murder.

He drove off. Moth stood speechless, watching him disappear.

Kate heard them open the front door and she ran down the hall with the diary. Trevor trotted along behind her and watched his mother stuff the notebook between the mattress and box spring. They both heard Moth's light tread on the stairs. Beryl sounded like she walked on her heels but he crept like a burglar. Kate tickled Trevor just as Moth entered the bedroom.

We were just playing, she said.

It's okay, said Moth. Dad had to go back to The Plant.

Kate straightened up and Trevor ran past Moth and down the stairs, looking for Beryl.

How do you know?

We saw him on the way home, Moth said.

He drove here and went back and he didn't even come inside? asked Kate.

He said he went to the club.

Kate walked past Moth, tight-lipped. She went into her bedroom and closed the door. What a god damned hypocrite. At the club, seeing her friends. She lay on the bed, got up, lay down again. He had gone to the club and then gone back to work and he hadn't even stopped at the house. The nights had become unendurably long since she'd stopped going to Joanna's and now he was going out on his own. He'd come home every night and fall asleep sitting up and she wanted to shout in his ear when he did. It was worse having him home than not seeing him at all.

There was nothing to do in Valentine and she hated it. Television disgusted her. She could walk out the door in Bresby and she'd be somewhere. You were nowhere, here.

She heard Beryl go into the bathroom and start the shower.

Everything Moth had written about this place was true. Robbing the club suddenly made perfect sense to her. She wanted to return to his room and sit down and tell him all about women and girls. The conversation that Tim had delayed and would never have. Moth played naked in the field with Donna Mesrine and the picture was permanently fixed in her mind. It would never change or vanish. Kate had spent most of the afternoon reading about it, catching up with what she'd missed since Joanna.

Donna took him in her mouth. She knelt for it and the image made Kate livid. It was so unbelievably sluttish for a young girl and it was giving Moth the wrong idea. Nothing he thought was right. He thought that when a girl was wet she was having an orgasm. He seemed to think there was a tunnel that ran at a right angle to the rest of the body and he couldn't understand why he couldn't push himself straight in. Kate could see her son, muscular and naked and straining on top of this girl. She thought about teaching him and the thought snapped her awake. She'd been drifting while she lay on the bed. You weren't responsible for what you thought, then.

Moth was already downstairs, hanging up the phone, when she walked into the kitchen. Trevor stood at the window with his face against the glass, looking for his father.

Were you talking to Donna?

Moth looked at her in surprise.

No, he said. I called Bresby. I'll get the money for the phone bill.

She moved Trevor away from the window, which was already covered in his handprints.

Daddy's going to be late, she said.

Trevor smiled at his mother and put his face back against the glass. Kate sat down at the table and watched him.

I called Terry, Moth said. Henry Godin killed a guy. Did you know that?

No, Kate said. Henry Godin?

She nearly asked if he was the same Henry as the one in the diary. She looked at Moth attentively instead.

He ran the boxing club, he said. Terry's father said he killed a guy who was trying to steal his bike.

Your father hates long distance calls.

My father hates everything, Moth said.

He left the kitchen and she heard him make his quiet way up to his room. The shower had stopped running. She wished he would go out so she could finish reading. It was barely dark and Tim was at work and the night was too long. Beryl would have nothing to say and Moth wouldn't leave his room again. Trevor would go to bed soon.

She wondered what was on TV.

Her husband was parked in the lot outside the shopping plaza and he debated whether or not to return to The Plant. There was nothing else he could imagine doing. He was hungry and he could take Kate to dinner or they could go to the club.

She had taken off all her clothes at Joanna's and Bill had seen the picture and Tim stopped thinking about dinner.

He kept forgetting about the painting until he thought about going home. He didn't want to tell her he knew, but he wanted her to know. More than anything, he didn't want to fight. No one was ever going to tell him the truth about the nights she went to Joanna's. Even if the truth was only what he'd been told, it was bad enough. More than bad enough. He was hungry. He could go home and eat and tell Kate he'd gone back because of the paint shop. She would want to know why he hadn't phoned.

He called her from the tavern across the street.

Your dinner's in the oven getting dried out, said Kate.

I had to go back to The Plant, he said. I just stopped for a beer with one of the engineers.

It didn't sound like he was at the club, but wherever he was it was lively. He never went anywhere with anyone and it sounded like an effort to spite her. Like going to the country club on his own. The house was so silent it made her nervous and there wasn't as much as a single bottle of wine tucked away.

I'm not a child, she said. You can't make me stay home.

I don't want to fight, Kate.

I didn't do anything wrong.

Yes, he said. Yes, you did.

They listened to each other breathe for a count of six.

I'm coming home, he said.

Kate carefully hung up the phone. She called Joanna's and let it ring twenty times, then hung up and redialled. She counted ten rings, then put down the phone. He knew about the picture. If she said nothing, he would say nothing. It would never be spoken of again even if they both lived another hundred years.

The house was so quiet she wished that Beryl would turn on the radio. She wanted to hear someone say something. Tim would come home and his silence would add an even deeper, ear-splitting hush. She could call Judy Arnold and listen to her slur out bits of gossip that wouldn't shock a village parson.

At least in Bresby they still killed people.

ii

Moth thought about prison every night. He had no idea if it would be full of guys his own age or old, fearless veterans refusing to let him have a bunk. He wondered if he was ready to fight to the death over small insults or if he would cower and quake. It was the French teacher dilemma writ large. Some nights he imagined attacking huge men who feared nothing and other times he saw himself bent over in the showers. He wiped off his stomach with one of his socks and felt his face burn in the dark.

He would be in the company of men, maybe for years, and he had never penetrated a woman. Moth didn't know if he could stand it. He would probably be the only inmate who had never felt a girl surround him, joining them together. Wherefore they are no more twain, but one flesh. Even God wanted it to happen. God wanted you to get married first, but He wanted it to happen. God wanted too much.

Moth had stopped praying and reading the Bible every night. Everything had started happening at once and there was too much to figure out without the impossible language and insane restrictions of that haunted book. Job lost everything because God made a bet. Moth had committed abominations with other men and he couldn't honour his parents. He stole,

148

he coveted, he wasn't interested in turning the other cheek.

They said God wasn't an old man with a beard, but how else could you see Him? Moth had begun imagining God as the group of scientists in *Our Man Flynt* instead. They sat at a table somewhere far away and watched his progress with great interest. He was a free spirit. God liked free spirits.

Moth had apologized to Donna because the school was too small for him to avoid her and there was no one else waiting to take her place. She was cautious about everything now, and wouldn't go to the field at lunch hour. She never got babysitting jobs and he was starting to think his apology had been a waste of time. More than that, he was sick with her again. The last time he'd walked her to the bus he thought she was a faster walker than he was, but he managed to keep quiet about it. For the rest of the day he tried to think of why he walked so slowly. Sometimes he hated the idea of making love with her. It would become an experience of hers, not his. That was just the way it worked.

He was going to prison for something that was almost a joke at the same time as Terry was involved in a murder. Moth had robbed the country club and it was less a real robbery than a b & e with a gun. The rest of his legend was a figment of his imagination. Valentine was unreal. Moth felt like a kid creating monsters at bedtime out of piles of laundry. There were no dangers, no enemies, no grudge fights. Terry was taken downtown and interrogated because someone had been killed and Moth talked to detectives in his kitchen while his father listened. Montreal had gunfights and gang wars, corrupt cops shooting innocent people. He wasn't ready for Montreal. Or prison.

You had to live in your imagination in Valentine because there was no life outside your mind. It was the only country you had. He could see why anyone would become insane, watching the world from home. You could be saving kids from a fire, foiling a bank robbery or disarming a mugger, just sitting there thinking about it. If none of these things ever happened, you would start to believe in your imaginary self. You would become a madman.

Moth got off the bed and pulled out his journal. This was it, the whole problem. He had come here and lost his mind. He didn't know why he'd taken a gun to the country club or why he'd even wanted to break in. He knew nothing. All he did these days was watch himself do things and maybe it was all he'd ever done. Maybe he'd become a living newspaper, a record of his own actions, an observer. He had to divine his motives after the fact and it was impossible.

Donna was killing him and he did nothing. Moth began writing it down. He could see the scientists at their table, nodding in approval.

Downstairs, the front door opened and shut. Beryl was home. Moth wrote.

Beryl felt the strain immediately. Her mother was looking at the television as though she was having an argument with it.

Where the hell have you been?

I'm not late, Beryl said.

Kate gave her a long look of warning from where she sat, but it only made Beryl angry. She'd made her decision after Terry's phone call and everything was about to shift. In a few hours the channel would be changed for good and all her mother had to do was stay out of the way.

I stayed late at school and played badminton, Beryl said. I had to walk home because I missed the bus and I stopped at the store and talked to some kids I know.

Her mother had the branch of a willow tree on the floor at her feet. Beryl didn't see it until she stepped farther into the room and a weak, empty feeling took everything else out of her mind. Kate smiled when she saw Beryl's mouth go slack. She reached for the stick and spent no more than a second looking for it. When she looked back Beryl was standing right in front of her, crazy with rage. Kate felt her own mouth begin to quiver.

If you hit me with that stick I'll kill you, Beryl said.

Your father, her mother said.

I'll tell him. I'll tell him about the stick and I'll tell him what you're like.

Who the hell do you think you are? Kate shouted. You haven't even been going to school. They called me. You're a god damned liar.

Moth opened his door and came down the stairs.

Get away from her, Beryl, he said.

She stepped back, watching her mother. Kate stood up, her face blotchy with wrath and the stick shaking in her hand. She could smell the liquor on Beryl's breath. Moth was suddenly between them and had taken the willow branch away and Kate wondered fleetingly if this was another bad dream.

Jesus Christ, Moth said. You think I'll let you do that again?

I don't need you to help me, Moth, said Beryl.

I'll do whatever the hell I want, Kate shouted.

No.

Try it, said Beryl.

Moth bent the stick in half but it didn't break. He opened the front door and threw it out onto the lawn.

You're brave now, Kate said.

Listen, Moth said. Tell Dad. I'll tell him myself.

Dad doesn't even know about it.

Go ahead and tell him, Moth said. What do you think he'll do?

Kate sat down because in another minute they would see that her legs were trembling. The injustice left her speechless. She was their mother and they didn't understand that. Tim had always said a good beating would do them both a world of good and now it was too late.

You use a stick on her and I'll use it on you, Moth said.

Kate felt herself turn red when he said it. They would think it was because she was angry, thank God. She shouldn't feel the way she did from Moth's words and even she knew it. Moth was insane, a murderer, and Beryl was no better.

She wondered if he would really use a stick on her. Would he make her undress?

Go to your rooms, she said.

You'd better call Dad, Moth said. Tell him to come home.

Tim would be home soon enough and he had finally settled down about Joanna. Kate wasn't going to give him more reasons to sulk. She had planned on beating Beryl before he arrived and now that had been taken away from her. He would find out about Beryl tomorrow in the early afternoon and he'd expect her to have solved everything by then. Every fresh problem was like a wound to Tim, an arrow she had deliberately fired into his heart.

Go to your room, she said. I'll tell your father all about this in the morning.

Don't try anything tonight, Moth said. I'm not kidding.

You're threatening me, Kate said, very calmly. It had better stop or I'll call the police before I talk to your father.

Moth was short of breath. He knew she could call the cops and destroy his pre-sentence report and he knew it wasn't beyond her. He turned away and went back up the stairs to his room.

Call the cops on me, Beryl said. Maybe they'll make me live with foster parents. I'd rather live with anyone but you.

I'll talk to your father about it, Kate said. Both of us are sorry we have you. We're sorry you were born.

It was as though she'd uttered magic words. Beryl's face contorted and she covered it with both hands and began crying. It was as deep and terrible as the night she'd been beaten and once Kate realized that, she felt happier. Justice was served. She heard Moth's door fly open.

I didn't do anything, she said.

Beryl turned from her and ran up the stairs, crying without restraint. Moth watched her, confused. He looked down at his mother.

You must have upset her, Kate said. You're so violent.

Beryl's door slammed shut. Moth took two steps down the hall toward it, then backed away. He returned to his room without looking at his mother again.

Kate went into the kitchen and picked up the phone. She bit her lip when Joanna answered and almost cried telling her how awful it had been and how much she missed her. Joanna told her to come right over.

Kate left the house without waiting another minute.

iii

Beryl slammed the back door and woke up her father. She ran across the lawn, carrying an old gym bag Moth kept in the basement, and quickly navigated the lot behind the house. The car was idling near the streetlight and Marcel leaned over and opened the passenger door. Beryl climbed in and threw the bag into the back seat, then gave him a kiss. He gave her a kiss. The car smelled of ashtrays and air freshener. Marcel drove to the end of the street, turned around in the last driveway and headed for the road out of Valentine.

Tim Watson got out of bed and dressed in the dark. Kate hadn't been in the house when he arrived and he was sure she wasn't home now. He left the bedroom and went downstairs as quietly as Moth. The living room light was on, as he'd left it, but Kate wasn't sitting in front of the television and she wasn't in the kitchen. He turned on the basement light and went halfway down the stairs without any possible justification. He knew where she was.

152

He took his coat from the hall closet and put on his shoes, then stopped in the middle of lacing them up. It was going to be a drunken, overwrought mess, full of tears and cursing. Bill worked for him. He went into the kitchen and checked the multicoloured numbers copied on a sheet of paper taped above the phone. He picked up the receiver and dialled and Joanna answered.

Is she there?

Hello to you, too, stranger, said Joanna. Come over and have a drink.

Is Bill still up?

You want to talk to him?

I'd like to speak to Kate, Tim said. He focused on the tape that held up the list of phone numbers. It had turned a dark yellow and thickened, like an old man's toenail.

Tim, Kate said.

Come home, Kate.

You can't treat me like a child, she said. I need friends.

We'll talk about it.

You won't. You won't even speak to me.

Can everyone hear you? Tim asked.

I need friends and I need a glass of wine and I need to go to the club.

And you need to take off your clothes for Joanna, he said.

He heard someone else pick up an extension.

Please get off the phone, Tim said. This is a private conversation.

He stood still, waiting for her to speak, wondering where she kept the scotch tape. It wasn't until he heard the dial tone that he realized no one had picked up another phone in the house. She'd hung up.

What? he said.

He felt ridiculous, an actor in a movie talking out loud. The Webbs were laughing at him and Kate was imitating his voice. He could see it. Calling back would make them roll on the floor and hold their sides. She had hung up in his ear. It was worse than posing naked, worse than Moth robbing the country club. He replaced the receiver and waited for her to call back and apologize.

When had he ever seen an old man's toenails? At the community centre pool, it must have been. Beryl had taped up the paper when they first moved in and it was supposed to be temporary. There was never a pen or pencil close at hand.

The phone didn't ring.

The car belonged to a friend of Marcel's and it was unclear to Beryl whether or not the friend knew he was using it. Her only concern was the cops, but the highway into Montreal made her feel anonymous and invisible. It wasn't an empty stretch of road, like the main drag in Bresby. People were out on the streets in every small town they passed through, even towns as small as her own. She felt like she'd discovered a dark secret, the truth of what happened in the rest of the world when it got dark in Valentine.

She was excited, but it was a tight, closed ball in her stomach. Marcel seemed happy and relaxed, which she hadn't expected. She hadn't been sure he'd even show up.

I love driving, he said. I love driving at night.

Beryl had a scared moment, wondering if she had fallen in love with him. Maybe it was just tonight. Marcel looked handsome and dangerous and completely at home. Terry always looked like he was on his way to a fight unless they were lying down together. Not tough or violent, just the grim look of a guy who knew what was coming. That wasn't the point. She was meant to be with Terry, no matter how Marcel looked right now. Marcel was better-looking, but Terry was Terry.

She rolled down her window and tried to swallow fresh air and clear her head. It was like trying to sober up with a cup of coffee. Maybe she loved Marcel. Maybe Terry was already in love with somebody else and couldn't say it over the phone. Even if he loved her, what she was doing was stupid. She wanted to get out of Valentine, but where would she hide in Bresby? What was she thinking of when she planned this? It wasn't a plan, it was a picture. She was sitting in Terry's car with her head on his shoulder as they drove down the highway. It went no further than that. She had believed the map of their future was written in the stars and would unfold when she presented herself at the appointed place. Now it made her feel like she was made of water. Her insides were loose and liquid and her face was hot and burning. She was embarrassed and afraid and she could say none of it to Marcel. She wished she was drunk.

They pulled into the bus station and Beryl said nothing.

Tim rapped on the door instead of banging it with his fist. From inside, his knocking sounded timid and apologetic. Kate smiled over her drink at Bill, who raised his glass and smiled back. Joanna was beaming with expectation. She walked gracefully to the door and opened it.

Bill and Kate watched her from behind, seeing her lean forward and then slump. Tim wasn't visible. Bill put down his drink and was getting to his feet when Joanna backed into the room and turned around. Behind her, a car door slammed. The door stayed open and there was nothing to be seen but the night.

He just handed him to me, Joanna said.

Trevor was asleep in her arms. Kate stood up, not sure of what she was seeing. Trevor, here. She looked at Bill, who stared at the child as though at a sea serpent. Joanna hurried across the room and handed him over to Kate.

I can't hold him, Kate, she said.

That fucking bastard, Kate said.

She took Trevor from Joanna and wanted to give her face a good smack as she did.

Jesus, said Kate, it isn't a bomb. He won't explode.

You have to go home, Kate, Bill said.

I know.

Clever Tim. She wanted to go home and stab out his eyes. Vomit on his clothes. She wished she could make Bill have sex with her, right this minute. He and Joanna stared at her like people watching an operation. Maybe she should take off her clothes and walk home naked. They'd be back in Bresby before the first snowfall.

Clever Tim. Trevor opened his eyes and saw his mother, then turned his face against her breasts. Kate kissed him lightly.

She walked through the open door and went home.

A skinny guy with hair to his shoulders got on the bus at Kingston and sat next to Beryl. Two men sitting together near the back laughed at the sight of him, and a woman in front of Beryl woke up her husband.

Look at this, she said. Look.

The driver shook his head, playing to the audience.

Beryl thought he looked like Jesus Christ. She wanted to feel his hair.

Is it real? she asked him.

He frowned at her, then smiled when he took a closer look.

Oh, yeah, he said. Are you a runaway?

Beryl hadn't expected the question to be posed so bluntly this early in her adventure. She had answers for every variation of it, but she gave none of them.

Yeah, she said. I'm going to Bresby.

He looked surprised, then nodded.

All roads lead to Rome, the guy said, but there's some heavy detours along the way. You take years finding your way home. I was in my first year and what happened was, I was open to the vibe. Like, there's a school vibe, a family vibe, vibes like, I don't know. Like a tambourine. It's close to your ear and you can hear it fine, but you can't hear the drums, the bass, the guitar. You're not digging the *song*, right? That's the vibe you have to hear. The song. So I can hear the song, I hear singing and I said fuck it. Most of the time, most things come down to saying fuck it. You do that, you have to do that, you say fuck it and you don't end up in some place like Bresby. You don't need the karma, baby.

Beryl understood nothing he said. He talked like he was famous. She loved his hair and the sound of his voice. She loved the way he said *fuck it*. What she intended to say was that her boyfriend was in Bresby. She was going there to be with her boyfriend. She just couldn't bring herself to say it.

Is it a family thing? That was my trip. Kingston, the guy said. I had to cool out my mother. My father is about five lifetimes away from even being on this fucking planet. Don't let your family hang you up. You're a runaway, right? You're not going to Bresby for your family.

He giggled like he was five years younger.

I had to eat a gram of hash at the station, he said. It's hard staying linear.

iv

Moth felt like he was peering out of a porthole on a foggy night. He was watching his bedroom through one eye, the side of his face mashed into his pillow, half awake and still stuck in a nightmare. All his life he'd had a recurring dream of waiting to be hanged. Tonight he was in a cell, looking out a high window at the sky and imagining never seeing it again. The thought of being trapped in a dreamless sleep without end was terrifying. The police entered the cell, which became an interrogation room resembling his bedroom. They asked him for a confession and he saw it in flashbacks, like a movie. He had never confessed in a dream before. He was always about to be hanged but he never knew why and it never occurred to him to ask.

He saw a woman, as white as cream, almost glowing in the dark. She wore no clothes and stood with her back to him. He groaned as she bent over Trevor's bed and she turned and looked over her shoulder at him. He had killed his mother. She was naked in his bedroom and he wanted to tell the police he didn't know why she was there. She turned around and he reached out his hand. It made him break the surface of the dream and he saw his hand stretched in front of him, felt himself put it there. He was awake.

His mother was there, wearing no clothes, smiling at him.

I was putting Trevor back to bed, she said in a whisper.

She stepped over to the side of his bed. His arm stuck out and her hip rubbed against it as she leaned over. He was paralyzed by the light thatch of pubic hair near his face. He wanted to cry.

His mother pulled his bedsheets up around his chin.

Your father, she said. He isn't as smart as I am.

She turned away from Moth and walked to the bedroom door. He didn't close his eyes, but watched her without knowing how he felt. His mother left the room and closed his door lightly behind her.

Moth was wide awake. He looked over at Trevor, who was sleeping with his mouth partly open. He tried to think of something else besides his naked mother. Dempsey being knocked through the ropes by Firpo. He couldn't sustain it. His hands were trembling and he grabbed the blanket tighter near his neck. He was afraid of touching his own body anywhere. His mother.

Moth was scared but didn't know it. He knew he should be angry and in daylight he would become furious. Much later he'd be excited. Here and now he felt like hiding under the bed. He was afraid to cry.

He picked his pants up off the floor and pulled them on while he was still in bed. His eyes never left the door. If she came back again, he would turn on the light. He'd yell for his father. He'd pretend she had woken him up and scared him and it made him yell. Moth sat up and leaned back against the wall. He wanted to go down the hall and wake up Beryl, but it would mean passing his parents' room. As soon as he saw daylight, he'd wake her up. He knew he wouldn't be able to sleep for the rest of the night.

Moth nodded out sitting up. He slept heavily and fell back into a dream of waiting to be hanged.

Chapter Eight

Buster wouldn't wear dark glasses. He wore a blindfold covering his face from his eyebrows to the bridge of his nose and knotted at the back of his head. Terry thought he should have worn something black or even a different colour for every day, not a scrap that looked like a dishcloth. It was stiff and spotted and it was never replaced. It looked like Buster was playing a game of Blind Man's Bluff with little kids and had grabbed the first available rag.

Buster wasn't playing. He had come out of the rumble with Soldier unable to see, the details closed to discussion. Now he stood behind the counter wearing a dirty band around his face and he made a horrifying exhibition. Randy Zed said it made guys scared to fight.

Buster wore two straight razors, one in each pocket of his vest, and he hooked his thumbs beside them at any sound of approach. He spoke even less than he had before and the pool hall had a hushed, suspenseful feel, as though Soldier was about to burst through the back doors at any moment.

The old, fat guys no longer came to read their newspapers. There was one small man about Buster's age no one had seen before and he sat on a bench and watched customers shoot pool. There was no question in anyone's mind that he carried a gun, and debates centred on how many of them were hidden under his coat. His hands were very large for a man his size, and they were always open and unoccupied. He didn't read and he never spoke.

Terry and Randy Zed shot pool. Terry wasn't drunk, but he'd had enough to keep his hands steady when he took a shot. Randy never seemed drunk, no matter what he drank or how long he drank it. He beat Terry three games straight and they paid up and walked out. It was cold and smelled of snow, but there had been no snowfall. Neither of them said another word to each other once they were outside and they separated at the mouth of the alley. The air was making Terry feel the booze. He got into his car and tried to start it, tried to start it, tried to start it. He waited and looked out through his windshield and his mind felt as colourless and static as the view. He started the car and turned up the heater and then leaned over onto the seat and fell asleep.

The detectives who'd questioned him at the station had shown up at his door that morning. It was so cold outside that Terry had let them come in and they had spotted Beryl immediately.

She's underage.

No, Terry had said. She isn't. She's my cousin.

Beryl wore one of Terry's shirts, a white striped one that almost reached her knees. Her legs were bare and she had hockey socks on her feet.

Jesus Christ, the cop said. Have some fucking sense.

Look. It's a long story.

You ought to start thinking, Terry.

She's my cousin, Terry said.

The cops stared at her and she looked back with an expression devoid of defiance. She looked curious and interested in them.

Aren't you wondering about your old man? the cop asked Terry.

The rug made a thick, wet sound under his feet, as though he was squashing dead June bugs. The air in the living room was getting as sharp as smelling salts.

Look at this, the other cop said. It looks exactly the same in here. Can't you smell it?

My father should clean it up, Terry said. He won't.

Your father. He hasn't been home.

No.

You're not too worried about it?

No.

Beryl stepped back into the bedroom, closed the door and pulled on her pants. She very slowly lifted up the window. It was too cold outside. She needed her coat or at least a sweater. She decided not to escape and she closed the window and locked it. There was a brief rapping on the door and then one of the big cops opened it and looked in on her.

You must be a detective, she said.

How do you know?

You just look like one.

He laughed and stepped into the room, closing the door. This room hadn't changed much either, except for a small bundle of Beryl's clothes on top of a gym bag. There was a transistor radio on the floor beside the bed and it took the cop a second to realize it was playing.

The batteries are almost dead, Beryl said. I hate that.

My partner has to talk to Terry, he said. What's your name?

Cheryl. I'm his cousin.

No, said the cop, You're not. I don't care if you lie, but you're really going to get Terry into some deep shit. Where do you live?

My parents live in Quebec.

Go home, the cop said.

Anywhere Terry is, that's my home. You can send me back, but I'm just going to come here again.

The detective sat down on the edge of the bed and scouted the room for an ashtray, but nothing would serve. Sonny and Cher sang in a tinny whine near his feet.

Can I see your gun?

No, he said. Does his father know you're here?

He's been on nights, Beryl said. I just sleep here.

Who pays for gas, food, everything else?

His dad leaves out money for him.

The detective liked the way Sonny and Cher sang, but he was torn over their marriage. While he liked the idea that a young, beautiful woman would marry a funny-looking older guy, he resented Sonny being able to have her at all. Sometimes he felt slow and old and despaired over ever meeting a woman any better looking than himself and other times he'd see his belly in the morning and know he still looked better than Sonny. It made life more active with possibilities.

You're not my department, the cop said, but I'm making a call. You understand? I want you out of here by the end of the week. I want you out of Bresby and on your way back home. Call your folks.

Beryl looked at her feet and said nothing. These cops were as big as the ones who had come for Moth. Maybe the guys in uniform couldn't get promoted because they weren't big enough. Why did they say that women loved men in uniforms? It wasn't true. A guy in uniform isn't the boss, not even the boss of his own life. It was an old saying, probably from the war. It was most likely a commercial, trying to make guys join the army. An ad. They didn't have commercials then because they didn't have TV.

Do you watch *Gunsmoke?* asked Beryl.

Yeah, the cop said. It isn't my favourite show, but I watch it.

You look a little bit like Marshal Dillon.

He took out his cigarettes and hunted through his pockets for matches. The house was dirty enough to be a giant ashtray, anyway. There was something about the way the kid talked that made him want to laugh.

Men like you, I'll bet, he said.

It surprised her, but he was so friendly she smiled back at him.

Yes, Beryl said. I like them, too.

Do you like Sonny and Cher?

No, Beryl said.

The detective lit his cigarette.

In the living room, the other cop told Terry that his father had been arrested at The Plant during the Friday night shift. He had broken another worker's jaw and nose with a wrench. Terry was impressed.

What was the fight about?

It wasn't a fight, the cop said. Your old man walked up to him in the cafeteria and let him have it.

What does he say about it?

I don't know, it isn't mine. I just recognized the name, the cop said. I know you.

Yeah, well, thanks.

Roy Godin hasn't been around, has he? Any of the bikers?

Terry went from a high idle to ninety-five, no hands on the wheel. His eyes felt dry and scratchy in their sockets as he stared at the cop.

I forget your name.

Bishop, the cop said. Detective Bishop.

I don't know anything, Terry said. I gave Soldier a ride. Why is anyone going to bother me?

Bishop looked at the rubble near his feet, at the dresser lying inside the father's room, at the stuffing coming out of the cushions on the couch. He had come to tell Terry that his father was in jail, which wasn't necessary, especially since he'd probably be released today. Now there was no reason not to leave. He felt like he was waiting for Terry to give him information and he needed none. He didn't care if Barnes had been killed by Godin or felled by a rock falling from a plane, as long as Henry Godin went to prison. The girl had seen Barnes near the bikes and saw Henry Godin reach him before anyone else. Clarence Barnes was dead, Henry Godin was in jail. Roy Godin and all the bikers on earth couldn't change that. Bishop didn't have to be in this tiny house where there was nowhere to sit and not enough air to breathe.

You know why I'm here, he told Terry.

It was an old gag, as old as telling a guy that his partner had just come clean. Bishop had no reason to say it, but said it anyway. He felt like saying he was there because Terry reminded him of himself when he was younger – a television answer. Terry didn't remind him of himself at any age. Usually you said it when a young guy did something crazier than you could ever have imagined doing. Terry had killed Clarence Barnes and they were both pretending he hadn't. That was crazy enough.

Yeah, Terry said, I know why you're here.

Say it, Terry.

You think I killed Soldier.

I didn't, Bishop said, but I do now. I knew it and I didn't even know I knew it.

I'm not saying I did it, Terry said.

No, you're not.

They looked at one another from across the room and for the first time the detective realized that being scared made no difference to Terry. He could be frightened and he could be hurt, but he couldn't be reached. You didn't have to break down a tough front and then gut him like a perch. There was no front. He was right there in front of you and nothing was ever going to make him confess. He just acted like himself, which is what separated him from the South End gang and what made you think he was telling the truth. He acted like Henry Godin. It made Bishop uncertain and furious. He didn't want to see Henry Godin on the streets, but he didn't want this kid thinking he was tougher than the police. Tougher than Jeffrey Bishop.

You're going to tell me, Bishop said.

Maybe, Terry said, if you help me.

You're lucky I don't just take you downtown and handcuff you to a chair. How long do you think it'd take me to make you talk?

I don't know, Terry said. I want you to find out what happened to my mother.

The cop could hear both of them breathing loud, shallow breaths. He wished Terry had asked for something else, anything else, because he could have grabbed him, cuffed him, backhanded that expression off his face. The kid wanted to know what had happened to his mother.

Okay, he said. I'll find out.

Beryl and Bishop's partner came out of the bedroom together, smiling like secret lovers.

You've got a nice girlfriend, the cop said. Too bad she's so young.

Terry's face went blank and Bishop wondered if he'd actually start swinging. Maybe the kid was crazy.

We're finished here, Tony, Bishop said.

Terry and Beryl hadn't walked them to the door. She had pushed herself against him as soon as the cops left and he had ripped open the shirt she wore and bit her on the mouth. They had dragged each other back into the bedroom and he had heaved her onto the bed. The room smelled of the cop's cigarette. Terry pulled off her pants and had her with his shirt pushed up and his jeans to his knees. He had her again twenty minutes later when they both wore nothing. The third time, Beryl knelt on the edge of the bed and Terry stood behind her, his bare feet on the cold floor. After that, they had slept.

Terry woke up in the front seat of his car and felt for Beryl before he opened his eyes. His head ached and he saw Randy, saw Buster in a blindfold, remembered the pool game. The seat under his head shook and his throat was so dry it felt like it was made of paper.

Terry climbed out of the car and pissed endlessly, leaning against the door and gulping down cold air. A minute of breathing took away most of the pain behind his eyes but didn't make him any less thirsty. He wanted a pitcher of lemon kool-aid, a pitcher like the one in the commercials with the face drawn on it. He shook at the thought of anything so cold, but he was thirsty enough to drink from a puddle. He got in the car and drove down the alley and up the street to the Pinklon.

He had to call Darlene and he didn't know what he'd say. He hadn't seen her since Beryl had arrived tapping on his bedroom window. His father had been on nights, which meant that Beryl shared his bed that night and every other, climbing out the window in the morning. It made her feel like they were married and it made him feel like an outlaw. Terry had a kitchen chair

164

jammed under the doorknob, but his father had stopped prowling since the house was smashed up. It was the only thing that had changed. Neither of them discussed that night and neither of them would clean up the mess. Terry still crawled under his bed and he realized it no longer had anything to do with his father. He couldn't stand the idea of being unconscious and exposed, vulnerable to attack from any quarter. When Beryl was in bed with him, he had her to protect. He didn't feel like the target.

He had to call Darlene. He had to pick up Beryl, find out how long his father would be in jail, get some money. It was too late for everything and he had to run just to reach the starting line. Terry wanted to go to the Pinklon and drink until it was over. He pulled into the parking lot behind the hotel and sat in the car without moving. He didn't want to drink until it was over, that was just a thought, a first thought his mind broadcast in case God was listening. He knew by now that thinking wasn't pointless, it was just the thinking that sat on top that had to be ignored. The thoughts that sat on top like foam on a glass of draft.

There was a building in the old movies that broadcast news in letters that appeared like magic on a strip that ran around the top of its wall. Words moved all the way around it, right around the corners, and men in fedoras pointed at them in excitement. That's how he imagined his first thoughts. They were broadcast to everybody and immediately understood because everyone had heard them before. Drink until it's over. I want to hide in a bottle, he would say. He needed a cop or a priest who'd step in and tell him it was a crutch and the coward's way out. He had the thoughts, that was true. But the thoughts were lies and maybe you just broadcast them to yourself.

What did Soldier's thoughts look like?

He got out of his car and thought about calling Darlene, knew he had to call Beryl, wondered who to call first and what to say. He wondered why the hell he was here if he didn't want to drink until it was over.

Beryl wondered if Terry was going to phone or if he'd just show up. She'd have to leave within the next half hour and it was making her nervous. She'd spent the day with Susan, as usual, but there seemed to be no reason for it now they knew that Terry's father wasn't coming home. Susan seldom attended school and both her parents worked. Her parents were Beryl's proof that she overreacted to her own.

She told Beryl that her friends used to come by, but they smoked so much she couldn't get rid of the smell before her mother and father came home. Some of the boys stole liquor. Susan was being punished every day for the crimes of her friends and now she didn't let them into the house. Beryl wondered whether she had any friends and what her punishment would be when her parents saw her attendance record.

Susan's bedroom had pictures of John, Paul, George, and Ringo scotch-taped to the walls, singly and as a group. Most of the pictures had been cut out of magazines and there was one colour poster that stood alone above the head of her bed. It was a concert photograph showing everyone except George in high spirits.

George makes me feel funny, Susan said. I had a dream he punished me for fucking Paul. He was just like my dad.

Beryl could see no resemblance between George and Susan's father except that George hardly smiled either. When he did, he looked like he was imitating somebody smiling.

My parents like them, Beryl said. Maybe that's why I don't.

You don't like cute guys, said Susan.

Terry's cute.

No. He's good-looking, I guess, but he isn't really cute. Paul is cute.

Beryl didn't say anything and she didn't smack Susan's mouth. She hated not being able to hit her or scream in her face. It was a bad idea, spending all day with somebody, especially when they got to make all the rules. She needed a better plan.

George made me take my clothes off and bend over, Susan said. My father makes me bend over a chair, but I had to touch my toes for George.

He still does that? Beryl said. Your dad?

It's only about four smacks. I don't care.

Beryl couldn't imagine standing naked in front of her father any more than she could imagine him demanding it. Her mother, yes, but she'd rather be beaten to death than co-operate in humiliation by her mother. It had always made her feel funny when she saw Susan's dad and imagined it. She didn't want to get hit with a belt and she decided that undressing was punishment enough. She would misbehave at Susan's and make the father angry and he would make her take off her clothes for a lecture. She had thought about it today, talking to that big cop.

Herman's Hermits, Susan said. That guy is cute, too. Really cute.

166

I don't care what they look like, Beryl said. It's the way they sound.

That's ridiculous.

The cop liked Sonny and Cher. He had looked a little disappointed when she said she didn't like them. She wished she'd lied when he asked. It would have been a friendly thing to say and he wasn't a bad cop. Sonny wasn't cute, unless you were an old woman. Her mother thought that chubby, silly men were cute. It was the only time she ever used the word.

Beryl heard a car pull up and looked out the bedroom window. It was a station wagon and a bald man rummaged through the glove compartment before getting out of the car. He didn't look up and his head shone yellow under the inside light.

It isn't Terry, Beryl said.

This is making me nervous. I'm not allowed to just have people over.

Beryl picked her coat up off the bed. She was afraid that something terrible had happened to Terry and she didn't want to get angry in case it was true. Maybe he'd done something stupid, trying to get them some money. He might be in jail with his father. That cop might have changed his mind and told on them and now Terry was in trouble and they were looking for her. The cop was mad about Sonny and Cher and he broke his promise to wait. Anything could have happened.

Susan shuffled between the front window and the back door while Beryl put on her boots.

I don't stay home every day, she said. I have to go to school sometime.

It's okay, Beryl said. We have a plan.

She stepped out into the backyard just as Terry called. Susan answered the phone while Beryl was walking around the side of the house and told Terry that she'd left. He was in a corner of the Pinklon and had just spent his last dime. Beryl would take the bus, walk to his place, use the key that was kept in a rubber boot near the front door. She'd be mad as hell. He'd just promised to see Darlene and couldn't see how he'd manage it. He didn't even know why he'd promised.

Terry picked up the phone and dialled numbers at random. The dial tone disappeared and he turned and faced the room while he held the receiver to his ear, trying to stave off a decision. Randy Zed sat with a woman in her late twenties who wore one of those fuzzy, fluffy sweaters and a pair of tight black pants. Not exactly pedal-pushers, but the same idea. She had stiff, wavy hair that barely covered her ears. She might even be in her thirties, he thought, now that he was giving her a good look. Randy wouldn't want his company.

He saw two or three guys he knew to greater and lesser degrees and then he saw his father. Jerry Delaney was sipping on a glass of draft and looking at him from the far side of the Pinklon and he didn't smile or nod or otherwise acknowledge recognition. Terry hung up the phone and took the long walk across the room.

Thanks for coming to see me, Jerry said.

How the hell did I know you were in jail? They just told me today.

Try answering the phone once in a while.

There was somebody I didn't want to talk to, Terry said. Look. It isn't my fault you were in jail. It's your fault, not mine.

I'll bet you called the hospital, too.

Are we supposed to be friends or something?

Jesus, Terry, said his father, I'm your father.

Buy me a beer.

He sat down and Jerry waved to a waiter. Terry thought he looked younger, as though he'd just returned from a vacation. It was either being locked up that agreed with him, or violence.

This guy, Walter. I've been seeing his wife.

Terry watched him and breathed lightly. He no longer even imagined his father with any woman other than his mother and the possibility had never been discussed between them. Now he knew. A married woman, probably some barfly, and a sleazy affair. His old man even knew the guy.

The waiter put another draft in front of Jerry and scooped change off the table.

One for yourself, Jerry said, and the waiter took another coin.

Walter, Terry said. This is the guy you hit with the wrench?

Yeah. I had it in the back of my belt. I walked right past him and he gives me a look, you know. A real look. I turned around and came back and he turned his head and looked at me. Right across his fucking nose, I let him have it. Then I gave him another one. Big, tough Walter.

Well, shit, Terry said, you could lay out anybody that way. I mean, George Chuvalo.

Maybe not Chuvalo, Jerry said, but pretty well anybody else. It wasn't supposed to be a fight, kid. You understand? She met me in the parking lot on Thursday night and she had two black eyes. She told me he knew. He was going to get me.

168

Okay. You got him first.

No, Jerry said. I got him for those black eyes. I want him to know that he's going to get killed if he tries that. Right in the fucking cafeteria at work. He never thought I'd have the balls. Now he knows.

Terry and his father drank their beers.

Really, Jerry said, when you get right down to it, who gives a shit? I lose the job, I go to jail, what? The right thing to do was what I did and you can't let things get in the way. Everything tries to stop you doing the right thing. You understand me?

Terry wished he had money. He wanted them to drive to the liquor store and buy two bottles of whiskey and sit up all night drinking. He wanted to grab his father and hold him close, like a kid saying goodnight. You never understand your father when you're young. Terry was glad he was older.

Dad, he said. Let's go home.

Jerry signalled the waiter.

Home? he said. Shirley's meeting me here. Right after she finishes her visit with Walter at the hospital.

Jerry paid for two more beers, then tossed a coin onto the empty tray. He and Terry took a mouthful of their drinks.

Terry, get rid of that girl. I can smell her around the place. You're asking for trouble.

So look who's talking, Terry said.

They both laughed. Terry raised his glass toward his father and Jerry touched the brim with his own.

Women, he said.

ii

Beryl had been in the house for nearly an hour when the phone rang. No one spoke when she answered, but no one hung up.

Who is this? they asked each other in almost perfect unison.

Both of them waited. Darlene knew it must be Beryl, even though it wasn't possible. Beryl couldn't see a face or a name, but knew it was an enemy by instinct alone.

Are you calling for Terry?

Is your name Beryl?

169

Who's asking? Beryl said, taking a line of Moth's.

My name is Darlene Bain. You're Beryl Watson.

So what?

I want to talk to Terry, Darlene said.

Why? Who are you?

Let me talk to Terry.

You can talk to me, Beryl said. I live with him. I'm practically his wife.

Darlene moved the phone away from her mouth in case she started crying. It could be a lie, but it made sense out of everything. He loved her and then she never saw him again. He never phoned and never answered the phone. She saw the whole wordless picture. It was a puzzle that assembled itself before her eyes and displayed indestructible logic.

Who are you? Beryl asked.

We started going out before you moved to Quebec, Darlene said. I see him almost every night.

Bullshit. He's with me every night.

Before you came here, Darlene said. Every night.

Come and see him, Beryl said. I'll kick your head in. Liar.

When you do it with him, he puts his hands on top of your head.

Big deal, Beryl said. He knows I don't care about sluts.

I'm going to have his baby.

Beryl dropped the receiver, then knocked the whole phone onto the floor when she tried to pick it up. She knew that Darlene would think she'd dropped it because of what she'd said and Beryl wanted her to know it wasn't true. It must have slipped. She couldn't seem to pick up the receiver and didn't know why she had become such a klutz all of a sudden. It was embarrassing. She straightened up and looked at the phone on the floor and had to remind herself what it was. A dog was whining, maybe over the phone or outside the front door. She ran into the bedroom and heard the Monkees celebrating their tiny passions and she stomped on the radio as though it was on fire. The face caved in and the music stopped. It was her. She was making noises like a dog. She sat down on the bed and made herself quiet, then got up and went back to the living room.

Beryl picked the phone up off the floor and hung up, set it down on the edge of the couch, then lifted the receiver to her ear. She heard the dial tone and realized what she'd done. She tried to remember Darlene's last name and nothing at all came to mind. It was as though she had never heard it.

She tried to think of anyone she could call who might know who she was or have her number. Moth. He might know, but it was too crazy.

Her mother picked up the phone on the third ring and Beryl hung up. She wondered whether it sounded like a long-distance call and if her mother knew it was her. Maybe they could trace it through the phone company. The cop had told her she had to leave by the end of the week anyway, so it made no difference. She had talked to the cop this morning and Terry had been gone all day and now he wasn't here. They needed a plan.

She thought about him with his hands on top of Darlene's head. He pressed you down like that, held you still while he was inside you. Darlene was tall and had very long legs that she'd lift and wrap around Terry's back, high up near his shoulder blades. She looked like Audrey Hepburn. They had sex in her four-poster bed every night, every single night, even when Beryl had to crawl down the TV antenna to meet him. Terry was with Darlene the night she was trying to climb up the hill with a monster behind her. The night Jiminy Cricket rescued her. Beryl ran away from home to be with Terry.

The facts and the fiction swamped her, drowned her, cut off her breath. A pipe had burst in her brain. Darlene was as lean and tough as Ida Lupino and Beryl was caught on the hill, raped and devoured. More than anything, she wanted Terry to hear about the night she had gone to the arena. There were a hundred things she needed to tell him and now he was in love with Darlene. Maybe.

She thought about Marcel that very moment and immediately tried to stop thinking. Terry had left her no choice with Marcel. No choice. He wouldn't write and she had no boyfriend. Marcel wasn't in love with her and she wasn't going to have his baby. Darlene was lying. Maybe.

The phone rang and she knocked it off the couch with the heel of her hand. She leaned over and picked up the receiver, stretching the cord tight.

What the hell was that? asked Terry.

What the hell was what?

Are you all right?

No, Beryl said, I'm not. Darlene is pregnant. She's sitting here and she's really upset.

Terry said nothing.

No, Terry, she said. You have to talk.

We broke up, he said. You moved. Same thing.

You were seeing her before I went to Quebec.

She isn't there, he said. Put her on the phone if she's there.

You told her you loved her.

Look, Terry said, she isn't pregnant and I wasn't seeing her before you moved. She's jealous.

Beryl's thoughts had slowed to a walk. She wanted to go back to Susan's then come here and try this again. Marcel was smiling while he drove, making her think she was in love with him, and she knew Terry was right. The rules had changed when she'd moved. Something like that. She was walking through treacle, but they didn't have treacle in Canada. Mud. Her thoughts were wading through thick, sucking mud that was like treacle. Darlene was jealous and lying about everything and that was no surprise. Anyone would do the same thing. Beryl was here and Darlene was alone and she knew how awful Darlene must feel. She was home eating and eating and really getting big.

Beryl saw it all and it made her feel sick and sad.

Are you there? Terry said. It isn't my fault that she called.

Where are you?

I saw my father and we went for a drink. I called Susan's but you weren't there. You can ask her.

Come home, Terry.

I'm with my father, Terry said. He just got out today. I've got to talk to him.

Talk to him here, Beryl said.

And what are you going to do? Hide under the bed?

It felt like hide-and-seek. You're squished in the corner of a closet and it's dark and you don't know where your friends are hiding or if the girl who's It is going to suddenly open the door. Maybe they've all gone out to play and left you there as a joke.

What am I supposed to do, Terry?

She could hear him breathing while he tried to think and that's when she knew. He had nothing in mind, no ideas, probably hadn't even expected to find her there. Just checking. His father might be in the bar or he might be in jail, but Beryl was hiding in the corner of the closet and that's where he wanted her. She had nowhere to stay and no money and he hadn't made a plan. Darlene might not be pregnant, but he wasn't finished with her yet. Maybe she called because he was supposed to meet her. Maybe Darlene

172

saw him every day while she was with Susan. She wanted to scream. She screamed.

You can't do this to me, she shouted.

I'm not doing anything, Terry said. I'm trying to figure things out.

Where am I supposed to sleep tonight?

Listen, Beryl, Terry said, I killed Soldier.

Beryl let herself cry, exhausted from holding it back.

Do you love Darlene? she said.

I killed Soldier, Terry said. I hit him with a rock. Twice.

I don't even like being here, Beryl said, sobbing. This place is so creepy and dirty. I just don't know what to do, Terry.

Do you even know what I just said?

Yes.

Say it.

You killed Soldier, Beryl said. You hit him with a rock.

Okay, Terry said. I'm going to be about an hour.

The radio's broken.

Go and lie down, he said. You're tired. I'll be there in an hour without my father.

He hung up and Beryl leaned over the couch and replaced the receiver. The phone wobbled on the spongy carpet and began ringing again. It had almost never rung before and tonight it never stopped. She went into the kitchen and opened the fridge door. There was nothing to eat, but there were three bottles of beer lying down on the shelf. She wasn't looking for food, although she knew she must be hungry.

She opened a beer and took it with her into the bedroom. It tasted like the first beer she'd ever had. They hadn't been drinking together since she'd arrived, but Terry sometimes had a couple while she was at Susan's. Nothing would make Susan raid her father's liquor supply. God knows what the penalty was for that. Beryl sat on the bed and took a long pull and could see Terry slinging a rock at Soldier, like David and Goliath. There was nothing wrong with killing a guy with a rock.

It took her half the beer to appreciate his confession. He was an outlaw, a bad man, a killer. If he'd been there the night of the monster, Terry would have killed him, too. He turned every other guy she knew into a kid. She had been going to school with children, guys who stole snowmobiles. She wondered why the cops didn't take him off to jail. They would know he'd done it,

173

cops knew things like that. They even knew she wasn't his cousin.

She finished her beer and went back to the fridge for another. It must have been like this for the pioneers, living without music or TV. At least this place had lights, but what were you going to do with a light when there was nothing to look at anyway? Terry and his father didn't even read magazines. They were both violent men. Maybe they got that way because they didn't have magazines or a stereo or a television set. It must have been after the TV got smashed that Terry had killed Soldier. Now his father was attacking men at work. Maybe the world would be more violent without television.

She wished Terry would kill Darlene.

The big difference between Terry and her brother was that Moth said he hated television but watched it all the time and Terry said he hated it and didn't watch it ever. Moth wanted to kill people and Terry killed them. She didn't know what had made her think about Moth. Television. They used to talk about television. She thought about Terry being an outlaw and herself being Beryl and she was trying to find a place where it fit. She wanted to look at it, but she was stuck in the centre and it was hard getting a picture. Movies were so much better than TV, but she couldn't find the right movie this minute and she needed it.

When she had first met Terry, she was a nice girl and he was a rebel. Not a really bad guy, just a rebel, like the song. She was the blonde waitress and he was that actor, the leader of the bike gang that came to town, except her father wasn't the cop. It was never a perfect fit, no matter what movie you saw. She was some kind of hostess and he was in the army, hated by the officers. She and Moth loved that film. Burt Lancaster holding a broken bottle, ready to fight Ernest Borgnine. Terry was more like Burt than Montgomery Clift, but that would make no sense, changing parts. She loved the scene on the beach but it didn't fit her. She could see Terry racing cars to the edge of a cliff and fighting over being called chicken, but nothing else made sense in that story. There was enough to piece together a relationship, though, if you snipped your way through the movies. A nice girl and a tough guy and she was the only one who understood him. It was no fantasy. Terry was a tough guy and Beryl was the only one who knew him.

Darlene was ruining her life retroactively. There was never another woman in a movie unless the hero's wife was horrible or crippled or else she was the heroine and the husband was involved with a slut. She didn't want to see herself or Terry like that.

Westerns always had the answer. It was too bad, but it was true. The guys fought over things guys really fought about and nobody blamed parents or teachers or the whole world for whatever they did. The bad guys wanted to be bad, just like in real life, and the good guys weren't very exciting. Beryl didn't want to live in the woods and ride horses, although she liked the idea when she had met Terry. It was a kid's idea.

Who was she now? Who was Terry?

She tried to remember who David had married after he killed Goliath. He was just a boy when he did it. If there was a girl, she wasn't hiding from the law. David wasn't seeing two girls, she was sure of that. That was the whole problem. Darlene made every movie and story impossible. There was no such story ever written. It left Beryl nowhere but here.

She started feeling better on the third beer. She took off her boots and stretched out on the bed and wondered what they were saying in Valentine. They had called the cops, of course, and neither one of them would understand why the whole police department wasn't out looking for her. Her father believed in everything except reality, Beryl thought. He probably imagined it would be like *Dragnet*. Her mother was afraid Beryl would say why she ran away. Unless she'd been telling the truth and both of them were sorry she'd been born. She drank from the bottle. Sorry she'd been born.

She took off her socks so the rug wouldn't soak them and tiptoed around tiny bits of glass on her way to the couch. Marcel's father answered the phone, told her to call back after eleven and hung up in her ear. Beryl tried to think of people to call. She didn't know how long ago she'd talked to Terry and she wouldn't be able to tell when an hour was up. She needed more beer. Tonight she'd have to go somewhere else to sleep and there was no plan, no fucking plan at all. There was no money and nowhere to go and Terry didn't do anything except get through a day. He got up and they had sex and then he went downtown and later picked her up and they had more sex. If he had any ideas or dreams, he was quiet about them. Maybe he spent the whole afternoon at Darlene's, eating things she cooked for him and having sex. Maybe Terry did nothing except fuck girls all day long.

Terry killed Soldier, she remembered.

She thought it was probably a lot to have on your mind.

iii

Jerry Delaney called Shirley's place and let the phone ring and ring and ring. He hung up and did it all over again. She picked up the phone.

Jesus Christ, Shirley.

I thought you were coming over, she said, thick and indistinct.

No. I said I was at the Pinklon. You were going to be here an hour ago, after Walter.

Walter, she said. You really hurt him, Jerry.

You got drunk and passed out, Jerry said.

No. No, no, no. I did not. I've been making myself pretty.

What are you doing, Shirley? I can't go over there.

Why not?

He had no answer. It wasn't as though her husband didn't know. The worst that could happen is a neighbour could tell Walter and then what? Jerry had hit him with a wrench and he could hit him with a hammer. He could shove a chisel through his eye. Walter was going to watch his step.

Anything to drink over there?

I think so, Shirley said. I think there just might be, you know that?

Jerry felt his face flush and his body swell, his hand getting thicker on the receiver. She was waiting for him with her face and her voice and he had her all to himself for as long as he wanted.

Keep it running for me, he said and hung up.

A woman was sitting at his table and drinking his beer. Jerry could only see her back as he walked over to get his coat off the chair, and he wondered who might be this bold. When he saw it was Olive from The Plant, he didn't sit down. He only saw her in the cafeteria when he was on days, and on the nights he found her in the Pinklon he ignored her. If he was asked why he didn't like Olive, Jerry would have said that no one liked Olive, which was untrue. She was neither popular nor unpopular. She was just another woman from The Plant who had no kids and drank at the Pinklon when her husband was on nights. Like Shirley.

Just on my way home, Olive, he said.

Too bad. I wanted to buy you a drink for the job you did on Walter.

Everybody thinks I lost my mind.

That happened a long time ago, said Olive. I don't think they realize how long ago you lost your mind. I'm still happy you nailed Walter.

I'm going, Jerry said, pulling on his coat.

Jerry, you should sit down for a minute. Just for a minute.

I don't like talking to you, Olive, he said. You should know that. And I don't have the time.

Sharon Dudar came in last night, said Olive. Here. I hadn't seen her for fifteen, sixteen years and she walked right in and sat down and had a couple of drinks.

Sharon Dudar?

Sharon Ticehurst. She married the mechanic, that guy in Bowmanville.

I don't know her.

Who do you think you're talking to? Olive said. Sit down.

Is there something you want to tell me?

God damn it. I really think you don't know who the hell I'm talking about.

Right, said Jerry.

Sharon, she used to work at The Plant, she came in last night and stayed about an hour and then she left. They were here visiting her family and usually he doesn't let her come to the old spots, Olive said.

Bowmanville. She could come here any time she wanted.

They live in Kirkland Lake now. You know who I mean, don't you?

No.

She worked with me. She was seeing that general foreman, Grimes. She dated a few guys from hourly rate, too.

Sounds like any of you girls.

She knew Betty.

Jerry sat down, looking off to one side as though he could see Betty and this stranger working together.

Sharon Ticehurst, he said. I know the name.

Jerry, Olive said, she wanted to know about Terry.

Sure, he said. Makes sense.

It does, doesn't it? Olive asked.

What else?

That was all. I just thought you should know.

Jerry blinked, still looking in the same direction. Olive drained the glass of beer and watched him carefully. He turned and looked at her.

Sharon Ticehurst was a real cunt, you know that? Jerry said.

No, said Olive, She wasn't. She really was not.

Jerry stood up and walked past her, quickly. Olive turned and watched him move through the bar in a straight line, all the way to the exit doors. Nobody should drink as much as they drank, but Jerry really should stop before his head became a sponge, she thought.

She was still happy about that god damned Walter.

iv

Terry parked near the corner of the street and waited for twenty minutes before he saw Darlene walking toward the car. He knew she'd be sullen but he didn't think she'd launch an all-out attack. It wasn't her style. He'd have to tell her about Beryl and act like he had no idea she already knew. He'd make it look like that's why he was meeting her, to tell her to her face. He owed Darlene nothing. He didn't ask himself why he was there, prepared to wait another twenty minutes for her and twenty minutes after that. Neither did he question why he had to race back home afterward.

She got into the car and looked straight ahead, as he'd imagined she would.

Darlene, Terry said, I killed Soldier.

She turned toward him, her script obsolete. He saw her face lose its authority and take on her actual age. She was a pretty girl.

I hit him with a rock and I killed him.

You killed Soldier, she said.

Yeah.

You killed him.

Yes, said Terry. I'm not going to say it fifty times.

Darlene stared at him, unsure of her expression and in no control of it. It seemed terribly important to have the right reaction, but what she really wanted to do was smooth down his hair. It stood up in a comic tuft near the back of his head and she wanted to make it lie down and then hear him say this all over again. He was telling the truth and she wanted to smile at his hair. She wanted to get out of the car slowly and go back to her room or maybe drive with him to California. Terry killed Soldier. Darlene wanted to push Richie's face in it.

Why did you have to kill him?

178

I didn't have to, Terry said. I just couldn't think of any reason not to kill him. It didn't feel like it would make any difference. Do you see what I mean?

She shook her head, trying to see his eyes clearly in the dark.

Everything felt so important, he said. Then we were just a couple of guys on the beach and it didn't mean anything at all. It was just going to go on and on.

What was?

Everything. I could hit him or not hit him. So I hit him.

She nodded as though it all made perfect sense. Terry moved closer to her.

Darlene, he said, Beryl is here. She just showed up and she's been sneaking into the house while I'm out. My father gave her some money so she could eat, but I've only talked to her for about ten minutes. I don't want her making trouble for us.

Good idea, said Darlene.

What?

I don't know, she said. Whatever you just said.

Are you upset?

I don't know. It's too late to go to our place.

She's going home this week, Terry said. I haven't laid a hand on her.

I could do it right here, if you want.

Do it? he said. Here?

It's dark enough, said Darlene. Would it make you happy?

I thought I should tell you about Beryl.

I trust you, Terry.

She held herself still while he kissed her. Terry tried again and this time she let her lips open and kissed him back. She touched the side of his face, then ran her hand up through his hair. The piece near the back was springy and wouldn't flatten out under her fingers. She kissed him again with urgency and stopped him from moving away from her.

Let me do it, she said.

Terry pushed himself back behind the steering wheel and unbuckled his belt. He scanned the street while he lifted himself and pulled his pants down to the top of his thighs. He thought he should probably move the car away from the streetlight.

You aren't afraid of anything, are you? Darlene said.

179

She held her hair back with one hand and held him with the other. He felt her breath and the dark warmth of her mouth. Different from Beryl. He tried to remember whether he'd showered that morning. Yes. Beryl did it in the shower and she was forceful and direct. Darlene opened like a flower anywhere you touched her. He closed his eyes.

Darlene raised her head, panting, a minute later. She leaned over and wiped her mouth with the bottom of his shirt, then sat up. Terry straightened his legs and pulled up his pants.

I wish I could kiss you, Darlene said.

Terry buckled his belt and said nothing. He wondered where Beryl could sleep tonight.

Are you going to jail?

Maybe, Terry said. I don't think so.

Soldier was a monster, Darlene said. Even Richie was nervous about him.

Even Richie, Terry said with a snort.

He used to hide at the creek and chase kids that went to the arena, she said. Hide in the dark and then try to scare them to death.

That's kid stuff.

No, Darlene said. For Soldier, it was like sex.

Well, said Terry, he won't be doing it any more.

He looked through the windshield and tried to see the sky. There was no moon visible tonight. The sky was only small patches of darkness between streetlights when you tried to see it from downtown. He opened his door and leaned out, looking up.

What are you doing, Terry?

Maybe if he saw the moon he would know whether or not he was in love with Darlene. Or Beryl. Maybe he could be in love or not and he would just decide to be in love. Maybe he'd decide not to be in love. It was all as simple as Soldier.

But there was no moon tonight. If it was there, he couldn't see it.

CHAPTER NINE

i

Moth got a suspended sentence from a man who wore a common grey suit, not long black robes. The little man peered at him through the thickest glasses in existence. His face was strange and mantis-like, frowning from the other side of a desk, his narrow skull dominated by huge, distorted eyes that seemed wider than his head. Lines ran deep from forehead to chin and it reminded Moth of a thumb wrinkled by hot water. There was a metal nameplate on the desk that read *Georges Georges*. It must have been terrible, receiving a prison sentence from Monsieur Georges, he thought. Like being sentenced in a cartoon. You would leave the room in the company of a soft, fat guard and with less dignity than you were given in gym class.

Georges Georges had told him that he could have been sentenced to fourteen years, then paused for effect. He spoke in English with an accent so dense that Moth could only nod blankly, guessing at the content. The fat guard touched him on the upper arm and he realized it was over, but he wasn't at all sure what it meant.

It means you got away with it, his father said outside the courtroom.

Am I on probation or something?

His father said nothing. Moth wanted to ask him whether he'd have been happier with fourteen years, but he didn't. Some of his teachers and one or two guys from the football team gave him the same problem as his father. He could either hit them or ignore them and even Moth understood that hitting any of them would be worse than doing nothing. Violence was as pointless as talking.

The day was bright, but the wind made both of them fasten their coats at the neck as they crossed the parking lot.

Winter wasn't this cold in Bresby, was it? his father asked.

There wasn't as much snow, Moth said.

I want to stop in at a couple of places on the way back.

Moth censored a complaint. His father would visit hardware stores and cavernous warehouses that sold automotive accessories wholesale. It was worse than being stuck with his mother, but it was better than fourteen years in prison.

Sure, he said.

I'm thinking of buying a rifle, his father said.

They got into the car as he said it and Moth asked him to repeat it. His father settled himself behind the steering wheel and started the engine.

A rifle. Maybe a shotgun, I'm not sure. What do you think?

I think you're kidding, Moth said.

There isn't anything mysterious about it. You buy one in a store, just like anything else.

What would you do with a gun?

I'm not sure, his father said. I know a couple of foremen who go hunting. The Plant manager shoots skeet. I think he hunts ducks as well.

You want to hunt?

No, his father said. I don't think I want to hunt. In the war, we had .303's, Lee Enfields. You see them around now for about ten dollars. I thought about getting one, but I was never in battle. I'd feel like one of those heroes at the legion who never saw any combat, but they all talk like they're Audie Murphy. Of course, he was American. They used to say that Americans gave medals for regular bowel movements.

Look, I used a gun, Moth said. I know it wasn't the right thing. You're trying to show me some kind of lesson, right? Like, what is the point owning a gun.

Why do your kids always think everything is about them? asked his father. I thought it might feel good finishing work and then blasting twenty clay pigeons out of the sky.

He put the car in gear and manoeuvred out of the lot. There were teenage boys with new haircuts and suits hurrying to catch up to angry and embarrassed parents, boys being nearly dragged to the courthouse by bigger fathers, boys who looked like they hoped the old man would try laying a hand on them. Tim Watson and his son watched them crossing the parking lot as the car nosed slowly onto the main road.

Moth wanted to get out and leave his father talking to himself. He didn't want to give any opinions and he didn't want to hear what his father thought. They had established the rules long ago and there was no need to change them. Guns. It must have been a toss-up between guns and boxing when his old man searched for a topic. Moth had a vision of a conversation beginning and then lasting for years, literally years, so he would end up talking to his father for the rest of his life. It was a frightening idea. It scared Moth how much it appealed to him.

Dad, he said, don't buy a gun.

I'm not going to shoot anyone. I've heard the recoil on a twelve-gauge shotgun is fierce. Have you ever fired one?

Yeah. You remember those guys stole those guns, I was just a kid? They let me shoot them.

I don't remember it, his father said. I'm not sure if I want a shotgun. The manager told me the recoil knocked him flat on his back the first time.

No, Moth said. I've heard that, too, and I was a skinny kid. I hadn't even started boxing. It's one of those things you say, you know? It knocked me flat. It didn't. I don't know why guys say it.

Where do we go? A sporting goods store, I guess.

Any big store.

I don't know anything about guns, his father said. What about a .22?

You can't shoot clay pigeons with it, Moth said. It sounds like breaking a twig when you fire it. A .12 gauge makes a big noise and it has a lot of power.

You need a permit from the police for a revolver, don't you?

Dad, let's go home.

Let's go to the tavern.

They drove to the highway and over to St Lucy. Moth thought about Donna and prison. Tim pulled into the parking lot of the tavern across from the shopping plaza and it immediately made him think of Kate naked with Joanna Webb. He crept the car past the front doors, but didn't stop.

I don't know what I want to do, Moth.

Moth felt a needle of panic. He wanted his father to shut up. If they were going to talk, he wanted to fight about his sentence or crime or his attitude toward the judge. His father made him feel cold and scared.

You're just tired, Moth said. You're tired, aren't you?

Yes.

I don't need to drink, said Moth.

You're not going to jail, his father said. Don't you want to celebrate?

He stopped the car. They were parked beside a Mustang and facing the entrance to the tavern. Moth thought he should buy a new car instead of a gun. A man with a full beard and an enormous belly came through the doors and immediately turned and vomited. They watched the steam rise from it, while the man shouted in French.

I really don't want a drink, said Moth.

A gun, his father said. You'd probably take it, if we had one. Have you ever met Bill Webb?

Yeah.

He's a nice guy, don't you think?

I don't know, said Moth. Does he have a gun?

I have no idea, Tim said. He might, I suppose. You'd never guess Jake's father had all those pistols.

Mr Webb isn't the kind of guy I imagine owning one. His wife is some kind of artist, isn't she?

We should have stayed in England. Your mother never liked it here, not from the first day. Women miss their families.

Moth found no comment to make. He could have told his father that none of them had been happy with the lousy places he'd picked, but he didn't want to hear about the infinitely worse circumstances of the old man's upbringing. No one else chose Canada, Bresby, or Valentine. His mother had nothing to do with anything they were talking about.

The man who had been vomiting in front of the car straightened up with his back to them. He wiped his mouth with his sleeve and went back into the tavern.

Protecting the family, his father said. That's one good reason.

I guess so.

You don't want me to get one, do you?

The thing is, Moth said, I thought you hated guns.

I do.

It doesn't make any sense. You hate them. I don't know what you're talking about.

Moth felt his lower lip give a quick tug on the last word and he closed his mouth tightly. He felt weak and helpless, the way he felt when he couldn't stop laughing. He might begin laughing right now, like a demented child, and he was afraid it would make him start crying. All of it made him angry, but he couldn't muster any force or focus behind it.

I don't know what we're doing here, Dad.

Well, I wanted to buy a gun, his father said. Now I'm thinking about it stuck in the back of the closet and never getting oiled or whatever it is you have to do. It would be just like one of those presents you kids carry on about until you get it and then you never use it. Always the most expensive present, too. It would end up like that god damned fishing tackle in the basement.

So what are we doing?

We could go inside for a drink. They'll serve you here.

I don't want a drink.

Then we'll go home, his father said.

He no longer looked tired, but had the same sulky expression of mute forbearance he always wore, crushed beneath an evil burden he hadn't asked to shoulder. Moth relaxed into the familiar everyday tension.

They headed back to Valentine.

ii

It wasn't Kate's fault, it was his. You'd have to be from Bresby or worse to think of it as an acceptable place to live. Couldn't even go for a pint after work. The pubs were all in cheap hotels and none of them had any windows. Even a prison had windows. Every patron looked lonely and suicidal or on the brink of committing murder and they drank as though it was their first time ever, without caution or control. Country music shrieked through cracked speakers and everyone screamed at each other to be heard. The people he worked with and those he met in the neighbourhood were incapable of carrying on a conversation that didn't involve the personal lives of human beings they barely knew. It was hateful. The god damned kids became honorary citizens overnight, indistinguishable from every other delinquent on the street. He had taken the family there, to Bresby. He had taken Kate.

Valentine had nothing and no secret was made of this. It was defined by what was absent. It had no pubs, no pool halls, and no street corners crowded with unemployed, drunken men. There was almost no traffic, there was no noise, and there were no bikers. The real estate people used what it lacked as its greatest selling point. Unless you went to the club, there was no reason to leave the house. Of course Kate would hate it. She could take Trevor to the community centre or stay home and watch television. The Webbs were the only couple even vaguely engaging and he had embarrassed her with them. He couldn't take her to Montreal during the week or when he worked nights and he wondered what the hell he'd imagined it would be like for her, living here. A woman couldn't spend all day looking after one child and Trevor didn't need constant attention.

He thought of himself sitting on the front lawn in the summer, cleaning an enormous shotgun while the neighbours sneaked looks at him through the space at the bottom of their curtains. It was as good as a billboard saying Leave Us Alone. Cars drove slowly past, everyone eyeing Tim Watson with his gun. He wished he could shoot targets in the yard, the shotgun rattling windows like a sonic boom. Leave Us Alone.

He knew it was an irrational picture and he had no idea of its source. Whatever their flaws, the populace of Valentine most definitely left the Watsons alone. Stupid thought. No one had invaded the house and whisked Beryl off into the night, and Moth hadn't been forced to rob the club. Neither had Kate been held down while the clothes were torn from her body and wine poured down her throat. It gave him a feeling of quiet pride, having the intelligence to discern this. Laying blame was not his province, Tim thought. He dealt with the consequences of his own actions. He'd brought the family to this god damned place and then everything fell apart. It was due to nothing he'd done, nor was it a crime of the town. Beryl and Moth had no excuse. Kate was his failure. He had given her no options at all.

Tim saw himself shatter the mirror and explode the bottles behind the bar in waves of machine gun fire. He'd do it like they did in all the gangster films. You couldn't buy a machine gun, could you? He could use the same cowboy gun as Moth, fanning the hammer. You didn't see that in movies any more, or maybe he didn't watch enough westerns. Fanning was probably a lost art. It may never have existed. He raised his arm and sighted along his extended finger. Just like that. Pull the trigger and smash the bottle that sat on top of Marc Cloutier's head. Turn quickly and hit Bill Webb in the face with the barrel of the gun. Good God.

Kate. She deserved better. He was going to have to endure the Webbs and the wine and the club, all the consequences of moving to Valentine. They were nearly impossible to contemplate.

If you decided to shoot yourself with a rifle or a shotgun, you would have to pull the trigger with your toe. He couldn't imagine taking off his

186

socks and inserting his big toe between the trigger and the guard. Maybe the big toe was too thick. You would sit there with the barrel in your mouth, trying one toe after another. It was altogether too Beverly Hillbillies for Tim. Too Jethro, Hemingway be damned.

It wouldn't be fair to Kate, either.

iii

Donna turned off the TV and the rec room became too dark for her to see her own hand.

We need some kind of light, she whispered to Moth. Just a little bit.

Moth didn't know if he wanted any light or not. If he could see nothing at all, he knew he'd be able to speak everything on his mind. Total darkness was too intimidating to endure for any other reason. They wouldn't be able to find the light if they needed it and he'd never know if someone sneaked into the basement, rubber-soled shoes moving silently toward their voices. He wasn't sure he wanted to tell her everything or anything at all. He wanted to see her body.

Turn the TV back on, he said.

She crawled back to it and it came on with a hum. A few seconds later the picture appeared and he watched her from behind as she turned off the volume. He wondered if you were allowed to kiss a girl's ass.

Donna crawled by the light of a black-and-white movie. He hadn't seen her naked in so long it felt new and unlawful and he was terribly excited by it. They were in the basement of the Bouvrette home, a sleeping child overhead. It was Donna's first babysitting job in weeks and Moth wondered if she'd taken it just because he'd been to court. They whispered hoarsely to each other as though there was someone else besides a sleeping child in the house.

I didn't bring a rubber, Moth said.

Pull out before it happens, Donna said. It'll be fine.

Moth didn't bring up what they'd learned in health class. One drop, they said. He felt like a sissy. She wanted him to do it and he had always wanted to do it and there was nothing in his way. Donna put her hand on his shoulder and he touched her face and then she was underneath him. Her legs lifted and her knees touched his ribs. She had him in her hand and he

187

didn't know how she'd done it. They kissed. Her fingers were guiding him and she licked his lips.

Moth felt his stomach tighten, like it was waiting to be hit with the medicine ball. He tried not thinking and began thinking. This isn't a fight and it isn't a contest. She's done this before. Everyone in the world has done it except Moth. She opened her eyes and looked into his, asking. Her hand tried to encourage him and he wanted to reach down and smack her wrist. There were too many things to think about and she was so sure of herself. She knew everything. Even the way she looked at him made her seem adult, a grown woman. He had to do it.

He rolled onto his back without letting go of her. She leaned over him and kissed his neck and then moved herself down his body. There. He watched shadows and light flicker on the ceiling and reached down to touch her hair. All he had to do was stay like this and everything would be perfect. Roll her over and do it before there was any time to think.

Donna made a sound that was muffled and urgent and Moth groaned loudly and grabbed her hair. An instant later he felt too sensitive to be touched and he pushed her away.

Moth, she said, crawling up beside him. You're supposed to tell me.

Sorry.

He felt as slim and nimble as a bantamweight. He wished some intruder would burst into the house so he could protect her. He could fight all night.

That wasn't the plan.

No, he said.

She wiped her mouth on his shoulder, then rested her head there. He wrapped his arm around her and watched the TV. It was an old movie. A man and a woman seemed to be arguing, but even with no sound he could tell the argument wasn't serious. They wore movie expressions of exaggerated response and their eyebrows were never still. Both of them took turns walking quickly to a door and then turning around and talking. It was a bad movie for tonight.

Are you watching the TV?

I'm thinking, Moth said.

Everything began creeping its way back inside him and there was nothing he could do to stop it. He could crawl over and turn off the television and then hold her in the dark. That was as far as he could think. There was nothing he could put into words.

I'm quitting school and going back to Bresby.

She seemed to stop breathing. She lay as still as a corpse, then moved away quickly and sat up, blocking the TV set and becoming a solid black shadow in front of him.

What are you talking about, Moth?

I'm quitting school, he said. I've been waiting to go to prison and now I'm not going and I just can't go back to high school. Not after that. It's bullshit.

What do your parents say?

It doesn't matter what they say, Moth said.

No. Nobody else matters to you.

I'm telling you, aren't I? You're the first one to know.

Thanks, she said. That's a nice plan. Fuck me and then tell me you're leaving town. I'm glad we didn't do it.

He had had no idea he was quitting school or leaving Valentine until he said it. He wondered if it was true. His heart began pounding and he was grateful she didn't have her ear against his chest. He wanted to shut up.

I don't understand you, she said.

Okay, I'm moving to Texas. You understand that?

Donna picked up her skirt and got up, stepping into it. She looked for her sweater. On the TV, the man was showing surprise by sticking his head forward like a turtle stretching its neck. Donna pulled her sweater over her head.

I have to check the baby, she said.

She crossed the room carefully and found the door. He watched her and heard himself call her back, but made no sound. This was awful and wrong and he wanted to make it disappear until the morning. He was stupid.

Somebody should kill me, he said.

He felt himself naked in a way he'd never known. It felt new and familiar, like seeing an old picture of yourself for the first time. He wanted to shout out that he loved her. He wondered if he should marry Donna instead of leaving town. When she came back downstairs, he would do it with her. He could do it now, this soon. It was because she looked the way she looked. She had on all her clothes and he wore nothing at all. She had on all her clothes and she was angry. Moth wanted her to come back right now and do it and then he'd do whatever she wanted. Leave town or stay in school or get married. She would leave her clothes on.

He crawled to the TV set on all fours and changed the channel. He wanted Donna to see him do it like this, the way he had seen her. One other movie was playing and it was black and white, too. It looked like a musical.

Donna was taking too long upstairs. Moth was getting cold but didn't want to put on his clothes. He didn't know what to do.

iv

– ran away from home.

Kate Watson stopped and looked at the words, trying to think of a better way of putting it. Left home, disappeared, vanished.

I didn't mention it at the time because I thought she would likely return soon. Off with her friends or some damned older lad and that sort of nonsense. I think she has gone back to Bresby so I am not so worried. She is a young girl but I don't think much can happen to her there. Beryl is not really wild but thinks she is as we all did. Mum, I don't blame her even if she has made us mad with worry because this is a bloody awful place to live. It sounds nice to you and I know you want me to be happy and God knows I will lie in any bed I make. I liked it to begin with but the people here are no better. Canadians are farmers. I have written this to you many times but this lot is worse than I am able to say. You would have to be here to see for yourself. Tim just won't tell his work to go to hell no matter how I feel about it.

She put down the pen and moved the blue airmail paper out of the way while she poured another cup of tea. Her penmanship was slow and precise and it took Kate a long time to write a letter. She wrote her mother every two or three weeks and wrote Tim's mother every couple of months.

I feel like hell over Beryl. We had a row the night she left and now I wish she was here and I had just left her to herself. She hates school and won't go and she lies about it. I didn't like school either but I didn't have to lie. I wish she didn't have to and I know it is my fault she does. This place has made me

Damn it. She couldn't think how to end the sentence. Made me crazy would mean she would have to tell too much. She wasn't crazy, anyway. Made me realize that I should never have left home and I should have made Tim stay. Too young to stand up to him. They get you too young and then when you're old enough to tell them to go to hell it's too late. You're already in Valentine.

190

This place has made me

Stark, staring mad. There is too much time and too many people. Or too few. None of it would make any sense to her mother, forty years in the same house and no one moving in or out of the neighbourhood. You couldn't know this unless you lived it.

Moth acted like it was all about the beating Beryl knew she deserved. If that was true, she would have run away after the first one. There were children who were beaten with a stick every time they misbehaved and Beryl had been punished only once. She must have known what she'd get for missing school. It seemed like a silly reason to run away from home, Kate thought. There would be hundreds of runaways if that was all it took. She picked up the pen and wrote.

This place has made me randy as hell. I don't know if it's from drinking wine more than I used to or if it's from sitting around the house. Perhaps because I take off all my clothes at Joanna's and I think about her husband biting my bum. I think about Joanna naked and I think of giving Moth a good hiding when he's lying in bed. I did think about Moth never mind he is my son. Tim would never take a hand to me his mother made him timid. Tim is tim-id I hadn't thought of that. A spanking really is all I mean or a very quick thrashing and then being fucked half to death. I take myself to bed in the afternoon and wrap my legs around the pillow.

She put down her pen and crumpled the letter, then straightened it out and tore it into little pieces. She didn't want Tim to smack her, spank her, or thrash her. It would shock her mum and it shocked Kate to read it on the page. Maybe when you're randy it makes everything else part of itself. Beryl needed a beating and next she is thinking of herself and Tim. Herself and Joanna. Moth would make anybody think strange thoughts because he had those muscles and always looked like he was going to attack you.

Kate scooped the scraps of paper into her palm and dropped them into the teapot, then stared at the pot and wondered what the hell she'd done. She emptied it in the sink and rinsed it, watching tiny pieces of thin blue paper gather in the drain. Trevor was in the backyard with two other kids and she watched them pulling wire and broken appliances out of the vacant lot and piling them onto the lawn. No one was crying or in any immediate danger.

The letter home couldn't be delayed any longer. Kate filled the kettle and plugged it into the wall socket, picked the paper out of the sink and dropped it into the garbage bag, then dried off her hands on a tea towel. She fetched another airmail envelope from the living room, then resumed her seat at the table.

Beryl isn't living with the family. What about that? Better than ran away. She isn't here and we are concerned. No. Beryl has done a damned fool thing, but she's a headstrong girl. As though it were of no great concern. I know I am very late replying to your letter but. It is because.

Beryl ran away from home because we had an awful row about her missing school. I don't know what ails the girl but it was like trying to talk to Penny Holmes' mother. The same mad talk. Penny's mum had the war but Beryl has no excuse. I woke up in the morning and she had gone without so much as a note. We are very worried but I am sure she is fine and will return soon. I was going to give her a good beating over school and now she'll come back and have to get it anyway. More now because she ran away. They don't think of these things.

The kettle had stopped making its noise and was now boiling all the water away. Kate left the table and carefully made her pot of tea, watching everything she did. There was a slight tremor in her hands, but it was probably due to writing her mother about Beryl. Last night had been nothing spectacular.

She covered the pot with the cozy and carried it over to the table. Last night had been nothing to write home about, she thought. Imagine writing mum about the club, as though it were anything like a night at the pub. Joanna was there, but didn't give her much attention. Bill liked her and it probably made Joanna uncomfortable. He's seen the picture. He thinks about me all the time.

Kate remembered saying something in the parking lot that made Joanna laugh, but she couldn't remember what it was. Bill was being as charming as ever, but she didn't know if he had laughed as well. They were in the parking lot. She tried to remember what happened next. In the lot and then she was home. Kate couldn't recall coming home. She had undressed and gone to bed, but her memory held no evidence of these things. No idea of what time they'd left or when she'd arrived here. It made her palms sweat.

She had to write this damned letter.

You need a daughter because you need someone to talk to and they need you to tell them what's what. You need a daughter. Moth is too old to run away but he's another man in the house. It will happen with Trevor as well. They pluck the heads off the flowers next door to give you a present and soon they don't want you in their room any more. They get bigger and stronger than you and they pick girls who would be hanging about the docks if they were back home. Moth wears his shirts until they are full of holes.

Beryl is just at that age. You forget that. She is at an age and I will wait for her to get past it. I can't live here without a daughter at least there's two of us in the house. She will get past this and then we'll be able to talk to one another. Of course your mother always seems old and daft when you're young but it will change. She will change. If Beryl won't come home I might as well

God damn it. She had to start thinking out the whole sentence beforehand. Might as well what? Cut Tim's head off while he's asleep. Join a nudist colony. Anything I damned well please. She doesn't have any idea how much I miss her you never know that until you have kids. They were raised over here too damned slack but that wasn't Kate's fault. You couldn't abandon your own standards because you lived with farmers. Maybe Beryl believed the rot she saw on television, kids talking to their parents as though they were chums. They didn't help with the housework and they came and went as they pleased. Never so much as a cuff on the back of the head.

If my mum hadn't talked to me I'd have no sense at all.

Kate pushed the letter away and wept. She folded her hands on the table and rested her head on them. Beryl shouldn't do this to her.

When she heard the front door open, she pushed back her chair and hurried over to the sink. She turned on the cold water tap and splashed palmfuls of water over her face.

You're still in your housecoat, Moth said behind her.

Kate took a paper towel off the roll and dried herself. She turned around, wiping her hands.

Have you been crying?

No. I have a headache.

Were you in bed all day? Moth asked.

Who do you think dressed Trevor and put him out? Women can't stay in bed all day, Kate said.

Moth walked out of the kitchen and she heard him climb the stairs. She turned both taps on full and resumed crying. It was worse than ever having Moth when Beryl wasn't here. You would think the police could find one girl in Bresby when they had her picture and the names of all her friends. They should take that god damned Terry and beat it out of him. He knew where she was. Young girls leave home because of boys like Terry, not because of their parents.

She turned off the taps and wiped her eyes with the sleeve of her housecoat. Trevor waved to her from the backyard, a broken hockey stick held beside him like a spear. Kate waved back and turned away before he broke his neck trying to do something to impress her. She went to the sheet of phone numbers taped above the phone and found Terry's, written neatly in blue ink.

A man answered on the third ring.

Terry?

No, Jerry. Terry isn't here.

Are you his father? Kate asked him.

Who's this?

My name is Watson and I'm looking for my daughter Beryl. I think Terry knows where she is.

You're from England, Jerry said. Whereabouts?

The north. Have you seen my daughter, Mr Delaney?

Nope.

I need to speak to Terry, Kate said.

Listen, Jerry said, I know some girl came here, but she isn't here any more. The cops sent her back home. She's probably already there.

Do you think I wouldn't know if she was here, you god damned idiot?

Kate heard Jerry say something but it was muffled, as though his hand was over the receiver.

She's there, isn't she? Kate shouted. Put her on the phone. Put her on right now.

Who do you think you're talking to?

My son is coming there and he's going to break your neck, she yelled.

Oh, I think my son is probably tougher than your son, Jerry said.

Kate tried to hang up, but the receiver kept falling off the hook. She couldn't understand how it had ever stayed on before. She left it dangling by the cord and went into the living room. One end table had a small cupboard beneath the drawer and Kate found the Bristol Cream in it. Barely enough left for a glass. She wondered if Tim was drinking it behind her back.

Kate held the bottle in both hands and drank what remained. There was only a few gulps' worth and she had taken her last when she heard the car in the driveway. She put the empty bottle back and hurried into the kitchen. Trevor was nowhere in sight, but had probably run around front when he heard the car. She hung up the phone effortlessly. It rang immediately.

Mom, Beryl said, I'm coming home.

Yes. Good.

I'll be there tomorrow.

Beryl, her mother said.

What?

She heard Tim and Trevor come in the front door, having a loud discussion over killing bears with a spear.

You know, Kate said. You must know.

Know what?

The things I said. Sorry you were born, those things.

What about it? Beryl asked.

I'll see you tomorrow.

Kate hung up the phone.

ν

Beryl couldn't imagine Terry didn't love her. It felt like she'd lived her whole life in love with him and now he didn't love her any more and she couldn't believe it. She didn't feel empty; she felt like she had never existed. There wasn't enough inside of her to cry. He had scooped out her vital organs and left her with nothing to feel.

You understand, Jerry said to her, I could go to jail just having you here.

Beryl nodded without looking at him. She hadn't even seen Jerry until today and he made her nervous. She could tell that whatever came out of his mouth had nothing to do with the way he felt. He drank beer without offering her even one drink and he talked about anything that jumped into his head. He seemed annoyed that she'd been staying there without cleaning up the mess.

I don't care about the couch or the dresser or beer on the rug, Jerry said. What bothers me is the TV.

He guzzled down the rest of the beer in the bottle and then leaned forward and began shouting, his face red and veins appearing like worms on his neck.

He can pay for that fucking TV! He can pay!

195

He tried to catch his breath while he stared in fury at Beryl.

It was your fucking letters that made this happen, Jerry said. Your dirty mail.

I'm sorry.

I wonder what your mother would say about that?

I don't know, she said.

Jerry got to his feet, every breath making his chest rise and fall.

Don't come near me, Beryl said.

He smiled at her and shook his head, then walked into the kitchen and opened another beer. Beryl felt like she could be killed or beaten or raped or all of those horrors and no one would know or care. Terry didn't love her and his father was a horrible pig of a man who wouldn't leave her alone. He had promised to pay for the train back home and Beryl wondered what would happen if she grabbed her coat and fled. She'd have to hitchhike. Or she could call that big cop, Marshal Dillon. That would probably mean going to court and talking to social workers and she couldn't face any of it. Maybe Marcel would steal a car and come and get her.

Jerry Delaney came back into the room and sat on the arm of the couch, looking calm and insane.

Sharon Ticehurst, he said. You ever watch a movie and about halfway through you know you've already seen it? It just kind of clicks?

No.

It isn't exactly like that, Jerry said. I can't explain it. Sharon was in a movie with me, sort of. I can't remember it very well.

Terry opened the front door and stepped inside. He looked from Beryl to his father.

Did he do anything to you? Terry asked.

Oh, fuck you, tough guy, said his father.

Beryl shook her head, but she didn't go to him. She couldn't tell friend from foe tonight.

He kept banging on the bedroom door, Beryl said.

It's my house, said Jerry.

You never even came back here after the Pinklon. I didn't know you were going to show up, Terry said.

I'm here now. What are you going to do about it?

My mother called, said Beryl. He talked to her and she hung up on him and I called her back. I'm going home.

When?

Tomorrow. Your dad said he'd give me the money.

You want to go home? asked Terry.

I might as well, Beryl said. You and Darlene don't need me around.

She started crying before she'd finished talking. She covered her face with her hands and stepped quickly over the spongy rug to the bedroom. The door closed silently behind her, worse than a slam.

See what you've done?

Shut up, Terry said.

His father pushed himself to his feet.

You want to say that again? You think I'll let you get away with that?

Terry walked past him and went into the bedroom. She wasn't lying on the bed, but standing with her back to the wall beside the door. Her eyes were wide open and crying and it was something he had never seen before. It made him feel young and guilty.

You're Satan, she said. You're making me live in hell.

Beryl didn't know what was coming out of her mouth, but the effect on Terry was impressive. His mouth opened but didn't speak and he backed away from her and sat on the edge of the bed. He stood up again, as though sitting made him vulnerable to attack.

I went to the Pinklon, he said. I wasn't looking for Darlene. I got confused.

You killed me, Terry. You're going around killing everybody and trying to act like a little boy.

You showed up here at the worst time, he said.

There's no good time in hell, Beryl said.

Stop saying that. What's the matter with you?

I'm leaving tomorrow, Beryl said, But there's a curse on you for the rest of your life.

She felt inspired. There was no name-calling or telling of lies. No need to raise her voice. She didn't as much speak as hear her own words. Maybe it was all true. She knew she had no power to deliver a curse, but she also knew one hung on Terry's shoulders like a shroud. He was being dragged to the bottom of the sea as she watched from the deck of the ship.

You might as well be dead, Terry, she said.

Beryl, listen. Everything is happening. I can't make a plan until the next thing happens. I can't explain it.

197

Darlene was the last thing and she'll be the next thing, Beryl said.

No. Soldier was the last thing. Everything else has just been just passing time.

He sat on the edge of the bed and didn't look at her. Beryl knew the routine from her father, from Marcel, from all of them. They were doing the real suffering, having so much more to deal with than you could imagine. Your problem with them was small and stupid. They suffered and you genuflected in the presence of their suffering. Once she had the image, it unlocked the answer: they thought they were God. Terry was Satan and thought he was God. Sent by Satan, then. The real Satan had other things to do besides breaking her heart.

What if he, the real Satan, thought he was God? What if everything happened in the world because he thought he was God?

You know something, Terry? she asked. I'm too smart for you.

Yeah, he said. You're so smart. You come here without a dime or a clue and you think like a little kid. Fuck you, Beryl.

Fuck you, Terry.

She felt better, knowing his real identity. What had happened between them wasn't her fault. She didn't know she'd thought it was her fault until now, when the feeling disappeared. He was the cheap version of evil, like a delivery boy for Satan.

I saw her that one night because she was upset, he said.

Where do you go? You leave here like you have a job, Beryl said. I think you see her all the time, ever since your dad got out.

No.

You leave me here every day and you knew he'd show up sooner or later.

You should go home, Terry said, but it has nothing to do with Darlene.

Don't even say her name.

Terry got up and walked out of the bedroom. He went into the kitchen as his father silently measured him.

That's my beer in there, his father yelled.

Terry came out with an open beer in his hand and Beryl looked at father and son from the bedroom doorway.

Are you going to give her money to leave?

I didn't ask her here, his father said.

You said you'd pay for the train, Beryl said.

I don't remember.

The cops are going to come, said Terry.

They already have, Beryl said. I don't answer the door.

Why don't you get a god damned job, Terry? asked his father. Pay your own fucking way.

She needs the money now. Tomorrow.

Call her parents.

You said, Beryl said.

I told you I don't remember.

Jerry Delaney stood up slowly and looked at Terry in a way he thought fathers looked at their sons during serious disagreements. It was supposed to be a grave look of concern and warning, but Terry saw menace and regret. He felt his insides turn hollow and small tremors in his joints and made himself breathe normally. The next one wasn't supposed to be his father.

I don't want you drinking my beer, his father said.

Okay.

Terry took a couple of gulps from the bottle while they eyed one another.

Your mother is Sharon Ticehurst.

Terry took the bottle away from his lips and held it loosely in his hand. For a dizzy instant he thought his father had called his mother a dirty name in a code he didn't understand. He wished his old man would take a swing at him so they could begin. Talking was becoming too difficult.

You understand?

I understand you're drunk, Terry said.

Sharon Ticehurst. I couldn't even remember her. Kind of skinny, but a girl who was like that up top but still has hips. You know what I mean? An overbite. I remember that. Kind of a roundheels, even for a girl at the Pinklon.

You're giving Beryl the money, Terry said, Or I'm taking it off you.

See, I was already married. Wouldn't you think she'd just get rid of the kid?

How much is the train, Beryl? Terry asked her, looking away from his father.

She had the fucking baby. Like I was going to leave my wife because Sharon had a baby.

She had your baby, Beryl said.

199

He turned his head and smiled at her and Terry dropped the bottle and took a step forward. He threw his right hand straight from the shoulder as his father turned toward him and it landed right on the button. It was a perfect punch. Jerry reached out as though he was trying to embrace his son and fell to his knees. Terry stepped back and watched him fall over onto his face.

Beryl ran from the bedroom door and kicked Jerry in the ribs, then steadied herself and kicked him again. Terry touched her softly on the head with his left hand and she moved away.

One punch, Terry said. One fucking punch.

Kill him, Terry.

Jerry Delaney rolled onto his back and groaned as broken glass cut through his shirt and into his shoulders. He opened his eyes and blinked at his son, then closed them. When he opened them again they were round and terrified.

Please, he said.

My mother's dead, said Terry.

I have just about enough money for the train, said his father. I can get the rest.

My mother.

Sharon, said Beryl. Her name is Sharon.

She tried to scream as Terry grabbed her by the throat with one hand, but it cut off her breath.

My mother's name is Betty, he said.

Beryl backed away as soon as he let go of her. Terry was looking down at his father and she took small steps until she felt the edge of the bedroom door. She needed to get her coat and get out. Close the door and then sneak out the back window while Terry killed his dad. The house looked bright with colour, as vivid as a musical. She owned every feeling existent and couldn't decide which one ruled the moment.

Hell was a place full of fear and bright colours. Terry lived here and was going to be king. Her life was stupid without him. It was small and whiney and too much like the lives of everyone else.

Terry rested one foot on his father's chest and looked down at him with no expression at all.

Beryl closed the bedroom door.

I don't like it when I can't remember the night, Kate Watson said. I want to be careful after last time.

You were a devil, Joanna said. Wasn't she, Bill?

Bill smiled from across the table. The club was already getting crowded, even though it was before nine and there was no band. Kate sipped at her glass of wine, carefully. She felt like dancing on the tabletop.

You're my friends, she said.

Of course we are.

Tell me why I couldn't find my knickers the next day.

Knickers, said Bill. You must mean those tiny little black panties.

Tim would kill her. She couldn't look at Bill. It didn't make her feel quite so playful now, knowing Beryl was coming home. She had to drink less, much less.

Don't be embarrassed, Bill said.

The stories I could tell, said Joanna.

I wish, Kate said and downed her drink, feeling her face grow hot.

Yes, sure.

I wish we could just do something and get it over with, said Kate.

The Webbs stared at her without exchanging a glance or blinking their eyes. Joanna's hands lay flat on the table and she began a very faint smile. Kate looked back at her and felt suddenly older than anyone else at the table or in the club. It was a room full of noisy brats, snickering and smirking.

Don't you get tired of playing? she asked.

Relax, Kate.

No. The suspense is killing me.

How much have you had tonight? Joanna asked in the kindergarten teacher's voice people use on the sick and the drunk.

I'm your little joke, Kate said. I take off my knickers and I run around your living room naked and fall asleep. What do we do now?

We act like friends are supposed to act, Bill said. You know how to be-have. I don't imagine it can be so much different in England.

No, Kate said, I suppose it isn't. I have my mum in England and my sisters and all the girls I knew when I was growing up. Just like here. We all get together in the pub with our men and have a chat and go home and have sex and raise children. You can go for walks. There are stores and people and cinemas and everything you need. You can't make a lot of money, but what's the point in making money if you're somewhere that has nothing you want to buy?

You're just feeling sorry for yourself.

Yes, Kate said. I am. I've never been with a woman, Joanna, and you're a lovely woman. I've never been with another man since I met Tim. I think we should do it. I can do it with you or with Bill or with both of you. But I can't keep on getting pissed in this rathole every night and do nothing. I just can't.

Don't burn bridges, Bill said. We're your friends, but you can't become too naughty.

Stop, Joanna said. She's right. You took me unawares, Kate.

What do you want to do, Joanna?

I don't want to rush into things, Joanna said. I like it when they unfurl on their own.

Kate leaned back with a heavy sigh.

Thank God, she said. You said it.

Bill started to stand and then actually jumped to his feet. He smiled meaninglessly at them and walked over to the bar.

He isn't good at this, Joanna said. If it just happens, he doesn't feel like such a villain.

You've done it before.

Think about the first time you made love with a man, Joanna said. Did you wonder how often he'd done it before?

Yes.

Joanna laughed merrily and put her hand over Kate's.

Beryl's coming home tomorrow.

So you'd like to celebrate, is that it?

Joanna, do you fancy me?

You're making me dizzy, said Joanna. Yes, of course I do.

Bill likes to watch, doesn't he?

He likes watching me with men, Joanna said.

Nice for you.

Bill isn't queer. Don't think it for a minute.

I don't know what to do with a woman, said Kate. I have no idea.

We're not going to rush, Kate. It ruins everything.

Well, how fast can we take our time?

Joanna lowered her head and shook it slowly, as though marvelling at an outspoken child. Kate looked past her and saw Bill talking to Tim at the bar. She felt herself deflate. The night went as flat as ginger ale left on a bedstand.

God help us, she said.

Joanna turned and looked toward the bar, but neither of the men noticed her. Kate wondered if she was relieved.

Well, said Joanna, I suppose that closes this little chapter for now.

Kate saw Bill balancing drinks and nodding toward their table. He liked to watch his wife with other men. Maybe they called her Tim's wife and she had nothing to do with it. They wanted Tim.

A glass of wine appeared in front of her and the two men sat down.

Just stopping by, said Tim.

Following a whim? Joanna asked him

Oh, he's a spontaneous sort of lad, Bill said.

Tim looked at Kate, who gulped down the fresh drink without stopping. She put down her glass and caught her breath.

Tim, she said, I want to go home.

I just got here, said Tim.

I don't mean back to the house. I want to go *home*.

Kate reached over for Tim's drink and he picked it up. She almost punched him in the face for doing it.

I want to go home, Kate repeated. I miss my mother.

She put her hands in her lap to show she meant no mischief. There was nothing left to say on the subject and she couldn't understand why they couldn't just move along. She leaned over and gave Tim a kiss, but he didn't even turn his head.

She knew she had ruined the night. Ruined it, and there was still hours and hours left to go.

What nobody understands, I'm sure, is there's a different set of rules for an artist than for a pipefitter, Joanna said. Whatever the hell that is. A pipefitter, I mean. You know what I mean? I'm not a lesbian. I don't hate men. People want to force you into a box they understand. It makes you less of a danger. Do you know how much we threaten these people here? Because we're free. They're threatened by our freedom. No fucking children. They hate that. They talk about kids like they've been brainwashed and don't have any choice how they speak. It's true. They beat the shit out of them and scream at them on the street and almost pull their arms off when they're shopping. Then they ask you why you don't have kids.

Bill was in the bathroom and she yelled loudly as she paced the house and drank. She wore only a pair of white panties and she kept returning to the mirror on the living room wall. Who else her age could look this damned good in plain white panties?

Her husband sat on the edge of the bathtub, reading John O'Hara and trying to outlast her.

Bill, she shouted, I have great tits. That would make them hate me, anyway. I fly in the face of convention. I'm not a nymphomaniac. We just aren't like them, hon. Never will be. Come out of there.

The room turned black around the edges and she sat down, catching her breath. Too much shouting. There was a swelling beneath her navel that was prominent now that she was in the chair. She poked it with her finger. She wasn't pregnant and her period was too far off to account for it.

Jesus Christ, she said, I'm getting fat. It's happening to me. This place is making me fat.

Joanna stood up and walked cautiously to the mirror. It made her realize that she was drunk. She stood in profile and looked at her stomach. White makes you fat. She tugged down the panties and kicked them away. It was there, that curve all the way up to her belly button. Men get theirs above it and we get ours below. She pinched the flesh and produced a thick roll between her thumb and forefinger. Not really thick, but thick enough.

What if you get fat, anyway? What if you never have kids and your ass still spreads and your tits hang down? she said without raising her voice. Then what?

She hit the corner of the coffee table on her way to the bathroom. Too much to drink. Maybe it wasn't the booze at all, maybe she was dying.

Bill, come out. You have to come out of that fucking bathroom. I'm dying.

Go and lie down, Bill said.

What if we end up bringing home old drunks from the bar because no one else will even look at me? Jesus, Bill, we have to stop this. I'll lose my teeth and all my muscles will turn to fat and I'll be watching you with whores. No one will ever buy my paintings. Open the door.

He opened the bathroom door and rapped her sharply on the head with his book. It was a paperback, but thick enough to make her head bob. She backed away from him and whimpered.

You have to be nice to me, she said.

Shut up and go to bed. You're drunk.

Do you think I'm getting fat?

You're gaining weight, he said. What do you expect? You sit on your ass all day long and you drink too damned much. Are you happy now?

Bill, be nice to me. Tuck me in.

He grabbed a handful of her hair and twisted it. Joanna fell to her knees with a scream and grabbed hold of his wrist with both hands. He yanked harder and stepped away from her and she put her hands down so she wouldn't fall on her face. Bill took a step toward the bedroom door and she had to crawl to catch up. He took another step and another. Joanna crawled after him, naked and crying.

Everybody feels so threatened, do they? he asked. Look at you now. You know what they're afraid of, Joanna? They're afraid you'll fuck their husbands.

She cried as she crawled.

I'm bad, she said. I'm sorry I'm so bad.

Too late for that now.

He loved her like this. He couldn't wait to get her into the bedroom.

vii

Kate Watson sat up in bed immediately when Tim shook her.

Is it Trevor?

It's Beryl, he said. The police have her in Kingston. I have to go fetch her.

Kate tried to think. Beryl was in Bresby, coming home later today. Where the hell was Kingston?

What happened?

She was driving here with that Delaney boy and the police stopped the car, Tim said.

Why was she bringing him here?

Kate, I have to go to Kingston. Do you want to come with me?

205

I'm not leaving Moth to look after Trevor, she said.

She turned on the bedside lamp. It was just before four o'clock. Her clothes were in a pile on the chair and seeing them made her more alert. She wondered if her underwear was in the pile. Tim was wearing the same clothes as he'd worn at the club and she looked at his side of the bed. The pillow showed no dent and the sheet was still tucked in on his side.

I was downstairs when they called, he said. I wasn't sleepy.

Kate pushed him aside and climbed out of bed. The room felt cold and she got her robe quickly from the back of the door. Tim didn't watch her. She was dying of thirst and urgently had to use the bathroom, but she stood at the bedroom door and looked at him without moving. He looked up at her.

You were drunk last night.

Yes, she said. You brought me home. And then what?

I had another drink with Bill and Joanna.

There's nothing to drink here.

I went to their house, he said.

Kate went down the hall to the bathroom and locked the door behind her. She turned on the tap and sat on the toilet while the water ran. It was as though she didn't want her husband to hear her pee, she thought. Like it was their first night together. The idea made everything sadder and uglier. She was sorry she'd ever met the Webbs. She hated Joanna.

She flushed the toilet and cursed herself. It would take forever to fill a glass now. He had gone to their place for a drink. Had seen her picture, probably. She took the drinking glass from beside the sink and held it under the tap. Maybe it made him angry enough, the picture. Bill watched. Joanna had such a strong, full body she'd make anyone wild. Kate drank the glass of water without stopping. The bathroom was freezing.

When she went back to the bedroom Tim was getting changed, carefully folding his pants. He would taste of her. She thought about kneeling in front of him and pulling down his underwear and wondered if he'd know. He'd think it was bloody odd, no question of that. She watched him put on a pair of dress pants.

What are you doing?

I'm not seeing the police dressed like a tramp, he said.

You're never dressed like a tramp, for God's sake.

Kate, just let me dress the way I want.

He took a clean white shirt from a hanger and put it on while his pants were still open. Tucked in the shirt and closed the pants and Kate watched her opportunity vanish with his shirt-tail. Joanna all over him, her taste thick on his foreskin. He must feel so pleased.

You had a drink at their place, she said.

Yes, he said, taking his black shoes out of the closet.

Then you came home and the police phoned.

He nodded, sitting on the end of the bed and putting on the shoes. Same black socks as last night and they probably were the only things that really needed changing. Kate tried to remember what had happened after the club, but her memory was like a dream on TV. It was too bright and too fuzzy, the edges of everything smeared. She saw the four of them sitting at a table and there was nothing but silence.

I only had about three glasses of wine, she said.

Maybe you should have only have had two.

He stood up and they looked at one another. She wanted to touch him and she wanted to rip off his face. This wasn't a good night for him to go anywhere. A long drive without words wasn't thinkable, either. God damn Beryl.

She followed him downstairs trying to find the right question to ask or the correct way to behave. It was impossible without knowing what had happened. Tim opened the closet door and took out his coat.

Jesus, Tim, what did you do over there?

I told you, we had a drink, he said. Two drinks. I can drive.

You know what they want, don't you? They hate me.

Let's go to Kingston and get Beryl.

Don't start this, she said. You'll lose. You know you will.

Tim buttoned up his coat and she heard him breathe through his mouth while he did. He raised his head and looked so calm and unfamiliar she almost stepped back.

Don't threaten me, Kate. You have no idea what I'll do. Don't make me show you.

He walked past her and opened the front door and they both watched snow falling out of the sky like feathers from a pillow. The ground had a thin white cover that was getting thicker every moment.

Tim gave the deep, groaning sigh she knew so well. Just his luck. Another disaster for poor Tim in his endless battle. Life was too cruel for the poor sod and it was a wonder he could live at all.

He stepped over the threshold and closed the door behind him without looking at her. Kate locked it after him. She thought he might have an accident on the highway, he might be killed, the police would have to call again. Maybe it would happen on the way there or maybe on the way back.

She couldn't decide which she'd prefer.

viii

Bill Webb was tired, but he didn't want to go to sleep. He loved having the hours to himself when Joanna was in bed and there was no one to talk to and nothing to hear. It was the magic moment of his day. She'd stay up too long when he worked the day shift and sometimes she was already eating toast and jam when he came home from graveyard. He liked finishing the night shift and having just a bit too much to drink when he came home. It was the only time he could think anything he wanted. He enjoyed turning out the lights and sitting in front of the window, looking out at the street. Like he was letting his mind out of its cage.

The police car drove slowly past, its little emblem on the door. The snow was falling too quickly for its windshield wipers. It must be the young guy working these hours. Frightening to think of him carrying a gun. There must be no standards at all for these little places, beyond a driver's licence. It would have been him that showed up when Moth was caught. Poor Tim. The man probably hadn't jaywalked in his life and his son was breaking into places armed with a pistol. Kate's side of the family. The other boy was Jack? Jacques? Neither one of them looked like thugs.

Moth was a boxer. Wasn't Henry Godin a boxer? He ran some sort of club besides the motorcycle gang. A boxing club? He had that ridiculous machine, making sure everyone at The Plant knew who he was. Anybody would get attention riding that bike. Joanna said that she'd always wanted to paint him. Where had she ever seen him? Of course, everyone in Bresby was aware of Henry Godin. Always wanted to paint him. She mocked men like Godin, but wanted that. Maybe she made things safe by having them posed and under her control, trapped forever in the same position on the canvas. Maybe not. She would want him with his clothes off. She wanted a sensitive, unconventional man and she yearned for criminals on motorcycles. It was confounding. Henry Godin would go nowhere she wanted to go and

208

he'd hate everyone she knew. She wanted his very opposite. She had always wanted to paint him.

He thought about Joanna naked, straddling the chromed Harley.

Moth. That's how he'd arrived here. Maybe Moth knew Godin, maybe he belonged to his boxing club. So what? He couldn't remember his point.

Was Tim molesting that little girl of his? That would be something to shout about. Fucking hypocrite. You always know a girl will put out if she hates her father and Beryl prowled around giving off heat like an alley cat. Running away. She had some reason to hate Tim, so what was it? He probably wouldn't smack a housefly. Kate is a slutty mess because he's ignoring her and having their daughter. It's the Watson family secret.

Joanna is standing on a street corner admiring the motorcycle. Godin offers her a ride and she gets on and wraps her arms around his waist. Women love riding motorcycles. He turns off the main road and travels so fast she has to bury her face against his jacket, all the way to the lake. She is wearing tight shorts and a sweatshirt and she takes them off – no, he pulls them off – behind a boulder on a hill. He pulls down her shorts and sees the curve of her hips and the field of flesh from the light curly hair at her crotch all the way up to her full breasts. Her nipples are already hard.

Bill drank his drink and imagined Henry Godin looking at his naked wife. She turns around in a circle, displaying herself. Maybe she playfully sticks out her ass to him. Godin would be surprised at how fit and beautiful she was.

Bill saw the hard torso on top of her, Henry's arms bulging with muscle, his hands cupping her ass and his fingers leaving marks.

He topped up his drink from the bottle beside him and unbuckled his belt. He opened his pants and eased his hand inside. Lifted the waistband of his underwear and held himself. Start again. Joanna doesn't just meet him by accident. Could there be any possible reason he'd come to the house? She goes to his house. The whole bike gang is there.

The police car again, going home this time. She would never meet Henry Godin here or anyone else. The sun shone on every nook in Valentine and revealed every secret. The snow was forming a ledge along the bottom of the window and he wondered if he'd have to shovel. How many men from The Plant would keel over with heart attacks after shovelling their driveways? Not Henry Godin. He was in jail now, but if he wasn't. Moth probably did all the shovelling. They couldn't get Moth over there. Far too young and besides. I mean, good God.

He should take up photography. He would need models, the same as she did. Build a darkroom in the basement. He was an artist at heart but had never found his medium. He could see black-and-white shots of identical homes, rows of them, their innate fascism laid bare. Well, the innate fascism of the builder, if not the buildings. Overweight women laughing beside the pool, thighs bulging out of their bathing suits. Close-ups of wrinkled flesh and broken veins, stretch marks just above the top of their white shorts. God, yes, he could see it all. Naked pictures of young, muscled boys walking beneath the street lamps and embracing girls on the golf course, the police car driving past in the background. He could easily fill a book. *Valentine's Day.*

Music was an attractive idea, but it took too long to learn. If he bought a camera tomorrow, he could be taking pictures before sundown. The piano would take years to master. God knows how long before he could begin composing.

He would take pictures of Joanna lying underneath strangers. Kneeling for them.

Someone was walking through the snow in the middle of the road. He realized it was a woman and then saw it was Kate. Walking along the road and coming to his house. He felt paralyzed, watching her. He put down his drink and took his hand out of his pants and fastened the top.

It was beginning to feel like the longest night of his life.

Spring

Chapter Ten

i

Jake drove his father's car around the perimeter of Valentine and pulled into the club's parking lot. It took him less than five minutes to back into a spot between two station wagons. Moth looked unimpressed.

Not as easy as it looks, Moth. Try it sometime.

We should go in and wreck the place, Moth said.

Sure. And I'll never get the car again.

See? You get something and then you're afraid of losing it. Pretty soon you'll take all the shit in the world just to keep what you've got.

Bullshit.

Not just you, I mean anybody.

My mom went to driving school, Jake said. When they finished, they sent their best driver for the test. He passed and they gave the whole class their licences. Like he represented them.

Your mother told you?

She told me I could do it, but it costs you. You know how you hear you can pay off the cops if they catch you drunk driving? True. I always thought that was bullshit.

My old man would never let me use the car, anyway.

Get a job, Jake said. Get your own car.

I read this thing about heavyweights, Moth said. The champions. This guy traced them all the way back to John L. Sullivan. He went back like they were links on a chain. You've got one champion who hit the last champ who hit the champ before all the way back to the beginning. See what I mean? Ali throws a right hand and it travels through time all the way back to Sullivan. Before him, if you keep on going.

Your father could get you on at The Plant.

Did you understand what I said? Moth asked.

Okay, so?

So think about it. Everybody who ever hit anyone else is probably connected.

Everybody who ever had a conversation is probably connected, too, Jake said. I talk to my grandfather, he talked to his father, pretty soon someone is talking to the Indians.

That isn't a chain. This is fighter to fighter, this is history.

You could do it with fucking, as well.

No, Moth said. It isn't the same thing at all.

You want to drive down to St Lucy? We could.

Jake, can you stop thinking about driving the car for a second?

Look, Jake said, I don't think it's an amazing idea. Sorry. And I like the car. I like driving. There's nothing wrong with me driving this car.

Moth watched a man leave the club, skidding and sliding on his way to his car. It wasn't anyone he recognized. They should at least walk in and sit at the bar. He felt ready to fight, but he knew it would pass and take too long returning. He always felt ready after the moment had gone.

Jake watched the same man and saw the blast of exhaust when he started his engine. The car began backing up and Jake almost honked his horn. No time to warm up at all and the guy was already backing up.

I should get back home, Moth said.

Jake inched the car out of its spot as though he were transporting a trunk full of nitroglycerine. The other car roared past, the back end waving like the tail of a snake.

How is she? he asked.

They've got her on tranquilizers. She's the same, but calmed down. I think she just got drunk and everyone went nuts.

Big Frank does the same shit when he's drunk.

Exactly.

They must have done something to really piss her off, said Jake.

Look at them. She looks like a fucking amazon and the guy's queer. They're weird.

Did she get shock treatments?

Is that what you heard? Moth said. That's bullshit. She was only in there for a few days. Is that what they're saying?

I just wondered, said Jake. No one's saying anything.

Too much booze, that's all.

Maybe you can trace drinking all the way back to the first grape.

You know, Jake, you can eat shit.

Yeah, okay. But I'd be thinking about getting a job if I were you.

He stopped the car outside Moth's house and it fishtailed briefly before standing still.

That happens to everybody, Jake said.

Moth got out and slammed the door and walked through the snow to the house. It was worse here than in Bresby. Snow piled so high it looked like one of Trevor's drawings, a child's idea of winter. Snow up to the rooftops and blocking the doors. Little men digging tunnels to find their cars. You could drown in snow.

Beryl was already home, sitting beside Trevor in front of the TV.

Mom's asleep, Beryl said.

He took off his boots and went upstairs. It was less than an hour since he'd left and he felt humiliated. He should have flattened Jake's snout for him. There was nothing separating Jake from everyone else now – all he needed was a good job and then he could find the right girl to have his kids. Moth had expected a long talk and was nearly ready to tell someone his secret. If not Jake, who? Maybe it was a sign that he wasn't supposed to tell anyone at all.

He lay down and then thought better of it. Lying down made him think about Donna and he couldn't face locking himself in the bathroom again. He sat up and looked at the mess between the beds. Trevor had dismantled the hockey game and tried to make soldiers out of the metal men. There was an orange tank crayoned on the board, its cannon starting at the blue line and reaching nearly to the goalie's net.

Moth had sparred with Lennie Sparks during the summer. It had been humbling. Sparks had boxed five of them that afternoon, one after another, with no breaks between rounds. They each went one round and then left the ring while the next man climbed in. Sparks put his hands on Moth's shoulders and let him throw punches to the body unimpeded. He was less yielding than the heavy bag. He was a Canadian champion and that fact alone made Moth feel he had participated in something historic. Now it had taken on a stranger meaning.

Sparks had fought Peter Schmidt, who had once gone ten rounds with Sugar Ray Robinson. Robinson had hit almost everybody, but if you wanted to connect with the heavyweights, he had fought Joey Maxim, who'd been up against Archie Moore. Moore had actually floored Rocky Marciano, who had knocked out Joe Louis, and Louis had demolished Max Schmeling in their famous one-round battle. You were already back to the Second World War with that fight. Schmeling hit Jack Sharkey during the dark days of boxing and the great Dempsey had belted Sharkey down and out. Dempsey won the title in 1919 from Jess Willard, who had beaten Jack Johnson or at least hit Jack Johnson, and Jack had beaten up Jim Jeffries. Jeffries fought James Corbett, who had lifted the crown from John L. Sullivan. There it was.

It was the dream, the funnel of time he had been launched through by the right hand of Travis. There were endless ways of seeing it. Jack Johnson had flattened Stanley Ketchel and Moth had seen himself as Ketchel during one trip down the tunnel. The same hair, anyway. Corbett had fought at least once on a barge. It was a thrilling and peculiar feeling, as though he was looking through the pages of a book and following God's finger along each line. Everyone who had fought in the ring might be part of the chain, but no one else had ever said they remembered it. It didn't count if you didn't remember.

Maybe it didn't stop at boxing. That might be nothing but the spine, running through the centre of time. They fought bare-knuckled before Sullivan. A long time before that, they fought in the Colosseum, hands wrapped with metal studs. Moth tried to remember the cestus. His history ran on a line of blood that stretched back to the Garden of Eden. That was his secret discovery. He'd hit Jake sparring, but it had only been a punch. Jake was connected to the beginning of time but would never know it.

He wondered whether his future travelled the same road. Some young fighter had hit and been hit and he would punch someone else who would eventually intersect with greatness. The punch would take all the blows Moth had inflicted and received and carry them to the end of time, when the final punch was thrown. He saw a dark, empty arena where the last two men fought to the death, but he didn't experience it. He couldn't remember the future existing in the fight against Travis.

Moth was starving. He wanted to go downstairs and eat toast and cereal all the way to dinnertime and then go on a strict diet tomorrow. It was a routine that played out every day and he tried to avoid thinking about it. He felt perpetually stuffed and empty and his stomach was still hard, but rounded. One of the Texas Rangers on *Laredo* had a muscular, dazzling physique that he maintained by riding a horse and shooting at outlaws. Men at the end of their ropes were unshaven and living in rooming houses until they were rescued by a crisis they alone could solve. They drank too much but never gained an ounce. No one got fat from despair. Some fighters became huge and bloated between fights, but you only saw them in the ring.

There was a light rapping on the bedroom door.

What? he said.

Beryl came in and stood by the door, looking unsure of herself. As though she had broken something of his and was trying to find the nerve to tell him.

How come you've stopped talking to me?

You haven't been talking to me, either, Moth said.

You haven't even asked me a question. What did I do to you?

Who said you did anything?

I didn't make her do it, said Beryl. She knew I was coming home.

She didn't know you were coming with Terry. She didn't know Dad would have to drive all the way to Kingston to get you.

I didn't have any choice with Terry, Beryl said. He beat up his father and then told me we were coming here. He scared me.

Oh, come on, Beryl.

You don't know him. You think you know him but you don't.

I quit school, Moth said. I don't know what I'm supposed to do. You and Terry just aren't that important to me right now.

What happened after they called here?

I was sleeping. I guess Dad left for Kingston and Mom went nuts. She must have been drunk.

Did she really go there with a knife and try to kill Mr Webb?

You're hearing that shit at school, he said. I was here. I woke up when she came back because she was making such a racket.

I like her better on tranquilizers.

Who doesn't?

Beryl looked at the broken hockey game on the floor and kicked at the little figures.

You believe in God, she said. Do you believe in the devil?

She took him by surprise. They had never talked about God and he no longer envisioned a panel of interested deities peering at his life. Moth knew there was one God and he was beginning to see it was a losing battle trying to please Him. God was a mystery, but the devil was easy to understand.

217

We're the devil, Moth said. We do everything they say the devil does. Something terrible happens and everyone blames God, but it's Satan. It's us. We do it. We're the fucking devil, all of us. You might as well say human when you say Satan.

Well, Beryl said, Terry is human.

I'm starving, Moth said.

He got up and walked past his sister without looking at her.

His mother had taken a rake from the Webbs' garage and smashed out the front window of their house. Bill Webb had been cut by flying glass, small gashes to the face that had bled copiously. He had gone outside when she started smashing all the other windows and she threw the rake at him, then her coat. She wore nothing under the coat. Neighbours woke up terrified by the noise and looked out their windows to see Kate Watson running through the snow wearing only a pair of boots, and Bill chasing her. He stopped when he realized blood was running into his eyes. She had lost her breath shortly after and walked the rest of the way.

Moth poured Cheerios into a bowl and Trevor came running into the kitchen.

I want some, he said.

Okay, Moth said, but I'm turning off the TV. You can have cereal or watch TV.

Moth had woken up when he heard the front door slam and his mother laughing as though she was being tickled. By the time he had got his clothes on and gone downstairs, she was sitting on the couch, crying. He wanted to kill her.

Go and put some fucking clothes on, he said. You have to stop this shit.

He felt his body shaking and he needed to sit down. It made him furious. The worst thing in the world was feeling one way when your body felt another. His mother could still make him cry. She would always win.

She wiped her eyes with her hands and looked at him like a confused child.

Take off my boots, she said.

Mom, look at yourself.

Please? she said.

Moth went to his mother and knelt at her feet. He didn't raise his eyes above her shins. She leaned slightly forward and ran her fingers through his hair while he unlaced her boots. It felt like the bell had sounded and everyone else had left the ring. There was no ref and no rules. You just made it up as you went along. He had unknotted the laces and tugged them free, making enough slack to slip off the boot without effort. He had felt graceful and skilled.

Moth ate the bowl of cereal and then filled the bowl again. He took a loaf of bread from the breadbox and put two pieces in the toaster. He saw his father's car mount the hump of snow in the driveway and he poured the cereal into the sink, then scooped out handfuls and stuck them in the garbage.

The police had come to the door just as Moth had put down the second boot and laid his head on his mother's knees.

Don't answer it.

Go upstairs, Mom.

He stood up and took her hands, then pulled her to her feet. Her eyes were still wet from crying. She was a beautiful woman and Moth wondered where his god damned father was. He was afraid to kiss her.

Go upstairs.

The doorbell had rung again. Moth had gone to the door and leaned against it as she went up to her room. He didn't want to watch. When he'd heard the click of her door, he had opened the front door of the house. It was the young cop, the one that had come to the club that night. The cop had had his mother's coat in his hands.

Moth popped up the bread in the toaster and dropped it into the garbage bag as his father entered the house. He heard Trevor say that he was hungry. The hangers rattled in the hall closet and then the door was shut and his father was in the kitchen.

Is your mother sleeping? his father asked.

Yes.

Where's Beryl?

I think she's in her room.

His father pulled out a chair and sat at the table. Moth wished he'd go upstairs so he could eat.

What the hell are we going to do about food? his father said. They take so long to deliver the damned thing.

There's stuff in the freezer.

Your mother's the only one who knows how to cook it.

We could have sandwiches, Moth said.

His father rubbed his face and sighed. Moth hated the sound of it as much as Kate did.

Let's see what your sister has to say, Tim said.

Moth left his father sitting at the table. He walked past the front door and had the urge to open it, walk outside and disappear. There was nowhere to hide in the house any more. Trevor was here almost all day long and now his mother was sick and there was no way to avoid speaking to his father.

Beryl was still in his room. She sat on Trevor's bed and looked at a tiny metal hockey player in her hand.

We can't all be Satan, Beryl said.

Why not? You can fight it, but that's your natural self.

There's good people too.

Moth stretched out on his bed. There was a speck on the ceiling he kept meaning to investigate every time he lay down, but forgot about when he sat up. Maybe a squashed mosquito from the summer. It reminded him that Beryl had thrown a rock through his window and that she was probably insane. His mother had smashed windows with a rake. It all meant nothing.

Dad says we can eat sandwiches for dinner, he said.

You hate me, don't you?

You're asking me weird questions.

We drove all the way back from Kingston and he hardly said a word. He didn't ask me anything, even. Just like you.

I'm not like him, Beryl, Moth said.

Terry killed Soldier.

Moth kept looking at the speck. He imagined that the room was tipped up on its side and the speck was on the wall across from him. He could just walk over and look at it. That wasn't true. It would be high up on the wall and he'd be standing where his dresser stood. There would be no room for the beds or anything else if that wall became the floor.

Okay, Moth said.

You don't believe me.

I don't know. I'm not a cop, why tell me?

His limbs felt like rubber and he didn't want to think about anything new. He wanted Beryl to go away and he wanted his father to order Chinese food. He turned his head and looked at his sister. She was turning the hockey player in her hands.

Terry is full of shit, Moth said.

Beryl nodded without raising her eyes. She stood up and looked at Moth.

Do you know a girl called Darlene Bain?

No, he said.

She turned away and he heard her walk down the stairs. He got up and closed the door behind her. Moth went around the side of his bed and knelt down, lifted the mattress and took out his notebook. He was about to sit down and instead he stepped up onto the bed and stood in the centre. He leaned over and put his hand against the wall for balance and looked up. It was a dark, round speck that looked like a drop of paint. It must have always been there.

He stepped off the bed and sat on the edge. He took the pen clipped to the top of his notebook and flipped through pages until he reached his latest entry. He put the book on his knees and wrote, *I would go crazy except for Bob Dylan.*

Moth closed his notebook and replaced the pen. He stuffed it back between the mattress and box spring, then stretched out on top of the bed. He thought about Donna.

ii

Maybe everything on TV was true and everyone Beryl knew was crazy. It was possible. Fathers weren't always bad-tempered and silent and mothers didn't act like they were prison wardens. Of course, you had to act the way the kids acted. That was possible as well. There was no reason why Terry couldn't have been a guy who went to school and had some ambition and didn't have a drunk pig for a father. Lots of guys played football and didn't get into fights at dances. Lots of girls didn't run away from home. They went to school every day and didn't get drunk at lunch hour. She could do it. She wasn't stupid.

She didn't think that Satan was everybody in the world. That was exactly the kind of thing Moth would believe. He liked being unhappy. Probably thought it meant that he was smart, which it didn't. There was nothing that smart about her brother. Rotten in school and he was always grouchy. Moth didn't have the guts to be Terry and he couldn't be his father and his only choice was to be Moth, which wasn't much. Stay in the house and feel bad all the time. People are not the devil.

She knew the attraction, though. Why you would go with the devil rather than God made perfect sense to her, even though it seemed so crazy when she was a kid. They were always selling their souls in movies or on scary TV shows and they always got screwed. He either tricked you or your life was short. Then you had an eternity in hell and it was impossible to see that as being worth it. The trouble was, you could see what the devil has to offer and nobody knew what heaven was like. It was scary to think it might be like church. Satan gives you money and clothes and a dream house and God lets you suffer and makes promises. The devil is here and the devil is now. He makes you feel like you're God.

Maybe Terry had no mother at all and never had. He might have grown like moss on the side of a tree. If he hadn't killed someone he'd just be a bad guy. If he didn't make you want him even when you knew what he'd done, he'd be like a lot of guys in the South End. Terry knew how to make you belong to him. It takes the devil's help to do that, when you're a killer. Darlene Bain was probably an evil bitch who fucked animals. Darlene wants to kill her parents and knows Terry will help. Darlene belongs to him and Beryl belongs at home.

She didn't believe that really wholesome guys could be good at sex. You heard that it was beautiful and holy, but you had to be married and they didn't say anything about feeling like the roller coaster had just flown off the tracks. Like you were at the very bottom of the loop going as fast as it was going to go and the whole train went right through the guardrail. You can taste the sweat on his shoulder and you just want to tear the skin right off his back. You don't care if you die right then. Maybe that's how you know it doesn't come from God – you don't care if you live or die. Sex was probably very nice with the right guy and she was sure it felt lovely. Guys like Terry just make you crazy. Making love came from God and fucking came from Satan.

You don't get the good stuff all by itself, either. It's like finding an ad for the devil and missing the tiny print at the bottom saying prohibited in some states or void in New York. Terry was like the end of the world when they were lying down, but the small print says he might kill you. He fucks other girls. He doesn't make any money and he drinks and he beats up his own father. He grabs you by the throat if you say something he doesn't like.

222

You want to be with a guy who won't take any shit, but sometimes he thinks you're the one giving it to him.

His foot was on his father's chest and his face had about as much expression as an insect. She could see right then that he was blind to everybody else in the world and the only song he heard was one that played just for him. She wanted him anyway. She wanted to ride with Terry forever, all the way down the highway to the end. Darlene was the one thing that destroyed every hope and dream. You could overlook what happened to Soldier, but Terry couldn't love her the way she loved him and still fuck Darlene. It was impossible. You can't ride to the end of the road with a guy who isn't completely nuts for you. Terry wasn't nuts for Darlene, probably, but maybe he wasn't nuts for anybody. Maybe Terry was just nuts.

She could change everything and she would. Marcel was never a match for Terry and she'd get along fine without him. She had to stop falling in love. It was the songs that made you fall in love, not TV. Well, that wasn't true. It was the songs that made you think about it and remember it and it was songs that made you cry. She wondered if anyone had ever cried over a TV show. You couldn't look at Ralph and Alice and say God, that reminds me of being in love. No, it was the Supremes and the Beatles and Jackie DeShannon who reminded you. Gene Pitney and Roy Orbison and the Animals and not the songs Moth played over and over in his room. He probably doesn't think there is any such thing as love, either. People are the devil and music is probably mud. It sticks to his feet and makes him swear and lets him enjoy his lousy mood.

She would be a daughter. Her mother was obviously crazy and she should have realized that a long time ago. It wasn't her mother's fault. She could be a daughter to her mother and ignore all her insults and stupid ways of making fun. Her mother had lost her mind and Beryl could handle her. No wonder her father was so wound up all the time. She was going to go to school every single day, she was not going to drink, she was not going to have sex on the golf course. It was over. If you act like that, you've made the devil your friend. You trust him and then he screws you. Just like Terry.

He was on the side of death. God had opened her eyes and let her see and now everything was fine. She knew better. If you leave the road, before you know it you're lost. Things happen to you like they did in her mother's magazines. You get raped and tortured and buried in the sand. You leave the road and it is always night in a strange place and there is never any town in sight. You leave the road and then you die. That was all the choice you had. You could stay on the road or leave it and die.

iii

Bishop told Terry his mother was dead. She had died in Massachusetts in a head-on collision when Terry was less than a year old. There were two people in her car and three in the other and everyone had been killed, then burned. Killed immediately. No one had been trapped inside either car, burning to death. He made sure Terry knew that. It had taken the police a long time to make an identification.

I'm sorry, Bishop said, but there it is.

I need to find a woman named Sharon Ticehurst.

Good luck to you. Our deal was that I find out what happened to your mother.

This woman, she might be my mother, said Terry.

Jesus Christ. You can forget it. Your father was married to this woman and she left when you were already born, so you can fuck yourself, kid. I did what I said I'd do. Now it's your turn.

I killed Soldier, Terry said.

How?

I picked up a rock and hit him with it.

The whole thing, Bishop said.

He was standing right in front of me, looking at everyone by the fire. They were maybe, I don't know, a hundred feet away? The bikes were just a little bit in front of us. I hit him and I ran down the hill and back to my car.

What was Henry Godin doing? He wasn't just standing there looking at Barnes.

I couldn't see anything, said Terry. I looked up at the moon and then I looked at Soldier and then I picked up the rock.

You hit him to impress Godin, said Bishop. So why run?

Why do I want to impress Henry Godin?

I don't know. I'm asking.

The moon had a lot to do with it.

What are you, a fucking werewolf? Bishop said.

He stood up and walked the width of the office and then sat down again.

He stood up. He walked. The kid had sat right there and lied to his face when they picked him up the first time. He looked more scared then than he did now and there was no reason for him not to be terrified. He was confessing to a murder. Bishop stopped walking. They could hang him.

I'm going to write down what you've said, Bishop told him, and you're going to sign it.

No.

Yes.

I said I'd tell you what happened, Terry said. Well, I told you.

Bishop unclipped the holster from his belt and lay it down on a desktop. The short-barrelled revolver was held fast by a single strap beneath the hammer. He unlocked the bottom drawer of the desk and put the holstered gun inside, then locked it again. He tucked the key into his pants pocket and walked over to Terry, who stood up when they were just over an arm's length from each other. Bishop's jaw tightened and Terry was expressionless.

Sit down, he told Terry.

If you're going to get rough, do it while I'm standing up.

You're not going to fight me, you fucking asshole. I'm the police.

I can't just stand here, Terry explained.

Bishop moved his face closer. He had a couple of inches on the kid and a lot of pounds. He waited for a crack in the bravado, but none appeared. This guy was crazy.

Do you know how long you'd last in a fight with me?

How long?

Bishop would have dropped him on the spot if there'd been any hint of a challenge or dare, or even if the kid was angry. Terry looked grave, not unconcerned. He had no arrogance and no fear. He had delivered what he'd promised, but he wasn't going to give any more than that. Beating him up wasn't going to change his mind or make Bishop feel any better. There was no point to it, now he knew the kid was crazy. You could beat up a tough guy and turn him tender, but you got nothing but broken hands from the insane.

He hit him anyway. Faked a right and then hooked his left hard into the kid's cheekbone and watched him stagger two paces before he caught himself. Bishop raised his hand, palm out, as Terry took a step forward.

That was for your father, he said.

He had it coming.

It doesn't matter. You can't punch your old man in the head.

I'm not signing anything, Terry said.

They stared at each other and Bishop watched the kid's eyes. He hadn't gone down from a pretty good shot and he looked like he was ready to throw one of his own. Terry was going to lose, but he was seventeen years old and even landing one was the same as winning. Getting beat up by a cop wasn't losing a fight.

You hit like a girl, Bishop. Like a fucking girl, Terry said.

He lowered his hands and stepped over to the chair, not even looking at the cop. Bishop felt himself blush, but made no move. Terry sat down.

You think you're pretty tough.

Yes, Terry said. We could step outside, you know? You take off your gun and your badge and tell me you're just another guy. I've seen cops do that. Like they don't have the whole department and the city and even the newspapers on their side. Like anybody would believe you guys grab guys like me just to beat us up. There's always two of you, at least. You call that tough? I don't.

There's only one of me here, said Bishop.

Yeah, here. In the fucking cop shop. You want to whale on me, you do it. But don't think you're tough.

It had become a bad dream for Bishop. He didn't understand how things had turned out this way. He would have to pound on this kid, but he was going to have to cuff him to the chair first. Even Henry Godin wouldn't try talking like this. Godin was too smart. This kid was suicidal.

He grabbed the chair behind his desk and pulled it over, then sat down a few feet away from Terry.

You're a tough kid, maybe, but you're stupid, he said.

Terry gave him a small smile, like he'd heard it all before. The kid's asshole father had made everything impossible for every other guy who would ever have to deal with him. Bishop knew it was too late. He'd clocked the kid and there was no turning back.

I could make you sign anything, Bishop said. Admit it.

Try it.

No. Think before you open your mouth. I get my partner in here, we cuff your hands, we start whacking you in the balls. See?

You can't make me sign anything, Terry said.

Bishop heard his own breathing become erratic. They were going to have to hospitalize this guy and he didn't want to do it. It was stupid. Terry was leaving him no choice.

Your girlfriend got sent back home, Bishop said. We'll bring her back.

So what?

So if she knows anything, if you told her about this, then she's an accessory after the fact. We'll have to keep her locked up until the trial. She already has a record of flight.

Bishop was inventing it as fast as he could. Terry's expression didn't change.

Even if you didn't tell her, how do we know that? We'll charge her.

All right, Terry said. Write down what I told you. I killed him. I'll sign.

Bishop tried not to show his relief. His muscles unknotted and he leaned back in the chair. Terry would sign a confession. The crime had been solved and the case was closed and Bishop had done almost all of it on his own.

Henry Godin, he said. You know that piece of shit is a rapist? Picks a girl up and then turns her over to his buddies. He'll break her nose or knock out her teeth if she gives him any trouble. Some kid tried to protect his girlfriend and Godin had him held down and yanked out his front teeth with pliers. I'm not making this up.

I've heard about it, said Terry.

Think about the things you haven't heard about. If everyone knows this stuff, what is it you don't know? That cocksucker is a killer.

I'm a killer, said Terry.

You killed a guy, one guy, a lunatic. He was just like you. Henry Godin, he's a different kind of guy altogether. Him and his fucking gang.

I'm tired, Terry said. I've been tired since Kingston.

You'd better listen with both ears. You're not going to sign a confession. You understand that? You're not going to tell anybody you killed Clarence Barnes. Right?

I already told my girlfriend.

Yeah, well, Bishop said. Henry Godin is going to prison for it. I'm going to make sure he goes there for a long time. Am I going to get any trouble out of you?

Terry looked into the cop's face, trying to discover what this was all about. It felt unreal, but it was exactly what he'd known would happen. He wasn't going to sign a confession and Henry Godin was going to the pen. All he hadn't figured was the co-operation of the police.

What's going on?

Henry Godin, said Bishop. He's the only thing that's happening.

What about me?

Are you listening? Go home. Go back to school. Keep your mouth shut, even to other cops. Quit hitting your father.

I need to know about Sharon Ticehurst, Terry said.

Bishop laughed.

You're pushing your luck, Terry.

I'm not trying to make a deal, Terry said. I'm asking for a favour.

We're finished here, Bishop said.

He stood up and went back to the desk and unlocked the bottom drawer. Terry got to his feet and watched him. The holster snapped onto his belt on the left side, the handle facing backward. Bishop was left-handed, Terry realized. He should have noticed.

Go home, Bishop said.

Terry walked out of the office and went home.

Jerry was on the phone when the front door opened. He hung up, then picked up a baseball bat that was leaning against the couch and held it like he was expecting to swing at a pitch. The bat still had the white price sticker showing.

I thought, he said to Terry, but lost the rest of it.

I was with the cops. Who is Sharon Ticehurst?

Jerry looked confused, as though he knew the name but couldn't attach a face to it.

Why is everybody talking about her all of a sudden? he asked. It's a girl Olive knows. Olive at The Plant.

You told me she was my mother.

I was drunk.

You're drunk right now, Terry said.

You try me again, I'll open your fucking head.

You went out with this Ticehurst woman, right?

Terry. You don't know. Somebody was just on the phone and I can't remember who it was. See what I mean?

Dad, Terry said quietly, I'm going to kill you. You're too drunk to use the

228

bat and I'm going to beat you to death with it. You want to count to three or should I?

One, his father said, grinning.

Two, said Terry, taking a step toward him.

Hey, hey, hey. Just a second. You're not giving me a chance to think. Sharon. I knew her from work. We went to a hotel a couple of times, she still lived with her parents. I mean, she wasn't a kid.

You went with her, but you were married.

I was drinking a lot, Jerry said. Awful fucking fights with your mother.

My mother.

Look, we were married. Wasn't she your mother?

Terry saw that he was genuinely baffled. He looked afraid and wounded, as though he'd just woke up screaming and couldn't remember the nightmare. Jerry looked at him for help.

You got this woman pregnant, Terry said.

It was Shirley. On the phone. I just need a second to think.

Pregnant.

Who?

Terry slid closer and kicked the bat out of his father's hands. It bounced off the wall and then hit the floor with a damp thud.

Terry. Please.

Who was my mother?

There's only one woman I ever loved, Jerry said.

He brought his head down nearly to his knees and made a high-pitched squeal like a pig in a slaughterhouse. His body shook and he squealed again. Terry backed away and felt his mouth go dry. He saw his father digging his fingers into his face and watched the veins bulge in his temples and he turned and ran outside. He slammed the door behind him and kept running. It was worse than listening to Richie Bender. He was in the car and halfway to the Pinklon before he even knew he'd turned the key in the ignition.

He reached for the radio but didn't turn it on, afraid of what might be playing. Music saved your life, but it could kill you as well. Richie and the Righteous Brothers. "Needles and Pins." His father liked all those old songs they never played any more. There were songs they sang together when he was a little kid, but Terry couldn't remember them now. "Sixteen Tons." He knew that one, he knew the cowboy one, he knew too many. Darlene liked "I

Got You Babe." Everybody liked the fucking Beatles.

It was early to be at the Pinklon and the lot was only half full. Most guys with a job and a car would turn up after they'd gone home and had dinner. He dug through his pockets and found enough change for one beer, if he didn't leave a tip. He wondered if Darlene was home.

Terry thought he should fight Jimmy O'Hara or maybe Randy Zed. Jimmy would just be a fight, but Randy would be a real test. He needed sleep or liquor. What he really needed to do was go toe to toe with Bishop. He tried to rest his head on the front seat, but he could feel every muscle stretching like he was hanging from a ledge. Randy Zed. Beating Jimmy would mean nothing. He had felt just this way the night he had met his father accidentally and he'd gone over to see Darlene instead. That's how it all started, or ended, with Beryl. Girls aren't what you need. It just feels that way. You need your mother.

He crossed the alley, where no serious disputes were ever resolved, and entered through the back door. He couldn't fight Randy behind the Pinklon, it had no standing whatsoever. Men so drunk they could hardly stay upright swung and kicked each other into bloody submission in the alley after closing time. Only a coward started a fight in the bar. You could blindside a man and land a storm of unanswered punches before the bouncers came and pulled you away. Unless you were Soldier.

Terry went directly to the bar, where a waiter was loading up his tray.

Do you know a woman named Olive? Terry asked him. From The Plant?

The waiter nodded toward the middle of the room. Terry saw women with men, women with women, at least two women sitting alone. He hated waiters. He went to the table of a very thin woman who sat unaccompanied.

Is your name Olive?

Are you trying to be funny? she asked.

Terry.

He turned around and saw three women sitting together a couple of tables away. They wore skirts and sweaters and the one who waved at him looked older than the other two. He'd seen her here many times before. She stayed late and her shoulders became hunched when she drank and Terry remembered her because she stared right into your face when she walked by. Older women never seemed scared of anything. Not in the Pinklon, anyway. He walked over to the table.

You're Terry, the woman said.

Is your name Olive?

He knew she worked at The Plant because of the way she dressed. Olive got to her feet and looked at her friends, who were staring at him.

Jerry Delaney's boy, she said.

She took Terry by the sleeve of his coat and led him to a vacant corner, balancing half a glass of beer in her other hand. They sat at a table that tilted an inch when she put down her beer.

Don't touch the table, Olive said. You want a drink?

Sure.

Terry counted out his change and laid it carefully on the table while she flagged the waiter.

I can't tip him, he said.

Olive watched his face and smiled. She wasn't so bad-looking. She stared like a vice-principal trying to make you crack. Not quite like a cop. Maybe mothers looked at their kids this way, finding out their secrets. The waiter arrived and put two glasses on the table and Olive paid him with a bill from her purse, ignoring Terry's nickels and quarters. The waiter put down her change and left.

You can't tip them every round, Olive said. Who could afford to drink?

My father said I should talk to you.

I doubt it.

He said you knew somebody called Sharon Ticehurst.

He might have said that, Olive said, but I wonder how it came up?

Can I call you Olive?

She smiled and sipped her beer. He saw that her eyes were wet.

You'd better tell me how much you want to know, she said.

My father said that Sharon Ticehurst is my mother. I don't know if you know this, but he's crazy. He says different things about my mother every ten minutes.

Everybody knows Jerry is nuts, she said. Sorry.

Do you know her?

I shouldn't tell you anything, Olive said. If your father wasn't the way he was, he'd do it himself. I don't want to be mean. When Betty left him, he went to hell. Every guy goes to hell, but your dad just stayed there. Do you know what happened to Betty?

She was killed in an accident.

Yes. Jerry always thought she'd come back.

Can you tell me the whole thing? Do you know it all?

I knew Betty and I know Sharon. That's more or less the whole story, don't you think? Do you want to know it? Olive asked.

Terry drank his beer without pause until the glass was empty. He gasped and caught his breath. Olive waved to the waiter and poured half her fresh glass into Terry's. He drank it.

You don't look like him, but you sure drink like him.

I only have enough money for one beer, Terry said, but I need to drink.

Don't worry about it.

The waiter came, delivered and left. Terry and Olive both took a big gulp from their new drinks and set the glasses down.

Your dad got involved with Sharon a few times. It happened before he met Betty and then it started again after he was married.

What a son of a bitch, Terry said.

It happens. Sharon's a sweet girl and she always liked him. She got pregnant and that's when the trouble happened. Sharon would have killed herself before she would have tried to have a miscarriage. It had already happened before and it's just the way she was. It's the way she is.

He got her pregnant. My mother, Betty, was she pregnant, too?

No. Sharon got pregnant by Jerry and you were born. She couldn't keep you on her own. She already lived with her parents with her first kid and they weren't going to take on another one.

How many kids does she have?

Well, that's a whole different story. She was a widow. It was an accident at The Plant. The point is, she thought your dad should marry her. Nothing in the world would ever make Jerry leave Betty. He was working nights when Sharon showed up with you and told her the whole story. She left you with Betty and then Betty left you with your father. That must have been a hell of a night.

This woman, Sharon, she left me there?

There wasn't much she could do, Terry. You think you would have been better off in an orphanage?

I want to meet her, he said.

That's going to be kind of difficult, Olive said.

I'm not going to hurt her, Olive.

I don't mean that. She finally got a guy who married her. He's a moron, but she likes him. They live in Kirkland Lake now. Also, this moron doesn't know about you.

Terry took out his wallet and tugged the pictures of Betty Delaney free. He handed them across the table.

Oh my God.

Why don't you keep them? She was a friend of yours.

Olive looked at the pictures one after another. She didn't look sad, but surprised.

She was a kid, Olive said.

What is Sharon Ticehurst like?

Olive handed back the photographs, but he didn't take them.

Give them to your father. Don't be so awful, she said.

He saw Randy Zed come into the bar alone and watched him scan tables. Their eyes met but they didn't acknowledge each other. Randy went to the isolation zone and sat down. Terry didn't feel like fighting him. He took the photographs from Olive and stuck them back into his wallet.

What she's like, she's a woman who wants kids. Her husband didn't get along with her other boy and look what happened. What I'll do, I'll write her and tell her you want to talk to her.

I can't wait that long.

You can't go making trouble for her. She's had a hell of a time of it.

Betty would never have done what she did, he said.

Grow up.

He didn't know what to say or do next. His mother was nothing more than a name to him, a name spoken in a smoky bar by a drunk office worker. He didn't even like the name Sharon. Betty was a mother's name. He had nowhere to go and he needed to drink. He reached across the table and held Olive's hand.

I don't know what I'm saying, he said.

She waved at the waiter and smiled at Terry.

That's all right, Terry. You just need a drink.

He wondered if he'd have to have sex with her. She probably wouldn't expect it, but he'd seen old strangers maul one another after closing time. The alley wasn't solely a domain of violence. He saw she wore a wedding ring and wondered if her husband would show up. Maybe he knew everything about his life. Maybe everybody knew.

Does everyone know about this? Sharon is my mother?

233

Not many people, Olive said.

The waiter arrived and she made a quick negotiation. Terry forced himself to wait until she picked up a glass before taking one for himself.

Thanks a lot.

She was here a while ago. Sharon. She just came down for a day or so. He won't let her see old friends, her husband. One of those guys. And it was just so damned sad.

Did she see me? Was I here? Terry asked.

No. She asked about you and I told her you were a big, handsome kid. Which you are.

She came here to see her other kid, right? That kid knows her.

It was so sad, you can't even imagine. Her boy was killed. You must have heard about it. Somebody killed him down at the lake.

Terry stopped drinking.

Her poor parents. They had nothing but trouble with him since the day he was born and now he's dead, Olive said.

Murdered.

Yes. Sharon couldn't take him with her, but she loved him. Can you understand that?

Yes, he said.

She wants them to hang the guy that did it. I hope to God they do.

Clarence Barnes, Terry said. Everyone called him Soldier.

God. You knew him, said Olive.

CHAPTER ELEVEN

i

Moth worked at the carpet factory for almost three months. All he had to do was change spools when the wool disappeared and wheel around long spindles of jute twice a night. The factory was two miles from The Plant and Moth got a ride from anyone in Valentine who was working nights. Anyone but Bill Webb. Most of them took him right to the factory and all of them asked him why he didn't get a job through his father and make some real money. The men he worked with lived north of the factory and he had to hitchhike to get back home after his shift. The police approached him on two different nights while he was standing at the side of the road and never bothered him again. Sometimes he flagged down a cab, but they were rare and he hated spending the money.

It changed and then ended after one Friday's shift. He was picked up by a young guy who had almost no English and who drove him right to his door. His name was Yves and Moth explained his situation in horrible French and simple English words. Yves did something and lived somewhere and Moth smiled and nodded as though he understood everything he heard.

Yves picked him up on Monday night and drove him home again and Moth gave him a closer look. He was probably in his early twenties and a little on the thin side. Not skinny and soft, that dreadful combination, but more like – he tried to think. Terry. It was a weird comparison. More like Terry when he was younger. Taller than Moth and with a leaner, less bulky look about him. Yves had full lips and beamed when he smiled. It made Moth smile back. He wished he knew the language.

On Tuesday Moth showered and washed everything twice. He cut his fingernails and looked for a different shirt than the two he wore all week. He chose a black t-shirt and wore it under his blue sweater. The green sweater was for work and it was thick and had a multitude of loose threads. He wished he had stopped being such a glutton. He considered doing push-ups but the effect would be lost by the time he finished working that night.

Yves was waiting in the parking lot when Moth left the factory, and he got into the car without changing his grim, tired expression in case enthusiasm made him transparent. He sneaked a glance around the lot and no one was paying any attention. Moth tried a bright, sunny smile. It made him feel like a girl in the ninth grade.

Music? Moth asked.

Yves shook his head and jabbed the radio with his index finger. He hit buttons and turned knobs and nothing happened. He talked while he demonstrated and Moth understood it was broken. That mystery was solved. Most drivers had to shout to be heard over the screaming, stupid deejays playing the same six songs every hour. Yves asked him a question and laughed when Moth smiled but didn't know what he'd been asked.

Bob Dylan? asked Yves.

Moth almost shouted. They both started naming titles at once. Yves ran off a long sentence very quickly and said, God said out on Highway 61, in clear and perfect English. Better than perfect. With an accent. Moth loved the way he said "Like a Rolling Stone" and wondered how he could make him say it again. Yves asked a question and then repeated it very slowly, as though the words could be understood at half speed. Moth held his hands out, palms up, and shook his head.

No? Yves asked.

Again. Say it again. Encore.

Yves repeated it, paused, and then said, My house?

Go to your house? Moth asked. Now?

Now? Yes.

Maintenant?

Oui, Yves said, maintenant.

He saw that Yves wasn't quite as tall as he'd thought, once they were out of the car. The house had a gravel driveway and was as utterly dark and silent as every other home in the neighbourhood. It was a bungalow with a small front yard and a hedge no taller than a row of tulips. Yves led him past the garbage cans at the side of the house to the backyard and then down three concrete steps to a basement door. Moth felt anxious and alert and looked him over again, from the back. Lean, but he appeared strong across the shoulders. If it was something strange, he could take this guy. Get inside those long legs and arms and take him down, then hit him so his head smacks the floor. One good shot would do it.

He followed him into the basement, which was as dark as a cave. He could hear both of them breathing, but couldn't see a thing. And then there was light. Yves turned around and motioned Moth to close the outside door. He looked different under the overhead light than he had in the car. Moth wondered how he looked to Yves.

There was fake wood panelling and not a single poster on the walls. The shadows were as dark as paint. Yves turned on a small lamp and flicked off the overhead light and the room lost its hard edge. There was a single bed, a throw rug, a small stereo in the corner. The ceiling was only inches above their heads and four paces would cover the distance from the door to the back wall. Moth loved it. Yves picked up a stack of albums that leaned against the stereo and handed them over, one at a time. Dylan, Dylan, and Dylan. Moth wondered how they were going to play a record when people were probably sleeping six feet above them. He smiled and handed the LPS back and Yves leaned forward and kissed him softly on the lips.

No man had ever kissed him before, or attempted to. The thought made Moth sick, but reality trampled his expectation. He had never done anything other than lower his pants in the front seat of strange cars and now it had all changed. Ricky Charles, but that was kid stuff. Yves wasn't going to motion him to pull down his pants and Moth wasn't going to convince himself that he was bored and making a trade for a ride home. This was this.

He stood on his tiptoes for a long, deep kiss and felt their chins scrape. Yves wasn't so much taller, but Moth wanted the feeling of standing like that and being kissed. Girls did it in comic books. He and Yves pulled off each other's coats and he held the narrow hips and closed his eyes while his shirt was unbuttoned. He would have stayed in shape had he known this was his future. Tomorrow he was going to begin. He felt a light touch on his chest and then a kiss. Yves had him by the arms and was trying to move him toward the bed. Moth opened his eyes.

The light, he said.

Light?

Turn off the light.

Yves looked at the lamp and back at Moth and shook his head. Moth gave up any idea of control and then he was shirtless and being kissed on the neck and he fumbled open the buttons on Yves' shirt. He was sitting, then lying, on a thick blanket and raising his hips for his jeans to be yanked off. He reached for Yves and his hands were gently moved away. His heart pounded as though he was fighting the last round and even while he was dizzy with romance his body was still taking a dip in cold water. Anything he said was going to make even less of a difference than usual.

Yves was leaning over him, one denim knee between Moth's bare legs while he held down his wrists. The knee moved higher and rubbed against him and it all began to work, just like it worked in his dreams, better than his own hand in the bathroom at home, better than Donna. He was naked and helpless and about to be possessed. He hoped Yves made him do things he had never even heard about before.

I feel so dirty, he said.

It was the greatest feeling he'd ever known or would ever know and he wished he could speak French just for tonight. He wanted to say that people talked about this like it's something you do in a starched collar with classical music on the stereo and feeling like you've just planted roses in the garden. They talk like it happens on a warm, bright day when bread is baking and love is written in pink, gothic letters. Moth saw the pictures but didn't have the words. He wanted to say whatever it is you say when you feel so dirty and so glad to be dirty and the night is dark and the room is awful and neither of you understands what the other one is saying. Yves kissed him so hard he thought his lips would bruise. Maybe they would. He wished Yves would look and see how well it was working.

His body felt hard and muscular and his stomach was fine when he was lying down like this. He wished he could see himself and watch the soft hands and long fingers trace the shadows along every contour. He wished he could be Yves. Their chests rubbed together with hardly a hair between them. The denim-covered legs knelt on the bed and one wrist came free as the hand holding it dropped away to unbuckle and unzip. Moth was conscious of his mouth being open and he licked his lips with the tip of his tongue. Their hipbones touched, his wrist was held, he felt Yves force himself between his knees and Moth raised and separated his legs. He lifted his head and kissed and was kissed and he moaned.

There was nothing to understand. He knew the way it made him feel and he silently sang praises to the Lord. Yves held him down and kissed his neck and slid his stomach over his and Moth raised his legs higher and wrapped them around the thin, hard body and silently sang praises to the

Lord. This was here and now and everything. It all belonged to God.

ii

Moth got home just a few minutes before his father left for work. Tim wondered whether there was a graveyard shift at the carpet factory.

I went out with a couple of guys, Moth said.

How do you like the job?

I don't know.

He took a box of Shreddies out of the cupboard, then pondered it. Maybe he should start eating fruit in the morning. They never had any in the house. He decided the cereal was okay, but he'd have to forgo the toast. They should get skim milk.

He wished his father would disappear.

A shift is eight hours, said Moth. You're supposed to sleep eight hours, too. The rest of the time, when you're not travelling to work or getting home, you're supposed to have your life, right? That's insane. You get a third for yourself.

You can't still be on about that?

Moth hadn't even thought about it since he'd started working. It was an old complaint that had become more compelling ever since boxing stopped making sense. He would never be a professional fighter. God had given him boxing and it had stopped school from being a nightmare. He had given it to him so that Travis could hit him and take him through time.

Just because I'm doing it doesn't mean it isn't nuts, said Moth.

Well, Tim said, I've been doing it a long time. I shouldn't have to explain it to you at your age.

They take your life away from you.

You are what you do. That's who you are. If you're what you do, then you get two-thirds of a life. That's as much as you can get without giving up sleeping.

You think a general foreman is who you are? Moth asked.

I have a trade and I was promoted. I'm raising a family. I'm a husband. That's what I do and it's who I am.

Moth was shocked. His father had no need to defend himself and had never engaged him before. Even Moth didn't expect him to take it seriously. It was embarrassing.

239

You want to think about what you're doing, Moth, his father said.

He got to his feet and went into the hall for his coat. Moth heard the sigh. He took milk from the fridge and poured it over the Shreddies, then put the bowl on the table. He had to learn to shut up. He knew the answers about working and he knew the secret: don't have children. Everyone used kids as the excuse for everything. If you didn't have them, nothing could make you live where you didn't want to live and do things you didn't want to do. He wouldn't have any children. Especially if he was queer.

I'll see you later, his father said, exhaling in the hall.

Yeah.

He heard the front door open and close and watched his father walk past the window. You want to watch what you're doing. Maybe it showed all over his face in ways that only an adult could see. His lips might be swollen and his face rubbed raw. His father might think he'd had a fight. Maybe you could smell Yves all over him. Or maybe he looked like a different guy altogether.

He went to bed just as Trevor was waking up and fell asleep being shot at with a bent cardboard tube. He woke up in the early afternoon feeling drugged and beautiful and wanting to sing. His bedroom door was open and he pulled his jeans under the covers and dragged them on. He picked up his T-shirt and smelled it, but there was no hint of Yves. He wished he had taken something of his.

Moth stood under the shower for five minutes before the water turned cold. Wash day. He got dressed and went downstairs.

His mother sat at the kitchen table in her dressing gown, a magazine held open with an empty plate. There was an overexposed black-and-white shot of a woman in her underwear crammed into the trunk of a car. It spread across two pages. The woman's hands were tied behind her back with what looked like nylons. The usual indistinct faces of men in fedoras stared down at her.

Tea in the pot, his mother said.

Moth thought there were two reasons why his mother had changed. At least, changed as much as she was going to change. She treated him differently because he was working and no longer a school kid, and she had a new attitude toward everything else because of the pills she took.

You slept in today.

I went out with some guys after work, Moth said.

Bludgeoned to death, his mother said. I've never liked that. Why not say she was hit over the head and she died? Bludgeoned.

Moth poured a mug of tea and wondered if the magazine used the same pictures for different stories. The corpse was a Pretty Co-ed or Missing Housewife or Blackmailing Secretary, whatever they needed. Maybe the stories themselves weren't even true.

Your magazines always have that picture, he said. Or one just like it.

Yours have men being punched in the face. I can't tell them apart.

He wanted to argue, but didn't. Anyone could tell the difference between Willie Pastrano and Flash Elorde. He saw Yves wearing boxing trunks in the ring with him, jabbing while Moth ducked and charged. He should have asked for his number. Pointless. Yves on the basement floor, a black pool of blood spreading from his head to the rug. Sex Deviant killed by Hitchhiker. His room looked like it was waiting for the right subject before it could be photographed. A close-up of Moth's dead face, one eye mysteriously missing and the socket filled with dried blood. Slain Hitchhiker.

He wondered what a picture from last night would look like, a picture of the two of them. If you could even get pictures like that.

Doris Summerhill takes Valium, said Kate. She told me she started taking it because she peed her pants whenever she had to talk. Whenever she had to talk to more than one person at a time. I asked her if it worked and she said she still pees her pants, but it doesn't bother her any more.

Nice story.

It's perfect, said Kate. Valentine doesn't bother me any more.

Moth didn't want to hear about his mother and Valentine. He didn't want to know why she'd run naked through the street or smashed windows at the Webb house. She was quiet most of the time and it made everybody happier, except his father. Nothing made his father happy.

Beryl came home from school every day and helped with dinner. Moth knew it couldn't last, but it had, Beryl and her mother side by side in the kitchen. She couldn't cook but she did it anyway. The house felt strange without his mother and his sister in it. The two of them had become copies of the originals, but without the grotty substance. It was like living in a place haunted by their ghosts.

He took his tea back upstairs. If he counted the cereal he'd eaten when he came home, then he'd already had breakfast. Maybe he should move directly to lunch. He squeezed a thumbful of flesh next to his navel. Maybe he shouldn't eat at all.

He lay down on the bed and tried to think of any Dylan lyric that might support what had happened last night. None of his favourite songs were rooted in that kind of flesh and blood reality. Mr Jones didn't know what was happening, Johnny's in the basement, the chimes of freedom were flashing. The reality stuff was standard: girlfriends went to Spain and black maids were murdered by rich guys.

Two young guys meet on the road and travel to the end of the universe, flesh against flesh, but it wasn't natural. It was strange and it was wrong. Dylan could have made it right.

Moth knew he should write it down and figure it out, try to remember everything he'd ever read. Weak father, strong mother. He didn't know whether he'd classify them like that. You do it when you're a kid, as an experiment, and maybe he had gotten stuck there. Waited too long for a girlfriend. Maybe Ricky had been just a substitute for a girl and you couldn't count the guys hitchhiking because that had been for money. He hadn't done anything, just sat there. If your eyes were closed, who could tell the difference? Last night had happened because of Donna. Maybe.

It tired him out, made him feel like he hadn't slept at all. He sat up and took a gulp of tea and wondered whether Yves would meet him tonight. It razed every thought and left him hungry. If Yves came and took him home, he could endure anything in a day. He could be a creel boy at the rug factory for the rest of his life or even take a job at The Plant. It was a delirious notion that erupted without preamble and made him smile. He knew he should see it as pathetic. It made him feel like it was Christmas Eve.

Moth.

His mother was standing at the bottom of the stairs, looking up at his door.

Would you like a sandwich? she said. Salmon?

Moth hated the round, soft bones in every mouthful of salmon. He had started to think of tuna as being Canadian and salmon as English.

Sure, okay.

His mother walked away and he felt like running down the stairs and holding her. None of it was right. She didn't ask to move to this shit hole. She'd hate him if she knew about his night and she would clamour about it at every opportunity. She'd tease – no – she'd *bludgeon* him over Tab Hunter or Guy Madison or any man who was good-looking. Bill Webb.

My mother loved me but she died, Moth said.

He went back into his room and sat down, looking into his cup. Hud said that. Paul Newman. His mother would bug him about Paul Newman, if he gave her the chance.

iii

Moth told himself to take it like a man. If he hadn't been suffering such frightful pain, he would have laughed out loud. Take it like a man. The hood of the car was warm against his palms, but his legs and his back were cold. His pants slipped lower an inch at a time, whenever Yves made a thrust. He didn't know how his shirt had been pushed up to his shoulders.

The pain was unbelievable. The night before, Yves had stopped and repeated a single word, soft and urgent. He'd massaged Moth's stomach and thighs and didn't try to go any farther until he was understood. Relax. He was telling him to relax, not to stiffen up, and Moth had willed himself limp. Yves gained another inch, Moth froze, he was massaged and heard the whispered word. He relaxed. Yves sunk into his body.

He'd forgotten about the pain until the moment Yves bent him over the hood of his car and began the assault. He couldn't relax and Yves didn't speak or stop pushing or attempt any massage. Nothing Moth said would make any difference unless he said No and he knew he wouldn't say it. Vlad had him straddling a sharpened stake in the courtyard of his castle. Nazis were trying to make him renounce Jesus. It was a prison nightmare, the line at which he would die rather than let anyone cross. Moth was alive and Yves bored into him.

The car was parked behind the loading dock of a cement company, just a few feet in front of a chain-link fence. Enough time to pull up his pants if the police came around the corner, but no explanation would be convincing. He hoped they'd think he was a burglar. Moth nearly screamed as Yves forced his way inside, cock without end. He wanted to pray but knew he'd be damned. He wasn't going to say No or Stop or anything else. He wished the police would arrive.

Yves gave three quick, excruciating prods and then shuddered and dug his fingers into Moth's thighs. He moaned like he'd just finished a heavy bench press and slowly fell forward. Moth felt a kiss to the back of his neck. He felt Yves straighten up and withdraw and he embarrassed himself with a couple of high-pitched gasps. He tried to breathe normally before turning around and pulling up his pants.

243

He was alone, staring at the dark weeds pushing through the fence. Moth took his coat from the hood of the car and felt the heat of the engine on its lining and then jumped back at the bleat of the horn. He looked through the windshield, but Yves was gazing into the rear-view mirror, straightening his hair with his fingers. The interior light came on and Moth saw that he wasn't handsome at all. Hawk-faced. He looked like a guy at a dance trying to find a girl who was drunk. Yves saw him staring and stared back, almost a tough look.

Moth got into the front seat and twisted himself around so they were face to face. He couldn't just let the look pass. Yves gave him his beautiful smile and darted in for a quick kiss. He rubbed Moth's hair and kissed him again, then turned back and started the car. Moth straightened himself out on the seat, accepting the kisses as an apology. You couldn't look at him that way just because he'd done what he'd done. A look was a look.

Yves began whistling, then singing. They drove out from behind the building and navigated an unpaved road back to the highway. There were no cars or people in sight and Moth remembered how excited he'd been on the way there. He thought it was probably less than an hour since he'd left the factory. Yves was singing the first verse of "Ballad of a Thin Man" and Moth wondered if he was giving him a message. He looked over and got a brilliant smile and a nod to join in. They turned onto the highway and he hoped they were going to the tiny apartment. This had been an onslaught of passion that Yves couldn't control and now they would lie down together and whisper words that would disappear like shouts on a windy day.

They rode along the highway and Yves kept singing. There was a turnoff he'd taken the night before and he drove right past it. They were heading for Valentine.

Moth had never been so small. He shrunk into the car seat and held one skinny wrist in his fingers, crossing his hands the way he had in Sunday school. His mother used to open tightened jars of jam and get his bowl down from the shelf. His father carried the bicycle up from the basement while Moth did nothing but hold the door open wide. He was that boy, without boxing gloves or a Colt revolver, sitting next to a stranger in a car. Smaller, even. When he had crossed the ocean, he'd seen large eggs in the water with bright lights inside them. His mother told him they were buoys and Moth imagined little boys floating alone in the dark reading comic books beneath the white light. He had wished he lived in the middle of the sea, too small to be noticed by anyone except God and the gulls.

They were driving to Valentine. Yves had finally stopped singing and Moth didn't delude himself with fantasies of boot and fist. He wished Yves would touch him. He'd been losing ground ever since he left work and anything he said or did now could only make it worse. He looked out his window at St Lucy and watched the last hour all over again. It's the end that decides the beginning. If they'd fallen against each other and tumbled onto the ground afterwards at the cement plant, every minute that had gone before might have been thrilling. Even the pain was a price worth paying, no worse than being hit in the ring on your way to victory. Had that been their end, the beginning would have been a heart-stopping preliminary.

Yves had grabbed him by the back of the neck and pushed his head down as soon as Moth got into the car. One minute he was changing wool and the next he was the wanton whore of the highway. Moth did what he was supposed to do as best he could. Did Donna like doing it this much? Maybe you had to have one of your own. He felt like he'd scaled a fresh summit, like he had reached his own name in the clouds. The bad boy behind the bad boy. He had come up to breathe and rub his jaw and he saw concrete buildings that weren't illuminated except by security lights. They pulled into the driveway beside the cement company.

This was the end. A hard look through the front window and Moth hadn't even stared him down. He was being taken home like one of the girls who went on the bus with the football team. It made the beginning a cheap, terrible chapter in the night. He had been useful and now he wasn't needed any more. Maybe Yves would drive all night, looking for other hitchhikers who knew the words to all the Dylan songs.

Moth let his head hang when the car stopped and didn't lean over for a kiss. Yves waited, but said nothing. He didn't reach out and cover his hand or ask a soft question Moth wouldn't understand or do anything at all. The end. Just another sulky girl waiting for her date to say I love you. The thought made his skin contract and ripple over his arms. Jesus Christ. He couldn't even muster a threat.

Moth got out of the car and it rolled away as soon as he slammed the door. He went into the house and directly to the kitchen and began eating before he'd taken off his coat or boots. He ate and ate and ate.

Have you heard it was because I was sleeping with Tim? Joanna asked. I have.

I thought I was sleeping with Bill, said Kate. You found me there and I had to run home without my clothes.

I haven't heard that. I like that one.

I don't want you to be angry with me, Joanna.

This place is too small for that, said Joanna. I'll tell you what, why don't we get together for lunch sometime soon?

I'd like to see you now.

Oh, Kate, no. It's too early yet. We have to take our time and we must proceed slowly.

Joanna spoke each word separately with almost a pause between them. More a comma than a full stop. Must, proceed, slowly.

I've stopped drinking, said Kate.

That's good. That's very good.

She waited, but Joanna didn't keep talking. The position of the telephone was hateful and she didn't know why it had never bothered her before. You had to stand up to have a conversation and it discouraged a talk of any length. Tim would never notice because he only got calls from The Plant and none of them lasted more than a few minutes. He would never dream of considering anyone else.

She could hear heavy breathing on the line. It sounded anxious. Kate wanted her back, but she liked the idea of Joanna being nervous about her.

You sound funny, she said.

I was doing my exercises when you called. Bill says I'm getting fat.

You're perfect, Kate said.

Kate, I really have to go.

She hung up without even waiting for a goodbye. Kate held the receiver to her ear, expecting she would somehow be reconnected. The dial tone began its drone and her eyes started to water. Beryl came into the kitchen with Trevor and took the milk from the fridge and filled half his mug with it. Kate listened to the dial tone and watched the two of them. Moth was suddenly in the doorway, as though he'd worked his way downstairs by crawling over the walls like a fly. Too damned quiet.

What's for dinner?

Stew from last night, Beryl said.

Joanna had hung up on her. Maybe Kate should go over and break another window. That had got their attention. This time they'd probably lock her up for good. Right in the middle of the thought, it happened: she felt a wave of noiseless static move up her neck to the top of her head and she hung up the phone. This was the good part, but it didn't last. Twenty minutes and then she would even out. She had learned to drink coffee with the tranquilizers and they worked to much better effect. Without the coffee you just got sleepy.

She walked over to the kitchen table and sat down next to Trevor, who took a piece of newsprint from his pocket and smoothed it out in front of her. She looked at the thick crayoned lines and saw a purple pumpkin with antennae. Tiny wheels beneath the pumpkin and a smudged circle touching one side. Trevor looked up at his mother and waited.

The Easter bunny, Kate said.

Trevor laughed and nodded his head. He picked up his picture and handed it to her.

For you, he said.

Kate took the newsprint and gave him a kiss.

He made a picture for everyone, didn't you, Trevor? Beryl asked.

No, Trevor said, frowning.

Well, you made one for me and one for Mommy.

Is there anything else besides the stew? asked Moth.

No, Beryl said.

It's the Oscars, said Kate. We'll be having snacks all night.

Moth walked out of the kitchen without saying another word. He wouldn't watch the show any more than Tim would. Stew was better the second day anyway and they could both go to hell. Moth should have kept his job.

We should get popcorn, said Beryl. Besides the chips. I'll make it.

You could take Valium as much as you liked and for as long as you wanted and it never became a habit. It was a little yellow miracle. She had started on three a day and stuck to it except for special occasions. She never took more than two at a time. You needed to drink coffee, not tea.

Trevor, she said. Do you love your Mommy?

Yes.

He closed his lower lip over his upper and knelt up on his chair to kiss her. Kate wanted to cry. You should be able to start having children when you were fifty. It would take you right to the end, then, and you wouldn't have to worry how to fill the thousands of days left before you died.

I love my children, she said.

v

You can call it a betrayal, but you've already betrayed yourself, Tim Watson said. Do you see? You betray yourself first, then you betray others. You'll always betray them after that if you don't take care of the first one, which is yourself. I don't mean to say that's an excuse, but it's a fact. I betrayed myself. The damned word is starting to sound funny now, I've said it too often. What I shouldn't have – it's a long list. There's things I should have never done, starting with leaving home. I mean England. There's nothing to be done about that now, except find a way to survive. Even that's too dramatic. In India you have to find a way to survive, it has meaning, that word. Here you find a way to go on. Just go on. There's no point in feeling bad because there is nothing left to do except go back ten or twelve years and that's impossible.

It's times like this I wish I were spying for the Russians or living off counterfeit money, anything at all but the same old tired things you'd see on the late show. If I were a doctor, I'd have work I could devote myself to and not even consider my home life. Or a scientist. Maybe that's all late show ideas, too. Maybe it would be the same if I were a butcher, baker, candlestick maker. You spend – well, even my son said it – you spend two-thirds of your life at home. It can't be war all the time and it can't be a secret code you can't decipher. She was high-strung to begin with, at least since we came here. She was always on a high idle, you might say. And then it became strange and now it's, I don't even know what I'd call it. Now it's like they say in the old westerns, it's too quiet. I don't know what she thinks about, although that's nothing new. This is different than it was. I don't know what she thinks about but I don't think it would make any difference if I did. I can't use her as an excuse. That isn't fair. You see, it's a betrayal, but I'm trying to blame her. It isn't her fault. This is my own doing. I don't know what to think of myself and I wonder what you think of me. You think I don't love her, naturally. Anyone would think that. You have no reason to believe otherwise, do you?

248

Tim was putting on his shirt while he talked and he kept stopping at every button. The shirt was white and so long that it covered his underwear. Joanna had never heard him talk so much and she wondered if he was really just as chatty as Bill, once you knew him. Maybe there were no strong, silent men.

I thought you might like it, she said.

Once you were on the phone I felt like I was rubbing her nose in it for nothing.

She called, Joanna said. We didn't call her.

You didn't have to answer.

Of course I did, said Joanna. I thought it was Bill. I want to fuck you while he's on the line. And I won't feel one bit guilty, either.

Tim was a few feet from the couch, his pants a puddle at his feet and the shirt still open. She couldn't cover herself even had she wanted to, unless she put her own clothes back on and she wasn't ready to do that. The first time was always too quick and crazy and she wasn't prepared to get dressed just yet.

Joanna slid off the couch and onto her knees and crawled across the floor to Tim's feet. They always liked that. The damned phone rang again and she couldn't afford to ignore it until Bill called from The Plant. She smiled up at Tim and crawled back to the couch. Joanna picked up the receiver from the coffee table and stayed on her knees, her back to him, hoping it would stop him from buttoning his shirt.

No, dear, she said. Not today. I don't have the time to talk.

She hung up and turned around.

Was it her again? Tim asked.

No. It was that god damned Marc Cloutier. One of our little mistakes.

Tim wondered when everything in the world had changed. This wasn't real life or living in Valentine or even having an affair. She was a woman who held reality like a piece of clay and you had to contend with whatever she made of it. Each new moment made him want to sit down and master it before the next instant occurred. Marc Cloutier, a manager posing as a Las Vegas club owner, friend to gangsters, punisher of misdeeds. He could imagine Moth ripping away at him in brilliant fury.

What is it?

I want to feel self-righteous, Tim said, but I really can't, can I?

I wouldn't think so.

249

She stood up and came to him. He didn't know whether he'd say she was beautiful, but it would be a simple step to take if you fell in love with her. She had breasts that rode high and perfect, but it was her neck that fascinated him. You didn't have to touch it like it was made of china. It felt solid and slightly thick and he already loved the feel of it straining against his palms whenever she moved her head. He watched her neck, her breasts, her body. He saw the muscles appear and diminish in her thighs as she walked toward him. Tim looked at her face when it was right in front of his. Maybe she was beautiful.

What did you do with Cloutier? he asked.

Why don't I show you?

Does Bill know?

Joanna laughed, leaning her head against his chest as she unbuttoned his shirt.

Does he know? she said. He was *here*.

I can't understand that. I can't.

She helped him out of the shirt, pulling it down at the back while he jerked his arms out one at a time. She dropped it on top of his pants. Someday they would make underwear for men that was attractive, even a different colour. Probably about the same time they stopped making back pockets.

What don't you understand? she asked him. You've never thought about Kate being taken by another man? By a gang? Standard fantasy.

He wanted to say, Maybe in your world, but for all he knew she was right. Maybe every man he knew thought about it. He didn't. He didn't even want to think about Joanna with anybody else. Marc Cloutier did it to her in this house, right in front of her husband. He would never understand Bill, but he tried to think about Cloutier. Another man watching. You are naked and you have an erection and there is another man there.

Joanna pulled down his underwear and went down with it, her mouth on his chest, on his stomach, her breasts against his thighs. Tim knelt down before she could make her next move and kissed her opened mouth, arms around her. She put her arms around him and they hugged and kissed and knelt like the poster for that movie. The title escaped them both.

250

What was so great about Dylan? Moth didn't know how to answer that. Maybe because he didn't sing that you had to be true to your school and he didn't sing about his girlfriend or his car. He didn't sound like the Beatles or the Beach Boys. Maybe the great thing about Dylan is that he didn't sound any better than you would. He wrote the things you would write and he felt the same as you'd feel. The greatest thing about him might be that he was you.

He didn't say any of this to Donna and wouldn't have, even if she'd given him the chance.

I like Dylan, too, she said. Did you call me to find that out?

I haven't talked to you in so long, he said.

Let's see, you were leaving town, weren't you? You were quitting school and leaving town. Leaving me.

I had to get a job, Moth said. I can't leave with no money.

Leaving me.

Do you want to move to Bresby? Well, then.

You know what hurt? It isn't even a big deal for you. I'm no big deal, Donna said.

You don't know. What am I supposed to do? Cry?

Yes.

Come on, Donna.

Why are you calling me? Why now?

I miss you.

How much? Enough to cry?

I want to see you, Donna.

Fat chance. You're just horny, that's all it is.

Moth was hungry. There were chips and popcorn in the living room, but he'd have to watch the Academy Awards to get at them. He picked black pieces of unpopped corn from the bottom of the pot and tried to eat them silently.

I want to talk to you, he said.

Talk.

Not like this.

Okay, Moth, you might as well know I'm going out with someone else. You probably already know.

Moth spit the popcorn kernels back into the pot. He wished he'd moved a chair over to the phone. Jake should have told him, or Beryl, and they didn't and now he was making a fool of himself. Calling like he wanted her back and it was too late. She'd tell everybody.

Yeah, I know, he said. So what?

I don't think he'd like it if we got together. I wouldn't like it if he did it.

That's okay, Moth said. Let's forget it.

You're leaving for sure?

You know something, Donna? What does it matter?

I don't hate you, Moth.

Okay. Listen, I've got to go.

When are you going to Bresby?

I don't have the exact day. Beryl will tell you.

You're mad, she said.

I'm just mad because he's pushing you around. But that's your business.

He's not doing anything like that.

So long, Moth said.

Don't hang up. You call out of the blue and I'm supposed to decide everything in like a second.

Listen Donna, Moth said, wearily, I'm not trying to talk you into anything.

I couldn't go to your house.

Maybe you're right. Maybe it isn't such a great idea, anyway.

Can I call you back?

Moth paused for effect. He didn't want to overdo the weary voice, but bullying Donna wasn't the way, either. Just a little bit more than neutral was the right tone.

I might be going out, he said, which was preposterous. When do you want to call back?

An hour? Donna said, even though she had meant the next day.

Talk to you in an hour, Moth said and hung up the phone.

He rinsed out the pot and replaced it on the stove, then went into the living room. Beryl and his mother were sitting together on the couch, Trevor at their feet. Trevor was eating handfuls of popcorn and trying to ask questions with his mouth full.

Can you take him upstairs? Beryl asked.

Moth leaned over the end of the couch and took potato chips from the

252

bowl on his mother's lap. Beryl had the barbecue kind, which he preferred, but he saw them too late. They were watching a car commercial as though it contained a message meant only for them.

I'll have to take the popcorn, too, Moth said.

Take it, said his mother.

Trevor? Let's go upstairs.

No, Trevor said.

You can bring the popcorn.

Trevor immediately stood up and lifted the bowl. He raced up the stairs ahead of Moth and ran into their bedroom. He knelt down on the floor and tried to keep his hands on the bowl of popcorn while he looked under the beds. Moth watched him crawl underneath the bed and drag the bowl with him.

Are you going to eat under there? asked Moth.

No.

Trevor pushed out the bowl and then dragged himself after it, holding a fistful of broken crayons in one hand. He put the crayons on the floor and picked up a piece of newsprint, turning it over. Both sides were covered in his drawings of bunnies, eggs, and a mysterious princess who lived with the bunny. She was a stick figure with a crown and a wand. He began hunting through every piece of paper on the floor, trying to find one that had space still uncoloured.

Just leave the bowl, Moth said. I'm not going to eat all your popcorn.

Trevor had picked it up but put it down. He searched the paper scraps quickly, keeping a close watch on his brother. You could buy dozens of sheets of newsprint for pennies, but the holidays had devoured them. Reindeer, trees, many Santas, and now the fabled egg-bearing rabbit. He tried to throw the last piece of paper, but it floated harmlessly two feet from him, then rocked itself back and forth down to the floor.

I want to draw, he said.

Moth sat on the bed and watched him. He could meet Donna here, but his parents never went out any more. His mother got too tired and marble-eyed and seemed content enough to stay in front of the tv. He might get her over when his father worked nights, after his mother went to bed. That was too far away, at least another week. If he had a car, he could take her behind a factory and bend her over the hood. It was warmer now. They might be able to meet outside and take a walk on the golf course.

He'd quit his job the night after the cement company episode. All night long he'd thought about Yves showing up and wondered what to say and how to say it. It was impossible. Even if he spoke French, they'd reached the point where only violence would achieve a balance. Moth felt ashamed that he didn't want to beat Yves senseless and he wondered whether he was secretly afraid. Too scared, even though the guy was skinny and probably never had a fight in his life. He should have hit the man at the arena, the night he saw Sweet Daddy Siki. He was a faggot and a coward. Terry would have killed Yves. Terry would never have let it happen.

Terry would have knocked down that little asshole who worked the number one loom, too. Shoving you out of the way every time he wanted to check the creel. The hallway monitors would lie bleeding. Bill Webb. He must have done something to his mother to make her smash the windows. Where were her clothes? Jesus Christ. He couldn't understand why his father didn't get that shotgun and use it on Webb. Maybe he had raped her. Terry would go over and find out. Go over with a knife or a crowbar. No. His bare hands.

Moth had quit his job an hour before the shift ended. He had said nothing to the foreman and it was assumed he was leaving to use the washroom. He walked outside and hitchhiked and got a ride from a kid his own age who wanted to prove he was a fearless driver. Moth walked the last couple of miles and thought about beating up Yves if he came to the house. He thought about standing on his tiptoes for a kiss. No one was awake when he reached home and he had sat in the kitchen, wanting to phone someone, wanting to eat and unable to sleep. His father had pulled into the driveway and Moth had gone up to bed.

His father was late tonight. He hated it when the old man worked days. It seemed like the house was full every minute from the time Moth woke up.

Trevor was behind him, gasping and straining. Moth saw that he had shoved his arm between the mattress and the box spring and he was pulling out the notebook.

Paper, said Trevor.

Moth came around the end of the bed and took the notebook out of his brother's hands. He flipped through it and saw no torn fragments. Trevor hadn't taken paper out of it before, but he knew where it was. He knew where it was.

Moth pulled out two sheets near the back and handed them over. He opened the door of his closet and stuck the notebook on the high shelf, out of his brother's reach. Trevor lay on the floor and began drawing immediately.

That's all the paper you get, Moth said.

He went downstairs and into the kitchen, not looking at his mother. She was saying something to Beryl about how Elizabeth Taylor looked so damned awful and she didn't believe it had anything to do with making that movie. Moth went into the kitchen and phoned Terry.

They both heard Trevor start to cry and tried to ignore it. They were still miles away from Best Picture but neither of them wanted to miss a minute. Kate thought Moth should be upstairs, not on the phone, and to Beryl it sounded more like whining than real crying. Trevor probably couldn't find any paper or he was just overtired.

He didn't become louder, but more insistent. It started with Mommy, repeated three or four times, then became Beryl. Kate poked her in the arm.

You'd better go and see.

Don't poke me, Beryl said. He was calling for you before.

He's calling for you now.

In a minute, Trevor, Beryl yelled.

He called her name. Kate poked Beryl and Beryl gave a stab to her mother with a stiff finger. Kate swung and Beryl lifted her arm and caught it on the wrist.

Damn you, said Kate. Now I've broken my hand.

Pretty soon Moth will be off the phone.

You learned that from your brother, said Kate. Don't do it again.

She swung the same arm in a clumsy backhand and hit her wrist on Beryl's. Kate held the wrist and began to pant.

I told you not to do that.

I'm not sitting here while you hit me.

You'll do as you're told, said Kate.

Beryl tried to watch the tv and her mother at the same time. This hadn't happened since she came back home. Maybe her mother hadn't taken a pill tonight.

255

If you're going to be like that, you can go to your room.

Stop it, Beryl said. I'm not going anywhere.

Trevor called out for his sister.

At least go and see after your brother, said Kate.

You go. He wanted you. He's your child.

I'm not well.

You're well enough to hit me, aren't you?

Kate was going to threaten her with her father, but she knew it wouldn't work. The whole house treated her like a leper, including Tim. If not a leper, then like one of those slow people who have funny faces. Weird eyes and thick lips. Like she was stupid or insane and she was neither one. Tim was late and if he ever got home he wouldn't listen to her complaints. Working late because he knows it's the Oscars. She had made one mistake and now he acted like everything she said was strange and false.

Go and see what the matter is with Trevor, Kate demanded. And then you can go to bed.

Why are you like this? Beryl said, almost shouting. I'm not going to bed. I'm going to tell Dad that you're out of your mind and I was afraid to leave you alone. He'll believe me. Just sit still or I'll smack your face.

Kate grabbed Beryl by the hair and pulled her head down. Beryl swung at her mother blindly and landed a slap high on the side of her head. Kate hit Beryl on the ear, then lowered her head and kept swinging with her free hand while Beryl dug her nails into her mother's arms and tried to rip off the flesh underneath her housecoat. They called each other bitch, whore, and cunt. Beryl pulled her head free and saw a handful of hair in her mother's fist and Kate leaned away and tried to catch her breath.

Beryl lunged in at the very moment Kate tried another backhand and it landed hard against her nose. Beryl grabbed her face and leaned over. She began crying and Kate saw blood seep under her hands and roll down her chin.

You see what happens? said Kate. You see what happens?

Blood started falling in big drops from Beryl's chin and splashing onto her jeans. Trevor was crying and calling her name.

Go upstairs and wash your face, Kate said. Don't let Trevor see all this blood.

No.

Beryl took away her hands and Kate saw the stream of blood that ran from her nostrils across her mouth. It was already slowing down and the nose didn't look broken. She smiled at Beryl's wet, red eyes. Beryl took the corner of her shirt and lifted it to her face. She dried her eyes and then wiped up the blood.

Not with the shirt, for God's sake, said Kate.

Without changing expression or position, Beryl smacked her mother hard across the cheek. It sounded like a clap of thunder. It knocked Kate against the cushion at the end of the couch and she got to her feet as quickly as she could. Beryl stood up at the same time. Kate was too shocked to cry.

They both sucked air and waited nervously. Trevor was crying upstairs and the TV boomed its pompous awards music while they looked each other over. Time sat like yesterday's stew, thick and heavy. Kate laughed.

Aren't you naughty? she said.

Beryl watched her mother, waiting for a fresh attack, but Kate laughed the way she did at one of those British comedians. Her mother was crazy. The idea wasn't new, but it made Beryl start crying again. Kate stepped toward her but stopped when she flinched.

Oh, don't. Come on, Beryl.

Kate gave her a hug and Beryl cried against her mother's shoulder. Kate started to cry with her.

Look at us, for God's sake, she said.

She helped Beryl back down on the couch and sat beside her as before. Trevor cried and cried and cried.

Where the hell is Moth? Kate said.

Tim came in and hardly gave them a glance. He took off his coat and hung it up in the closet.

It was the paint shop, he said. I sweated like a horse. I need to shower.

He noticed they were crying when he took off his shoes. Beryl was leaning over and he couldn't see her face. Some sobbing actress talking about her dead mother, probably. He could hear Trevor crying upstairs and wondered why the hell Moth hadn't shut him up. He imagined Moth in tears somewhere, the whole house weeping over a secret he knew nothing about.

He went upstairs and opened the bedroom door and saw Trevor hanging almost upside-down. He'd caught his foot on the headboard, between the slats, when he'd tried to crawl off the bed. His hands and face and tiny chest pressed against the floor and one leg was held high in the air. His face was a red as the Bouvrettes' Corvette.

Tim pulled the foot free and kept hold of him at the same time. Trevor turned his face against his father's shoulder and dug his fingers into his shirt. Tim hoped it wouldn't make the child smell of Joanna. Trevor kept crying without changing the pitch or volume. Tim rubbed the foot that had been trapped and it felt icy. He went to the bedroom door and shouted downstairs.

Trevor was stuck on the headboard. Couldn't anyone hear him?

He trembled with outrage. There wasn't any sound below him except for the television set, and then he heard laughter. Beryl and Kate laughing.

You went and got him! Kate yelled back.

You lose! shouted Beryl.

They laughed like actresses portraying the insane in old movies. Moth walked slowly up the stairs, looking at his father.

What's going on? Moth asked.

Don't have children, Moth, his father said.

He handed Trevor over and walked into the bathroom. Moth carried his brother back to their room.

How would you like it if you had this room all by yourself?

No, Trevor said, crying.

The whole room. You'd never have to be quiet.

No.

Well, Moth said, that's too bad.

Chapter Twelve

i

Bresby hadn't changed much. Moth saw a Tamblyn's right next to the bus station that he was sure hadn't been there before and it looked like they were adding a store to the shopping centre. There was a fresh rubble of brick and wood on a corner near the centre of the city, but he couldn't remember its previous life. He was glad the bus hadn't passed anywhere near Melody Creek.

The houses looked ancient, after Valentine. The buildings and homes he saw downtown were constructed of dark brick and looked as though they were built to wage perpetual battle against cold. Winter in Quebec was endless and iron-fisted, but the houses in Valentine were bright and covered with windows. These were gloomy, grimy little structures that might have been the offspring of The Plant. Each of them had a small, dark picture window that stared like a dead eye. Moth had never seen Bresby this way and he wondered if Valentine had ruined him. He might be too soft for his old town.

Roy Godin lived with his mother in a narrow house that was stuck to the one beside it. It had two upper floors and there were three bedrooms on the top storey. Roy had one of them and two movers shared the other, each with his own bed. The smallest room had been vacant a week, ever since its tenant had taken a job up north. Up north was where real guys went, Moth knew. They made fortunes working impossible hours in exhausting jobs.

He had saved two hundred dollars from the carpet factory and the rent at Mrs Godin's was ten dollars a week. She was an unfriendly woman who had her own room on the second floor and Moth knew it wasn't the kind of house that would allow him to stay in bed and read magazines. He had to make a decision soon, but not today. His clothes and razor were in an old suitcase his father had used in England and Moth had learned that the suitcase was a stupid invention. You had to haul its entire weight with one hand on a little handle. He wished he'd asked Jake for a duffel bag.

He left the suitcase under Roy's bed and they went down the street to a restaurant Moth had never seen before. It had a counter and three tables and smelled like burned meat. There was a man about Roy's age having coffee at the counter and a couple of teenage boys eating fries and gravy at one of the tables. The waitress looked like one of Henry's girls from the front and reminded him of Donna when she walked away.

Last night I waited on a golf course for about three hours for this girl, Moth said. She never showed up.

Look at those arms, Roy said. What have you been doing?

I was on the wrestling team. I lifted weights.

Jesus. You look strong, Moth.

Yeah. I'm a little heavier than normal.

Your old man can probably get you on at The Plant, can't he? Roy asked.

I'm not sure what I'm going to do. I came here for a wedding.

The waitress brought them two coffees and smiled at Roy as she set them down. She handed each of them a menu printed on brown paper that opened like a Christmas card.

Nice day for sailing, she said.

Too bad I have to work, said Roy.

She walked back to the counter and Moth saw that she was too wide across the shoulders to be confused with Donna. He wished he'd found out the name of the guy. It would just be one more detail to drive him crazy and he didn't know why he wanted to know. She was probably seeing some guy who didn't even think about where she'd been or what she knew or how she did everything she did. Moth had thought about every one of these things all the way to Bresby on the bus.

I told her I had a boat, Roy said. I was drunk.

Terry Delaney is getting married, said Moth. You know who he is?

No.

He was with Soldier the night by the lake.

Oh, yeah, okay. You know the guy?

Yeah, Moth said. I heard he killed Soldier.

Sure, said Roy.

I mean I heard it from somebody he told it to.

Every guy wishes he'd killed some guy, Roy said.

I thought you might want to know. I mean, I've known this guy a long time but he fucked over my sister. I don't owe him anything. Henry was always a good guy, as far as I'm concerned, Moth said.

Oh, sure. Good guy Henry.

Moth didn't know what to say. He'd debated telling Roy all the way here, when he wasn't wondering whether or not Donna had travelled the same highway and seen the same things as he was seeing. He tried to memorize every detail because she would have noticed something he hadn't even seen. Roy didn't care about Terry, and Moth didn't understand.

Two thousand bucks for a fucking motorcycle, Roy said. How much money do you think he gives my mother? Nothing. When does he come by the house? Never. When Henry was good was when our father still lived there. We were kids and the old man would slug my mother and we'd jump on him. Stronger than hell, my dad, he was a cook in the logging camps. He'd beat the piss out of us. Henry got the boot in when he was about sixteen and he gave the old man a beating so bad it made him cry. My father, not Henry. When he was finished, Henry did it all over again. I had to go upstairs. My mother and I cried in her room and we could hear my father begging and trying to get away. When Henry let him go, he never came back. That was good. It was the right thing to do and Henry did it.

The waitress returned and asked them if they wanted to order. Moth asked for bacon and eggs and Roy settled for another coffee.

You think my mother likes it that he runs a bike gang? That doesn't impress her. She's embarrassed every time one of those assholes rides down the street. There's nothing she can say to her friends about it and they hear every fucking story. You ever hear that Henry yanked out a kid's teeth with pliers?

Holy shit, said Moth. No.

Never happened, but everybody believes it. Henry's a bad guy but he doesn't need pliers or anything else. He's too vicious.

I thought he killed Soldier with a rock?

Yeah, Roy said. So maybe he didn't kill him. Maybe this other guy did it and Henry is waiting to get out and kill the guy himself. I don't know. The main thing is, I don't care. I hope they don't hang him, but Henry has it coming. Whatever he gets, he's got it coming. If he was going to do all this shit, it would have been better if he'd left our old man alone. What he's done to our mother, fuck him. At least in the pen she can visit and she'll know he didn't do what they say he did. That's perfect. He's a good boy in a terrible place and she can make him food and see him every fucking week. I'll tell you what happened to Henry. He ran out of luck. He had a hell of a lot of luck and he used it all up doing all that crazy shit before and now his time is up. Too fucking bad.

Roy drank the rest of his coffee and Moth took a sip of his own. The waitress hurried over with the pot.

Breakfast is on the way, she said, filling their cups.

No hurry, Moth said.

Maybe I should call you Captain, she said to Roy as she walked away.

What would you do? Roy asked him. Tell her it was all bullshit or make some excuse about somebody borrowing the boat?

I don't think she really cares if you have a boat or not, Moth said.

You've got a lot to learn about women, said Roy.

ii

It took Terry all morning to pull up the carpet. It was never going to be cleaned and now it was home to armies of dark bugs he didn't recognize. The bugs didn't leave the rug, but he slept with a blanket jammed against the space under his door in case they became restless. The house was dyed with the smell and his clothes seemed to carry it everywhere he went. Darlene said he was imagining it.

His father had been to court twice and was going again in a month. The union was fighting for him to keep his job, but he didn't go to The Plant any more. He drove to Kirkland Lake and then went to the police station to find out why he was there. They sent him back to Bresby. Terry sometimes heard him, but only saw him in the house every few days. His father would hide and leave the house when Terry went into his own room. The same bills began appearing in the mailbox and the mail was never opened. Terry wasn't sure how mortgages and taxes and the rest of it worked, but he knew the days of the house were numbered.

He had applied for a job at The Plant. They were supposed to start hiring soon.

He towed the TV set outside and set it against the garbage cans and then used the rake to get all of the broken glass into the centre of the room. He had to push the couch out the front door to rip up the carpet and then decided to leave it out there. He shoved it down the steps and around the corner until it was next to the TV. It looked like it had been chewed by monsters. Once he'd pulled up the edges of the carpet all the way around, he folded it in on itself, covering glass, bugs, and cushion fillings. He folded it up like a large envelope and then tried to haul it outside, which was slow and maddeningly awkward. He couldn't keep it closed going through the door, so he walked over it and pushed it out instead. It unfolded on the front porch.

Terry grabbed one foul corner in two hands and dragged the whole mess around the side of the house and into the backyard.

The living room was almost empty. He left the front door open and then lifted his bedroom window to let air through the house. He wasn't sure what product cleaned floors and what equipment was needed. They used a mop with a sponge on TV, but it was usually on linoleum. Maybe they didn't imagine you could have this kind of disaster in your living room.

Sharon Ticehurst had sent him money. Olive handed it to him in the Pinklon one night when he was nursing the only beer he could afford, and told him she'd called Sharon. Everyone knew that Jerry was on the ropes and neither Olive nor his mother could stand the idea of Terry going to school without eating breakfast. Now the money was gone and both breakfast and school remained sights unseen. He avoided the Pinklon so that Olive wouldn't see him drinking his mother's money and started asking strangers outside the liquor store to buy him a bottle. Most of them refused, but the guys who looked like they needed a drink would do it for a buck. A large, heavy man wearing a hockey jacket took his money and then came out of the store and refused to hand over anything. When Terry blocked his path, the man hit him full in the face without moving him. The man hit him again. Terry touched him lightly on the arm.

Don't make me kill you, he said.

The man returned the money and looked over his shoulder all the way back to his car. Terry got a bottle half an hour later and his left eye was almost swollen shut by then. The young guy who bought it asked him who had given him the eye and Terry said he got it from his brother.

He heard himself say it, just like he'd watched himself get punched without fighting back. It gave him a weird feeling of upset, not quite panic. He didn't like it.

Maybe the house was never going to smell normal again. He went into the bathroom and found his father's aftershave, then came back and poured it over the floor. He mopped it into a wider area with one of Jerry's socks. The room smelled less swampy, but more like a locker room. He was afraid of even buying disinfectant in case it ended up making the house smell like school hallways.

Darlene wouldn't be coming here. Her mother and father had rented them a motel room in Niagara Falls and when they returned they were moving into the parents' basement. It was a terrible thought, but it took no time to make money at The Plant. Terry tried not to think about tomorrow or the Falls or especially moving into the basement. He would be a father by the time everyone went back to school.

Randy Zed demanded a party. He knew two girls who would dance and have sex with each other and anyone else for a hundred dollars. Randy would buy the beer and invite Jimmy O'Hara and Buster and his bodyguard. Terry thought about asking Bishop and his partner and he invited Moth over the phone. Randy wanted everyone to chip in for the girls.

The plan became darker to Terry every minute. He couldn't possibly ask a couple of cops to attend and he didn't know anyone who wasn't at odds with some other member of the group. Buster would scowl under his filthy bandana and have the proceedings described to him by his armed guard. It would be a night of flesh and blood and Terry had no heart for it. He wanted to tell someone about Soldier and their mother and he wanted to find out about Beryl. This was his night. Tomorrow was Niagara Falls.

The living room was finished. He moved the dresser out of the doorway to his father's room and closed the bedroom door. He had less than five dollars. He wanted to lock the front door and drive down to Blue Arch. He phoned Darlene.

iii

Moth walked into the house without knocking. The front door was wide open and he could see Terry beyond it talking on the phone. He didn't know how you were supposed to greet an old friend, but he nodded when he walked in and Terry nodded back. In movies they always said, How long has it been? He sat down on the vacant straight-backed chair in the empty room and waited for Terry to finish his call.

The house smelled like the roots of a tree that had just been pulled out of the ground. Maybe not. Mossy, but there was alcohol in the air and it gave a sweet and heavy aroma that lay on top of everything. The odours had nothing to do with each other. Maybe Terry's father had died and rotted here.

Terry hung up the phone, got up and walked over to Moth. He held out his hand and Moth stood up and shook it.

How long has it been? Moth asked.

What are you talking about?

I haven't seen you, Moth said. It seems like a long time.

Does Beryl know I'm getting married?

I didn't tell her.

Don't, Terry said. Did you bring anything to drink?

You want to get some? Moth asked.

He took out his entire life savings and thumbed a ten from the roll. He saw Terry's face relax.

I can get it, but it takes a little while.

In Quebec, you can buy it in corner stores. They never even ask your age.

Well, Terry said, this is Bresby.

What happened here? asked Moth, looking around the room.

It's a long story. Everything is a long story.

I've got a story or two myself, said Moth.

You'll have to wait here. A couple of girls are coming over to put on a show.

Moth felt his face burn. He imagined the kind of girls who would come to something like this and what they might do. Visions flashed like photographs on the back of a thumbed card deck. He could see the girls in the middle of the living room, naked and surrounded and laughing about it. His tongue felt thick.

You been lifting weights?

Not today, Moth said.

Terry watched Moth lick his lips. He looked nervous and stunned. There were headlines in the *Bresby Times* about people using drugs. They quit school and came to Toronto and lived like rats. Moth was weird enough to use drugs.

Terry put the bill into the pocket of his jeans. Moth might be the wrong guy to talk to, now that he thought about it.

265

What are we drinking?

Anything you want, Moth said. Is that enough money?

Sure. Sit down. Those girls will be here soon.

Terry left him there. He walked out of the house and got into the car and thought about having sex with Beryl. He backed out of the driveway and drove downtown.

Moth closed the front door and looked into the bedrooms. There'd been a fight, obviously. The couch and the TV he'd seen at the side of the house weren't being retired due to age, they had been destroyed. He wished Terry had told him about it. Somebody attacked him and they had fought from room to room. His father. Beryl had said something about it. He felt like calling her right that minute and finding out. He looked in Terry's room and saw that nothing was broken except the radio. Maybe his old man had broken it and then Terry attacked him. Their boots ripped the couch, they fell over the TV, they fought across the room and into the bedroom and tackled each other against the dresser. Maybe the house smelled of blood.

He sat down on the chair and thought about the great fights Terry had fought. He tried to remember his own and realized he hadn't had a street fight since he started boxing. It couldn't be true. He worked his way through all the guys he wanted to hit and those he should have hit, but he had hit no one who wasn't wearing boxing gloves. That still left plenty, Moth thought. He must have faced fifty guys, maybe a hundred.

He wondered if Terry was connected to the thread of violence and blood that led back to the beginning of time.

Nearly an hour had passed when there was a short rapping at the front door. Moth opened it and found a woman in her late twenties wearing tight black pants and a white blouse covered by a suede jacket. The pants were too tight and looked like they might burst apart. She had a round, chubby face and brown eyes and her colouring made her makeup look conspicuous and overdone. Her hair had been swept up and covered in a transparent yellow scarf.

Are you Terry? she asked.

Moth stepped aside and let her in.

Randy Zed and Jimmy O'Hara were the only customers in Buster's. An hour after they had arrived, Randy hit Jimmy across the face with a pool cue and knocked him down. The small man with the big hands hit him across the forehead before he could put the boots to Jimmy. The man used a homemade leather blackjack with a spring in the handle and he missed the temple when instinct made Randy turn around. The blow threw Randy against the pool table as Buster began feeling his way out from behind the counter and the small man swung again.

Terry walked in the back door just then and he watched without moving a muscle. The lead tip of the blackjack hit Randy Zed high on the head as he tried to duck and knocked him a couple of feet to his right. Buster took out his razors. The small man stepped forward and Randy leaned away and kicked him in the face with timing so perfect it begged for applause. The man sprawled backwards and Randy booted him in the mouth and the man screamed as though he was howling through a pillow. He curled up on the floor, his hands covering his face. Randy steadied himself against a table with one hand and stomped on the small man's ribs. Buster was using the tables to guide himself toward them, an open razor in each hand. His head was tilted back as though he was trying to see from underneath his blind-fold.

Randy picked up the cue ball and set himself when Buster was only a table away. Terry watched Jimmy O'Hara get up and smash the heavy end of a cue across the back of Randy's neck. Randy fell onto the small man as though he had no bones. Buster stopped and sniffed the air.

Who is it? he said.

Jimmy.

Help me get him downstairs.

Jimmy crossed the room and opened the door to the cellar. He heard the scuff of a boot behind him and gave the back of the room a quick scan. It was empty. Jimmy's nose was broken and his eyes were starting to close. He saw that he was leaving a path of blood wherever he walked.

Buster had tucked his razors back into the pockets of his vest. His blind-fold had started to slip. Jimmy tried to avoid looking at it as they grabbed Randy Zed by the shoulders and legs and pulled him along the floor to the cellar stairs.

The small man stayed between the tables, moaning and holding his face.

Terry was already a block away.

Terry changed his mind just as he was backing into a spot in front of the liquor store. He shifted gears and drove down to the Pinklon, went right past the parking lot and turned south for the highway. It would only take him three days to reach Vancouver if he travelled non-stop. Ten dollars and change wouldn't get him there.

He was navigating the same route he'd taken with Soldier. He stopped the car after crossing the tracks and turned it around. Beryl knew and Darlene knew and he had told Bishop as well. Too many people. Terry wanted to talk to somebody, but not about Soldier or his mother or his father. Maybe he didn't want to talk at all. Whatever he wanted didn't involve a couple of girls. It didn't involve Moth.

He drove back downtown and went right past Francine, then stopped the car and backed up. She kept walking, looking straight ahead. When he called her name she turned around and walked over.

You want a ride?

Thanks, Terry.

She got in and closed the door. Her hair was longer than he remembered and health radiated from her like heat.

You smell like spring, Terry said.

I go swimming at the y, she said. But that's a nice way of putting it.

I'm trying to find somebody to buy a bottle. Moth's in town.

I hear you're getting married, or is that just a rumour?

Okay, Terry said. Moth's in town *and* I'm getting married.

God, married. I can't imagine.

Me neither.

Francine had two brothers, both older. They weren't part of the South End, but showed up for every dance. They almost never fought, but when they did it was in tandem. Everyone knew them because they were funny, not tough. Terry liked them both and they seemed to like him and everyone else.

Where are we going? Francine asked.

Aren't you going home?

268

I don't have to. They'll serve us at the Pinklon.

No, Terry said. I want whiskey.

Do you want to be alone?

Terry gave her a glance. She was looking straight at him and he saw that she was gorgeous or maybe it was a night where any nice girl looked gorgeous. Maybe she liked him. It didn't matter who liked him any more. A hundred beautiful girls could breathe in his ear and it wouldn't matter for the rest of his life. Tonight he could say he was going to get married and after tomorrow he could say he *was* married. That was the end of it. He wished he had stepped back and thought about it instead of grabbing Darlene just because she got into his car. He might have thought about Francine and called her up. He almost told her, but he kept his eyes on the road and his mouth shut. Now he wanted to grab Francine just because she got into his car, he thought. Whoever he met was the one he wanted.

You know Beryl Watson? She was my girlfriend forever. Then she moved and I met Darlene and she was my girlfriend. Now I wish you were my girlfriend. It's nuts.

That's a stupid thing to tell me, Francine said. You're saying I could be anyone.

No, I'm saying that if I had just waited and thought about it, maybe you'd be my girlfriend, Terry said.

Keep going to Oak, then take a left.

I mean, if you liked me.

You've got a strange way of talking to a girl, Terry. Now you're getting married, so what's the point?

I can tell you just because I feel like telling you, he said. I can't do anything about it. That's the point. I can say anything and it's safe, right?

He turned on Oak, a street with no trees at all. The houses were only a few steps from the sidewalk and he drove slowly, bouncing through potholes.

You moved up here?

No, she said. That white house on the right? With the hedge. Stop there.

Terry double-parked on the street. He watched Francine get out of the car and his eyes followed the back of her jeans all the way to the front door of the house. Someone let her in and Terry sat and waited. Moth had once had a crush on her that lasted for months. While he and Beryl were undressing in the field Moth was running after Francine, begging to carry her books.

He didn't know whether he really felt like he could say anything or he was just finding an excuse to say he liked her. If she asked him what he wanted to do, he didn't know what he'd say. What he wanted had nothing to do with girls. You always wanted girls, but there was something else at the bottom of the pond. He didn't know what it was, but it wasn't any girl he had ever met or would ever meet.

It wasn't any of the guys, either. Soldier was as far as you could go and everything after that was just treading water. You swam the lake and now you're seeing how long you can keep from drowning. Beating the shit out of Randy Zed was the same as fucking Francine. It would be great, but then what? What then? He'd have plenty of space at a dance if everyone saw him beat Randy. Shit. Was everything he'd seen at Buster's a dream? No. He would never beat Randy now and neither would anyone else. If nobody knew who you beat, it was pointless. It must be why guys always told you about the girls and why they lied. You couldn't lie about a fight. Someone would come looking for you.

Francine came back to the car with one hand inside her jacket. When she got inside, she showed him a nearly full twenty-sixer of vodka. Terry started driving.

Her mother hides bottles all over the house. If you find one, she can't say it's missing, she said.

Where we going?

Where do you want to go?

Terry took the next left off Oak. He knew a place.

v

Moth and Connie sat on the chairs in the bare living room and waited for Terry and his friends. Moth had looked for coffee or tea and hadn't found so much as a clean water glass. They had exchanged names and observations about Montreal. It was peculiar, making small talk when they both knew why she was there. Peculiar to Moth. Connie looked at ease, but uncomfortable with the chair. Once in a while she'd sniff the air.

She stood up and took off her coat and her face kept the same sweet expression she'd worn from the outset.

I think you'd better tell me what's going on, honey, she said.

It's like I already told you.

Randy said I'd be dancing. There isn't even a radio here. Irene couldn't come, so it's only fifty dollars, but I haven't been paid yet. And that's fifty for the dancing. Everything else is extra. Are you Terry, really?

No, Moth said. I'm really not.

Who's going to pay me?

Moth got up and took out his money. He counted off two twenties and a ten and handed it to her. It changed her smile.

You can see how a girl would worry, she said.

Connie put her hand on his shoulder. Pleasingly plump, Moth thought, an expression that had never made any sense until this moment. He wondered if the fifty included her taking off her clothes.

Are you a little nervous, sweetie?

Do you take off your clothes for that money?

Yes, I do, she said. Not these clothes, I have an outfit in my bag. I strip, but you need music to strip.

Would you just take off your clothes, these clothes, if I wanted you to?

They only come off once. Your friends show up and they get me just the way I am.

I don't care.

No dance or anything?

You said other things would be extra. How much extra?

If you wait for Randy, I'll bet he's going to pay for everybody, she said. What's the matter, am I too irresistible?

Yes.

She gave him a quick, firm kiss for that. She could see he was nervous and she liked teasing him, but he deserved a kiss for being sweet.

Randy hired me, she said.

Does that mean we have to wait?

Unless you're Terry, said Connie.

You win. I'm Terry.

She put her head back and laughed the way people don't laugh in real life. They don't throw their heads back and their laughter doesn't sound like ha ha ha. Connie's did and he didn't care.

I knew it, she said. Aren't you silly? You're shaking, sweetie. I don't bite unless you want me to.

271

Maybe we could go into my room?

His hands trembled. He had only just met her and she was going to take off all her clothes. It didn't seem believable. She took his hand and he led her to Terry's room.

I don't want to sound tough, but we should talk about money, she said. You give me another twenty for french or another fifty for everything, french included.

How much if you stay the night?

They were in the bedroom and he closed the door. His hands shook worse than ever, but all he needed was time. French must mean with her mouth, he thought. She was so bold.

The whole night? she asked. Just with you?

I don't know.

We'd better wait and see, honey. You like me, don't you?

Can I kiss you?

Connie moved against him and they kissed. She was a bit shorter than Donna, about the height of his sister. She pushed too hard with her lips and her mouth was opened too wide. Her tongue smeared his lower lip and chin.

Everybody thinks you won't kiss them, she said. I'll always kiss a sweet boy.

She unbuttoned her blouse and pulled it out of her pants. There was a soft roll of flesh above her belt and her breasts looked enormous beneath the lacy bra. She reached behind her with a small grunt and Moth saw a tiny gold cross swing on its chain. He held it between his thumb and forefinger as the bra fell away and her breasts lowered by an inch. Her nipples were a soft pink and barely protruded.

Aren't you afraid of hell? he asked.

You must be Catholic.

No. But God scares me sometimes.

Connie opened her belt and Moth began unbuttoning his shirt. She unsnapped her pants.

God scares me, too, she said, finally. I go to Mass, but I'm still scared.

I don't even go to church.

Let's not think about it right now.

Do you ever think that this is hell?

Oh, honey, she said. Are we going to have fun.

272

She pulled her pants down and sat on the bed to free her legs. Her thighs were wide and white, bigger than Moth's. Her panties were black, but mainly obscured when she leaned over.

She looked altogether womanly.

vi

They held their noses and took gulps right from the bottle. After the first couple, Terry stopped playing. He wanted the taste and the burn. Francine took the vodka from him and asked him to pinch her nose. He held it gently and squeezed while she drank. Her nose was narrow and he was afraid he'd break it just by squeezing. He liked touching her face.

Lucky this is vodka, she said. I'd be in trouble at home.

They kept walking. The hill was inhabited by uneven rows of shadows, some taller than himself and others the height of a tool box, the smallest beginning to lose their outlines to the night. Terry squinted at each one and didn't tell Francine that vodka smelled as much like liquor as whiskey. The people who made it must have started that fairy tale about not being able to smell it.

Do you think it's too cold to go skinny-dipping at the Arch? Francine asked.

Is that what you want?

What do you want, Terry?

I didn't even know you liked me, he said.

Now you know.

It was cool outside, but not so cold they couldn't undress. The idea of her naked made him feel colossally powerful. The bugs weren't in season and he knew if they went to the Arch he'd take her right on the grass, before either of them ever touched water. Or have her while they were both wet and shivering. He looked at her and couldn't tell whose breathing he heard.

This was better than the Arch. They could lie down six feet above the remains of people who hadn't known passion for fifty years. Ghosts would look on in envy. Terry imagined the tiny spirits of dead children and then thought of his mother. She wasn't his mother any more, just another dead woman in the ground. You shouldn't fuck in a cemetery.

I have to find it, he said.

273

Francine moved into him and pressed against his chest as smoothly as a shadow. It felt like she was listening to his heart. Terry gave her a tight squeeze and then let her go and resumed his slow walk. Too dark to read anything clearly, except near the streetlights outside the fence. He would know it because it would be new.

You should have brought a flashlight, she said.

It'll be one of the new ones.

Can you smell the earth? I can.

He smelled it, too. They walked between the carved and inscribed stones and followed the smell until they found a headstone so white it almost glowed. Francine bent over and looked at the chiselled letters.

It's a long name, she said. Foreign.

Terry walked behind it and ran his hands along two other monuments, short and tall. The older ones had a more porous feel to them and there weren't many that were new. The big cemetery, Heartwood, would have been impossible to search. Soldier wasn't buried at Heartwood.

Francine took the section to his left, trying to make out the names in the decaying light. In a few more minutes it would be too dark to see anything except spooky black silhouettes.

Terry walked in a large half-circle and found himself next to her as she straightened up in front of a marble slab that was beginning to tilt. He put his hand on her back without thinking and felt her move with every stroke he gave her. Skinny-dipping. It was the worst idea of the night. He could imagine the phone call. She'd call Darlene just like Darlene had called Beryl. Like Sharon had talked to his mother. Betty.

Her hair was in his face and it smelled like something he recognized but couldn't name. It smelled like her. He wanted to tell her everything he had done and everything he'd thought and then ask her what she thought of him. He wished she didn't like him. What he wanted was someone to look him over like he was a wrecked car or a broken piece of machinery and say he was insane or give whatever judgement they chose to give. That was a mad thought. All he wanted was to find Soldier.

The ground felt as solid as a sidewalk and his foot slipped on contact. Solid and smooth, like the floor in a government office. You'd never stay on your feet if you wore half moons. A step later and the earth was soft and covered with grass. He moved his foot back where it had been and squatted down. There was a rectangular piece of marble, maybe two feet long, set right into the ground. Francine's face was beside his own, nearly cheek to cheek.

Move back, she said.

She knelt on the ground and leaned over the piece of marble, then ran her finger over the inscription.

It's him, she said. Clarence Barnes.

Terry looked at it and saw nothing except dark lines on a light stone. He looked just beside it and the words became visible in the corner of his eye. He wasn't sure if he really saw the name or just wanted to see it. He handed Francine the bottle and she drank. He took two big gulps for himself when she handed it back.

Let's sit down here and drink, he said.

She kissed him when they sat on the grass. It was the deepest, most incredible kiss he'd ever had. He knew immediately that Francine was the girl of his destiny and just as quickly realized that girls weren't his destiny. He felt sick and blind. Sex was like a pink worm crawling through the middle of your plans. Soldier lay beneath them, anchoring the past and pointing toward the future.

He was a lunatic, Francine said.

Maybe.

If he wasn't crazy, then nobody's crazy, she said.

Maybe everybody's crazy.

Touch me, Terry.

I'm getting married tomorrow, he said. Nobody's going to like it much if we do it tonight. Even your funny brothers.

She moved away from him, but only a couple of inches. Terry drank.

I can tell you a secret about my brothers, she said.

He handed her the bottle and she took a big drink without holding her nose. Terry watched her and imagined marrying her in the morning.

Everybody likes them, Francine said. They're a couple of comedians. One of their jokes is they come into my room while I'm asleep and Gary holds me down while Jimmy rapes me. Then Jimmy holds me down. They've been doing that since I was eleven years old.

Terry could barely breathe. Speech was impossible.

You do anything to them and they'll just take it out on me. They have dirty things they do, too. Worse than what I told you.

He slid farther down along the grass until his head rested against the nameplate and his body was stretched out full length. Francine gave him a sad smile and took another drink. Terry knew she was drunk, then. Her eyes were beautiful and liquid and trying to focus.

He wondered whether he should kill her brothers or just beat them until they were broken. She wouldn't like it, no matter what they deserved. She wasn't that kind of girl. Francine had handed him a reason, a perfect reason no one would ever be able to dispute and they'd all think it was about her. She'd think it herself.

Where are they? Terry asked.

She whispered something too softly to be heard. He pulled her closer.

Say it again, he said.

Francine whispered. Terry turned his head and tugged her over until her mouth was an inch from his ear.

Again.

They went, she whispered, to the marge of Lake Lebarge.

She laughed so suddenly and loudly that he jerked his head away and right in the middle of a laugh she coughed a huge geyser of vomit over him. Terry jumped to his feet and gagged as he pulled off his coat. Francine was still coughing and throwing up over herself as she tried to stand up. She'd stopped laughing. Terry leaned over and pulled her up by her shoulders. The patch of grass smelled worse than his house.

She leaned against a headstone, bent double with dry heaves. Terry took off his shirt and used a sleeve to wipe off his pants, then the other sleeve to get the worst of it off his coat. Francine had a strip of whitish puke running from her breasts to her knees, like a streak of pigeon shit on a statue. She'd vomited all over Soldier's grave. Terry pulled her by the arm and sat her down under a tall, thin column of stone that felt no more solid than a sponge.

Sit still for a minute, he said. We'll go for some water.

I can't laugh because it'll make me sick, she said. It isn't true about my brothers. I made it all up.

Bullshit.

Terry, I'm sorry. It was a joke.

I don't believe you, Francine.

Yes, you do.

Terry looked at her and believed it. She was drunk, but she wasn't lying. It scared him that she could make up a story like that. She'd teased him with violence the way girls, some girls, would tease you with their bodies. Let you see a little, feel a little, and then run away. He could almost feel himself hammering Gary and Jimmy, but there was nothing but shadows and ghosts in front of him now.

I don't get it.

It makes most guys excited, she said.

She coughed and choked, then took shaky breaths, watching her feet. Terry walked the few steps back to where Soldier's body lay buried. He reached down and felt wet patches and lumps that hadn't dissolved into the ground. It smelled terrible and there seemed to be lots of it. He had no choice.

He spread his shirt and stretched out on the grass, his head resting on the marble. He looked at the sky and felt the shirt turning damp while he wondered whether to wish on a star. Everything was upside down. He'd been hit in the head with a rock when he was a young boy and for a moment before he collapsed he had seen himself from above, as though he was hovering over himself. Tonight he lay on the grave and saw himself from below. He saw his back, nearly close enough to touch. It was Soldier seeing him. He lay on top of his brother and watched through his brother's eyes.

Suddenly there was light from the sky. Terry didn't know his eyes were closed until then and he opened them as the moon came out and shone. It looked like the moon, but he couldn't understand where it had been all night. Maybe it was an eye in the sky. He saw himself from its surface, the only living man in a graveyard. Francine counted for nothing. He saw Soldier behind him and then he was watching the moon from beneath himself, his body blocking out most of the light. He closed his eyes and he was under the ground and he opened them in the middle of space. It was a delirious journey. Buried in the earth or standing on a dead rock in the sky, but never was he lying on the wet grass of the cemetery.

I killed myself, Terry said.

The moon would stay the same and Soldier could never change. Francine groaned from her tombstone and Terry saw a kid's cartoon of a pink worm wiggle its way into the gravity of the night. Like a plane flying over when the TV was on. A buzz, a bending of the image, then everything back as it was.

Terry, she said. Terry. I feel better now. I do. I'm just so thirsty.

He stood up and went to her, scooping up his coat and the bottle. He wanted to run all the way to the fence and over it into his car. He wanted to talk, but he didn't know what he'd say. Francine held out her arms and Terry wrapped one of his around her and pulled her to her feet.

Are you taking me home? she asked.

I'm taking you to Blue Arch, Terry said.

He hoped he was drunk.

vii

Connie wrapped her legs around Moth, pushed her mouth against his, dragged her nails down his back. He kissed her and touched her but he stayed as limp as a strand of spaghetti. He strained until his face was red and it made success even less possible. Moth found out that french did mean oral and it worked for as long as he was in her mouth. He rolled on top and he was back where he started. She was baffled.

Something about me scares you, she said.

This happened with my old girlfriend too. It isn't you.

Is this what you always do? Just lie there?

She felt his whole body tense, but she'd been with bigger and stronger men than this kid. She stroked his biceps.

You've got a nice body, Connie said.

Moth rolled over on top of her. He kissed her neck and moved his head down to her breasts. It embarrassed him that he hadn't done anything be-cause he didn't think you did it with whores. He didn't want to break any rules. Now he pushed his face into her flesh and she felt soft and harmless. He lifted her heavy thighs and she opened her legs.

You're a sweet boy, she said.

It was different than being with Donna, from the way it looked to the taste of her in his mouth. He pushed his hands under her buttocks and they had a round, irresistible feel. She'd let him try anything, he was sure. If she refused or made him stop, it didn't matter, they had no one in common. It occurred to him that he didn't need to act or imagine the rules. He was anonymous.

Moth climbed back up her body and enjoyed her kiss for the first time. Her face had lost its forced cheer and she looked at Moth like they knew each other. Nothing had changed where change was needed.

They lay on their sides, nose to nose, and she talked to him in a low voice.

Tell me, she said.

It isn't you, said Moth.

Tell me what you like. Tell me what you think about.

Her hand held him, but without urgency. She rubbed him slowly and with just enough tension. Moth didn't know where to begin.

Do you like being tied up?

I've never tried it.

Are you a bad boy who needs a spanking?

No, he said. Don't talk that way.

Tell me, Terry. Tell Connie what you want.

He thought about Donna in the basement. He'd wanted her in her clothes and straddling his lap but she'd been too upset with him. He knew that it wouldn't work tonight, Yves had that side of the street. Moth had thought about almost everything at one time or other, but nothing from home had power here. This wasn't the bathroom or his bed after midnight. Connie was too big and too present. He didn't know what would work with a real girl. Imagination was like all the phantom fights in the dark, where you recovered from every punch and felt no pain or fear and never suffered fatigue.

Why don't you just lie there and do nothing? Moth said.

How?

Just don't do anything. Don't help me. Close your eyes.

She turned onto her back and spread her arms and closed her eyes. Moth sat partway up and looked at her. He felt like he could spend as much time as he wanted looking anywhere at all without being asked why he was looking there and what he was thinking about. He spread her legs and knelt between them. He could do anything at all.

Moth grabbed her by the hips and rolled her over and buried his face in the wide curve of her bottom. He kissed her as sloppily as she kissed his mouth. He ran his lips up her spine and pulled her onto her back and climbed on top of her. It made no difference. He knew he was trying to manipulate himself into entering her and he had to believe it didn't matter if he could or not. It didn't matter. But if it didn't matter, he wouldn't be doing all this.

Open your eyes, he said.

His face was just above Connie's. He kissed her on the nose.

I love your ass, Moth said.

You are kind of a bad boy, aren't you?

Yes.

Did your girlfriend ever sit on your face?

He felt his throat closing and heat washed through him. He could do it if he wanted. They had all night and she wanted him to do it that way. She liked it. He couldn't imagine anything more outrageous.

You like that, she said.

Oh, God.

I'll make you get on your knees and you'll do anything, you'll do anything, he said.

Yes. Yes, please.

Anything I say.

She reached for him and touched him so lightly he hardly felt it and then he was inside her.

Yes, please, Connie said.

Moth rammed himself into her for less than a minute and collapsed. He sobbed, catching his breath. Connie ran her hands down his back and gave him a pinch.

Now you know what you like, she said.

I like you.

I like you, too, she said. But what you really like to do is talk.

Moth didn't speak. He held her and kept his head on her shoulder without looking at her face. She didn't know anybody and she didn't care what he said.

What I really want to do is disappear, he told her.

He climbed off Connie and lifted his pants off the floor.

Sure. I'll swallow you up. Guys spend nine months getting out, she said.

And the rest of their lives trying to get back in, said Moth. Yeah. I know that joke.

He took out his money and began laying bills on the bed.

viii

Terry got home just before the sun came up. The living room was empty and Moth was sleeping in his bed. He took a white shirt and dark dress pants out of his closet, then found a pair of dusty black shoes in the corner. He would be married in four hours.

There were a couple of inches of vodka left, but he thought he was probably still drunk anyway. He could take a belt just before he went to Darlene's house. They'd invited him for breakfast and he planned to change there. Moth. There was no point at all waking him up.

He sat on the floor and leaned against the wall and took a large swallow of vodka. It had no bite. He wanted to call Beryl, but it was too insane. He wanted to see his father. He thought about waking Moth up, but there was nothing he could say that Moth would understand.

He had slept in his car at Blue Arch after taking Francine home. They'd stripped off their clothes and waded in up to their knees and washed themselves off. He had never seen a body as exciting as hers and he had never wanted anyone less. He would never forgive her that stupid story and he didn't know or care how she felt about him.

It didn't matter. She'd lie to her parents, but her brothers would find out she'd been with him and it would get around. Darlene would hear it and never believe he hadn't laid a hand on her.

It was kid stuff. You could commit every crime and leave it behind you, but kid stuff stayed forever.

Terry finished the bottle and set it down. He went to the bathroom and steadied himself against the sink while he shaved. The blade was too old to make it really close, but it didn't cut him, either. He thought about a shower, but the towels were as stiff as cardboard. Niagara Falls and then that god damned basement apartment. Maybe he'd come back here for his clothes and maybe he'd never see the place again. He missed his father and he missed hiding under the bed.

Terry left the house and drove over to Darlene's. He was so early her father kidded him about nerves. They hated each other.

Terry wanted to tell him that he had killed Soldier Barnes, but it had happened a long time ago and had nothing to do with today.

281

Moth woke up and saw a strange face looking at him from behind the bedroom door. It was a man's face in desperate need of a shave and his hair
stood out at odd angles from his head.

You're not Terry, the man said.

No, said Moth. I'm not Terry.

The face disappeared and Moth climbed out of bed and pulled on his
pants, then fastened his shirt. He heard the front door open and close.
He checked the pocket of his jeans and then the other pocket. He'd been
robbed. No. He had given the money away, fifty dollars at a time. Moth bit
his tongue then stopped before he could bite it off.

He walked into the living room and saw nothing except an empty bottle
on the floor. The woman was gone, Terry wasn't home, no one had come
over all night. He had no money at all, not ten dollars for Mrs Godin and
not bus fare to get there.

He used the bathroom and smelled Connie. You couldn't pray after a
night like that. You couldn't even pray. Moth covered his face in cold water
and scratched his skin with the towel. He smoothed down his hair with his
hands.

There were movies where a guy wakes up and has no memory and has
to spend the rest of the film finding out who he is and what has happened.
Sometimes they woke up next to corpses. This wasn't that. In movies, they
always had money to take a cab and have breakfast or they knew secret tricks
about getting cash and clothes and places to live.

He felt an odd, empty tingling between the legs and he grabbed himself
with one hand and squeezed. If only she would come back and lie with him
for a few minutes, he could face everything after that. It was the perfect day
to turn into a fly or a fork, unnoticed or unremembered even by the people
who saw you. He wished he could step into the whirlpool of time and vanish. He would let it carry him all the way back to the Garden of Eden. Or
England.

Moth sat down in the same spot as he'd sat the night before. He was
having trouble catching his breath and his heart banged against his ribs like
a gate in the wind. There was this room and there was outside this room and
there was nowhere else. He couldn't go upstairs and force Trevor out of the
bedroom and he couldn't eat until he felt disgusted. He couldn't fall asleep

or make plans he would never implement or call Jake on the phone. There was no whirlpool or ocean or river of time. He knew it now. If he was part of history, so was everyone else. Roy Godin had how many connections to all the fighters who had ever lived? Anyone who'd ever hit anybody had it. Or done anything to anyone at all. The idea made him breathe faster and his heart made a dull thud in his ears.

He was nothing special. Moth was nothing special. It was a terrible thought. Nothing special. He wished Connie would come back. He wished he was standing beside his locker with Donna.

Maybe this was like Job. You hold on to what you believe and eventually it all turns out. All you have to do is keep the faith.

His own mind was making him sick. He believed he was scared and he had faith that he was nothing special. This wasn't a Bible story and he wasn't a hero and all he wanted to do was pick up the phone and ask his mother to send him some money. Moth was terrified he might really do it. He had to walk out the door and not even think about it. Walk out the door and hitch a ride and tell Roy he'd been robbed. Roy would lend him the rent and then he could find a job. It was simple. All you had to do was keep the faith and don't panic.

He put on his jacket and opened the front door and one look at the alien neighborhood told him he was lost.

Tom Walmsley won the first Three Day Novel contest in 1979 with his novel *Doctor Tin*; its sequel, *Shades*, which also contained the original novel, was published in 1992. Heís also the author of the poetry collections *Lexington Hero* and *Rabies*, the plays *The Jones Boy*, *Blood*, and *Something Red*, the screenplay of the film *Paris, France*, and many other things. He lives in Toronto.